PRAISE FOR ST

"In *Stone Mother*, a young girl, born during a WWII bombing raid, struggles to solve the mysteries of her mother's abuse, her father's absence, and the strange silence about what happened during the war. Beautifully written and emotionally true, this novel deals with the damage caused by secrets and the need to discover the truth."

Barbara Esstman, author of The Other Anna and Night Ride Home

"A harsh mother, a kind-hearted father. A young girl is brought up with her siblings in a castle. This should be a fairy tale, but the bombs of WWII have only recently stopped falling. Set against the backdrop of Germany's defeat by the Allies, the author pulls us into the confusion, magic, horrors, and yearnings of an unraveled world for the girl and the wider society. What does her future hold? How do we survive trauma and learn to thrive?"

Maureen Roberts, author of My Grandmother Sings to Me *(Bogle-L'Ouverture Publications, 2004) and* The Penguin Book of New Black Writing in Britain *(Penguin Publications, 2000 & 2021)*

"*Stone Mother* is an emotional rollercoaster where we get to ride shotgun as Marie explores a medieval castle, is shipped off to a home for 'children of criminal parents,' is left to her own devices at 15 waiting tables at the Alaska Highway — this book will take you through majestic language from one astounding place to another, and back. Marie's journey, an echo of the author's own, navigating a stylish, unpredictable and cruel mother, yet we are privileged to come along, seeing an owl family on a windowsill and hearing her father's magical lectures about life — all while being surrounded by a family and country trying desperately to cope with dark secrets and the horrors of past sins. Unforgettable."

Hildie Block, author of "People" *and editor of* Not What I Expected

STONE MOTHER

MALVE S. BURNS

atmosphere press

To Arnost, Bradford, and Maura

BOOK ONE

Falkenburg Castle

1

FALKENBURG CASTLE, 1948

To a child, parents are like weather—all around you and constantly changing. They come and go at will, are the spring rain and autumn fog, refreshing cold and blistering heat. They're the gray days that last forever or star-filled nights after a drenching rain. My own mother was both a firebolt and freezing cold, and constantly around me—often breathing right down my neck.

I'd just turned five when Mama grabbed me to wash my hair. Wise to her fierce fingers that would yank my roots this way and that and push my face underwater until I almost drowned, I broke free and ran—out the front door, across the courtyard into the horse barn of Falkenburg Castle. The barn door slammed shut, and I dove into darkness.

The air smelled of leather, horse hide, and hay. I stood, just for a moment, so my eyes could adjust to the dark. The horses ground grain in their own rhythmic way, as if all was right with the world. But it was not.

I stumbled toward Chestnut, our brown mare, crawled under the curve of her belly, and heaved a sigh of relief. Chestnut would kick anyone who came close—except me. I heard footsteps. Chestnut snorted. I burrowed deeper into the straw, hushed my breath, and listened. Mama's perfume was tainting the air. My stomach heaved.

Chestnut moved ever so slightly. I kept my eyes tightly shut, my face low to the ground. Mama's steps came to a halt. Chestnut stomped her hoof and snorted like a dragon. She kicked the stall.

"You filthy, wretched beast!" Mama hissed.

Her steps moved away. *Please God, keep them moving.* Next, I heard them outside. I'd been spared for now. When I finally dared head home, I saw our father's car parked outside the gate and breathed a sigh of relief. Whenever Vati was home, Mama attacked with words only. I opened the gate and made for the front door.

Was I punished the next day? I don't think so. Mama's anger flared up like wildfire but rarely lingered. And each new day brought her an abundance of fresh provocations—animate or inanimate, such as the car door that "refused" to close tightly. Mama pummeled it with her umbrella with such ferocity, she dinged it all up.

Talk of "the war" was another, smaller constant of my life at Falkenburg Castle, a kind of background murmur. I might hear one woman in the shops say to another, "Exactly three years ago today, Erwin, my oldest, came home from 'the war.'" Or "My husband Peter would have turned 40 today had he survived Stalingrad." Or "The communists have turned our lands into a collective farm."

My parents stood in the flesh before me, but "the war" had no body for me. I had no images, no sounds or scents that I could recall. I could not remember the nights when bombs almost killed our family. I could not remember Sudetenland where we had lived at the end of "the war." I was a year and a half when Vati, Mama, my 10-year-old brother Bastian, 4-year-old sister Ingrid, and I fled west on a horse-drawn wagon, hiding in the woods by day and moving by night.

I knew nothing of Hitler, Nazis, or mass murder. Nor could I recall Falkenburg's Duke offering our Vati the Castellan's house at the Castle because the town needed another doctor.

But I knew every crack in my Castle's six soaring towers and in its massive, defensive walls. I bathed in the light of its voluminous chapel, breathed in the scent of vellum manuscripts, and slipped into the hum of its whispering halls. Safe within the stone arms of this medieval fortress, so solidly anchored on rock, I was inhaling the musk of time and marveling at my Castle's treasures—its paintings, tapestries, sculptures, and manuscripts.

Our benefactor, the Duke, did not live in the princely residence of the upper courtyard, but in a palace some ten miles away. He'd given us shelter when housing was impossible to come by because millions of Germans from the East kept pouring into the Western zones on tractors, on horseback, and on foot. Many had trekked hundreds of miles, some merely limping along—all of them fleeing the victorious Russian Army. The Duke opened his outbuildings, storage houses, and other parts of his estates to refugees and handed us first prize with the castellan's house.

Because Falkenburg Castle was the one and only home I had ever known and because its chapel and halls provided a refuge from Mama, I was convinced that I had always lived within its protective walls. My older brother and sister, and Mama, too, tried to tell me otherwise, but the Castle and I knew better. We belonged together.

2

Back to 1943:
Bombs Falling

Long after we had left Falkenburg Castle, I asked my father how he'd dared request a week's home leave in the middle of WWII, as he had often told me. "What's more important than delivering your own child?" he had replied. "Asking was easy. I helped your sister into this world and was determined to usher you in as well." My father's request for a leave was granted. In October of 1943, Vati boarded a train and prayed that his timing was true. Three days after his arrival, my mother went into labor.

Vati told me the story of my birth so many times that I could call it up at will as if I had been present. And, of course, I had been—if only as a red-faced bundle of flesh and bones that slid from her mother's body into her father's outstretched hands.

Vati was worried about the clear sky that October night because good visibility often brought on air raids, but he kept his thoughts to himself. While dabbing Mama's glistening forehead, he told her she was doing just fine. That it wouldn't be long now. Then he went to the kitchen to check on my brother Bastian and my sister Ingrid.

He was trying not to consider the worst, he told me—bombs killing his soon-to-be-born child, along with its parents. But how could he not? Our family lived three miles from the city's center. That provided some protection from the worst, but not enough. Often, when the pilots were ready to return to home base, they dropped their bombs willy-nilly on whatever was in their path.

In the kitchen, Vati asked Anna, barely eighteen then, if Ingrid and

Bastian had had their dinner. She assured him they had and were now getting their belongings together "just in case."

"Well done," Vati told her. "The clear night worries me. Stay by their side."

Only minutes after Vati returned to the bedroom, the low drone of bombers broke the evening's silence. Sirens blared, men, women, and children spilled into the street to head for the shelter, while Mama, in the grip of contractions, pushed out short thrusts of breath. Vati took her hand and held it firmly. He told her it sounded like they were flying somewhat east of town.

From the bedroom window he watched Ingrid and Bastian as they hurried with Anna to the air raid shelter. Basti, Mama's son from her first marriage, was holding Ingrid's left hand, Anna clutching her right. Ingrid had blown out three candles on her birthday cake just three weeks before.

Everyone was rushing to safety while our mother was clenching her fists and crying out as bombs began exploding over our town.

The blinds covering our bedroom windows didn't fit tightly, showing the red rim of the sky. *What madness to bring a child into a world of fire.*

The block warden spotted the candlelight from below and called up from the street, "Lights out! Extinguish all lights!"

Vati let him shout, rushed back to Mama, and took her hand. "Push, Lily, push!"

Mama pressed down, and Vati pulled me into the exploding night with that irrepressible sense of hope he felt at every birth. "A girl, a perfectly formed girl," Vati told Mama and made his way back to the kitchen to fetch warm water. For the blink of an eye, my father told me, the world had been set right. While he was cleaning me up, the all-clear sounded. He dipped the cloth into the water one more time, he said, but stopped midair. "You were looking at me with your big blue eyes as if you saw right through me and our deranged world," Vati said. "Your knowing took my breath away."

When he heard the scuffling of feet from the street and the voices of people returning from the shelter, he listened for the footsteps of Bastian and Ingrid on the staircase, eager to show off their newly arrived baby sister.

What wouldn't I give to have seen Ingrid and Bastian's faces when they first set eyes on me?

And what wouldn't I give to remember what I, newborn Marie, had seen that night? My father's excitement and tender care? Mama's sweat-drenched exhaustion? The rim of a red sky beyond Vati's out-stretched hands? I don't know because my unfolding brain could not yet record what my eyes took in. For all intents and purposes, I might have been born blind.

3

FALKENBURG.
THE JEWISH CEMETERY

While I remained ignorant of the war and my people's past, I *did* know enough to look for escape routes whenever I found myself alone with Mama.

One day, when Vati was at his surgery, my brother at boarding school, and my sister in elementary school, I tiptoed to the front door of our house, slipped out quietly, and hurried through the outer gate of the Castle into the heath.

As soon as I set foot on the shepherd's trail, a long gray stick caught my eye. Intrigued by its perfect straight line, I picked it up. 'Now I can be a blind person,' I thought, closed my eyes, and began tapping. I squinted at first to make sure I was not headed for a thorn bush or a patch of thistles, but quickly got the hang of it and tapped along briskly—until my stick bumped against something solid. When I opened my eyes, I was standing before the high walls of the Jewish cemetery.

I'd never been inside before and tried the massive gate. It was locked. Why was this cemetery so far from town? I wondered.

Anna had told me once, "That's where the poor souls buried their own."

"What poor souls?"

"The Jews. They...they've been cursed since time immemorial, that's what the chaplain told us in school...but they need their peace." Anna had lowered her eyes.

"Why have they been cursed, Anna?"

"Because they crucified Jesus. Now, don't you trouble your head. That was so long ago," Anna had said, making the sign of the cross.

Did God curse the Jews? I wondered, but did not ask my question out loud because I felt Anna's turmoil.

I pushed along the cemetery wall until I came to a spot where the ground was elevated and I could find a handhold. I heaved myself up and over, landing in the soft mounds between gray headstones.

I saw no flowers, no candles or any other sign that someone cared about the place, in contrast to Falkenburg's town cemetery where people grew flowers on their loved ones' graves from early spring to late October.

In here was emptiness. The paths were covered with tall grass, the stone casings cloaked with moss. Perhaps even the spirits of the dead had left this place. I sensed a frightening unknown. The love and care that had created this place had long run its course, and a strange forgetting had set in as if the cemetery were an empty room in an abandoned house.

I traced the chiseled lines on the headstones with my fingers, slowly feeling my way. The letters were wavy, not at all like the print in my Bible or in *Grimm's Fairy Tales*, nor like the vellum manuscripts in the Castle's library. I wished my touch could unlock their text as Braille might if I were truly blind. I smoothed the tall grass that surrounded the mounds, careful not to disturb the graves, and knelt to pray the way I'd been taught, "Dear Lord, please open your arms and take in the souls of all who are buried here."

By the time I raised myself, shadows were falling across my shoes, the sun sinking low, disappearing behind the cemetery wall. I had to get home before blackness swallowed the walls, the headstones, and me. With dusk creeping in all around me, I was suddenly sure that the graves were filled with fleshless arms and bony fingers that would drag me down.

I paced the wall—it seemed so much higher on the inside—searching for elevated ground. I stretched as high as I could but in vain. With rising panic, I hurried away from the wall. Then I charged, running toward the graves and on top of them, and, terrified by this sacrilege, I leapt, reaching the top of the wall. I clung to it with all my strength, pulling myself up and over, and tumbled to the ground below.

As soon as I passed through the outer gate, I spotted Anna walking toward me and flung myself into her outstretched arms, pushing my face deep into her warm flesh.

"Hush, hush, Marie." Anna gently moved me away from herself so she could look me in the eye. "Where in the world have you been?"

"I climbed over the wall of the cemetery in the heath and then... couldn't get out again."

Anna winced when she heard *cemetery in the heath* so that I started shaking all over again. She put one arm around me and walked me toward our house. "From now on, don't ever leave the Castle without first getting permission from your mama or me. Understood?"

"Yes, Anna." She squeezed my hand.

"I won't tell your mama. You've had enough of a scare." She pulled out a hanky. "Now wipe your face and blow your nose real good before we go inside."

I did as she asked while keeping my eyes firmly fixed to the ground. I didn't dare look over my shoulder, afraid that the dead had risen up and were coming after me.

When Vati returned from making house calls, I heard him sing out in the hallway, "Lilybeth, I'm ho-ome," and make his way to the bathroom as he did every night to scrub his hands and forearms thoroughly clean. Though I couldn't see my father from the nursery, his firm step and the mere sound of his voice calmed my haunted heart. Even Mama's angry cry of "Why can't you for once be home on time?" could not upset me.

Before I knew it, Vati stood in my door.

He sat down by my bedside, kissed my cheek, and felt my forehead. "I hear you have a tummy ache. There seems to be something going 'round. How are you feeling?"

"Better." I was just like my father's patients. When Vati stepped out from the examination room, his inner sanctum, every face in the waiting room lit up. Men and women sat up taller, children stopped crying, and the patient called to follow him inside smiled or sighed with relief. Vati was not especially handsome nor of towering height, but he was a giant in the eyes of suffering women and men and a comfort to their souls.

Vati looked at me with concern. "Did you have to throw up?"

"No."

"May I listen to your tummy?"

"Yes." Vati put his ear against my stomach, palpated, and listened.

"I think the tummy is calming down," he said. "I'll stop by again after dinner to make sure it keeps behaving." Vati turned to leave.

"Vati?"

"Yes?"

"Why did they bury their dead so far from town?"

"Who's that?"

"The poor souls, the Jews."

"Oh?" Vati took a deep breath. "You mean the cemetery on the heath behind the Castle?"

"Yes."

"That's a long story." Vati stroked my cheek and said in a low voice, "I will tell you, Marie, when you are a little older."

"Promise?"

"Promise."

It is pitch dark. Someone is lifting me out of my bed. Not Vati. He would have lifted me ever so slowly while gently pressing me against his chest. "Ingrid," I call out. No answer. The arms are hard and steady.

"She awake?" whispers a woman.

"Gettin' there."

"Here, take this."

A moist cloth smothers my breath. I know the scent. Ether. Vati takes it with him on his house calls in case he has to cut someone or sew them up.

The face above me cackles, then grunts, "That's better."

Next, I'm on a mound of earth like a grave. Tall figures surround me, swaying above me like poplars in the wind. A moan. From me? Before I can tell, I feel the ether cloth pressing down on my nose and mouth again.

———

I woke from Ingrid shaking me. "Wake up, Marie!" Ingrid's forehead bumped into mine. I could have cried from joy. I was here, next to my sister. In our nursery. I looked for the swaying figures. They were gone.

"Slide over. You've been having a nightmare, moaning something God-awful." She slid into my bed. "There. Hush. I'm right here. Go back to sleep."

4

IN THE BEGINNING
WAS THE WORD

Come Sundays, our Anna braided her long black hair, coiled it into a chignon, and draped her best shawl around her shoulders. Next, she turned my sister's thick blond hair into twin Schnecken, braided buns, and pinned them over her ears. My own fine, ash blond hair—Mama called it lifeless—produced such meager braids that I was allowed to wear it down though Mama insisted on big hair bows. The metal clasps of the bows scratched my scalp, and the eye-catching colors of the ribbon—bright pink, red, or purple—vexed me something terrible. I felt like a box of assorted chocolates presented to Mama by one of the Duke's minions.

But I forgot about ribbons and clasps as we crossed the upper courtyard because the moment we stepped onto the cold stones of the chapel, the organ's vibrations set my heart atremble along with the pews and tall, clear-glass windows. When the music had come to rest, silence filled the air, a springboard for the word of the Lord that floated toward us through the preacher's voice. *Am Anfang war das Wort, und das Wort war bei Gott und Gott war das Wort.* "In the beginning was the Word, and the Word was with God, and God was the Word."

I sat up tall to lean into the beautiful words that echoed from the walls before settling into my heart—electrified by the interplay of "Wort" and "Gott," a "cross-stitch" that tried to pin the mystery down.

I wished the minister would never stop reading from the Holy Book. While I liked his sonorous voice, his sermons left me cold. He delivered straight talk, without mystery, whereas the Bible's verses surprised, seduced, and sang. Ruth's promise to Naomi, "Whither thou goest, I will go and where thou lodgest, I will lodge," made my heart swell so that I grabbed Anna's hand. She turned toward me with a hushed smile, which I took as confirmation that her heart had been touched by the same words, too.

Hungry for words and ever more words, I wanted to unlock stories and books on my own. To my sorrow, I was only five and would have to wait months and months before starting school. I felt desperate and wondered how I could lure my sister into helping me reach my goal.

I did know she loved to suck on wild sorrel that grew near the river Woernitz at the foot of the Castle's hill. We all loved that sour, refreshing taste. Basti had told us that Roman soldiers used to chew sorrel leaves on their long, exhausting marches through Germany, France, and Britain, which only heightened our enjoyment. I resolved to pick a big bunch for my sister in return for a lesson. My mood brightened, only to darken again almost instantly: I would need permission to leave the Castle.

Next morning, I was shooed out of the kitchen right after my breakfast with Anna because it was *Waschtag,* laundry day. And Mama had a fitting for a dress in town. That was my chance! I rushed through the small back gate leading toward the river and, keeping close to hedges and bushes, scurried to the river meadow. I had never picked flowers faster than I did the wild sorrel, turned on my heels, and was back on the footpath before I'd met a soul, and more importantly, before any soul had met me. All out of breath and torn by guilty feelings toward Anna but not toward the worthiness of my goal, I fetched my toothbrush container, filled it with water, and soaked my green treasure.

In the afternoon, I took a seat at the card table in the library where Ingrid did her homework. When I saw her packing away her slate and stylus, I jumped up, retrieved the sorrel jar from under the table, and said sweetly, "I've picked some sorrel for you, Ingrid, if you'll show me how to write letters."

The tip of my sister's upturned nose rose even higher, her green eyes scrutinizing me for a moment before she smiled. "Sure, but if I were you, I'd be out in the yard, jumping rope or playing hopscotch." She was already fishing out a stalk of sorrel and chewing away.

"Later," I said softly and pointed to a word on Ingrid's slate. "What does that word mean?"

"Sonne," Sun, said Ingrid.

"Can you write it out one more time, real slow?"

Ingrid brushed some thick curls from her eyes, picked up a piece of chalk, and formed each letter slowly, pronouncing it at the same time.

"Sonne," I read out to her with a feeling of empowerment, as if I had just made the sun rise.

Ingrid's nudge broke the spell. "Now *you* write it!"

I locked eyes with my sister, let the chalk hover above Ingrid's beautifully formed *S*, and finally, awkwardly, wrote: SONNE.

Ingrid studied the slate for a long time before pronouncing, "A bit wriggly but not too bad. Do it again." I couldn't wait.

We spent the next two hours—and many an hour over the following weeks—thoroughly absorbed in our task. To my surprise, Ingrid savored her elevation to teacher, even without fresh bunches of sorrel, and I was thrilled with my entry into the magic kingdom of words.

While Ingrid was in school, I lifted the heavy tome of *Grimm's Fairy Tales* from the bookshelf. I recognized the stories by their colorful pictures and heard the words of the tales in my mind. Fortified by my sister's teaching, I walked my fingers from letter to letter and soon deciphered not only fairy tales but, within a few weeks, verses in the Old and New Testament.

My heart soared when my fingers found "*Am Anfang war das Wort, und das Wort war bei Gott und Gott war das Wort.*" Though all was quiet in the library, in my mind I heard the organ infuse the words with power, making them swell and float toward the dome of the church.

As I worked my way deeper into the Holy Book—with Ingrid's help and stumbling on my own—I was stunned by Jehovah's wrath that rained burning sulfur onto Sodom, and I stopped breathing entirely when the Lord demanded that Abraham sacrifice his own son. What? Gott wanted Abraham to kill his own child? How could he demand such a heinous deed? I knew instantly that Vati, if put in Abraham's position, would not obey God. But what about Mama? My stomach cramped, for I knew when Mama was in the grip of the furies, she had no mercy.

For as long as I could remember, I had known *wrath*. From that day forward, I trembled before the Lord as I did before Mama.

5

RETURNING FROM AUNT JULIA'S HOUSE

But I did not tremble before Aunt Julia, Vati's younger sister and chief surgeon of the county hospital, or before her husband, Uncle Herbert, when we visited their large stone house in Dillingen, not far from the train tracks. Unlike our dynamic Vati, Aunt Julia was the quiet, observant type with fine facial features and calm, probing blue eyes. She and Vati had studied medicine together, which created a special bond between them for the rest of their lives, but I did not think about the nature of their relationship at the time. I simply breathed in the good will between them that felt like a caress.

After a brief welcome, we children would be whisked away to the "nursery quarters" on the ground floor of the house. There, we'd sip hot chocolate with our two cousins, Robert and Reni, while listening to the mournful whistle of passing trains. I fell in love with that sound and would have given anything to bottle it and take it home.

But the greatest thrill at our cousins' house was not their marvelous playroom, the whistle of a passing train, or our fast-paced ping-pong games. It was the calm. No one screamed at Aunt Julia's house. No one shed tears. Though the grown-ups met by themselves upstairs, we would have heard Mama's screams if ever she had lost it up there. What concentration she must have mustered. Restraint was not part of her nature.

The moment our car had crossed the river Woernitz on our return to Falkenburg Castle, Mama, seated up front, began smoothing out the pleats of her dress with nervous fingers, making near inaudible coughing sounds. Ingrid, Bastian, and I shot each other warning looks. We couldn't remember a peaceful ending to any family outing. To us, her stifled coughing cascade signaled disaster.

I snuggled closer to my athletic sister, famous at school for standing her ground. Bastian, meanwhile, kept shaking his head. He stared out the window while plugging his ears with his fingers.

"So, you think Evelyn Meyer is a good doctor?" Mama asked, her voice already shrill. "A good doctor and such an *attractive* woman!" She stretched the word *attractive* out into a taunt.

We children knew that Dr. Meyer was a friend and colleague of Aunt Julia's though she had not been at Aunt Julia's house that day.

"She's all right," Vati said, "a perfectly decent doctor." Our father's voice was calm. The calmer he was, we knew, the more upset Mama would become.

"You never told *me,* Vati"—Mama lingered on the word *me*—"that Evelyn Meyer is so *attractive!*"

"Let it be, Lilybeth. It was just a superficial comment."

"Superficial?" Mama slapped the dashboard with her flat hand. "Is that what you call this, you coward? You never tell *me* what you think and feel. At least I know now why you invited the Meyers to Bastian's birthday party. You are lusting after that *attractive* woman!"

The car shot forward because Mama had stomped with full force on Vati's foot on the accelerator. He struggled free and worked the brake pedal. The car slowed down.

"Lilybeth, please. The children!" We came to a full stop by the side of the road.

"The children? The *children*? As if you gave a damn about the children. You always put your darling patients first," Mama hissed. "And if it isn't your darling patients, it's that hussy of a colleague, the oh so *attractive* Evelyn, that's on your mind. You never think of me, or the children."

None of which was true. Only last night, it was Vati, not Mama, who had awakened me and carried me to the kitchen so I could see the owl with eyes of amber that had landed on the windowsill.

Mama yanked out the ashtray, launched it at Vati, pouring ashes and cigarette stubs all over his head.

"I wonder what the *attractive* Evelyn would think of *her darling* Vati now?"

Though the car was no longer moving, Vati kept a tight grip on the steering wheel. I was praying for a deluge, a flood like Noah's that would wash the car and all of us away. The more the windows fogged up, the more everything around me—the steering wheel, the car, the road, and my own mind—became a blur.

When Vati pulled up the hand brake in front of the gate to our house, I scrambled over Bastian's lap, pushed out of the car, and ran. I could still feel the Opel rock and lurch after Mama had grabbed the steering wheel, still heard the metallic scratch when Mama pulled the ashtray out of its casing. Then I saw nothing, until slowly, ever so slowly, Vati's blue eyes surfaced from under the streaks of ash and soot. They looked dark, as if they could no longer hold any light.

Clouds flung shadows onto the skull of the wolf nailed to the drop gate as I raced toward the upper courtyard. Oblivious to the wolf's bared fangs, I shot through the gate into the inner yard.

Finally, I was out of Mama's sight, her shrieks no longer in my ears. I started to breathe more freely and rushed up the stairs to the ramparts. The wooden steps were rickety, and the floorboards splintering. Mama never came near them because of her high heels and nylon stockings.

But I didn't feel safe until I was way up on my skywalk.

Now I was in a realm where I knew every stone—and where every stone, I felt, knew me. When I touched the ancient walls of the battlement, I felt their unyielding strength and imagined the hordes of enemy soldiers rushing toward them over time: British, French, Spanish, Austrian, Polish, and even rival German soldiers during the thirty-year war.

I turned. With my back to the town and the open plain, I looked into the inner yard of the Castle with its ancient keep facing east; its well at the center, and the great hall with its imposing exterior staircase. Surveying the barren courtyard, my eye was drawn to the lone willow by the chapel's door, its veil of green enlivening the bleak space.

When out-of-town visitors passed the willow and opened the door to the chapel, they gasped at its voluminous space, which still thrilled me every time I crossed the threshold. I felt at home in its echoing space with its clear-glass windows and stone sculptures, and was convinced that Count Gottfried, a life-sized stone figure under the choir, kept watch over me. He was flanked by his two wives—the three of them doubly captured, first as a sculpture in the vault of the church and then as bones in the crypt below. What had the Count's life been like? Perhaps he could never forget his first wife, the one with the soft face, who had died so young.

She'd been only twenty-five, younger than Mama, Bastian had told me. I often ran a gentle finger along the hem of her stone dress and would have loved to touch her cheeks, but the figure was so much taller than I. The second wife was big and imposing, a veritable pillar of strength that reminded me of Anna.

I turned again, looking from the battlement toward the town and open plain. Only four years after Germany's most devastating war, I saw no signs of destruction. Had I lived in Hamburg, Frankfurt, or Berlin, I'd be surrounded by ruins and rubble. Here, I surveyed upright church spires and small villages, not targeted by enemy bombs because this was a hinterland, rich in wheat fields, barley, and hops, and devoid of industry, government, and military installations.

When I lowered my chin as I peered through the embrasures, I saw Falkenburg's cobblestoned streets. When I lifted my chin higher, the land rolled away from my eyes into the vast plain as if into an endless ocean.

The plain had been scooped out by a meteor some nine million years ago—the bowl-shaped landscape a perfect match for the dome of the sky above. The world came together in this space, and I felt both embraced and swept out as if I were God's lookout, his eye between earth and the heavens.

6

THE LITTLE
MATCH GIRL

When I came into to the parlor after my nap the next day, Mama's eyes and composure betrayed not the slightest trace of her fit in the car. She looked up from the couch across from our tall tile stove and said, "You're just in time for fairy tales." She patted the space next to her. "Do sit by me but take care not to crush the pleats of my skirt."

"Yes, Mama." Mama adored fairy tales and when she had nothing better to do, which was not often, she read to me. I, in turn, loved those special times when her voice became soft, her lips relaxed, and her mind forgot about elaborate dinners, the newest dress patterns, or waxing the floors to such a shine—yes, Frau Doktor could be found on her hands and knees when Anna had *failed* to clean the floors to Mama's standards—that you could serve a meal on them.

Mama cleared her throat. "Today, we'll hear about Rapunzel and her tall tower." I was fond of that story and longed for Rapunzel's thick hair that was so strong it could become the prince's ladder.

"No," Mama interrupted herself. "I think we'll read *The Little Match Girl* instead to show you"—Mama stopped, her large gray eyes grew wider, her forehead shot up—"how some parents treat their children." With that she put *Grimm's Fairy Tales* back on the shelf and picked up Andersen's *Tales*.

"Snow was falling, and it was bitter cold," Mama began. "In the fading light, a small girl was walking through the streets. Her parents were so poor that she had to sell matches to buy coal for their stove."

Mama's voice softened. "Snowflakes fell all around her and her hands were nearly frozen from cold."

Mama let the book slide down to her lap and stared out the window. Then she shifted her weight, sat up straight, and continued in a voice that was cracked—as if pushing against something that wanted to come out. What could it be? I wondered, and leaned toward her.

"A fierce wind was blowing, cutting straight to her skin. The little girl's dress was too thin and threadbare to protect her from the icy wind."

Mama fixed her eyes on me; they were as large as the owl's that landed on our kitchen windowsill and were filled with a sadness that stopped my breath. Something in me welled up when Mama looked sad. I wanted to touch her cheek to console her just as I wanted to console Count Gottfried's first wife in the chapel, but the moment dissolved so quickly I didn't get a chance.

"How could her parents let that little girl brave the cold without a winter coat?" Mama asked in an angry tone. "Do you know how lucky you are to have parents who care for you?" Her eyes demanded an answer, so I said, "Yes, Mama," still wondering why Mama had looked so desperately sad.

Mama picked up the book again.

"Not a man, woman, or child was in sight as night fell over the town, but the little match girl did not dare go home. She needed to sell at least three boxes. Then her parents could buy a scuttle of coal. The wind was howling across the square, throwing sheets of snow into the girl's face."

There was a knock at the living room door. Mama wrinkled her forehead.

"Come in."

Anna's big frame filled the doorway. She smiled at me, a small conspiratorial smile.

"You asked me to let you know the instant I was done cleaning the windows, Frau Doktor," said Anna. "I have just finished the last one."

Mama's eyebrows shot up. She glared at Anna and made small coughing sounds before settling the book in my lap.

"I'll be right back," she snapped without looking my way. The door had barely closed when I heard Mama shout, "You call that clean? Don't you have eyes in your head, *Du faule Schlampe*! You lazy slob!"

I froze, then pulled myself together and put the book down. I peeked into the dining room just as Mama ripped the leather cloth from Anna's hand, marched toward the tall east window, and rubbed with fierce determination. She rubbed and rubbed, with ever greater fury—as if every single motion fueled her anger—until the window seemed to curve slightly, then shattered.

For a second, Mama just stood there. I was already trembling when I saw her move in on poor Anna, whose shoulders had dropped, making her look almost small.

"Now look what you've made me do, you dirty witch!" Mama screamed. "It's all your fault, you...you ungrateful, lazy slut!"

Mama grabbed the pail of water and threw it. Anna ducked, and the pail missed her by inches and hit the dining room wall. In shock, Anna leaned against the wall while Mama's fists rained down on her.

"Mama, please," I managed to beg though I really wanted to scream at Mama. Her fists stopped. She stared at me with wild eyes and ran off to our parents' bedroom, which was off limits to us. I followed but could not make myself barge in. Instead, and as so often before, I ran—out of the house, up the incline through Wolf Gate, slipping under the skirt of the willow by the chapel's door. I was still shaking when Bastian joined me.

"Anna's all right," he said quickly, his gray eyes widening like Mama's, "I checked. I wish I could have helped her. But that would have made Mama even more furious."

"I know." The scene kept replaying in my mind. "What about the window?"

"That's broken for good, which means we have to call Helfried, the glazer." Bastian made a face.

"Don't you like him?"

"He's the weird guy I told you about. Wanders about playing a black flute." Basti pushed a lone curl from his forehead—my brother had a wonderful mop of brown hair—and said, "People are whispering that he's a warlock."

"A what?"

"A male witch."

I didn't know what to make of Bastian's revelation.

"Just before we moved into the Castle, a girl fell from the upper town wall while walking in her sleep," Bastian said.

"Was she hurt?"

"She died. Some people swear Helfried lured her into the night with his flute."

"Really?"

"I'll show you the place where she fell."

"I don't want to see."

"We know from old church records that there were witches and warlocks in Falkenburg during the Middle Ages."

"No, Bastian," I burst out in desperation with goose pimples breaking out all over me. "Vati told me there are no witches. And there is no devil. He says that people invent demons so that they don't have to face their own cruelty."

Bastian tousled my hair. "You and Vati!" he mumbled and stretched his long, lean frame. "In the meantime, Mama has locked herself in."

Both of us let out a sigh of relief. Whenever Mama retreated to her bedroom from exhaustion—perhaps even from shame—we wouldn't see her for hours and were free to do whatever we wanted.

"You all right?" Bastian's eyes searched mine.

"Ja, ja."

"Gut. Then I'll be off to Bernard's house. We're building a kite." He grinned. "I can't wait for summer." My big brother hated school. But I envied him and Ingrid that they got to go and couldn't wait to finally join them.

After Bastian was out of sight, I listened for footsteps and voices. When I felt sure that I was quite alone, I headed for the Treasure Hall, one of my favorite haunts. Nothing moved in its hushed space, and yet I felt surrounded by life—life holding its breath. It was here that the Duke had assembled his finest works of art, his tapestries, and manuscripts for safekeeping during the war. And here, they still waited to be sorted.

They spoke to me, these canvasses, sculptures, and busts, all at a loss of where to stand, sit, or lie. Some paintings were stacked together like a fan, others shone their imposing, mysterious, or tender images right into my eyes, luring me into their world. Vellum manuscripts filled shelf after shelf or spilled from boxes among rolled-up tapestries.

I felt certain that the statues at the hall's center, carved by a medieval master, were not lifeless wood. If only I could steal in without making a sound, I'd catch them lowering their eyelids or breathing a sigh. Their gray-brown, worm-eaten wood wound its way in elegant folds up to their delicate faces, and their eyes and hands, the lines of their veins, looked so real that they must have just recently been alive.

The saints' faces did not look serene but burdened somehow. They were seeking something beyond themselves. "What are you looking for?" I asked them, waiting patiently for their answer, then probing again, "Can I help you find it?" They stayed mum.

I didn't dare touch paintings or rolled-up canvasses but couldn't stop myself from running a finger along the surface of the vellum manuscripts. First, I wiped my hands on the hem of my skirt, then, beguiled by its scent, I lifted a volume with tender fingers. I took a deep breath of the musk of time and pressed the treasure to my cheek, warming its cool skin. When I finally opened the cover, I saw a tangle of swirls that I recognized as letters but not as words; they were written in Latin. Bastian told me that Latin is a "dead language," no longer spoken today, except in his church. This couldn't be. The words were right before me, I felt their pulsating life and wanted to unlock what they hid.

The light around me was darkening. When I looked through the tall windows into the sky, I saw clouds balling up. Like Mama's fists, I thought and stiffened. Anna! The stone stairs cascaded before me on my way down. I almost tumbled, but caught myself, found the passage to my shortcut to the inner yard, and sprinted through Wolf Gate to our house. Anna was in the kitchen, tending to several pots on the stove, turning her swollen face toward me with a lopsided smile.

7

THE SPIRIT PRINCE

The summer of 1949 was marching on, though not fast enough for me who couldn't wait to enter school in the fall. I sometimes pinched one of Ingrid's school books and snuck into the chapel. I might even climb up into the pulpit and call out the words full force before they dissolved into waves of echoes unfolding like an accordion.

Founded during the Romanesque period, my chapel had been expanded in the Gothic style during the Middle Ages, and finally received Baroque touches in the 17th century. Before Luther's Reformation it must have had colorful stained-glass windows, depicting Christ's passion or scenes from the Old Testament. But after our Duke's forebears joined the Protestant Reformation as one of the first rulers in Southern Germany, they replaced them with sheer glass to capture God's heavenly light in its purest form.

Basti caught me declaiming full force from the pulpit one July day and invited me down to watch him sketch the apse and its windows for his art class. I sat next to him without moving a muscle while he recreated this sacred part of our chapel.

"What do you think?" Bastian held up his pad.

"Beautiful, Bastian. Like the drawings in *Grimm's Fairy Tales*."

My brother smiled, slid the pad into his satchel, and invited me to sit down.

"We had the best Latin class," he told me. "Dr. Schmidt brought in a letter that was written right here at our Castle some eight hundred years ago. In Latin, of course." I was all ears, especially since Bastian usually dreaded his Latin classes.

"Who was the letter from?"

"From Prince Henry, the son of King Konrad who was the Holy

Roman Emperor in the twelfth century."

To think that the son of a king had stayed here in my Castle! My skin started to tingle.

"What did Prince Henry say?"

"He told his father that he was about to set out from our Castle to conquer Castle Flochberg some ten miles down the road." Bastian leaned toward me. "And we know from historical records that he *did* win back Castle Flochberg for the Holy Roman Empire."

I clapped my hands, "Bravo, Prince Henry," while wondering in which room the prince had composed his letter. And had he given a victory banquet in the great hall?

"We don't know much more about him," said Bastian. "He died at age thirteen the following year from some battle wound or other."

"Died?" I asked, jerked out of my reverie, feeling such a profound loss over the Prince's death right at the point of learning about his existence. I looked up at Bastian. He was thirteen. What if Bastian... I shuddered so hard Bastian put his arm around my shoulder.

"It's okay, little sis. Don't take it so hard."

I leaned against him. "If there were a war tomorrow, would you have to go and fight?"

"Don't be silly. You have to be at least eighteen to be called up." Bastian fell silent, then cleared his throat. "Until the end. When the fighting gets desperate, when too many men have been killed, they do call up boys. In 1944, just a few months after you were born, they started calling up high school students. They gave the boys uniforms and guns."

"Who did?

"Hitler. Hitler and his generals."

"Didn't anyone stop him?" I looked up at my brother, who looked back at me with such a strange expression that I worried I'd offended him.

"He was *Der Fuehrer* with absolute power," my brother burst out. "People followed him blindly because he promised to make Germany great again." Bastian's hand brushed over his eyebrows. "Vati thought Hitler was mad. Mama was terrified we'd all be locked up if Vati said so in public."

"Locked up?"

"Thrown into prison or worse. Hitler didn't tolerate criticism."

"Like Mama," I said.

My brother broke into a bitter laugh. "Oh, Marie! He was much worse than Mama."

Worse? I couldn't imagine anything worse than Mama's outbursts.

"He had a secret police force, the Gestapo, who arrested, tortured, and killed people. Once the Gestapo got ahold of you, you were a goner." Bastian shook himself and took my hand in his. "I knew some of the boys who were sent to the Front."

"You did?"

"Yes." Bastian stared into the distance. "Andreas, who used to let me ride on his handlebars when I was little—he never came back."

I held the name to me. I would pray for Andreas before going to sleep. Every night I asked God to protect our family. And, of course, from now on, I would also pray for the soul of the Prince.

Blood drained from Bastian's cheeks. His eyes misted over. I wanted to console my brother, but felt helpless, because I'd never "lost" anyone while Vati, Anna, Mama, and everyone in Falkenburg had lost loved ones in the war or in the bombings. I thought of the men without an arm or a leg Anna and I sometimes encountered on our way to or from town. Some had no legs or arms at all.

War. The word itself remained a mystery. Though the war had ended years ago, I somehow felt that it wasn't really over. Like blood under a scar. If you scratch, it bleeds out.

Prince Henry's life had also been cut short because of a war. "Was Prince Henry buried in this chapel?" I asked. The crypt was the only part of the chapel that made my flesh creep. Winding stone stairs led down to a dark vault filled with stone coffins. Still, if Prince Henry's body was resting in the crypt far from his family and home, I believed I might go right down there and sit by his side.

"No," Bastian said. "He was royal, he'd been buried at court." I let out a sigh of relief, followed by an inner sigh of regret. Bastian picked up his pad and got up. I hardly noticed. Pushing my anger against that Hitler man out of my mind, I wondered if I could find a portrait of Prince Henry among the canvasses in my Treasure Hall.

"What did Prince Henry look like?" I asked, but my brother had gone, leaving me to wonder about the young Prince's likeness.

Everything around me was quiet. The light around the altar was glowing, almost breathing, the air felt expectant. Did Prince Henry pray in this chapel before setting out to conquer Castle Flochberg, I wondered? Kneeling on the very stones where I now stood? "Yes," I whispered, mesmerized by the light. "Yes, yes, he did."

I was sure of it and felt a presence, a shudder in the air.

"*I did not want to die*," Prince Henry whispered from behind the altar.

My heart contracted.

"You didn't?"

"Nobody does," he said. "I was only thirteen."

"I know," I said, thinking of Bastian. "That's far too young." I looked to the left and to the right but couldn't see anyone.

"And the pain, the searing, hot pain."

"Were you wounded?" I walked closer to the altar.

"*Yes*." Now the voice was moving away from the altar.

"What happened?"

"A lance pierced my shoulder. I hardly felt it in the heat of battle, but later when the doctor cleaned and dressed the wound, the pain was excruciating." Now the voice came from the aisle between the pews. "He said I would be restored, but the wound never healed."

I was already in the aisle, hoping to catch hold of the Prince.

"The wound never healed, and the fire coursed through my veins like the plague through villages and towns."

The Prince was moving toward the back of the chapel, with me following his voice.

"No one could help me. I was doomed."

"Oh, no."

"*I was but a leaf in...*" The voice was becoming weaker. Was the Prince descending the winding stairs? I walked up to the iron grille of the crypt but could not bring myself to open the gate.

"A leaf in what?"

"*...in the...wind.*" I could hardly make out his words, yet they moved me. They sounded so lovely...but when a person turns into a leaf, the wind can whip him about. And now he's become even lighter than a leaf—he is a spirit. While I pondered this, I felt the Prince leaving me.

8

LISTENING BEHIND
CLOSED DOORS

A couple of weeks later, I ran into Bastian on my way to the "throne room," as we children called the loo at the end of the hall. Wooden steps led up to a big one-holer that emptied on the outside of the Castle's wall. Bastian waved me on. On my way back I almost bumped into him as he knelt before the keyhole to the library.

"What are you doing?" I whispered.

"Trying to find out what's next."

"What do you mean?

"If we're going to Aunt Amalia's in Garmisch or not."

"Oh."

Our parents were building a house in Garmisch so that Mama could be close to her best friend, Countess Amalia. Barely a year after arriving at Falkenburg Castle, our brother had told Ingrid and me, Mama began prodding Vati to leave "this stinky little town" and practice in the renowned mountain resort of Garmisch with its "upper-class clientele." She hated Vati's "boorish" Falkenburg patients. Vati finally relented. Since the projected move was many months away, we children mostly pushed thoughts of our new house in Garmisch out of our minds.

"Amalia," we heard Mama say, "has invited the children and me for a long weekend, which means I can also check on how our house is coming along."

There was a pause. I thought I could hear Mama pick up her coffee cup and set it down again. "I do think it's important for the children to associate with nobility."

"Hmm," Vati said. Mama liked to bring up her *noble* background.

Her father, our grandfather, had been a Baron, making Mama a Baroness. Ingrid and I never knew him because he died before we were born.

"What's *Hmm* supposed to mean?"

"It doesn't matter that Amalia is a countess, Lilybeth, she's a gracious lady, and her children seem perfectly normal and well-behaved whenever I've seen them."

"Amalia's never forgotten what you did the night we fled west. Who knows what would have happened to her and her family without your phone call?"

"And to us. It's our Czech neighbor we have to be thankful to."

"Yes, yes. Do you think we could take Bastian out of his boarding school for an extra day?"

"*Yesss*," Bastian mumbled under his breath.

"Absolutely," said Vati. Bastian almost snapped his finger with delight but stopped himself just in time. "Maybe Marie better stay home with me," we heard Vati say. I leaned in with a thrill. "She seems a bit under the weather. I'll give her a course under the sunlamp and fortify her with vitamin shots." My parents were always worried about my health though I did not feel ill. Especially not now that I got to stay with Vati.

"Good. That child spends far too much time in the library and in the chapel"—I felt sure Mama was rolling her eyes when saying *chapel*—"and not enough in the fresh air. Besides, Amalia's boy is close to Bastian's age, and the girl and Ingrid could be sisters. Marie would be the odd child out."

"When do you plan to leave?"

"On Friday by train like last time—a pleasant two-hour ride."

"Does Amalia's brother still live with her?"

"Count Mergenthal?" Mama inhaled so deeply we could hear it from behind the door and she answered in a soft tone we didn't get to hear often. "Yes, he's still there. And still heartbroken over the loss of his wife. Poor man."

Bastian scratched his head. "She's been preening," he whispered to me. "Even got a new hat which she hasn't shown to Vati." I was pleased to be taken into confidence by my brother, but not quite sure what he was hinting at. Something to do with Aunt Amalia's brother,

I got that, but what? Mama was in the habit of preening for any well-born woman or man.

"It's been barely six weeks since we last visited Aunt Amalia, and now she can't wait to get back," Bastian told me and wrinkled his forehead.

We heard Vati clear his throat. "Don't forget, Lilybeth, we've been invited to my sister's for coffee this coming Thursday. It's the Assumption of the Blessed Virgin Mary, one of Julia's rare days off."

"Those Catholics! They've got more saints than there are fish in the sea."

Though Mama's voice was full of mockery, Vati, who came from a Catholic family, took no offense. His laughter was free and open.

"How about a small liqueur?" Vati asked.

"Ja, ein kleiner Anise taete mir gut—a small anise would do me good—but don't you get any ideas. I'm exhausted from keeping *your* dinner warm."

Too bad we couldn't see Vati's face or follow his thoughts. Today, I'm sure that Mama must have seemed like a child to him. And I can guess with near certainty that all his senses, and especially his eyes, were mesmerized by the flames from the fireplace reflected on Mama's forehead, shining back from her eyes and highlighting her cheekbones. He must have gazed at her beauty and let out an involuntary sigh. That's what I remember when Bastian took my hand, whispering "hush," and walking me to the nursery—Vati heaving a deep sigh.

9

SCHMIDT'S FARM

I feigned sadness that I was not going to Garmisch with Mama, Bastian, and Ingrid to visit Mama's friend, but was inwardly happy to have Vati all to myself.

"Would you like to come along to visit patients?" Vati asked me the day of Mama and my siblings' departure while filling his bag with syringes, bandages, vials, and pills in preparation for his rounds.

Instantly, I felt a new energy.

"It'll be nice to have company in the car," Vati said, "but you have to be quiet as a mouse while I'm attending to patients."

"I'll be quiet, Vati," I promised, sealing my lips with my fingers.

Sitting up tall, I stuck out my bony chest while Vati shifted into neutral. We rolled down the hill, away from the Castle, setting the car free, so that we flew forward at an ever-increasing speed in utter silence except for the swoosh of the wind. The wind caressed our cheeks and blew Vati's thin hair up into the air, and I wished I could roll down these hills with him forever.

Vati motioned toward the swaying wheat fields after we reached the plain. "These fields were burned down time and again during the Thirty Years' War from 1618 to 1648," he told me with a somber expression. "Some of the villages were Protestant and others Catholic—just like today. So, the Catholics marched in and burned down the Protestant villages and towns, and the Protestants did the same to the Catholic towns and villages. Not only here but all over Europe! And"—Vati raised one finger into the air—"in the name of God, not some old heathen god, mind you, but a *Christian* one!"

Vati snorted in disgust.

"You mean that people attending Basti's church were fighting and killing people attending our chapel?"

"Precisely. Both sides had their cannons blessed, prayed to Jesus to be on their side, then fired their guns off at each other." Vati slowed the car down and locked eyes with me. "Jesus preached love and forgiveness, not war. Never forget that, my dear." He cleared his throat.

I was still wondering how people who attended church and who knew each other like I knew my Catholic brother Bastian would want to kill Protestant people like Ingrid and me—not that I'd ever believed Basti would, but what about people in his church? Vati's upbeat voice broke into my thoughts.

"You can be sure of one thing, Marie! God is far more embracing than any narrow-minded sectarians. God looks at the *soul* of a human being, not their church affiliation." Vati stepped on the gas pedal. "But now we better speed up or old farmer Schmidt will tie himself up in a knot. His daughter Barbara is our first patient this afternoon."

In the farmyard, Vati lifted me out of the Opel and set me down in the midst of chickens scattering in all directions—except for a blustering rooster who eyed me from his cocked head, his feather coat shining in the colors of a rainbow. I would have loved to touch his iridescent feathers but recoiled from the rooster's fierce stare and the purplish-red comb that crowned his head like a piece of raw flesh.

Out of the corner of my eye I saw the barn door close. Just before it did, I caught the glare of a younger, red-faced man that burned right through me. Vati, on the other hand, didn't give the hens, the rooster, or the red-faced man a second glance. I knew he'd keep me safe. Old Farmer Schmidt's lined face relaxed, too, and he stood taller after shaking Vati's hand.

"This is my daughter, Marie," Vati said. "I promised her that she can admire your little granddaughter once my part of the visit is done. How is the baby?"

"Fine. The little one is fine. It's my daughter Barbara I'm worried about."

"I'm here to set her right," Vati said in a firm voice. "Lead the way."

Farmer Schmidt opened the door to a dark hallway that resembled a tunnel. I was used to the dim passages of the Castle, though none as narrow as this. The Castle's passages smelled of cold air and wet stone, while this one was filled with the scents of hay, boiled cabbage, and ham. Finally, light broke in when Schmidt opened the door to a large kitchen dominated by a massive stove covered with pots and a floor crowded with milk cans.

"Marie, you keep Mr. Schmidt company. I'll be back soon."

Farmer Schmidt offered me an apple from a wooden bowl on the table. "No, thank you," I answered politely, though I wouldn't have minded sinking my teeth into a juicy apple—I had promised Vati to be no bother. The farmer moved some of the cans about, picked up an apple for himself, and peeled it with a small, sharp knife. Just as he lifted the apple to his mouth, there was a powerful thud. Again, thud, thud. Something was making the wall tremble, not the one with the arch through which Vati had disappeared, but the one right behind Farmer Schmidt's shoulder. Schmidt's arm froze mid-air. His eyes flickered while I heard a terrible moan, followed by a muffled scream.

Before I knew it, Schmidt had taken hold of my arm. "Never you mind," Schmidt said in a hoarse voice, his eyes no longer unsteady but infinitely sad. "It's my son, his hellish infection, his leg. He...he won't let them amputate. It's rotting. He's in agony." Schmidt straightened his shoulders, looked into my eyes, and patted my arm. "He won't harm you. No, no. My poor boy. He's not been right since the war. He wants to die, but Death shows no pity."

I thought of Bastian's friend Andreas and of Prince Henry. Of Vati's brother whom I'd never known, and of all the names chiseled into the war memorial. Schmidt's shoulders straightened when Vati reappeared.

"I have given Barbara a shot and instructed her to stay in bed. Period. No lifting of any kind," Vati told him. "It'll be best if she sleeps *alone*. Her body needs to recover and gain strength. No lifting or touching by Fritz. Now where is Fritz? He needs to hear exactly what I told you."

The old man clasped Vati's hand. "Thank you, Doktor. Thank you so much." He paused, then went on in a whisper, "That son-in-law of mine, that Fritz—the man is ruthless! He's Helfried's brother."

"Whose brother?" asked Vati.

"Helfried, the flute player. Always hanging around school and the little ones. People say he's a warlock."

My ears pricked up. That flute player again.

Vati took Schmidt's arm. "Come on now, lieber Herr Schmidt. Nothing but old wives' tales."

Schmidt shook his head. "I don't know, Herr Doktor. There's something not right about that family."

Vati picked up his bag. "Is Fritz in the barn? I'll tell him to shape up. In the meantime, do show Marie your lovely granddaughter." Vati headed for the door.

The hand that took mine felt as rough as a scrub brush. Together, we walked into a dimly lit bedroom.

"Come in," said a pale woman. "Don't be shy, Rosa's asleep."

I curtsied. Still dazed by what Schmidt had said about his son and at the same time sheepish about intruding on Barbara's privacy, I tiptoed toward a hand-painted cradle. There, under soft blankets, I spotted the red, wrinkled face of a tiny baby. I was puzzled by its ugliness. How could Vati call this scrunched-up face lovely?

Schmidt's scratchy hand took mine again. We walked out of the room and through the kitchen to the hallway. The hall seemed even darker than before. Would I hear the thud again? My ears were pricked, but it was Vati's thundering voice and not the moans that stopped me in my tracks.

"I'll knock your teeth out if you so much as touch her!" boomed my father's voice. "Do you understand me? *She is to be left alone.*" The old man dragged me along, opened the door to the yard, and whispered, "Shh," though I hadn't uttered a sound.

There, in the light, stood Vati, towering over a shorter, stocky, red-haired man.

"And if she bleeds again and you don't call me, I'll do worse. Understand?"

"Yes, Doktor."

I started to tremble. I wasn't used to seeing Vati's face so distorted by anger. And now? The old man bent down to me. "He is a daredevil, Herr Doktor. Only he knows how to talk to that no-good son-in-law of mine."

Searching his wrinkled face, I saw a satisfied, almost triumphant smile. While I was trying to make sense of the turmoil, Schmidt led us into the sun. Vati's face relaxed and brightened.

"Ah, there you are!" And without the slightest hint of exasperation, he called out to me, "Now we'd better be on our way." Turning to Fritz, he said, "I'll stop by again tomorrow."

I looked back after Vati lifted me into the car. Red-haired Fritz was raising his clenched fist. I felt sure he was clutching a knife in that tight ball of his hand.

Before the harvest was brought in that year, Fritz would open his fist and smash life as we knew it to pieces. I could not have known that during our visit, though I had been thoroughly spooked by the man. But even if I could have looked into his heart, what could I, a skinny girl, have done to stop him? My ignorance had always been suffused with a sense of foreboding. I felt the uncanny all around me but could not get hold of its contour nor grasp what lay at its core.

10

THE COUNT

Mercifully, there were moments when the uncanny melted away, if only briefly. Upon my siblings' return from Garmisch and their visit to Aunt Amalia, Bastian, Ingrid, and I celebrated our reunion with hot chocolate around the kitchen table. Our cheeks were rosy, our tummies content.

"You should've seen their ponies, Marie." Bastian jiggled my nose. "I got to ride *Ivan Devar* who wasn't anything like his name, he was so steady and calm." While I hadn't really wanted to go to Garmisch, I sure would have loved to ride a pony, and let out a sigh just as Vati joined us on his return home. He put his black physician's bag down on a bench and hugged us.

"Welcome back," he beamed at Ingrid and Basti. "I can tell from your shiny eyes you had a good time!"

"Did we ever," said Bastian. "We got to ride their ponies."

Ingrid tugged at Vati's sleeve. "The Count kept feeding me treats, Vati, delicious sweets. And each time he gave me a chocolate he also gave me a kiss. Yuck, sometimes he slobbered on me! Which made Mama mad." Bastian and Ingrid could barely stop themselves; they were sputtering so with laughter, and I chimed in—Vati's eyes were no longer smiling.

"Mama yanked me off his lap where he had pulled me so I'd be closer to the chocolates, telling the Count, 'Play with girls your own age.'"

Vati cleared his throat. He took Ingrid's hand. "So, the Count paid you lots of attention and spoiled you with sweets?" Ingrid nodded gravely, then smiled at Vati. "But then he'd take Mama for a drive into the mountains or to the theater at night. And we got to spend most of the day with Freddie and Abigail. She's become my best friend, Abigail has."

Vati straightened his back. For a moment, he looked like a tin soldier. Stiff and no longer at ease. I was puzzled by his change in mood.

"Vati? Vati, you home?" Mama called out from the hallway. Vati picked up his black bag, waved to us, and called back, "Yes, Lily, I'm home. Be right there."

That evening, I caught my brother eavesdropping again, much to my surprise, making me wonder if dark clouds were gathering all about us. He straightened the moment he spotted me and put his finger across his lips as if I didn't know that I had to tiptoe and not let out a peep when he was up to his old game. I stopped next to him and put my ear to the door just as Vati said, "So you had a good time with the Count, Amalia's brother?"

"Yes," Mama answered. Her voice sounded defiant. Already we heard her small, suppressed coughs. Never a good sign.

For a while, there was nothing but silence. Then Vati asked, "Did the Count proposition you?"

"What...what makes you say that?" Mama's voice was shaky. We heard her taking a sip from something.

"I can see it in your face," said Vati. "And the children told amusing and yet revealing stories about him." Basti and I looked at each other in shock, then pressed our ears more firmly against the door.

"What?" Though I couldn't see Mama's face, I knew it must be red by now and her eyes shooting fire.

"Lilybeth," Vati said, "it's obvious."

"You and your damn diagnoses." Mama huffed, close to spitting. "Anyhow, you're right."

We heard Vati get up and walk toward Mama. "You encouraged his proposal?"

Mama didn't answer. We heard Vati light a cigarette; I could even hear him take a deep breath to suck in the smoke. Finally, he said, "Do you feel he'd be willing to take responsibility for three children from two other men?"

Mama coughed. "He adores me. He'll do anything for me—unlike other men I know."

"Spare me, Lilybeth! You can do better than that."

"That's precisely what I'm going to do. A whole lot better than wasting away in this shithole."

"You mean Falkenburg Castle?"

"Well, it isn't ours, is it? We're not even housed in the inner yard."

Mama was insulting my Castle. Anger welled up inside me, but I couldn't let it distract me. There was danger in the air. Mama and Vati's battle of words was beginning to overwhelm me.

"If I remember correctly," said Vati, "Count Mergenthal doesn't have a castle either. In fact, he's homeless and bunking with his sister. It is *she* who lives in a fine old villa that used to belong to her husband's family, according to you."

Silence. I was waiting for Mama's voice but heard Vati's again. "And how is he going to support you and a family? His estates are in the hands of the Russians, who—I should think—would be unwilling to pay him a retainer."

"I resent your mockery, Karl." Mama's voice had become shrill. "He consults for the steel industry and is friends with the Krupps. The Count knows *all* the influential people."

"And we know where *their* allegiance was during the war," Vati countered like a shot. We heard him walking, picking up something—a bottle or decanter, I thought—and filling a glass.

"So what is it to be, Frau Doktor?"

"I'm leaving." Mama's voice was triumphant. Basti and I stared at each other. My mind was racing. *What does that mean?* Before Bastian could explain, we heard Mama get up. Bastian pushed me toward the nursery, and I had just enough time to open the door and step into darkness when the library door was flung open, throwing a light on my poor, prone brother.

"Bastian! Have you been eavesdropping? Wait till I..." Mama yanked Basti into the library while I stepped back into the hallway.

"Young man, come along with me. You're in for a spanking!"

That was Vati's voice, but I didn't for a moment believe he'd hurt my brother and was sure that Basti knew that, too. "Off to your room! And make it snappy!"

Now Vati was in the corridor, but he quickly turned in the direction of the kitchen. Bastian's room was next to the kitchen. I was safe.

"Go to bed, Lilybeth," he called over his shoulder, "we'll talk again tomorrow when we're both fresher."

I'd gotten up extra early after a restless night and had been brushing my teeth at the kitchen sink forever in order to catch Basti before he left for his train to school. Anna was taking a breakfast tray to Mama when my brother finally made his appearance. I quickly rinsed. "Basti? What happened last night? Is Mama leaving?"

Basti took my hand. "I don't think so. She enjoys making Vati jealous." Basti stopped himself, then went on, "Heaven knows why, but she likes to torture him."

"Why would anyone want to torture Vati?"

My brother's eyes grew larger. "Beats me." He looked beyond me, his face darkened. "You know how she is."

I sighed. Yes, I knew how she was but was not any wiser and still felt unmoored. Basti patted me on the back. "This isn't the first time I've heard her make outrageous pronouncements, believe me. Vati will set it right."

Vati was the one in our family who could set things right, I knew that, but wasn't sure if his near-magical powers could be a match for our mother's fury.

I was too young to think about the relationship between the sexes then. But I had learned from fairy tales—and a little bit from observing the world around me—that women were bent on "finding their prince" and men on finding a beautiful girl. Men had to be brave and women beautiful. That much was clear.

I had even begun to suspect that I might not live up to that ideal because my hair was "lifeless," and I was "nothing but skin and bones." But I rarely thought about my looks and didn't have other girls to compare myself to at the Castle. I was far more intrigued by the awesome beauty of the stork's wide-spread wings, the flowing beauty of Chestnut in motion, the distinct beauty of the paintings and illuminated manuscripts in my Treasure Hall—and, of course, the power and beauty of God's word resounding from the pulpit. Mama, on the other hand, was preoccupied with looking beautiful and being admired. That was clear to me, too. She had to be "the most beautiful of all."

11

FINALLY, SCHOOL

Finally, my first day at school! Anna woke me with a big smile. "This is *your* day. After you've scrubbed your face and ears, come to the parlor where your Mama has laid out your pretty new frock."

Mama, dressed in her morning robe, held out the school dress for me as if it were a priest's vestment, and I fully expected school to be a consecrated place, a temple of wisdom. 'At last,' I thought, 'I'll get really good at reading and writing. And I'll learn more Latin than I have picked up from Bastian, so that I can decipher the illuminated manuscripts in my Treasure Hall.'

A delicious shiver ran through me. What would they tell me, those beautiful books? What secrets would I uncover? And, surely, school would help me unlock the mysterious swirls on the gravestones of the Jewish cemetery.

Mama's hands were trembling when she slipped the frock over my head. Just then Vati marched in, carrying a tall, colorful *Schultu-ete,* a three-foot paper cone filled with sweets, the traditional gift to a child first entering school. He handed it to me like a scepter—a reward and a challenge wrapped in one. With bright, shining eyes, he patted me on the back. "You're a big girl now, Marie! Already, you're off to a good start with your reading and Latin vocabulary. Weiter so!" he said.

Vati checked his watch. Mama was fingering the edge of the table-cloth. "I think you better be going," she said, without looking at Vati.

"Now where is Ingrid?" Vati asked. "I'll give you two a lift to school on this special day before looking in on a patient. But as of tomorrow, your big sister will lead you down the hill on the path below the wall."

"I will, I will," Ingrid said, entering right on cue and eyeing my

Schultuete. Vati resumed his Toreador's song and Ingrid followed him out the door. Mama turned to Anna. "Where has the time gone?" she asked. Anna was wiping her eyes with a hanky, and I thought I saw Mama tear up, too, when I turned to catch up with my sister on "our" way to school.

My classroom was on the first floor of the old townhall, a four-story stone building. Six wooden desks with carved-out grooves for chalk, a stylus, and a sunken inkpot formed a row. I counted four rows. Boys sat in the front row, girls in the second, then boys again, followed by a row of girls. The teacher's desk was centered before the blackboard.

On our first day, Fraeulein Huber, a stout young woman dressed in a woolen skirt, a starched blouse, knee socks, and sturdy hiking boots, entered the classroom with *"Guten Morgen, Kinder,"* in the peculiar singsong voice of grade school teachers. She stretched out her arms like a conductor and circled them back to her body as if to invite us to greet her back in turn. Our parents had received a letter informing us that our teacher would be *Fraeulein Huber* and the door to our classroom had displayed a large sign with her name. I was fully prepared to greet her as *Fraeulein Huber.* But my classmates sat motionless, merely staring at her.

"And now our prayers," Fraeulein Huber said.

A strange jumble of mangled words and bits and pieces of sentences filled the air until all joined in with, "Amen." Chaos broke out after the word "Amen." Two boys launched paper airplanes; spitballs flew through the air; a girl shrieked because the boy behind her kept pulling her braids. Miss Huber tapped her desk with a long hazelnut switch. "If you don't quiet down instantly, I'll call you up front for a healthy whipping."

I was dumbfounded by the theatrics and even more upset by the ruckus. Weren't my classmates as eager to learn as I? I wondered if I had landed in some strange, otherworldly realm, thanks to a trickster or a scheming witch. But the second and third day weren't any better than the first. Fraeulein Huber spent as much time keeping order and threatening us with punishment as she did teaching anything. When she did teach, it wasn't words or another language like Latin but merely one single letter.

A few weeks into the school year, Miss Huber said, "Take out your slates. Today we will learn about the letter *H*. Where have you heard that letter before? *H* as in what?" she asked Hilda in the second row.

"Handkerchief," answered red-cheeked Hilda.

"Very good," Miss Huber cooed. "*H* as in handkerchief. Or house. Or heart. Or holiday. Or what, Herbert?" She pointed to a boy whose face was an explosion of freckles.

Herbert just sat there with his mouth open. He could not think of another *H* or if he could, he dared not speak up. Miss Huber flashed an encouraging smile.

"Well, Herbert?"

By now spittle was running down his chin toward his collar. That was too much for me. I turned my head away to the window, whereupon Miss Huber called on me, "You there, Marie. Can you think of words beginning with an *H*?"

"Hallelujah, hunger, and hell," I answered.

"Good, but next time don't look out the window. And let's forget about that *nasty* term *hell*." She marched to the blackboard to write out a beautiful *H*.

"Miss Huber, Miss Huber," Herbert's hand whipped the air, "I know another word beginning with *H*."

"Let's hear it!"

"Hitler," the boy beamed. "Adolf Hitler."

A tall girl at the end of my row gasped, then blushed, as the boy in front of me snorted. Most kids just sat motionless.

"Yes, that last name does begin with an *H*," Miss Huber said in a very stern voice, "but we don't want to *ever* mention that *nasty character* again."

Hitler. The *nasty character* who had sent Basti's friends to their death. I shuddered.

The longer I attended school, the more disillusioned I became. At home I was reading fairy tales and the Bible, but here I was condemned to merely sound out letters and copy them ad nauseam onto my slate. My classmates spent literally hours learning about just one single letter. The next day, Miss Huber would repeat what she told us about that very letter, made sure every boy and girl knew how the letter sounded, and asked everyone to think of words beginning with the letter under discussion. We didn't read stories, not one single line, but kept chopping German words into little pieces.

Since the first shocking weeks, I became so bored that I fell to staring out the window, watching clouds move across the sky, often not even hearing my own name when Miss Huber called on me. This was not the fountain of knowledge I had dreamed of. Worse! School was a thief. It took me away from everything enchanting—the intricate faces of the saints, the vellum manuscripts, the view into the land, and my books.

I kept trying to think of ways to skip school. A tummy ache bought me a school-free day now and then, but it did not work in the long run. One weekend morning, I headed out the main gate just as the shepherd was leading his flock into the heath. I watched him place his crooked staff into the ground with every step and cheered the clever hooks of his dog rounding up stragglers.

Then it hit me! Time and again, the Israelites had offered God a lamb or a sheep when seeking his favor. If I sacrificed a lamb to the Lord, I could ask him to release me from school forever. I fell on my knees right then and there and prayed out loud, "Dear Lord, I will sacrifice a lamb to you if you will lift the scourge of school from me forever." I rose emboldened, filled with the knowledge of the power of the Lord who had smitten the enemies of Israel and who had parted the sea for Moses. His stunning miracles forced me right back onto my knees again. "And I will sacrifice a lamb to you from now on every year on the day you graciously granted my prayer!"

When I crept into the sheep barn at the bottom of the Castle's hill, darkness enveloped me, stopping me in my tracks. I held my breath and squinted. My ears picked up noises of rustling straw and faint bleats coming from one of the pens. Following the noise, I came upon a mother sheep with her newborn lamb.

I was thrilled, but only for a moment before dread filled my heart. How would I go about sacrificing the lamb? I looked at the mother sheep, who in turn looked up at me while sheltering the tiny lamb under her belly. The lamb nudged her body until it found a teat and sucked eagerly.

Don't dither, I told myself. *Lift up the lamb and run. You made a promise to the Lord. He has the power to set you free.* I bent over the pen that came up all the way to my chest. My arms were not long enough to reach the baby. Perhaps I should give up. I didn't even have an altar. How and where could I build an altar? I needed time.

But no! Jehovah is a vengeful God! He can turn me into a pillar of salt or throw me into a lion's den. The thought of roaring lions steeled my determination. Just then the lamb made a smacking noise that sounded like that of a baby. I squirmed, but the thought of my promise spurred me on.

I picked up a large field stone, moved it close to the pen, and steadied myself on it. Then I climbed in. The lamb was all softness and bones, its heart beating so recklessly as if it wanted to burst through its skin right into my hands. It nuzzled my cheek with soft lips. I pressed it closer to myself and knew—knew I could not cut the lamb's throat. My arms hurt, the mother sheep bumped against me as if asking, "And now?" Slowly, I set the newborn back into the straw, climbed out of the pen, and ran—ran with a speed that tried to outrun the Lord.

Of course, he knew, must know by now that there would be no sacrifice. He would smite me. The big thorn bush at the edge of the heath might burst into flames and resound with his voice, "Why hast thou broken thy vow?"

At night, I tossed and turned. I was no better than Peter, who denied our Lord. I was a weak vessel, a worthless sinner. Nightmares haunted me. Mama provided no comfort. I was just a puny nuisance to her, a skinny runt with lifeless hair who asked too many questions. I couldn't turn to my sister; she wasn't very keen on the Bible. Vati was never home. Finally, I asked Anna what happened to people who broke their promise to God.

"Depends on what it is," she answered. "But God forgives. He sent his only son to take on the burden of our sin."

I clung to Anna's words and repeated them to myself to help ease my obsessive fear. And they did—up to a point. For extra protection, I followed Anna wherever she went, even to the far fields beyond the heath where Mama sometimes sent her to collect wild blueberries.

On a crisp, clear day, when our berry bowl was almost full and our fingers stained blue, we came to a crossroad, marked by a towering cross with the crucified Christ rising above the heath.

Anna stopped, crossed herself, and moved her lips in prayer. I kept my eyes to the ground, telling myself not to look. If I did, I wouldn't be able to take my eyes off the writhing man, curling away from the cross as if trying to escape his pain. A crown of thorns drew blood from his forehead, nails cut into his hands. His head was slunk to his chest, but his pain never slackened. It clung to the lines of his face, it gripped every muscle and limb. The fixed eternity of Christ's agony tormented me. I wanted to pull the nails from his hands and feet and tried to nudge Anna to leave. At first, Anna resisted. When she finally looked into my face, she picked up her berries again.

"What a strange little thing you are, Marie. You love going to church but don't want to honor our Lord on the cross." I could not understand Anna's calm in the face of Christ's pain, and Anna could not understand my anguish.

In desperation, I focused on the letters carved into the cross. Letters were doors to words, and words had power. They could soothe and they could save. Blood rushed to my cheeks. Perhaps Christ could be freed from the cross if we could unlock the word.

"Anna," I asked excitedly, "can you see the letters on the cross?"

"Yes."

"What do they mean?"

Anna read "I. N. R. I."

"Yes, yes, I know. Tell me, what word do they spell?"

Anna looked at me with sad eyes. "I'm sorry, Marie. I don't know."

I memorized the letters, whispered them to myself, and hoped my sister or brother would know the answer when we got home, but they did not. And Mama just shook her head. "I have no idea, Marie. Now go scrub your hands and get rid of those nasty blueberry stains!"

12

BROKEN MIRROR

I woke with a start. The bedroom was pitch black.

I heard Mama scream.

Ingrid turned in her sleep. "Wake up, Ingrid." I stood barefoot by my sister's bed, unaware how I'd gotten there.

Mama yelled, "How could you? How on earth could you?"

Ingrid shot up. "What...what...?" Before I could answer, Mama was shrieking at the top of her lungs, "You worthless bastard! Caring more for your patients than for your family! *Du Schwein*!" I pictured Mama's fists coming down on Vati when we heard a terrible crash as if a window were breaking.

"Did you hear that?"

"Yes. Bad." Ingrid jumped out of bed.

The door opened. Anna was standing in the doorway. "Come on, you two. I'm making hot chocolate. Let's go to the kitchen where we'll have some peace." Anna took me by one hand and Ingrid by the other. Together, we fled toward the kitchen, the furthest place from our parents' bedroom. We kept listening, now hearing nothing.

Next day, Mama did not show her face until noon—not unusual after one of her storms. Vati was at his surgery. When Ingrid and I snuck into our parents' bedroom while Mama was having coffee, we saw that Mama had smashed the large mirror, leaving nothing but shards of glass in its frame. The rest of the room looked pristine; Anna had made the bed and hoovered the floor.

I shivered. "Mama's waging war," I whispered to my sister. Ingrid nodded. "In our own house."

Bastian burst into the nursery all out of breath. He'd jogged all the way up the hill from the train station. "Let's meet at the loft," he told us with a serious face. "Marie, you head out first." I retrieved a rope from under my dresser, headed for the horse barn, and had barely crawled under the trough of an empty stall when Ingrid slipped in. "You here, Marie?"

"Ja." I emerged, brushing straw off my knees.

"Did anyone see you?"

"Nein."

"Gut."

The barn door opened quietly. Bastian appeared. He and Ingrid each grabbed one of my arms and pulled me toward a tall ladder fastened to the wall. The ladder led to a hayloft and from there all the way to the roof. Immense rafters, accessible from the loft, crossed the barn at ever-greater heights, tempting my athletic siblings to walk on them above a dark abyss. They moved, arms stretched out like tightrope artists, as if falling were impossible. I didn't join them, because I knew I would fall. You had to believe in *not* falling in order to make it across.

Ingrid let go of me and glared at Bastian. "You know *now*, right? Even though you *slept through it*!" Ingrid sounded like a prosecutor.

"C'mon, sis! My room is the furthest from their bedroom. I could *not* have heard them if I'd tried." Bastian defended himself.

"It *was* pretty bad," Ingrid said.

"Terrible," I chimed in and handed the rope back to my sister.

"Yes, Vati told me this morning on the way to the train. 'It'll be tense for a while,' he said, 'but it will blow over.'"

Bastian raced up the ladder while Ingrid fastened the rope around my waist; my legs were not long enough to cover the wide spaces between the ladder rungs. Bastian pulled me up. That was the scariest part of our meetings. Once safely on the floor of the loft, I never looked down again. Snuggled against Bastian, I surrendered to this cathedral of darkness, split open every so often by streaks of sunlight—thousands of illuminated dots, dancing daggers, that sliced the dark.

Bastian tightened his arm around me. "There's another thing.

My father in Berchtesgaden had a gall bladder operation. He wants me to come. Vati already phoned the principal, and I'm leaving tomorrow after school."

"Is your father *critical*?" I asked. *Critical* was a common term in our father's household.

"No, no." Bastian didn't sound worried at all. "Vati called the surgeon whom he knows from his time in Berchtesgaden. My father is stable." Bastian sighed. "But I guess I gotta go."

"We'll miss you," said Ingrid, while I squeezed his hand.

"Anna told me that Mama will be off tomorrow, too. For a very short visit to Garmisch to meet with the builder of our new house," said Bastian. Whenever I heard the term *new house,* I felt queasy and bereft and pushed the thought of a home that was *not* Falkenburg Castle into the deepest recesses of my mind.

"At least we'll have some peace," said Ingrid.

Bastian laughed. "Good thing my father doesn't live in Garmisch."

We fell silent for a while. "The principal of my school," Bastian broke the silence, "called me into his office and said I'd be welcome to return any time." He scratched his head.

"That was nice of him, wasn't it?" I asked. "He means after your father is better."

"I guess so." Bastian's fingers drummed the floor of the loft. He was shaking his head to and fro as if conversing with an invisible presence. Then he looked up at Ingrid, who was leaning against the rail of the loft. "And Mama is as jittery as she was during the war before we moved east to Marienbad even though Vati pleaded with her not to move—what with our soldiers retreating and the Russians in pursuit." Bastian stopped himself. "But I guess you really don't remember, Ingrid. You were only four years old." He turned back to me. "And you were an infant in swaddling clothes." Bastian threw up his hands. "I wanted Mama to listen to Vati, but she believed the propaganda blaring from the radio that our soldiers would be victorious in the end and packed up all our things to move us east."

"Why did Mama want to move?" I finally asked the question that had been on my mind.

"Because like always, she wanted to be close to Aunt Amalia, who lived in Marienbad," he said.

"Well," said Ingrid, but didn't finish her sentence.

"Well, what?" asked Basti.

"Well, at least we met Aunt Amalia, Abigail, and Freddie back then and have become good friends."

Bastian's face flushed. He shot Ingrid a sharp look. "But we lost almost everything—and had to flee the Russians in the middle of the night."

Ingrid touched our brother's arm. "But we made it. Vati says not everyone was as lucky as we were."

"Yes," Bastian said slowly and thoughtfully, "we made it." He tousled our hair and took a deep breath. The barn door opened unexpectedly. The sudden light hurt our eyes. What if Mama had followed us? We didn't want her to know about our secret meeting place.

"Bastian, Ingrid, Marie!" It was Anna. "I know you're in there. Come along, your Mama wants you in the dining room. Dinner is served."

The barn door slammed shut, and we were once again enclosed by darkness.

13

FAREWELL TO ALL

With all the commotion, I headed for the kitchen to seek comfort from Anna after dinner. "Anna, please make sure Vati stops by the nursery when he gets home," I begged her as soon as the door had closed behind me.

"I will, dear—if I get to see him at all." I stepped out of the way as Anna hurried to the kitchen sink with a steaming pot of potatoes. "Herr Doktor is scarcely home."

"I know. I haven't seen him for days. Ingrid hasn't either, and *she* gets to stay up late." For a split second, I felt resentment toward my big sister.

"Yeah, what's happening, Anna?" Ingrid walked into the kitchen straight toward Anna, who had started to peel the potatoes.

Anna wiped her hands on the small towel that hung from her apron. "There are too many sick people about. And some are so poorly that Herr Doktor needs to consult with your Aunt Julia. That means driving to Dillingen."

"Maybe we could ride to Aunt Julia with him?" Ingrid thought out loud. "Then we'll at least get to see him during the drive. I'll talk to Mama."

Ingrid's forehead relaxed. She turned to me. "You coming?"

"In a bit."

Ingrid shrugged her shoulders and left while I was wondering how I could worm more information out of Anna.

"Those very sick people you talked about, what makes them so sick?"

"That depends," said Anna, looking out of sorts.

"Is it an epidemic?" I persisted. "Vati told me about those."

Anna looked perplexed. "Not sure about that, but he's battling what he's battling." Anna scrunched up her forehead and pulled her chin in. She was buttoning down. I saw that I could not press her any further.

Before Ingrid had a chance to ask Mama if we could ride with Vati to Aunt Julia's house, Mama sent for us.

"I need to talk to you." Her face looked pinched. "It's about Vati. He has been working too hard, caring for some very sick patients. He got infected, was treated, and then admitted to a sanatorium. Do you know what a sanatorium is, Marie?" I shook my head.

"That's where people go who need long-term care. It is not for people who need surgery, but for long-term conditions," Mama said.

"What about the infection? Is it dangerous?" I was terrified by the thought that Vati, who spent all his time and energy on healing people, had fallen ill himself. "Could Vati...die?" I asked.

Mama snorted. "Of course not. He's receiving Antibiotika, a new miracle drug from Amerika that is killing the infection." I breathed a sigh of relief. "But he's run down," said Mama. "You know how hard he's been working. All he needs is time and the special care a sanatorium provides."

Ingrid was biting her fingernails. "Vati didn't look *that* run-down to me," she grumbled.

Mama's eyebrows shot up. "He did not feel well *inside*," she said, "and as a doctor he certainly knew. In any case, your father will be well taken care of and will write to you as soon as he's stronger, which should be before too long. Now to us. Unfortunately, Bastian is at his father's. That means that we three and Anna have to manage the move to our new house in Garmisch on our own. I have ordered the lorry for next week."

"Next week?" Ingrid and I asked in unison. Ingrid looked undone, almost angry. "That doesn't give us any time to say goodbye to our friends."

Mama threw up her hands. "Can't be helped. And remember, you have Aunt Amalia, Freddie, and Abigail waiting for you in Garmisch."

Ingrid's face brightened. "Abigail and Freddie. Thank God."

My face fell. I had no father now, no brother, and no one waiting for me in Garmisch. Suddenly, a jolt ran through me, leaving me helpless and stunned. *Mama's taking away my Castle, my stone mother, my home.*

––––

Ingrid and I were shaken that Vati was in a sanatorium but clung to Mama's assurance that he would get better and join us before too long. But why, of all times, did Bastian's father have to have an operation when we needed our brother so badly? Everything felt out of joint.

As if that weren't enough, Ingrid told me, "Mama says Anna will stay here in Falkenburg."

"Why?"

"I don't know."

I felt sick. My sister, four years older than I, had mostly cut her umbilical cord to Anna, but I had not. "Why, dear God, why?"

Ingrid threw up her hands.

I ran to the kitchen. "Why won't you come to Garmisch with us?" I asked Anna, who was scraping carrots by the sink. Though I had grown considerably over the past year, I barely reached Anna's bosom as we stood across from each other. Big-boned and tall, Anna had always been my bulwark against a hostile world.

"I'm not coming because your Mama's friend, the Countess, recommended someone to your Mama and also"—here Anna stopped scraping carrots—"and also because I may get married before too long and start a family of my own." Anna took my hand in hers. Her brown eyes were aglow. "You know how Cinderella marries the Prince at the end of the story? Well, I have found my prince."

As hard as I tried, I could not imagine my Anna being carried off by a prince. She put her arms around me and patted my back, which felt good, but did not soothe the pain of Anna wanting to start a family of her own. All my life, I had believed that Ingrid, Bastian, and I *were* her family. I felt deserted—betrayed.

"You better run along and do your homework," said Anna after she dumped the carrots into a pot. "I have to start packing up the linen next. When you are done, you can come and help me." I couldn't make myself leave.

"Will you come and visit us in Garmisch?"

"I will."

"And will you visit Vati in the sanatorium?"

Pain flickered across Anna's face, her eyes filled with sadness. "I will,

Marie," she said, taking my hand into hers and pressing it, "I promise
I will."

The lorry had come and gone. The car, parked outside our gate, was
packed to the brim. It was time to say goodbye. Vati's new assistant, Dr.
Weiner, would drive us to Garmisch as Mama had yet to learn to drive.

I headed for the Treasure Hall and ran my fingers across the illuminated manuscripts. When tears filled my eyes—they appeared from
nowhere—I took my sweater off and wrapped it around one of my
favorite tomes.

"You cannot do that," whispered a voice inside my head.

"Why not?"

"Because it doesn't belong to you. It belongs to the Duke."

"The Duke never looks at it, would never know it's missing."

"Still."

"No one loves it as I do. I'll keep it from harm."

Clinging to my wrapped treasure, I looked around the hall and
caught the astonished faces of the saints. Keeping my eyes locked
onto theirs, I unfurled the sweater and put the book back on the shelf.
Obeying God's commandments did not uplift me. I felt coerced.

Frustrated, I headed for the chapel whose echoing space, suffused
with light, could flow into me and give me peace—at least for a while.
After saying goodbye to Count Gottfried and his two wives, I took a
seat in the first pew.

I felt the presence of lives come and gone and walked up to the
spot before the altar where Prince Henry must have prayed before he
set out for his fateful battle. I fell on my knees, buried my face in my
hands, and waited. Waited for the Prince.

He did not come.

BOOK II

Garmisch 1951/52

14

OUR IMPERILED HOME

Steep rock walls and craggy peaks rose before us wherever we went in our new hometown, Garmisch, a two-hour ride from Falkenburg. I was awed by the mountains' grandeur and charmed by the clusters of deep-roofed Bavarian houses dotting the foothills of town. They were embellished with carved balconies and colorful murals—St. Christopher carrying the child Jesus or St. Hubertus shouldering a stag. Imagine houses telling a story. Falkenburg's houses had been mute and mono-colored—except, of course, for my Castle.

At Garmisch's southern edge rose Germany's highest mountain, the Zugspitze, that formed the border with Austria. You could reach its top by cable car or cog train and look into three neighboring countries on a clear day: Austria, Switzerland, and Italy.

Satchels on our backs, Ingrid and I were on our twenty-minute walk home from school, Ingrid in fourth grade, and I, at seven, in second. We followed the gushing Partnach River from the center of town to the tree-lined streets of our quiet suburb, a mixture of Bavarian-style and modern houses, surrounded by large gardens. The houses on our side of the street backed onto the foot of *Kramer*, a stocky, saddleback mountain that lacked the rock massifs and sharp peaks of Zugspitze.

"It must have been smashing to be here during the Winter Olympics of 1936. That's when skiing became an Olympic sport." Ingrid's face flushed with excitement. Bastian had promised to teach her how to ski this coming winter. "I hope they'll hold the Games here again."

It seemed that everyone we met in our new town couldn't wait to tell us that Garmisch had played host to the Winter Olympics of 1936. But no one mentioned the name of the man who had presided over those games. We learned that years later: Adolf Hitler.

No one in Garmisch spoke of Hitler, at least not in front of Mama, Ingrid, and me. Not at school and not at home. It was almost as if by moving away from Falkenburg, where his name had at least come up, though rarely, we had also moved further away from this monster. Yet in reality, we had moved much deeper into Hitler country—closer to his home country, Austria, and closer to Munich where he had begun his fight for power, his *Kampf.* Bavaria had been an enthusiastic Nazi state. If Ingrid and I had been older we might have guessed why the townspeople now felt compelled to stay mum.

Ingrid wrinkled her forehead after opening our front gate for me. "Gee, they're still celebrating Aunt Amalia's birthday," she grumbled when we heard laughter and the clinking of glasses from the veranda.

Our mother had become more lighthearted in Garmisch, as if she'd been released from some heavy burden. She flitted about, lifting an end table here, exchanging one porcelain vase for another there, bringing fresh flowers in from the garden, or holding a bale of brocade against the window frame to gauge its effect as a curtain. Her brighter mood overlayed my own sense of loss at first as I kept longing for Falkenburg Castle and Anna, especially in the still hours of the night.

Once again, we heard the delicate ring of glasses as Mama and her friend toasted their new life together. The sound gathered in on itself, then floated up into the atmosphere all the way to the top of Kramer Mountain, I believed, that rose like a gigantic wall beyond our mountain meadow. If you stood stock-still on our veranda, eyes straight ahead, that's all you'd see, that gray-green hulk of a mountain gobbling up your view—the opposite of Falkenburg's sky walk. That had opened the world to me. Kramer Mountain closed it down.

Ingrid and I were on our way to the kitchen just as Mama said in an upbeat voice, "To your health, dear Amalia," and continued with her voice trailing off, "and that we can hold on to this house." I couldn't hear the words after Mama's toast and thus missed the first clear warning for the greatest challenge ahead of us from now on: *holding on to our new home.* The new house was just that for me: a house. In my heart, I kept dreaming of my beloved Castle, my one and only *true* home.

Mama had set out two glasses of milk and freshly buttered buns with honey for us in the kitchen. Ingrid took a bite out of a bun and shook her head. "And to think that Mama not once asked Anna to have coffee with her!"

What? Mama had never shared a cup of coffee with Anna? I had never given the matter any thought but instantly knew Ingrid was right and felt terrible for not having seen—and sad for Anna. If only she had come along with us. Cursed be "the Prince" who suddenly appeared out of nowhere. Ingrid kept saying, "it's only a two-hour car ride to Falkenburg," but we had no car since Mama couldn't drive. Anna might as well have been living in another country.

"I'll be in my room doing homework," I told my sister, and headed upstairs before Ingrid could see the tears in my eyes. Though I now had a room of my own with bookshelves and a small desk, the room did not uplift me.

To be fair, our place did have a beautifully carved balcony facing the street, and opened to a large veranda and rock garden in the back; its rooms were light and modern as Mama liked to point out, but the rooms could tell no stories since they hadn't been lived in. They could not inspire my dreams. Prince Henry's footsteps and the sighs of the saints had stayed at the Castle where I longed to be.

"Marie!" Ingrid called from the stairway. "Come down quickly."

I didn't like this—Ingrid issuing orders. "Come quickly, please." The "please" did it. "Why?" I asked without enthusiasm as I trotted down the stairs.

"They've left some champagne, in the bottle. Aunt Amalia said goodbye at least five minutes ago. But here they are, still gabbing in the front yard. Let's try this *Dom* stuff."

Ingrid moved swiftly through the living room onto the terrace, lifted up the bottle of champagne and took a big gulp, scrunching up her nose. "Yikes! The bubbles tickle my nose. Here, have some."

The drink tasted strange, bitter, and my nose got all prickly, too. "How can they drink that?"

"No idea," said Ingrid. "Weird, isn't it?" She took another sip. "But delicious!"

When Mama was not at home or when she was totally preoccupied, I snuck out of the house to the main highway that had brought us to Garmisch, looking for Vati and his car. So many days had passed. Surely, he *must* have been released from the sanatorium by now and be on his way.

Every step forward filled me with soaring hope. Each rise that cut off my view might hide Vati's Opel, heading straight for me once I reached the top. I imagined the thrill of our reunion—Vati's surprised face when he first spotted me, his joy when he recognized me, and finally his arms around me. But the green Opel didn't show. When the sun disappeared behind clouds and shadows moved across my path, I turned around and headed home.

Aunt Amalia was giving a dinner party for our mother that evening and Mama was trying on every single gown in her closet when I got home. Finally, she chose the beautiful silk dress she had tailor-made in Falkenburg. Ingrid hovered about her, picked a rosebud from our garden, and stripped it of its thorns. Mama placed it between her breasts. All you saw was a pink bud unfolding its leaves like a fan at the center of her décolletage.

Mama's cheeks were animated, her eyes lit up from within; her entire being seemed aglow as she smiled at us from her dresser mirror. Ingrid and I couldn't help but beam back at her. This must be the woman Vati had fallen in love with, we felt, someone we barely knew.

We heard the toot of a car horn—Aunt Amalia's husband had arrived. Mama dabbed on a little more perfume, one dab behind each ear, one in the center of her collarbone, and one between her breasts. She swept up her cape, swirled around on her high heels as if already dancing, and was gone before Ingrid and I had finished saying good night. All she left behind was a cloud of perfume.

"Whatever happened to Aunt Amalia's brother?" I asked Ingrid. Though I'd been to Aunt Amalia's house a couple of times, I hadn't yet met him. "You used to tell such funny stories about him."

"I think something strange happened between him and Mama. He moved to Cologne to work for some big steel company. He *was* a funny man and fed us the best chocolates."

Ingrid walked me to my room and read some pages from *Pippi Longstocking* to me until I fell asleep.

I was woken by thunder and lightning and wanted to head for my sister's room but was too drowsy. Then I heard the front door open and the click-click of Mama's high heels on the marble floor. Satisfied,

I closed my eyes, only to be shaken by the sound of sobbing. What was happening? I heard a howl, followed by a succession of sobs and muffled cries.

Ingrid was already standing in the hallway.

"What's the matter with Mama?" I asked, my voice a whisper.

Ingrid shrugged her shoulders. "Who knows? Maybe someone spilled a drink on her gown, or some man she fancied didn't pay her enough attention."

Ingrid was right. Our mother's moods zigzagged as lightning during a storm. And, like Snow White's stepmother, she needed to hear that she was "the fairest of all."

"Ingrid, please look in on her."

"Let her first get off some steam."

"Only you can help her. She won't listen to me." After Ingrid disappeared into Mama's bedroom, I heard Mama's desperate voice. "She's moving away. I can't stand it, Amalia's moving away, now that I need her more than ever with the lenders crowding in on us and your father leaving us in a lurch."

Then the voices dropped away. Did Vati leave us in a lurch? I felt he would never do that knowingly. I knew he cared for us, so what was going on? Ingrid wasn't any wiser when I asked her the next morning. "But don't ask Mama," she told me. "Mama's in a foul mood 'cause Amalia's husband has been called to Bonn, the capital of West Germany. He'll take on a leading position within the CDU party—the Christian Democratic Union."

With her best friend and family moving away so quickly after our arrival, Mama felt lost. We could understand that. And Ingrid was losing her best friend, Abigail. For once, I was not losing anyone. That almost felt like a gain.

15

CREDITORS

In early summer, well-dressed men knocked on our door. Mama asked them into the parlor and sent us outdoors while muttering, "Why can't they wait for their *verdammtes Geld,* their damned money?"

The men were friendly at first; they wanted to know Ingrid's and my names, pinched our cheeks, called us *Pueppchen* und *Engel*—little dolls, angels. Later, they looked at us with sad eyes, and finally, they tried not to look at us at all. Ingrid filled me in. "They are creditors. Mama and Vati owe lots of money—Mama cannot pay the mortgage on this house."

Coming home from school, I heard Mama on the phone. "Please, Herbert. I beg you. *Please* give it your full consideration. There are two wage earners in your family. Julia and you, but I'm all alone." Mama was sniffling. "10,000 Deutsch Mark would make all the difference. The lenders are turning nasty." Mama fell silent. I wished I could hear what Uncle Herbert was saying. I prayed he would come through.

"Thank you for giving it some thought." After a long pause, Mama said, "Why yes, of course you'll want to discuss this with Julia." I knew from the tone of my mother's voice that she did not want Uncle Herbert to "discuss this" with our Aunt Julia and wondered if Uncle Herbert could tell. Then I tiptoed back out the door, closed it carefully only to turn right around, enter, and slam the door behind me. Mama promptly stuck her head out, calling, "Don't slam the door, you impertinent child."

I mumbled "Sorry, Mama" and headed for Ingrid's room to fill her in.

The next day, Mama sat Ingrid and me down at the kitchen table. "We must be extremely frugal from now on. No lollipops, no ice cream. No new hair ribbons"—music to my ears—"no new clothes. If we're not careful we could lose the house!"

"What do you mean 'lose the house'?" Ingrid asked.

"The creditors will take it away from us."

Ingrid was all frowns. "Can they really do that?"

"Yes," Mama sighed. "They absolutely can."

Within a month, we left the upstairs and moved much of our furniture, our books, and as many of our household goods as we could and moved into the basement apartment, originally built for the household help. Whatever didn't fit into the smaller place was stored in the attic. Mama rented out the main and first floor to an older couple who traveled a lot.

"Maybe," Mama told us, "Maybe the banks will now be satisfied."

It all happened so fast; we two sisters kept heading for the main front door after school at first. Only when our key no longer opened the lock did we turn and make our way to the outdoor steps and our "new" back door.

Before we could even insert the key one Friday afternoon, Bastian opened the door from the inside. We hugged him enthusiastically, while he grinned from ear to ear.

"My old man in Berchtesgaden finally let me join you—under one condition: I must pass 11th grade with an overall B or return to my private school near Falkenburg where they're holding a place for me."

"You can do it, Basti." Ingrid's face was glowing. My sister and I joined hands and danced around our brother. Life was looking up.

Often, when I was moping, thinking back to the Castle, Bastian snuck up behind me and tickled me. Just as often, he presented me with a sticky bun, a meringue, or almond cookie—seemingly out of nowhere.

Ingrid and I didn't give his generosity a second thought until the baker rang our bell one Saturday. Bastian motioned to us after Mama had closed the living room door. We listened in.

"I must ask you to take care of this bill, Frau Doktor," the baker said to Mama. "We've let it ride for quite a while."

"What bill?" Mama asked in the cool tone of voice reserved for servants and tradesmen.

"The one young Herr Bastian has run up."

"Bastian?" Mama's voice was still regal. "My son?"

"The young man who just let me in."

Ingrid and I looked up at Bastian. We knew he was always hungry, and he had grown by leaps and bounds over the past year, but we had no idea about his solo trips to the bakery.

There was a long silence before we heard Mama's voice again. "Let me see the bill." Another silence, then a horrified gasp. "There must be a mistake. How can one boy run up a bill at the bakery of *hundert-achtzig Mark*, one hundred-eighty marks?"

The baker cleared his throat. "Frau Doktor is welcome to call in her son and check out every item. He's been coming in every day, charging sweets, pretzels, and buns. Believe me, I know how hungry young men can get. I have a fifteen-year-old son myself."

"Bastian?" Mama opened the door. Ingrid and I turned toward our brother, who was already gone.

"Where is your brother? Tell me this instant! Where is he?" First, Mama grabbed Ingrid by the shoulders, then she moved in on me and shook me so hard I felt dizzy; she kept shaking until Ingrid put her hand on Mama's arm. "Marie's knees are buckling."

Our brother didn't show up for supper. We stashed away some food to take to the tree house that Bastian had just finished building in the backyard, but Mama wouldn't let us go out. In the middle of the night we were woken by voices.

"You low-down, miserable thief! Stealing from your own mother!"

The door to our basement living room with its small kitchen area was open. Mama was running with the heavy cast-iron skillet, using both hands to swing it at Bastian. At first, I shut my eyes tightly, but I couldn't stand the tension and opened them wide just as Mama screamed at the top of her lungs, "You miserable thief," took a deep breath, and slammed the pan down, grazing Bastian's shoulder blades.

At 16, my brother towered over Mama. I knew he could wrestle the skillet from her and wished with every fiber of my body that he would, but he did not.

Mama's next thrust crashed down on the stove with a resounding metallic clang. Had it landed on Bastian's head, our brother might have been killed.

"I'll get you! Just you wait and see."

Bastian made a dash for the door and was gone for the rest of the night.

Like many abusers, Mama was shrewd enough to whack us when no one was around. I had always known that we were safe when Vati was home, but it took me years to understand why. He would have been appalled by her mistreatment of us and would have put an end to her savagery. She couldn't risk that. And Vati was our family's only bread-winner. Mama had no higher education, no professional training, and no independent means of her own. She needed him.

Vati was also Mama's ticket to society. In a small place like Falken-burg, the doctor, the priest, and the mayor were the leading citizens of the town. Thanks to Vati, Mama belonged to that privileged group. She loved being called "Frau Doktor," she loved being served in the shops before the "common" folk, to have men remove their hat as she passed by, take a low bow, and greet her with, "Good Morning, Frau Doktor." While I resented our privileged status in the shops—the injustice of it—I took it for granted that Ingrid and I were known and accepted wherever we went as "the doctor's daughters."

16

AMERICAN SOLDIERS AND EMILY'S BIRTHDAY PARTY

Fall had come and gone. The cows had returned from their Alpine meadows to their barns in the valley. Ingrid couldn't wait for the first snow to fall so she could learn how to ski. I was indifferent to the seasons while dreaming of Anna and Falkenburg Castle.

"Your father cannot support us, and his own sister won't let us have any money," Mama told us one October day, her large eyes filled with worry and anger.

"Where will it all end?" Mama cried. "Dear God, where will it end?" She wrung her hands as in a melodrama.

"But can't Vati come back and help us?" I asked.

"No, he needs more time to get well. Everything's gone wrong. I have to find a job and make money." Mama kept folding and unfolding her fingers. "Thank God, Irma works for the Americans. She's talked to her boss at the PX, and I've been offered a job on probation. I'll be a salesclerk. Imagine that—a common clerk. Who knows? Maybe next, I'll be a servant girl!" Mama's eyes widened with incredulity, her hands forming small fists.

"What's a PX?" I asked.

"A huge American department store where they sell everything from chewing gum to jewelry to bicycles." Mama's fists were uncurling.

"Candy?"

"Yes, candy." Ingrid winked at me and turned her face away so that Mama could not see her delight break through.

American soldiers were the lifeblood of Garmisch. Unlike Ingrid and Bastian, I had never seen soldiers before and was intrigued by the masses of men in olive uniforms, hopping into olive green jeeps or cruising in yacht-like cars past diminutive Opels and Volkswagens. When out of military dress, they wore bright shirts and jackets, laughed lustily, chewed gum with their mouths open, and spoke with booming voices.

Americans struck me as simply *full of themselves*. No wearing of subdued garb like German women and men, no downcast eyes or brooding faces. They even routinely smiled at children, something Falkenburg's farmers had rarely done.

I sensed that their loudness was not meant to upset or disturb; they simply did what came naturally: humming happy tunes, feeling the wind in the stubble of their short-cropped hair, tooting their horns at pretty Fraulein and showing off their convertibles, while spilling swing, boogie, jazz, and monotone fiddle sounds—called country music—into Garmisch's streets and market squares.

When I wondered out loud to Bastian why Americans were so much happier than Germans, he said, "Well, of course, they are. They won the war and can do whatever they like."

I knew that. But there was more. I was not experienced enough to express what startled me about Americans, though I felt it in my bones. The biggest difference to Germans was: Americans *liked* themselves.

Just as I was falling asleep, Bastian knocked at our bedroom door.

"Can I come in?" he whispered. Ingrid closed her book, and I quickly shut my eyes because I knew I'd learn so much more by letting the two speak among themselves.

"Yes," Ingrid answered, "but talk softly. Marie's already asleep."

Bastian pulled up a chair.

"Things are bad," he said.

"Really bad?"

"Really, really bad."

Ingrid scratched her head.

"We're losing the house—if we haven't lost it already."

"Oh, no!"

"Mama *loves* the house," said Bastian.

"I know. I do, too," said Ingrid.

I cringed.

"Oh, Basti! What happened with Uncle Herbert?"

"Aunt Julia got back to Mama to tell her they are building a new house themselves, a big one overlooking the town, and they didn't have a Pfennig to spare."

"Scheisse." Shit! "If only Vati came back. It's been a long half year!"

"I know," said my brother, "Vati makes people feel good and can persuade them to do most anything, but Mama..." They both let out a sigh.

Bastian, hung his head. "I'll see if I can get a message to Vati."

I wanted to shout a resounding "yes," but managed to stop myself in time.

"But I'm not too hopeful," Basti said.

"Why not?"

"The guards—I mean the nursing staff—monitor the mail at a sanatorium."

"For goodness sake! Why?"

"To protect the patients from anything that might upset them."

I did not sleep well that night. Where would we go? We had no other home, and our old house at Falkenburg Castle had new tenants, we'd been told by Irma. The thought of being totally shut out of my Castle made me want to sob, but I suppressed the impulse because of my sister.

Ingrid had made some friends at school, but I had not. A couple of girls had invited me to their home because our Vati is a doctor and their parents looked forward to meeting him, but I hadn't found any kindred soul. Maybe I would at the birthday party of my classmate Emily who sat next to me.

On the day of the party, the sun was shining. The bushes along the brook that ran through Emily's garden were decorated with red and blue streamers, and the water glittered like quicksilver. Everything sparkled. The chairs around the cake-laden table on Emily's large veranda were almost lifted off the ground by colorful balloons.

I ached when I remembered I could no longer sit on our veranda. It had become the domain of the "upstairs couple." None of my classmates had to live in the basement of their own home! The happy giggles and shrieks around me suddenly hurt my ears. I fled the veranda for the brook outside. There, at the water's edge, in a grassy hollow, lay Emily's new ball. 'Damn ball,' I grumbled, grabbed it, and tossed it into the brook where it bounced merrily out of sight.

I did not feel merry at all, hurried back to the house, found Emily's mother in the kitchen, and told her with downcast eyes that I had an upset stomach and needed to go home. Trotting along the puddle-strewn path of the Partnach back to our house, I felt like the criminal I surely was.

At night in the dark, I tried to recall my favorite paintings and manuscripts from my Castle's Treasure Hall. Just before falling asleep, I could almost feel the vellum covers between my fingers, but when I woke in the morning, my hands were always empty.

17

HITTING THE ROAD

In late October, when Mama offered to make hot chocolate for Ingrid and me after school, we knew something was up. Bastian's prep school wouldn't let out for another hour, which meant she wanted to talk to us behind his back.

"Your brother is doing poorly in school and needs to go back to his old school near Falkenburg," Mama told us with wide eyes while her lips formed a thin line.

I felt crushed. Bastian's presence had always reassured me. I wanted him to stay. Somehow, I understood that Bastian had been jostled about by Mama until she married our father. Now Vati could not help him anymore.

"Couldn't we get him a tutor?" Ingrid suggested.

Mama's face turned a deep red. "A tutor? When we cannot afford real coffee?" Mama's short, nervous cough was setting in. "When I haven't had a perm in half a year, and have to wear nylons with runs?"

Mama stormed out of the kitchen, slamming the door. When Basti came home, we breathed a sigh of relief.

"Look," he said, "I should've studied harder. Though even when I do, it doesn't seem to make much difference!" He threw up his hands. "Now it can't be helped!" Then his face brightened. "But the best thing is I get to live with Anna in Falkenburg while finishing prep school. She's moved into the house of her fiancé's parents and my father in Berchtesgaden is gonna rent a room there for me."

Ingrid's face regained some color. I took Bastian's hand. "Can I come with you, Bastian? Please?" I squeezed my brother's hand with all my strength.

"Silly you," said Bastian softly. "Of course, Anna would be happy to see you, and I'd be happy to have you nearby. But you want to be here in Garmisch when Vati returns." My hand went limp. I straightened my shoulders.

"Yes," I said firmly. "I want to be here when Vati comes back."

We'd become an all-female household in our basement where twilight prevailed over light, and the bare floors resounded from our steps. Ingrid and I didn't dare ask Mama what had become of our lush carpets, because Mama was so exhausted; she worked all day long and left many a night after supper to earn extra money babysitting her American customers' children.

We missed our brother the moment we opened the door to our empty basement apartment after school. There was no one to tease us, to cheer us up, and to comfort us with sweets when our tummies growled.

"I'm afraid we'll have to cut back on food," Mama warned us. "The creditors take all my money and leave us barely enough to subsist. But at least we are hanging on to the house for now." Mama spoke with a sadness that was almost devoid of anger. We couldn't recall any other time she had sounded like that.

"The Americans celebrate Thanksgiving in a few days and I'll get an extra day off," Mama told us in late November. "It's a big deal for them. Families get together from all over the country and celebrate over a meal of roasted turkey. The PX bought hundreds of turkeys. If they don't all sell, I'm allowed to buy one half price. Wouldn't that be wonderful?" Ingrid and I nodded enthusiastically.

"I wonder if Vati has enough to eat?" I asked Mama.

"I'm sure he does. Patients in a sanatorium get the very best food."

I wanted to hear more, but Mama turned away to light the gas flames of the oven for warmth.

In the end, Mama could not bring home a turkey, but she made hot cider for us on the American Thanksgiving Day as a special treat. We wrapped our hands around the glasses, grateful for their warmth. "I am sorry we missed out on the big treat," Mama said, "but Irma made us a nice potato salad and sent along a package of wieners."

The bell rang upstairs. No one answered. It rang again. Mama's face hardened.

"I'd better see who it is before we're driven crazy. As usual, no one's home upstairs."

Ingrid and I prayed that Mama wouldn't scream at whoever it was. To our surprise, we heard shouts of joy. We exchanged puzzled looks, while Mama and someone else clattered down the stairs; Mama was bubbling over with words in English that we could not understand. Her face was flushed, her eyes shining.

She carried a huge paper bag in each arm, followed by a burly American in uniform, wearing a red scarf and a red cap, who held more grocery bags. In no time, the kitchen table filled with oranges, apples, bananas, and a pineapple! With pies and canned delicacies. The sweet man who delivered these rare treats had a crew cut, the huge proportions of a bear, and a face that radiated good will. Ingrid and I had taken a shine to the posters of Coca-Cola Santas in the PX, and whispered "Santa" to each other. Santa waved at us and broke into a heart-warming smile. "Jim's the name," he said and charged back upstairs.

Heading back down, Jim's steps were firm and deliberate. No more clattering. He appeared with a steaming turkey in a large pan, surrounded by potatoes, onions, celery, and carrots. As the air filled with a heavenly aroma, our stomachs gurgled, mouths watering.

Jim and Mama exchanged more words in English, punctuated with oohs and aahs, and Mama kept gushing *wonderful*. The turkey disappeared into the oven to stay warm. Mama asked us in the same sweet voice she used for Jim to put the groceries away and help set the table. "But leave out the cheesecake and pudding for after dinner," she cooed.

Cheesecake? Pudding? Ingrid and I cuffed each other. Was all this wonderful food really *for us*? And was this really *our* Mama? Soon, we, too, had been infected by the sights and scents of this moveable feast. Santa Jim knelt before us, repeating our names in an awkward way—he couldn't say a crisp German "r," but we didn't mind. Anything this Santa wanted to say was "okay." I understood right away that he enjoyed bringing joy. By the time the heavenly turkey graced our table, we each lifted up a delicate glass filled with wine.

"Prost," said Mama. "And thank you, dear Jim."

Jim raised his glass in a toast and looked deeply into Mama's eyes.

I wanted Jim to stay for dinner, but Mama told us he had to be back for his shift at base. Jim left quickly, waving goodbye. "I hope to see you again soon."

I would have loved to see Jim again. The sooner, the better. Sadly, that would never happen. To me, Jim symbolized the kindness and spontaneous generosity of Americans. My fellow countrymen of that time were far too stiff, too insecure, and too stingy to have showered heaps of goodies on virtual strangers.

Within the week, while Ingrid and I were in school, Mama and Irma moved our things into a one-room flat of an old villa on the other side of town. It must have been a striking home once, judging by its wrought-iron gate, its turrets, and its bay windows. But now its stucco was peeling, its gate was rusty, and the large garden overgrown.

The new place had no living room, no bedrooms, no kitchen, no nursery. Mama, Ingrid, and I sat, ate, studied, and slept in one and the same room. Only the bathroom provided brief moments of privacy. Though we kept bumping into each other, the room felt vast in its strangeness.

Mama never said we *lost* our house. We all knew. We also instinctively knew not to speak of that loss in front of Mama—as if the house were a living person who had suffered a horrible fate, so horrible that it could never be mentioned.

Without Vati, life droned on—Mama left for work, Ingrid and I for school. One night we were woken by a squabble outside our door.

"I have to increase the rent if you keep using so much hot water," our landlady warned.

"What do you mean, *so much hot water*? The girls share a tub once a week—and we cook very little."

"Nevertheless, my bill has gone up considerably."

"That cannot be," Mama said in a loud voice. "I cannot pay one Pfennig more." Her voice was trembling. Mama began pounding the door as if to underscore her despair; she sobbed. Her sobs grew louder, her fists pounded harder. Ingrid slipped out of bed.

"Frau Dr. Bergen. Get a hold of yourself! We'll talk some other time," said our landlady.

Mama's sobs became gurgles. Ingrid quickly opened the door, took Mama by the arm, and led her past our red-faced landlady back into our room where Mama threw herself on the bed, face down, her body heaving.

Ingrid rushed into the kitchen nook; she was working her hands while she waited for the kettle to boil. Across the room, I gingerly patted Mama's back.

"I've fixed you some chamomile tea, Mama. It'll help you sleep." Ingrid stood by the side of the bed. Mama turned over. Her face was swollen. She sat up and rubbed her eyes. Suddenly, her face turned a deeper red. "How dare you use up *electricity*! You'll drive us into the *poor house!*" Mama ripped the cup from Ingrid's hand and threw it against the kitchen cupboard, the scalding water spraying the walls, and even us.

Ingrid and I froze, lips pressed together. We held hands while Mama paced. Before I knew it, she grabbed me by my shoulders and pushed my head into the cupboard door.

"Mama!" Ingrid's voice was filled with shock, pity, and something that almost sounded like a warning. I turned. I didn't yet feel any pain though every cell in my body pulsed. Mama was quivering, her face strangely vacant.

Ingrid put her arm around me. I leaned into her, away from the pain that began pounding in my head. Mama seemed to wake up, and blurted out, "Oh, I am so sorry, Marie!" She took a step toward me. I moved back. Ingrid held up her hand. Mama stopped staring at the two of us, and stumbled back to bed. Ingrid loosened her hold and stroked my cheek.

"Is it bad?"

"Yes, but getting better."

"We need Vati back! Why doesn't he come?"

"He's still in that darn sanatorium. Come sit down in the chair. I'll see if I can find some candy," she lowered her voice, "in Mama's handbag." Ingrid found a stick of chewing gum and broke it in two, offering me one half. I nodded thanks, but didn't stick it in my mouth, afraid to move my jaw.

After a while we made our way back to bed, snuggling as close to each other as we could, holding on to each other until we finally fell asleep, too.

The next day Mama surprised us with a small, artificial Christmas tree from the PX and a bagful of glitter. I thought the tree ghastly, especially since it couldn't give off the wonderful scent of the fir trees I remembered from Falkenburg Castle. Mama placed the miniature thing on top of a dresser, already crowded with lamps, her jewelry boxes, and a sewing kit. The kit moved to the ledge of our bathroom window and had to be lifted every time we opened the window for fresh air. If I could have mustered an iota of humor at the time, I would have said that our Christmas had gone to the toilet.

Fortunately, Irma invited us for Christmas dinner to her apartment under the roof of a splendid American resort hotel. She had a well-equipped kitchen with a good-size stove, while we had only an electric plate with two heating elements. Ingrid and I dug into Irma's Christmas goose with great gusto and toasted our hostess with the fine wine supplied by Irma's new boyfriend, as we had heard her whisper to Mama. Ingrid had cuffed me and raised her eyebrows at the mention of "my new boyfriend," and Mama had wagged her finger at her friend.

I was sad when we had to leave Irma's place and return to our single room where a fake tree-let and a supplanted sewing kit framed our existence; my heart sank every time I opened the door to our so-called home.

So, I hit the road, whenever the weather allowed, to look for Vati and his car. I was sure that Vati wanted to be with us, and I needed him to come home.

Driven by longing, an ache that sat high up in my stomach, I set one foot before the other, lifting my eyes off the white center line and fixing them on the horizon. Each hill, each steep curve, spurred on my hope, just as it had when we first arrived in town. Surely, the next hill and the next curve would reveal Vati's Opel. It'd be a dot at first, then grow bigger and bigger until Vati pulled up right beside me. He'd jump out briskly just as he had at farmer Schmidt's, put his arms around me, and lift me way up into the air. Though I walked for what seemed like hours, I couldn't set eyes on the green Opel. But I could not quit.

When I heard the sound of an oncoming car one chilly afternoon, I knew it would *not* be Vati's. I had looked for him too many times before—in vain. I stood still, perfectly still and listened. All the while the sound of the motor grew louder, the hum of the tires stronger. Some part of me jumped to attention. I was but heartbeat and muscle.

Hitting the road was one way to escape Mama, but there was so much more. I really wanted to run into my father's arms for protection and love. And if I could not, I wanted to run into oblivion. I needed to break out of our bleak existence, and if I could not, I no longer wanted to live.

When the car came closer, I leapt into the road—running with all my might, coming alive while I ran. The pain pushed me toward the wheels I was trying to outrun. The driver hit his brakes till they squealed and came to a stop just after I made it across, hitting the ground hard. He missed me by inches.

Covering my head with my arms, I curled up on the shoulder of the road. The man's face looked ashen, and his cheeks twitched while he bent down over me. I hardly dared squint between my fingers. He stared for an eternity. Finally, he extended his hand.

"Can you get up?" he asked and when I did, "Does anything hurt?"

"No." He looked me up and down, checking me over.

"What about your cheek?"

"Just a scratch."

His face relaxed for a second. "Have you done this before?"

I nodded. He swept his hand over his hair.

"I almost killed you," he said. "This must stop!"

I dropped my head.

"Can you hear me?"

I nodded again, keeping my eyes fixed to the ground.

"I better talk to your mother, your teacher—anyone who can help put a stop to this."

"Please don't tell my Mama! I won't do it again if you don't tell," I whimpered.

"Look into my eyes." I finally looked into his eyes with all the despair of my heart. His anger had melted into concern and his warm brown eyes reminded me of Anna. The moment Anna's face appeared before me, I straightened my back and said, "I won't do it again."

"You promise?"

"I promise." My voice had a new, firmer quality. I could hear it myself.

The kind man let me go. The next day already, running into moving cars felt like something I had done in another life. I started to breathe more freely. The man's concern for my welfare had melted something inside.

Ingrid and I looked up in surprise while doing dishes when Mama opened the door to a man in a black pastor's frock. Without Anna to take us, we'd never attended church in Garmisch. The minister put his hat on the table and took our mother's hand in his.

"My dear lady, such trying times for you. You are in my prayers. I can only imagine how painful life must be right now." He sighed. "And that sad business that caused all this grief."

Mama put her fingers to her lips, motioning toward us. The minister turned around. He smiled at Ingrid and me. "I see," he said. "Yes, sometimes we have to walk in the valley of darkness, but God's light is above us." He studied Ingrid and me. "What lovely little girls. Yes, I see." His voice trailed off.

Mama sent us out to play. Before Ingrid closed the door, we saw the preacher take our mother's hand again and pat it gently. I wanted to listen at the door, but Ingrid pulled me away.

After the minister left, Mama called us back inside. The moment I saw Mama's face, an eerie feeling took hold of me. It looked exactly as it had when she had told us at Falkenburg Castle that Vati had been taken to a sanatorium.

"Well, you two," she said. "Seeing how we three are living in only one room and that I'm at a stage of exhaustion, the minister suggested you two spend a few months in a nice children's home in Kempten, about fifty miles from here. We passed through it on our way from Falkenburg. Do you remember?" Ingrid nodded yes.

"That's good," said Mama. "So you won't feel like total strangers. The home is run by Protestant sisters." Mama turned to me. "You'll be able to go to church again," she said. "When I think back to how many times we had to collect you from the chapel in Falkenburg, I know you'll be glad to hear that."

No church in the world can replace my chapel, I wanted to tell her. But I did want to hear the Word of God read from the pulpit again. Maybe the place wouldn't be so bad.

"The minister thought that the company of other children would do both of you good," Mama continued. "I think so, too. So, we'll start getting you all packed up. The chaplain—that's the Pastor's assistant—has agreed to take you by train to Kempten next week, on Ash Wednesday."

Ingrid and I said nothing. We had always done what Mama wanted—and perhaps life would be more peaceful without her. Too much had happened, the loss of our father, our brother, and our new house. We were numb now, worn down.

18

Vati's Letter

Dear Bastian, Ingrid, and Marie,

I hope you three are healthy and well. Bastian, I know school is not always easy, but you can do the work if you tackle it daily and have faith in yourself. Marie and Ingrid, I'm sure you are still the fine students I remember. Keep it up so that you can enter College Prep School after fourth grade.

And take good care of your mother. She is going through hard times right now, for which I am very sorry. Thank you for being good little helpers. I really shouldn't say "little." At eleven and eight you are truly "big girls."

I'm doing better, but probably won't be able to see you until sometime in the new year. I can't wait. I miss and love you dearly. Stick together, you three.

In my mind, I'm hugging you with all my strength and squeezing you tight.

Bussi, Bussi,
Your Vati

BOOK III

St. John's

19

St. John's Children's Home

The trees were naked and gray on the dull, wintry day we arrived at St. John's Children's Home. The streets looked empty, the sky so low, and the earth so barren, that I wondered if all creation had died. The chaplain who had escorted us on the train to Kempten looked around as if lost.

Finally, we came to a stop before a high stone wall that blocked most of our view except for the top floors of a bulky stone structure rising into the gloomy sky. We shivered; even the aloof and dutiful chaplain shivered as he rang the bell at the gate.

A tall figure in black appeared, her broad face framed by a stiff white cap. I couldn't help staring at the woman's bushy brows and the shadow of a mustache on her upper lip. The figure studied us with the eye of a sentry who had the power to keep us out or let us in. I prayed she would send us away, but the woman's jaw was set, her beady eyes sharp as a crow's. There was no dead bird or crushed rodent before her—only Ingrid and me.

"Zo!" the woman said, and that "so" sounded much weightier than you'd expect a short word to sound. "Zo, *you* are the doctor's girls." She turned abruptly to our chaperone. "I expect you'll want to be on your way."

The chaplain mumbled and backed away. I looked around the barren yard that was blocked out by this bulky building without a single pleasing line. The chaplain disappeared, and I was left staring at the gate that shut with a clang.

"You might as well take a good look," said the towering woman. "That gate is locked. It will remain *zo!* You are forbidden to leave St.

John's unless accompanied by one of us. And when you are marched to school in the morning, there'll be a Sister in the lead, a Sister in the rear. Is this understood?"

"Yes, Ma'am," said Ingrid.

"Yes, Sister!" shouted the woman. "Always address me as Sister. I am Sister Hedwig. Is that understood?"

"Yes, Sister!" Ingrid's voice was respectful. "Don't we have classes here? We go into town?"

Sister's bushy eyebrows shot up, and she broke into a smirk. "Where do you think you are? A boarding school?" She let out a hard laugh. "Let me make it perfectly clear, your ladyship! We have only one school in Kempten. It's a *proper* school for the children of *respectable* parents. None of them pleased to have to put up with *the likes of you!*"

Ingrid and I looked at each other with a puzzled expression. I shook my head. People had always shown us respect. Vati was a doctor, and our mother a Baroness.

"Let's get going!" Sister picked up Ingrid's case and marched toward the big building, swinging the case as if it were a lunch box.

I turned when Ingrid turned and slowed down when my sister did. We followed Sister Hedwig through a dark foyer and up a set of stairs. Only my legs had volition; everything else was paralyzed. The animated, longing part of me that had roamed the ramparts and halls of the Castle, and ran through mountain meadows, was folding in on itself.

I saw how the steep stone steps were worn down in the center as if whole armies of children had marched up and down them for ages, sagging more deeply than the steps leading to the great hall of Falkenburg Castle, and I wondered how this could be since this building couldn't be more than a hundred years old. Sister stopped in front of a bench placed against the wall of the hallway. "Sit, Ingrid! I'll be back. You're twelve. That means you are in the hall for older girls. At eight, Marie will stay right here with girls from six to ten."

I cried out and threw my arms around Ingrid, but Sister pulled me off. "Stop that! You're only a hall apart." Ingrid stroked my back. 'I'll be here,' she mouthed.

"You may not fuss," Sister barked. "Understood?" She cut the air with her hand as if slicing it.

Ingrid nodded emphatically, urging me on.

"Yes, Sister."

Sister and I entered a large dormitory. A handful of girls sat on their beds made of white metal, arranged in two rows on a dark floor. The walls were bare except for a crucifix. Four windows looked down to the street where we entered, the other two into the naked yard. I shivered as I took in the big room that felt barren, even with people in it. Space had been a friend at the Castle, had embraced me. This space was threatening, empty, and cold.

Sister paid no attention to the girls on the beds but marched on. At one point I heard her tell one of them, "No, these new girls are not up for adoption."

What was she talking about? Sister's hand on my back pushed me on. We stopped by a window where Sister addressed a girl with soft gray eyes who looked older than I, perhaps almost ten. The girl had ash blond braids and fine facial features and wore an apron over her skirt and blouse.

"You better set a good example for her, Christel. Do you understand?"

"Yes, Sister Hedwig," replied Christel.

I felt small and exposed as Christel sat down beside me. Sister, without another word, strode out of the room. There were no screens and no curtains. Ingrid seemed miles away.

"Sister's a bully, but she leaves quiet girls alone," Christel said to me. "Try not to stand out. Most of the girls in our dorm are good girls," she went on softly. "Gretl over there still wets her bed—she's eight. We try to wake her whenever we can so Sister Hedwig won't beat her."

"Sister Hedwig *beats* her?" While Mama's outbursts were as much a part of my life as wind and rain, I couldn't imagine a stranger being allowed to lay hands on me.

"Don't *ever* provoke Sister Hedwig," Christel continued. "She hits hard, but she only beats you when you've done something wrong."

I didn't like what I heard, but I very much liked my neighbor. Christel's eyes were bright and filled with kindness, her voice soothing.

"I think the Sisters are a little nicer to us than to the older girls, though not by much," Christel said.

Sitting so close to Christel, I couldn't help noticing Christel's hair.

"Look, we almost have the same hair color."

Christel's face lit up. "Yes, we do. And you have a dimple when you smile."

"I keep forgetting about that."

"'Cause you can't see yourself."

Only minutes after Ingrid slipped in and out of my dormitory room to make sure I was all right, Sister Hedwig barged into the room and clapped her hands. "Let us pray!" she commanded. The girls stopped what they were doing and knelt on the floor.

"I thank you, heavenly father, that you have kept me this day," Sister intoned mechanically, and we all joined in, "and I pray that You would forgive me all my sins"—oh, how the memory of Gerda's birthday ball pained me—"and graciously keep me this night. For into Your hands I commend myself. Let Your holy angel be with me, that the evil foe may have no power over me. Amen."

A deep silence fell after Sister left the room. No one talked, no one moved until the sound of her footsteps had died away.

Christel had held up her finger, motioning me to be quiet. "She always listens for a minute or two," Christel whispered across the space between the beds. After a long lull, she asked, "So, why are you here?"

"To give our mother a break."

"That's not a reason."

"Yes, it is."

"Most of us are here because our parents did something." Christel stopped for a moment, then added, "Or they were sick or got hurt."

I thought about that. "Our father is sick; he caught a bad infection and is in a sanatorium. And Mama is exhausted from working so hard. She needed a break."

"Gerda's mother jumped off a bridge," Christel said, "and Gretl's father burned down a barn. My stepfather..." She stopped herself. I waited for her to speak again, but she didn't.

"Did your mother make you come?" I asked.

"I no longer have a mother," Christel said. "He killed her."

"Oh!" I swallowed. "I'm so sorry."

"Don't. How could you know?" One of the girls was snoring.

We lay quietly. No one else seemed to be awake.

"You see," said Christel, "my brother and I woke in the middle of the night from the screams of our mother. We ran downstairs. She was on the floor, bleeding, with our stepfather staring down at her, a knife in his hand. A couple of times her hand was moving, and then it moved no more. That's when my stepfather..." Christel was sobbing. "That's when he cried 'Mother of God!' and called the neighbors. We held our mother's hand, and I put a pillow under her head and kept calling her name, but she didn't answer. She died in the hospital that night, so they took us away."

I couldn't bear what Christel was telling me and covered my ears, but her words kept ringing in my mind.

"Oh, Christel," I whispered, and almost in the same breath, "When did that happen?"

"Two years ago." Christel sat up while I pondered her answer. Thank God, not yesterday or last week, I thought, and was instantly plagued by a new anxiety. Two years? Did that mean that Ingrid and I might be locked up in this place for years? A moan escaped me, causing Christel to lean into the empty space between us.

"I am glad you're my neighbor, Marie."

"And I'm glad you are mine."

We lay close, without seeing each other's faces, too far away to touch. The hall was pitch black. I couldn't help imagining the woman screaming, the man stabbing her, and the two children helpless and stunned. And out of nowhere, the hate-filled glare of farmer Fritz who'd raised his fist at Vati disturbed my mind.

Just as I was falling asleep, a knife came flashing at me. I shot up in cold sweat until Christel's steady breathing reminded me of where I was. What in the world was going on? First, we'd lost Vati, then Bastian, then the new house, and the new town. And now we'd ended up in a place that felt like prison.

The next evening, after prayers, I slipped out of bed and groped my way to Ingrid's dorm, counting beds as I tiptoed along. Ingrid's was the fourth from the door. "Get in," Ingrid whispered as if she'd been waiting for me. We threw our arms around each other.

"We need to go home."

Ingrid stroked my hair. "Listen, Mama *hatte einen Nervenzusammenbruch*—had a nervous breakdown. My teacher told me and said to be brave and understanding. Mama will recover. She just needs time."

"You never told me she had *einen Nervenzusammenbruch*!"

"The teacher made me promise that I wouldn't breathe a word to a soul—and you saw how Mama acted after she argued with our landlady about the electricity bill."

I felt angry—and alone. Why didn't Ingrid tell me? We both suffered from the same mother. So, we should both know what's going on with her. I swallowed. "Do you really believe all will be well at the end?"

"Of course! We just have to give Mama a rest. As soon as she's better, we'll go home. In the meantime, we have to be brave." Ingrid squeezed me. "Now, you better get back before Sister catches us together." The word *Sister* made me bristle.

"A monster."

"I know. But we have each other and you have the nicest neighbor." The thought of Christel alone lifted my spirit.

Most girls at St. John's were kind to one another—like Christel, trying to make the best of our own and everyone else's bad situation, though some had become listless and worn out. There was a pushy older girl, but she didn't bother younger and weaker children. It was the grown-ups we had to fear.

Gretl, the bed-wetting girl, sat shivering under the covers in the unheated hall one morning.

"Get going!" Sister Hedwig barked after she had checked the sack of chaff that served as Gretl's mattress.

Gretl followed Sister to her room, her shoulders slumped. Christel whispered to me that Sister would whip Gretl so hard she'd barely be able to sit down. The other girls stopped braiding their hair and brushing their teeth for a moment when Gretl let out her first howling scream. They could do nothing to help her. Slowly, they resumed braiding.

I couldn't help but listen to Gretl's cries from behind Sister's door. I suffered for her and at the same time I was grateful—relieved—not to be in Gretl's shoes. The terrible gap between pity and relief made me want to rush out of my skin—I was so ashamed.

Christel told me that Sister liked to inspect the girls' ears before letting them go down for breakfast, but that morning she sent us to the refectory with one sweeping hand gesture. The dining hall was lined with long tables and benches and was filled with gray light. It reminded me of Falkenburg's kitchen—except that I was not allowed to follow anyone about as I used to do with Anna. Christel led me to our assigned place. As soon as we had all filed in, the kitchen staff joined us, lining up against the wall.

When all were assembled, a slim, younger Sister with a calm face stood up. "That's Sister Elizabeth, our head sister," whispered Christel. "We don't get to see her much. She's always in her office." Sister Elizabeth bowed her head. "*Herr, oeffne meine Lippen, damit mein Mund dein Lob verkuende. Ehre sei dem Vater und dem Sohn und dem Heiligen Geist, wie am Anfang, so auch jetzt und allezeit und in Ewigkeit. Amen.*"

Lord, empower my lips so that my mouth may proclaim your praise. Praised be the Father, and the Son, and the Holy Spirit, as in the beginning, so also now and for all eternity. Amen.

I was still cold inside and out, when the staff dashed back to the kitchen after Sister's "Amen," and we all sat down. The surface of the wooden bench felt like ice. But I took heart as the first platter arrived, piled high with slices of bread covered in a thin film of margarine and jam. Though I could barely detect the jam, that sweet, thin layer unfolded on my tongue like a revelation. Each girl took exactly one slice when the platter was passed, another when it came for the second time.

While the jam dissolved on my tongue, the cold slid from my bones. The walls and bench reflected the morning light—even more brightly when the tin cans, filled with chicory coffee, were set before us. I wrapped my hands around the cup of coffee, letting its warmth stream into my fingers, and swallowed as slowly as I could. We had already prayed with Sister, but the meal was our real communion. The sweetness of jam and the warmth of the coffee offered more comfort than all the prayers the Sisters rushed us through from morning to night.

Slowly but inevitably, the word of God started to lose some of its shine in that heartless place, especially when it flowed from the lips of Sister Hedwig or the Protestant minister. In church, the minister spoke of love and compassion, but when did he ever look out for us children? When he came to Saint John's, he shoveled Danish and freshly baked buns into his mouth right in front of us while we had to make do with thin slices of bread.

Every morning after breakfast, we were marched to Kempten's school in the center of town like a group of prisoners on detail, commandeered by two nuns, front and rear. We passed housewives in drab clothes who stared at us, their hair covered with kerchiefs and shopping bags dangling from their arms. Others quickly pushed their children out of the way, as if the mere sight of the girls from St. John's could contaminate the souls of their little girls or boys. Still others turned away, if from pity or some sense of shame I could not tell.

No one ever smiled at us.

I had barely memorized the names of my classmates when Annie, the daughter of the Burgermeister, who sat in front of me, lost her ruler.

"Someone stole it!" she whined. "I know someone did because I had it for first period."

"I saw it too," said Annie's friend.

The teacher asked us students to look inside our desks and under our chairs. We all shuffled about, lifting the covers of our desks and rummaging around, but found nothing. The room fell silent. Slowly, inexorably, the silence tightened around me.

"All St. John's children out into the corridor!" the teacher demanded.

She did not address me by name, and I saw no connection between the missing ruler and the children from St. John's—so I did not stir.

My neighbor whispered, "You, too."

"Marie, out into the corridor," yelled the teacher while the butcher's son shot a paper wad at me. I was being collared without understanding why and got up slowly as if in a trance. Someone snickered. Blood rushed to my cheeks, my stomach churned. Just before I reached the door, Annie chanted, "Marie is a *thee-eef*, Marie is a *thee-eef*!"

Ingrid, Christel, and the other children soon joined us in the corridor, whispering among themselves. Christel came over.

"What happened in your homeroom?" she asked.

"Annie is missing her ruler, but what has that got to do with us?"

"Nothing," Christel said. "But they always suspect us first. Better get used to it."

"Why us?"

"Because we lost our parents and no one's defending us."

We were searched and sent back to our homerooms. The ruler had not been found. Everyone looked up when I entered. I looked straight ahead, not left and not right. My face was hot, my heart beat in my throat, but I made it to my chair without shedding a tear.

At the end of class, the ruler fell out of the trousers of the butcher's son. The teacher looked at me quickly—not kindly—before marching the boy to the principal's office.

That night Sister Hedwig and we girls once again prayed, "For into Your hands I commend myself, my body and soul. Let Your holy angel be with me, that the evil foe may have no power over me. Amen."

And suddenly it dawned on me, suddenly I understood that the "evil foe" was not the devil as I've been taught—but Sister Hedwig. In our life, Sister was the foe. The minister, too, and even my teacher acted like "the evil foe."

This new insight both haunted and liberated me. Every time the Minister read from *Revelations* or used that word, I jumped with a start, feeling both enlightened *and* stricken as if I'd been "condemned to know." As a result, I clung ever more to Christel, who remained unwaveringly gentle and calm. Inwardly, I thanked her for her constancy. Yet I worried about losing her because Christel—alongside all orphans at St. John's—was up for adoption.

Some of Kempten's honorable citizens were allowed to choose an orphan and invite her to their homes to get to know her better. Mr. Gruber, the baker, and his wife, Mrs. Gruber, were looking Christel over. Christel helped sell cakes and bread on Saturdays after school, and she washed the shop floors after closing time. She liked serving the public and looking out onto a busy street from her own bedroom where she stayed once a month for one night.

"What are they waiting for?" I burst out one Sunday night after Christel returned from her regular outing. The question had been on the tip of my tongue for weeks. I sensed that it might cause Christel pain, and I never wanted to lose her, but I was also filled with indignation that the Grubers didn't recognize Christel's goodness and worth.

"Herr Gruber said you can't be too careful with strangers," said Christel. "They are looking me over."

"What's there to see?" I asked myself. Anyone who had eyes could see what a gem Christel was.

"It's a matter of time. Herr Gruber says you wouldn't trust anyone in the Army until you had seen action together."

Mr. Gruber must truly be deaf and blind. And what was that "army action" mumbo-jumbo?

From then on, I pondered how I could help my friend—always with mixed feelings because Christel was my saving grace, my buddy. I was glad my sister was at St. John's, but in many ways, Ingrid's physical strength and self-confidence set us apart. She was famous in Falkenburg for wrestling boys and pulling their hair if they had been pestering her. I was famous for looking out of the window and dreaming the time away. Ingrid liked to swim, do ballet, and skate, whereas I was warned off sports because I was so "frail." Thank God I had my paintings, sculptures, and manuscripts; the stork's widespread wings, the spirit Prince, and my fairy tales. Here, at St. John's, I had Christel.

The months marched on. Though each humiliation, each thrashing of Gretl stopped time, almost as if it were a stitch in a tapestry of shame, the regimen of school, homework, and prayers left little room for thought. Ingrid told me that we'd be allowed to go home for Christmas in a little over two months.

"Mama writes," Ingrid said, "that her new place in the fancy American Resort Hotel has a small bedroom, a living room, and a kitchen. It's the same hotel where we had our Christmas dinner with Irma. Just think, a real apartment, not just one stinky room." Though neither of us said a word, each of us was reliving the scene when Mama broke down because of the electricity bill.

I should have been relieved about going home for Christmas, and I was. But the prospect of finally escaping this heartless place made it even harder to endure the endless daily grind. Sometimes I felt I'd explode. One morning, after bedwetting Gretl's screams had already pierced my day, I suddenly couldn't bear the thought of facing my smirking classmates and haughty teacher.

I broke rank when one of the girls delayed the morning march to school to tie her shoes, and dashed around the corner into a small mews while the rest of the group crossed the large town square toward school. I moved so fast—speed was one of my greatest strengths—that hardly anyone noticed. Those who did would not say a word. We did not snitch on one another.

Once out of sight, I didn't know where to hide. I couldn't roam the streets while school was in session. A café was too public. Besides, I had no money. My plan was to hitchhike to Anna in Falkenburg after school let out.

But where could I hide? Maybe I could slip into the church and wait for evening by crouching in the pews. That sounded like a good idea until the arrogant face of the minister rose up in my mind. No, I wouldn't be safe in church. Suddenly, the fountain caught my eye. It sat in the center of the square, with a large stone basin, a center column, and a smaller basin on top of that. It didn't spout water this time of the year and no longer attracted passersby. I dashed across the empty square, jumped over the rim—and landed in a foot of cold rainwater. My feet got wet, but at least I was out of sight. I crouched down. All was quiet.

Slowly the cold water put me in leg-irons, creeping up the bones of my legs, my veins, even the roots of my hair. I was trembling, gently at first, then uncontrollably. What if I lost my legs and could never walk again?

I shifted from foot to foot, trying to curl the toes I could barely feel. Then I heard footsteps and knew, almost instantly, that the unwavering gait belonged to Sister Hedwig. I ducked as low as I could, turning myself into a compressed parcel, but Sister headed straight for me. Her black form threw a shadow over the rim, her arms yanked me up. My feet and legs had become so stiff that I buckled under and fell to the ground.

"That's right. Prostrate yourself, you Godless child!"

Sister Hedwig dragged me back to the home and thrashed me with a switch, holding my skinny body across her knees. She lashed and lashed as if she wanted to make up for all the days, weeks, and months I had not received a beating. Until that day I'd been taken for a shy and obedient girl.

Though my better self wanted to endure the pain stoically, I screamed. Ashamed of my weakness, I sobbed even louder. I was furious at the world. Furious at Sister, but knew that I was too weak to defend myself. I hated my skinny self.

"Go ahead! Scream your head off. In fact, you can cry all night long because you'll be locked in the cellar."

Locked in the cellar? The dark, dank cellar all by myself? I'd always been terrified of the dark.

"I will never, ever run away again, Sister Hedwig. I'll do what you want. Please don't throw me in the cellar!"

"Oh, you will? Well, the first thing I want you to do is spend the night in the cellar!"

All my anger—my sense that I had been right in running away, because I had been so terribly wronged—began to dissolve. My knees started shaking and my heart raced.

Sister marched me down into the vast cellar that ran the length and width of St. John's. She picked out a coal bin, a dark catacomb-like enclosure, shoved me inside, and threw a blanket my way. Staring me down, she locked the lattice with relish. Then she walked away slowly and deliberately. At the exit, she switched off the light.

My enclosure became a black pit. I couldn't see the cellar walls, the lattice of my prison, or anything else, I only felt blackness open its jaw. My heart fluttered and beat against its ribbed cage. *I gotta get out of here.*

There! What's that? The muffled sound of a flute. Was it Helfried's black flute that had lured the sleepwalking girl to her death?

My tortured body, exhausted from its plight in the fountain, begged for sleep, but my tortured mind couldn't calm down. Something was creeping toward me. I wanted to run, bumped into a crate, backed up, and tried not to breathe so that my breath couldn't give me away.

"Marie? Can you hear me?"

A voice from above. "Marie!" The flute stopped playing.

"I'm outside by the coal chute ready to zoom. Throw down some soft stuff on the ground."

Christel. Wonderful, courageous Christel!

I looked around, amazed I could see again, and spotted some sacks folded on top of a crate. I piled sack upon sack and capped it with the blanket Sister had thrown at me.

In swooped Christel, landing on top of the pile like a rocket. I threw my thin arms around her and held her as if we had just been reunited after a lifetime apart. I buried my head in Christel's apron and let a wave of joy, calm, and warmth wash over me.

"Thank you, Christel. You are so brave."

Released from my own fear and trembling, I finally calmed down. Something was working inside of me. With the darkness swept away and Christel's heart beating against mine, I suddenly felt sure that Christel *did* have a chance to escape her misery. Her way out was to speak up—to reveal the truth of our miserable existence. The cold, the beatings, the horrid food, everything.

I understood that our own silence was part of our hell. But who would listen to us and our friends? The minister? Lost cause. Our teachers? No way. Their contempt for us showed in every gesture and look. But Christel had the Grubers who were treating her well. They must care for her.

I could feel myself flush with excitement, took Christel's hand in mine, and looked firmly into her eyes. "Christel, you must speak to the baker and his wife and tell them all about St. John's. Everything. They have no idea what's going on in here. How could they? And if Mr. Gruber brings up the army and seeing action together, tell him that you are fighting in the trenches of St. John's every single day. That you have stood your ground. If they don't take you in after that, we'll run away together."

Christel agreed. We began composing a speech and practiced it with me taking on the role of Herr Gruber and Christel speaking for herself until sleep whisked us away. Snuggled against each other, we were still in a blissful other world when Sister Hedwig rattled her huge key ring into our faces and cawed, "Just look at you two miscreants."

I wanted to beg Sister to whip me for both of us. As if sensing my thoughts, Sister quickly pushed me out of the way. "I don't even want to look at you. Get out," she shouted, condemning me to listen to the brutal whipping of my best friend from outside the door.

That beating convinced Christel to put our plan into swift action, as she told me after the fact with sparkling eyes. When she was done washing the floors at the bakery during her next weekend visit, she asked the baker and his wife if they could talk. The couple invited her into their parlor and offered her a plush, upholstered chair. Christel was nervous, she said, suddenly not sure if she could deliver the speech we had worked out together.

Finally, Mrs. Gruber encouraged her to go ahead. "I have never spoken up to my betters," Christel told me she began, "but now I have to." She spilled out all the horrors of life at St. John's and finished by admitting to Herr Gruber that she hadn't seen action in the army but that she had fought in the trenches of St. John's. She had taken her beatings and never run. Above all, she told them, she loved helping in the bakery and would always work hard.

At that point Mrs. Gruber hugged her with tears running down her cheek, followed by Mr. Gruber who declared, "It's settled then. You're moving in."

I was thrilled for Christel, yet also heartbroken over my own loss. I couldn't imagine the dorm room at night—and my life at St. John's— without Christel. At the same time, I was elated that our plan had yielded such spectacular results. I was proud of my friend and happy for her and felt sure that the Grubers would never regret their decision.

Ingrid noticed my inner turmoil. "Don't worry about anything from now on," she tried to cheer me. "Our time here is almost done. Just leave it to me. I know we can get Mama on our side and with the least bit of luck we won't return after Christmas." She didn't have to tell me to keep those words to myself.

A week before Christmas, Sister put us on the train for the half-hour ride to Garmisch. Mama had been informed of our arrival time and Ingrid had been firmly instructed to get off the train at the first stop. Our faces were pressed against the window as the train pulled in.

We spotted Mama on the platform in a new baby blue coat with white fur trim, her hands tucked inside a white fur muff, the most striking person in sight. Mama pulled her hands out of the muff when she spotted us and waved with one bare hand. We jumped off the train and ran to her. Ingrid threw her arms around Mama while my face landed in Mama's muff that smelled of her perfume and snow.

"You've lost weight," Mama told Ingrid, taking a step back to survey us.

"And you're still as skinny as always, Marie—a hopeless case."

"They don't feed us much at the home," said Ingrid. Mama's eyebrows shot up.

"They don't?"

"We never get meat, only chitlins."

"Chitlins? But the minister said they would take good care of you!" Mama's eyes filled with anger.

"Well, they don't." Ingrid took over. "Mama, please don't send us back. The Sisters beat us. The kids from town spit at us. Everyone hates us. Whenever something is missing at school, it's the girls from St. John's who are blamed!" Mama looked shocked. I began to shake while Ingrid described our experience, a perfect foil to her words. I took hold of Mama's hand and placed it over my heart. "Please don't make us go back, Mama. I will die."

Mama stopped in her tracks, her bosom heaving. "I'll talk to Sister Elisabeth and ask her to do something about that!"

"Sister Elisabeth spends most of her day in her office. We never see her in the dorms, Mama," I said. And Ingrid added, "If it gets out that we complained, the other Sisters will beat us even harder."

Mama's nostrils were flaring, and she chuffed in that anxious way of hers. She kept stroking her fur muff and shaking her head, then said firmly, "Let's go home. You can stay."

Together, we walked to the first coach in line, a horse-drawn sled, parked outside the train station. Mama raised her hand, and the coachman climbed down from his perch. He stored our suitcases and helped Mama, Ingrid, and me up into the sled. When we pulled into the road between high snowbanks, the bells on the horse collar began to ring out. They jingled all the way through town and up the wooded hill that led to our new hotel apartment home.

20

BACK IN GARMISCH
AND VATI'S RETURN

The peak of Alpspitze rose directly before our eyes when Ingrid and I looked out of the mansard windows of the American mountain hotel. The rock walls of Alpspitze formed an almost perfect triangle, a much more attractive shape, I felt, than that of Germany's highest peak, the Zugspitze, a couple of miles down the road. Ingrid and I fell in love with Alpspitze, the small lake outside the hotel's door, and the winding tree-lined path around the lake's shores.

Our Alpine view was almost as stunning as the one from Falkenburg Castle, though nothing in the world could truly match that. Still, the pristine grandeur of our new environment touched me in ways that the view from our house at the foot of Kramer Mountain had never done. Now I could look out and down on the world as I had done from my Castle.

The locked gates of St. John's were replaced by a revolving lobby door, the barren yard with a view of snow-capped mountains, the worn-down steps with shiny elevators, and the enforced silence with laughter and animated conversation. A sense of exhilaration filled the hotel lobby, fueled by the crisp mountain air, invigorating ski runs, and Bavaria's fabulous brews. The hotel was as lively as a train station and as colorful as a circus parade, albeit more elegant.

Ingrid and I were celebrating each day as if it were a holiday because we no longer woke up in an ice-cold dorm and were treated to freshly baked buns with plenty of jam every morning, the buns delivered to the hotel from the bakery at the bottom of the hill. To keep Mama happy and show her how grateful we were, we did our chores religiously.

When Mama came home at night, we wanted her to know every humiliation we'd endured in that God-forsaken Children's Home. "You should have seen Sister's face when she pulled me out of the fountain, Mama. Her ice-cold stare—she looked like a reptile." Mama gave me a tired look. "Yes, I know, must have been awful." Must have been? I felt like shaking Mama.

"And that fatso of a minister, shoveling hot buns and Danish into his mouth, and groveling, 'Thank you, Sister Hedwig. God Bless you, Sister Hedwig.' That same minister hissed at me in the funeral chapel where we had to sing if we girls so much as held hands with each other," said Ingrid. "'Stand up straight,' he'd demand, 'hands by your side.'"

"I know, I know, Ingrid, you needn't go into further detail." Mama tapped her foot and wrinkled her forehead, looking pained. "I could wring the neck of that minister who told me St. John's would be good for you. Thank God, your stay at that place is over. Now let the past rest."

Ingrid and I felt it was easy for Mama to say "let the past rest" as she didn't have to endure life at St. John's. We did not know at the time that she, along with millions of our countrymen, had practiced "letting the past rest" ever since Germany had lost the war, along with any mention or acknowledgement of the unspeakable atrocities committed by our people. My sister and I knew nothing about them and would not for several more years. We only wanted some sympathy for our own lived experience. We tried to move our mother's heart—without much success.

So we let ourselves be comforted by the bubbling American world around us and embraced it with all the enthusiasm of newly released prisoners. Ingrid grabbed her skates right after school and in no time was turning beautiful pirouettes and figure eights on the frozen Riessersee Lake among dozens and dozens of American skaters.

I, in turn, breathed and lived the hustle and bustle of the hotel lobby, where I ducked out of public sight and observed the world from an oversized chair—all eyes and ears. Colorful American ladies, dressed in orange, pink, or blue, paraded by, with fingernails painted in pulsating colors. Even older women wore bright red lipstick, blue eye shadow, and pink rouge, creating a fruit bowl effect, I thought.

To my utter delight, young mothers let their children run about freely, play tag, bump into furniture, even into complete strangers, causing Mama fits of exasperation. "Those brats. No manners whatsoever! Don't Americans know that children should only be seen but never heard?"

I loved to wonder about people. If they were American, I could make up stories about them. If they were German—hotel personnel mostly—I found a spot near them and listened in. That's how I learned that the head cook "likes to look deeply into his bottle," and that Helga, one of the maids, was about to be fired for stealing perfume from guests.

One afternoon, I spotted Mama sitting shoulder to shoulder with her friend Irma on the love seat by the elevator, their noses almost touching. I snuck closer, slipping into an enormous armchair.

"No, Irma, I will *not* ask my husband to break the law!" Mama's jaw was set. I'd never heard her speak so harshly to Irma before and sunk deeper into my chair.

"But why not? I'd never tell anyone. My life will be ruined if some doctor doesn't help me. My parents will kick me out, my friends will disavow me... No one wants an unmarried mother around," whined Irma. "And the child would be called a bastard."

What? What was all that about?

Mama snorted and threw her hands into the air.

"You know it's true."

"I'd be happy if I were you. I *love* babies," said Mama.

"That's easy for you to say, you're married."

"And look what marriage has done for me!" Mama's tone was scornful.

"Couldn't you at least *ask* him to help me when he comes back?" Irma whined.

"No, Irma. He is already ruined, and he's ruined my life."

What did Mama mean? Vati was ill, but he was not ruined. And Mama's life ruined?

"Please, Lilybeth!"

"Stop it! Not another word or I'll never speak to you again!"

I was beginning to wish I had never eavesdropped on them when the elevator door opened and the uniformed elevator boy stepped into the lobby. "Anyone up, going up?"

Cut short by the elevator boy, Irma sighed, turned, and looked directly into my eyes. Her hand flew to her heart, her face flushed and froze into a mask. I shot up and ran outdoors before Mama could catch sight of me.

The ice-cold air felt liberating. I leaned into the wind, letting it blow Irma's grimace away. Before I knew it, music and laughter enfolded me. On the ice before me, young men and women moved in time to the music below the magnificent mountains, their arms interlocked, gliding as if one body through crystalline air. I wanted nothing more than to join the dancers on ice. When I finally returned to the lobby, Mama and Irma had left. To my relief, Mama never confronted me, which meant Irma had not given my presence away.

The American PX, where I sometimes waited for Mama at the end of her shift, was a fairyland of glamorous garments and gleaming gadgets. My eyes moved from display cases filled with gold, silver, and emerald necklaces, diamond armbands, and rings, to a counter of lingerie which glowed with a silky sheen, to another with watches and cameras, to a third filled with crystal and china.

The air vibrated with music flowing from loudspeakers and gave off the scent of warm popcorn. At times, I was stirred by the rousing rhythm of a tango, called *Blue Tango*, that pulled me into an unknown world of strange longing. Mama's fierceness seemed to melt away among Americans at the PX as I could clearly see.

"Move along, Marie. Don't just stand there, glued to my counter," Mama scolded me one afternoon while I was waiting for her to close the hosiery counter for the day. "I'll be done here shortly. Go look at other displays."

I moved on unhappily, worried someone might speak to me in English again and I wouldn't be able to answer. Walking backward, I bumped into a pillar and hid behind it, out of Mama's view. I watched as Mama wiped fingerprints off her glass counter with a leather cloth when a tall, uniformed man approached. Though I couldn't get a good view of his face, I knew he was an officer because of the dark stripes on his slacks. Mama greeted him with a shy smile, her cheeks flushing, her eyes quickly looking away again. She opened a drawer, fished out a pair of nylons, and slipped them over her hand up her arm.

As the man took Mama's hand in his, the flush on Mama's cheeks deepened. Her bosom rose. She smiled the sweetest of smiles, reminding me of the time she was happily preparing for Aunt Amalia's dinner party after we'd moved into our new house.

Though I couldn't see the officer's face, I was sure he was smiling back. He was leaning toward Mama while she pulled out more nylons. The officer did not stir while Mama presented pair after pair. He bought them all. Bathed in the man's adoring glances, Mama looked like a fairy queen. If only that same smiling Mama could have come home to us at night.

But the glow of the PX had usually worn off by that time. Within weeks after our return, she'd drag us out of bed at night, yelling and screaming, for not having watered the flowers or ironed a pile of laundry. We fully understood that her smile was reserved for Americans only.

In March, the ice on the lake was no longer safe for skating. Ingrid filled the void by devouring some of Mama's *Romanhefte*, romances— *Das ist der Liebe Zaubermacht*, Such is the magical power of love, *Die Bettelprinzess*, The beggar princess, and *Nach dunklen Schatten das Glueck*, After long shadows, happiness. My sister often read the juicy bits out loud to me while I was dusting or doing some other chores, but rushed the Romanhefte back to Mama's bedside table the moment we heard her come down the corridor.

"Marie, be a good girl and bring this bottle of polish to Irma's apartment," asked Mama, hanging up her coat after work. She handed me a small glass bottle, with nail gloss of deep red. "Tell Irma it was $1.80, which I put in the till—she owes me DM 7.20. Can you remember that?"

"Sure!"

Ever since I had seen Irma pressuring Mama on the love seat by the elevator, I'd avoided her. There had been something so eager and pushy in Irma's face, and I couldn't forget that shocked grimace when she had spotted me. I wished that Mama would send Ingrid instead of me. My sister, meanwhile, was making googly eyes at me, motioning me to get going, so I took the bottle of polish and knocked at Irma's door. Irma, her hair in curlers and her lanky body in a bathrobe, opened quickly.

"Come in, dear."

"I can't. We're making supper. Here is the nail polish from the PX. Mama says she put $1.80 in the till. You owe her DM 7.20."

"Thank you, Marie. How nice of you to bring it to my door." Irma went to her table and picked up an envelope. "Here you go. Please give this to your mama."

I mumbled a muffled "thanks," and turned on my heels as fast as I could.

"Marie?" Irma called after me. "You must be so happy your father's coming back."

I turned, my heart galloping. "Vati?" I asked, and raced back to Irma. "When, Irma? When?"

"Why, hasn't your Mama…?" Irma's fingers loosened one of her hair combs, then slid it back. "I don't know when," she told me, taking a step back. "But I believe it's not too long from now." She cleared her throat and fluttered her eyelids. "Thank you again for your help. Have a good night."

My eyes were glued to Irma's closed apartment door. *Vati coming back?* To put everything right? When I heard the radio news coming on in Irma's apartment, I gripped the money envelope more tightly and set off. Every time my right foot hit the floor, I whispered, *"Vati coming back, Vati coming back."*

"Irma says Vati's coming back. Is this true?" The words spilled out of my mouth before I could hand Mama the envelope.

Mama pushed a lock of hair out of her face. She looked annoyed. Ingrid dropped the wooden spoon she'd been stirring mashed potatoes with and stared from me to Mama.

Mama sighed. "Well, I wasn't sure of the exact date. I was waiting for more details before telling you. Vati only wrote he'd be returning this spring."

It was almost Easter. Did that mean Vati could return any day?

Mama looked at us as if we were somebody else's children. "What he is most concerned about is your education," she said. "He wants you to be at the best prep schools in Germany so that you'll be able to attend university. He thinks Heidelberg has the best schools." Mama looked at the kitchen clock. "My goodness. I'll be late for the Colonel's children." Mama was still boosting her income with babysitting jobs. "I cannot tell you exactly when your father will be here."

Mama snatched up her handbag, stopped in front of the hall mirror, dabbed her nose with powder, applied more lipstick, and rushed out without locking the door.

"Wouldn't it be something if Vati came back on Easter?" I asked Ingrid. "Actually, I don't care what day he comes back just as long as it's soon."

"Oh, he will. I'm sure of that though Mama doesn't want him to. You saw how she squirmed."

"True, she didn't look happy at all."

"She can't stand Vati." Ingrid's cool comment made my face grow hot—I knew my sister was right.

The door opened unexpectedly. Mama stuck her head back in. "Be sure to wash all the socks before going to bed," she said, pointing at a basin where a bunch of socks were soaking. The door slammed shut. Laundry and housework, all-important to Mama, didn't matter right now. Even Mama didn't matter right now: *our Vati was coming back.*

Ingrid retreated to the bedroom to do some homework. My blood was still throbbing, my body felt light, as if it wanted to float—until I tried to conjure up Vati's face. When I closed my eyes, Vati's intense blue gaze and radiant smile appeared brightly before me. "The Doktor only has to smile and already you feel better," his patients often said to Mama. I hadn't seen Vati for two long years. While I remembered his energetic step, his upbeat voice, and the reassuring touch of his hands, I could not quite piece his face together—and felt like a traitor.

In my frustration and, without thinking, I jumped up and was out in the corridor in a split second. My old habit of running from painful feelings had taken over. "I'll be right back," I called over my shoulder in Ingrid's direction and scampered down the endless flights of stairs toward the lobby.

The familiar babel of voices received me, along with a veil of smoke, and the soft sound of music from the dining room. Every time guests were ushered to their table, the waiters lit candles rising from silver candlesticks, and soon the dining room was transformed into a sea of lights. The faces of the guests turned softer while the glasses and silverware sparkled more brightly. The band was playing *Blue Tango,* and I felt that familiar longing for I knew not what.

Suddenly I stiffened. Wasn't that Mama over there at the corner table? But that can't be because Mama was babysitting Colonel Smith's children. I moved a little closer, making strategic use of the pillars. The lady at the corner table was wearing the same blue blouse Mama had on when she left our apartment just minutes ago. She was smiling at a tall man in uniform.

Now I knew and needed no further proof, even though Mama's escort was intent on providing it; he was taking hold of Mama's hands and kissing them the same way he had done in the PX.

Vati was coming back and Mama was having dinner with a man she didn't want us to know about. Yesterday, the thought might have troubled me deeply, but now, I dared hope, Vati would bring us all together again.

"Let's get the dishes out of the way," said Ingrid a few days later. "Before we go outside today. I'll wash, you dry. All right?"

"Fine."

"Then, while you dust and water the flowers, I can read to us."

Ingrid had started on *Wohin, Du armes Herz,* Whither, thou Foolish Heart, the day before. We both thought the novel silly, but had no trouble whatsoever being pulled into the romantic entanglements between a poor orphan girl and the local Baron. Just as the Baron was approaching the poor girl's hovel with a bunch of edelweiss in his hand, there was a knock at our own apartment door. We stayed put and didn't say a peep, since Mama didn't want us to answer the door when we were alone.

A louder knock. We looked at each other. Ingrid shrugged her shoulders and got up. When she opened the door, there was Vati—pale as a ghost. His blue eyes settled on us with astonished tenderness. The moment his face lit up, our hearts pulled in. We ran.

He held us tight for the longest time. Before my face nestled against my father's chest, all his features had come together again in an instant, forming Vati's crazily beautiful face.

"Are you all well now, Vati?" asked Ingrid.

"Yes, Ingrid, I am."

"Will you stay with us?"

"Yes, I'll stay with you," he answered in that sonorous voice of his. He took a step back, still holding on to our hands, and kept looking at us as if we were a revelation. Then he pulled us in and held us for the longest time.

My heart was thumping, my blood flowing more vigorously, I wanted to burst. After Vati released us, he looked around our place.

"Let's go outside and walk around this beautiful lake of yours." We grabbed our jackets. With Vati in the middle, each of us enclosed by his arm, Ingrid headed for the servants' elevator that led to the back door of the hotel.

"No," I called out with newfound strength and steered us to the guest elevator. "Let's take the guest elevator to the main lobby, the three of us together for all the world to see."

As soon as we were outdoors, Vati said, "Your mother and I will no longer live together. *Wir lassen uns scheiden.*" He scrutinized our faces.

"Well?" asked Vati.

We were not upset. Scheidung—divorce—was something abstract, but Vati's presence was real. We knew no divorced people though we had been told that Mama had been married before to Basti's father and then divorced him. What mattered was that Vati was here, walking beside us. Mama had not hugged or held us since we returned from St. John's, and she never looked at us with tenderness.

"I knew it," sang Ingrid, and broke into a trot. Vati pulled her back and stopped in the middle of the path.

"Your mother wants to emigrate to Canada. Just like Bastian."

"Bastian? Canada?" we asked, dumbfounded.

Vati looked surprised. "Didn't you know?"

Ingrid and I clutched hands and looked beseechingly at our father. "He didn't tell us."

Vati stopped at a fallen log and invited us to sit down. "Basti told me he wrote to you at the Children's Home. Now, don't be too upset because it is a good move for him. Germany is reinstituting the draft, and Bastian is just old enough to be drafted, but your mother, Bastian, and I have had enough of armies and war. That's why he looked for a country without a draft." A smile lit up Vati's face. "And Basti wanted a place where he could ski. It so happens that one of his father's nephews is a builder in British Columbia, which has high mountains and great ski slopes. The nephew was looking for an apprentice and asked what Basti was up to. He became Basti's sponsor, Basti applied for a *visum* and received one in record time." Ingrid and I were still in shock but felt a little better. "I have his address and one of the first things we'll do together is write to him," Vati said. Ingrid and I nodded vigorously.

We resumed our walk. "Your mother is also starting the immigration process, which can take a while because she is older, but with Basti and his cousin vouching for her should work in the end." Vati paused. "That means that you two will stay here with me in Germany—at least for quite some time."

The haze around us was lifting. My heart sang. I am sure the mountains were standing taller than they had only this morning. I felt alive.

Ingrid and I took in a deep breath and, as if on cue, charged forward, leapt into the air, and touched the tips of the spruce tree branches, one of our favorite games.

"Will we *really* stay with you?"

"Yes, Marie. I've even found a housekeeper for us, my former assistant from Falkenburg, Mrs. Borodny—her husband was killed in the war. She has a daughter called Sophie who was in your grade when you first entered school in Falkenburg."

"Sophie? That *jolly* girl with an upturned nose and brown braids?"

"That's Sophie!" he laughed. Ingrid and I jumped, touching more branches.

Vati's face relaxed. His eyes, darkened by a shadow of sadness even during the joy of our reunion, brightened.

"Sophie and her mother, in fact, are waiting for us at the Café Edelweiss. Let's say a quick hello, and then I'll take you back to your place so you can pack. Tomorrow morning we'll all leave together for Heidelberg."

"Tomorrow?" we asked in one breath.

Vati nodded, and we headed, once again, for the tips of the spruce branches. We would have taken off for the end of the earth if Vati had asked us to do so. "Mama knows that I'll take good care of you and that you need better schools. She wants you to get ahead in life just as much as I do."

Vati left the path to get a closer look at a patch of water lilies. His face shone. "Look at this floating garden."

A raspy chorus of frog calls dimmed as we came closer. "Nature," Vati said, "forever restarting her cycle. Spring brings new life, no matter what we wretched humans do. Violets push through the bloodied earth of battlefields. Swallows build nests in bombed-out churches."

He put his arms around Ingrid and me and we all looked out onto the lake.

"Couldn't we go back to Falkenburg?" I asked, my hope rising despite myself.

"No." Vati's voice was firm. "There are no prep schools in Falkenburg. That's why we are moving to Heidelberg. I've made an appointment with the headmistress of one of the best girls' schools in Germany, the Elisabeth-von-Thadden-Schule. After Bastian and your mother have settled in Canada, you'll have a chance to join her if you want to." Vati stopped again. "But for now, we're Heidelberg-bound!"

As soon as we entered the Café Edelweiss, a middle-aged woman in a neatly ironed dress got up from her table and walked toward us. When she came closer, I recognized her pretty round face with eyes that bulged ever so slightly, giving her face the look of constant astonishment. It was Frau Borodny, who used to put goggles on my eyes before my sessions under the sun lamp in Vati's surgery where she was in charge of patients' medical records. Frau Borodny looked anxious yet friendly. "Good to see you again, Ingrid and Marie!" We extended our hands and curtsied.

"Where's Sophie?" I asked, looking around. Frau Borodny smiled. "She had to get something from Herr Doktor's car and will be right back."

The door to the café slammed shut and a girl, about my height, walked towards us. First thing I noticed was *no braids* but a short haircut that showed off a delicately upturned nose and high cheekbones. When Sophie stopped directly across from me, I looked into a pair of mischievous green eyes with sparks of light dancing like fireflies. I offered my hand.

"Hi, remember me?"

"Sure do, Marie," said Sophie. "You're the one with the far-away expression, looking out of the window a lot." Sophie's voice was as soft as Christel's.

"Mutti told me that you miss Falkenburg Castle so much that I snuck through the gate at dusk and broke off a piece of the wall." She opened her fist. I looked from the piece of stone to Sophie's eyes, and back, lifting the craggy stone as if it were a jewel.

A piece of my Castle to have and to hold, a piece from my own *stone mother.* I closed my hand around it. Perhaps it had split from the fiery meteor that had hit Falkenburg's plain ten million years ago, cooling for millennia, to be finally shaped, fitted, and put into place by a pair of hands in the eleven hundreds. Perhaps by an itinerant craftsman from Hamburg? Or by some ancestor of Falkenburg's butcher or baker who had spoiled me with treats when I was small. I let my blood warm the stone, while my eyes hugged it, and my heart spoke to it. I felt a slight rise in my hand, a barely detectable echo of the beat of my own heart. Then again, perhaps the beat of my heart was nothing but a faint echo of the pulsing core of Falkenburg Castle.

The touch of Sophie's warm hand on mine woke me. Sophie, Falkenburg's herald, broke out into a radiant smile, "Thank you, Sophie. You've given me the best gift ever!"

Ingrid, who watched the scene with bemusement, asked Sophie, "Miss Huber still your teacher?"

"Yes," Sophie said, "and the same mean old sergeant." I couldn't help but giggle. *Sergeant* was the perfect word for her.

"I wasn't terribly fond of her," I said.

"Me neither," said Sophie.

"We better be going," Vati broke in. "Your mother will be expecting us. We'll regroup for our journey to Heidelberg tomorrow."

That night, Ingrid and I couldn't fall asleep for a long time. We wanted to hold on to the joy of the day, a time of promise that made us look forward to the future. We felt wanted, embraced, and cared for at last.

Mama seemed calm in the morning. She lifted our suitcases onto the couch and invited us to choose "one little item" from the flat. I picked a framed photo of my Castle, and Ingrid a drawing of the lake.

Mama admonished us to study hard so that we would never be caught in a situation like hers. "You must never become a clerk or a secretary, but a doctor like your Aunt Julia or a lawyer like Uncle Herbert."

When Vati arrived, Mama fell silent and walked restlessly around the two suitcases, coughing ever so slightly. Ingrid and I were instantly alarmed. The room felt like an arena, with Mama, the matador, ready to go for the kill.

"So, Herr Doktor is finally making his appearance."

Vati hugged us. "We said ten o'clock, Lilybeth!"

Mama didn't answer. Her cheeks grew redder. Ingrid and I dreaded the storm building up inside of her.

"This is a special time for all of us, Lilybeth, especially for the girls," said Vati. "You have taken good care of them. Now I want to do the same"—he cleared his throat—"so that you can proceed."

Mama pressed her hands against her temples and walked to the sink. Scenes from the Castle rushed through my mind when Mama threw plate after plate out of the window in a fit of rage. Mama clasped the rim of the sink.

"But I'll miss them," she sobbed.

For a split second, foolish me wanted us all to stay together and be a happy family, although we had never been a happy family before. I was about to rush to Mama when someone knocked at the door.

"Lilybeth, you there, Lily?" a man's voice asked in English.

Mama stopped sobbing and dried her eyes. She turned first to Vati, giving him a long look, then back toward the door. "I'm busy," she said in a clear, firm voice and made no attempt to answer the door. We remained silent, as if in a tableau. The face of the officer from the PX and the dining room flashed before my eyes, making me blush. Just then the footsteps moved away.

"Yes, let's be civil about this," said Mama, her face no longer agitated. "The girls are ready." Then Mama's large, childlike eyes latched on to Ingrid and me.

"Will you be all right, you two?"

"Yes, Mama," we said as twins.

"Heidelberg is a beautiful town with a big castle and an old university. You'll like it. And tell your father not to drive so fast—you know how he steps on that gas pedal. I'll come and visit soon."

Ingrid and I ran to her. We worried that Mama might break down if we cried, and we worried that she'd break down if we didn't.

"We'll quickly do the dishes," Ingrid offered with tears in her eyes. Mama waved her off. "Never mind. You better be going." She hugged both of us. "I'll miss you. Remember I love you."

"We'll miss you, too, Mama."

Vati picked up our two new suitcases. "It is not a goodbye forever. Your Mama will visit soon."

"Call me Tante B.!" Mrs. Borodny suggested after Vati had stored our cases. "It's less formal and shorter. Why don't you come up front, Ingrid, and sit between your father and me?" Ingrid beamed, giving us the thumbs-up. "I'd love to."

"How about calling me Onkel Karl, Sophie?"

"All right, Dr. Ber...Onkel Karl. Thank you."

"Well, that's settled."

Sophie and I squeezed into the back seat between boxes and cases. As soon as Vati hit the open road, the same road I had walked in despair so many months ago, Vati started singing, "*Ich hab mein Herz in Heidelberg verloren*," I've lost my heart in Heidelberg, and we all chimed in.

Sophie was still humming to herself when I snuggled back into the upholstery and closed my eyes, lulled by the song of the tires on the road. Sophie touched my arm.

"What's your favorite color?"

"Blue."

"Mine, too."

"Do you like marzipan?" I asked.

"I *love* marzipan."

"And books and movies?"

"Yes, yes. But I've seen only two movies, *Bambi* and *Cinderella*."

"Mutti told me that Heidelberg has lots of movie houses," said Sophie. "Falkenburg had only one. Hollywood westerns are so exciting! And Charlie Chaplin. I love Charlie Chaplin."

I smiled and fell asleep with my head on Sophie's shoulder.

BOOK IV

Heidelberg

21

TANTE B., SOPHIE, AND THE BROKEN GLASS

"Wake up, Marie." Someone was jiggling my shoulder while I tried to hold on to sleep.

"Wake up!" I opened my eyes and saw Sophie smiling down on me, still in her pajamas, her auburn hair tousled. Now I remembered Vati singing *Ich hab mein Herz in Heidelberg verloren* in the car yesterday as we left Garmisch. I sat up and looked around.

"So, this is Heidelberg."

"Not really. It's *Merkdorf*, a suburb of Heidelberg. We have to take a small train into town. Takes fifteen minutes." Sophie lifted her arms and swirled around. "And this is our new home."

I saw two open bed couches—I was in one of them—in a good-size room with large windows. There was a round table in the center with two comfy chairs; Sophie followed my glance.

"We look out on Schulstrasse, in the middle of Merkdorf. I came here with my Mutti and your Vati before we drove to Garmisch. Some houses still have large gates, an inner yard, and barns behind the house because it used to be a farming village. It's *sooo* different from Falkenburg where most houses were just houses. Our house also has a barn. I'll show you."

"Where's Ingrid?" I asked.

"In the bath—it's really only a toilet with a large sink. If we want to take a bath we have to go upstairs where Mrs. Gumbrecht lives and have to pay her! She charges two Deutsch Mark per tub! She's a war widow, she owns the house, and Mutti thinks she's on the lookout for a husband, but I don't think anybody's gonna marry her because she looks like a bulldog. Your Vati called it a 'touch of goiter.'"

We burst into laughter. Sophie talked as rapidly as running water, and her eyes sparkled whenever she said something naughty like "she looks like a bulldog." She took me across the hall to Vati's room—totally empty.

"What?" I asked. "No bed for Vati?"

"Oh, your Vati is renting a room nearby until some of the furniture arrives from Falkenburg. Mutti is also waiting for her bed from Falkenburg. She's sleeping with me on one of the bed couches—you with Ingrid."

Vati's room looked out into a yard. I squirmed when I spotted a gray wooden outhouse next to the remnant of a manure pile, but was taken with the tall, wooden barn that rose behind them. It was beautifully proportioned, like a church.

"It's no longer in use," Sophie told me. "When people still farmed, it was used to dry and store tobacco. You can tell by the small slits in the wood, they let air pass through for drying."

"Beyond the barn is a wonderful garden," Sophie gushed on. "Frau Gumbrecht is a really good gardener, but she won't allow us to go there and pick whatever we want. So waaaaaaa!" Sophie's pretend-cry made me laugh again.

She walked me to the kitchen with a stove, a small fridge, a sink, cupboards, and a kitchen table with chairs. We ended up back in the bright living room, which doubled as our bedroom at night.

"Where will your mother sleep when the furniture comes?"

Sophie opened a second door off the living room. "Right here." I looked into a narrow room that might have served as a pantry or maid's room in the past. "Boy, that's small."

"I know, but Mutti's happy."

Sophie pulled me back to our bed. "Let's have a tickling war." Before I could protest, Sophie had pulled me under the covers and was tickling me like mad. I gave as good as I could until we both heard Tante B.'s voice. "Sophie, Marie. Where are you?"

We surfaced with red, sweaty faces.

"Your Vati and I have already been to the bank and gotten groceries," said Tante B. "I'm glad you are wide awake, Marie. You were out like..."

"The village drunk," Sophie butted in while her mother continued.

"Like a light. Your Vati carried you inside." I smiled sheepishly while scrutinizing Tante B.'s face. Was she upset that I had fallen asleep or that Sophie had interrupted her? No. Her face still looked friendly.

"Good morning, sis." Ingrid, all pink and scrubbed clean, snapped a towel in front of me. Tante B. handed me a clean washcloth.

"Oh, Mutti," Sophie begged. "We're having such fun. Couldn't we stay in bed a little longer?" I stared at her as if she were out of her mind. To my surprise—but not Sophie's—Tante B. didn't get angry. She simply said, "Not today, dear." Again, I searched their faces, looking for signs of anger or frustration, but Tante B. merely picked up her grocery bags again, Sophie rolled over, and I took my turn in the bath.

Vati's one-room flat was only ten minutes away. By the time he arrived, we had made the beds, unpacked boxes, and helped prepare lunch. Tante B. was cooking spaghetti and meat sauce, humming to herself all the while. We girls set the table.

When coffee was being served, Vati settled back into his chair and pulled out a packet of cigarettes. He shook one out, stuck it between his index and middle finger while keeping it at a distance, as if wondering what to do with it. Then, with phenomenal speed, he shoved the cigarette between his lips, lit it, and drew in the smoke greedily, as if he was only now breathing fully. When the air became filled with smoke and filmy layers built up around him, he sunk back into his chair, seemingly content.

But something was different about our father, I felt. A vague sadness hung about him like the blue smoke from his cigarettes.

Smoke drifted toward the cupboard, where we were doing the dishes. "Careful with the glass, Marie. It's fragile." I accepted a wet glass from Ingrid's dripping fingers, dried it painstakingly, and checked it for spots.

"Mine is so much shinier," Sophie sang triumphantly.

"No, it isn't!" I swirled around so fast that my hand hit the cupboard and the glass broke. Vati and Tante B. stopped talking. Sophie looked aghast. I froze, my stomach tensed. I ducked and waited.

"Did you hurt yourself, Marie?"

"No."

"That's a relief." Tante B.'s voice was calm as she took my hand to examine it before she bent down to pick up the pieces. I fell on my knees beside her.

"I'm so sorry," I whispered.

Tante B. looked up and smiled. She *was* smiling.

"I know you didn't do it on purpose. Broken glass means good luck. What do you wish for?"

Without a moment's reflection and stunned by my own response, I said, "For Mama to be as happy as she is at the PX." When Tante B.'s eyes filled with tears, so did mine. Tante B. raised me up and wrapped her arms around me, rocking me from side to side. I didn't know how to tell her that I felt sheltered and at peace in this new home; that I felt good.

'I'm not homesick for Mama,' I wanted to blurt out, but all that came out of my mouth was, "I just..."

"Hush, dear," Tante B. shushed me, "It's all right."

The next morning, Vati piled the three of us into the old Opel for our first visit to the famous prep school he had chosen. A former country manor with a beautiful park, the school was enclosed by a high wall. It had a respectable main house, the *Herrenhaus*, complete with a tower and balcony. A simple Romanesque chapel sat on a modest hill to one side.

"I want you on your best behavior," Vati said, fixing his intense blue gaze on us. "Because this school offers the most challenging academic program." He had already told us that the school had been founded by a forward-looking Prussian noblewoman, Elisabeth von Thadden, a Baroness like Mama, who believed that girls should have the same education as boys.

"Because of Miss von Thadden's background, the school has attracted the daughters of Prussian nobility such as the von Bismarcks and the Hohenzollerns."

"You mean the Kaiser's family?" Ingrid asked.

"Yes."

"Oh, Mama will love that, but you won't find me kowtowing to any Princess."

"Of course not. A noble girl is just as bright or dumb as any other girl," Vati said. "But there may be one advantage. Her parents are likely to have gone to university and you might as well be around children who have been intellectually stimulated."

While Vati steered the car through the school's massive gate, Sophie squeezed my hand. This was the first challenge the two of us were facing together and also the first time I saw my new, self-assured pal nervous. I answered with my own squeeze and an encouraging smile. If Vati was right, I would finally learn what Falkenburg Castle had inspired in me: the desire to decipher what was hidden within Latin or any other language such as the mysterious swirls from the Jewish cemetery.

Vati parked the car close to the manor, jumped out, and disappeared inside. Ingrid and Sophie were fidgeting.

"Let us pray," Ingrid said suddenly, sounding like Falkenburg's minister. I wanted to protest when I noticed Ingrid's tense cheek muscles and the sweat on Sophie's forehead. *How can Ingrid be so trusting in the power of prayer after all we've been through?* I wondered to myself with astonishment, but dropped my head in solidarity while Sophie fell to her knees on the floor between the front and back seats.

"Dear Lord, give us the strength and the wisdom to pass our exams." There was a long pause. "As thanks, we will willingly do our chores and write to Mama once a week. Amen." Ingrid lifted her head, and Sophie scrambled back into her seat.

As soon as we had settled, we saw Vati walk briskly toward us, accompanied by an elegant lady. Our father was gesticulating while the lady in a long, flowing skirt held herself straight as an arrow, her head slightly inclined toward him. Her posture was flawless, like that of a Prussian grenadier, her face open and handsome.

We girls quickly climbed out of the car, formed a line, and were calmly inspected by the lady whom Vati introduced as "your headmistress, Frau Sonntag." The moment Frau Sonntag's eyes met mine, I felt calmed. Their chestnut color and depth drew me in, and her warm voice reminded me of Anna.

Frau Sonntag seemed to suppress a small smile as she surveyed us, though I couldn't imagine what might be amusing about us. Today I can. Our faces were serious and somber, our clothes bright orange, purple, and green, the wild colors of the American PX—not the usual drab German garb; our bodies a mix of pudgy and gangly with Ingrid and Sophie solidly built and I thin as a reed. We were a motley bunch.

"Come along, girls. I have prepared some questions for you," said Frau Sonntag. We followed her into the refectory, a light-filled hall that smelled of floor polish and jam. Since classes were in session, it was empty. Frau Sonntag seated each of us at a separate table, passed out paper and pencils, and handed us written questions.

"I'll leave you now," she said. "Do not talk among yourselves. Try to shut out the world and concentrate on what is before you." She looked at us with those knowing eyes, as if she could speak with her eyes only, and left.

I was stunned. No teacher in Garmisch or Kempten would have *ever* left us alone during a test—children were not to be trusted. Frau Sonntag trusted us although she had only just met us. Her request, expressed without anger or arrogance, did the trick. We girls scribbled without exchanging a word.

If we were accepted, we'd have to tackle three foreign languages over the next three years, starting with Latin in the first, English in the second, and French in the third. Math, geography, history, religion, and sports would remain part of the curriculum throughout the nine years of prep school, along with all three languages. Biology would come on board in the third year, chemistry and physics in the fourth. All sciences, the three languages, math—including analytic geometry and calculus—and German would remain compulsory subjects until graduation at the end of grade 13, when we would graduate.

Frau Sonntag had asked us to write an essay about a place we'd love to get lost in, be it a museum, park, river, or vacation spot. My pencil flew across the lined paper as I recreated Falkenburg Castle for the headmistress. My mind was on fire.

The math questions were not too tough, and the Latin questions were fun because of my past practice with Bastian. Every so often, I checked on Ingrid and Sophie. Ingrid kept writing with stern concentration. Sophie was busy at first, then she slowed, and finally, I saw her chewing her pencil.

While Frau Eierman reviewed our work, we three compared notes. Ingrid and I felt the test was fair. "I'm sure it was fair," said Sophie. "But I've never had Latin. It just wasn't offered in Falkenburg, and the math questions were tough."

"I bet Vati explained that to Frau Sonntag," I reassured her.

Only now, with time to look around, did we notice the large grave with a prominent stone marker in front of the chapel outside. There were no other graves in sight, making us wonder who might be buried in that singular spot.

Frau Eierman returned. Her eyes rested on each of us for a moment. "Ingrid and Marie, I'm happy to say that you've been accepted outright. At thirteen, Ingrid will start Untertertia, the third year of Gymnasium (university track, which equals the eighth year of regular school), and at ten, Marie will start Sexta of Gymnasium (university track, which equals the fifth year of regular school). Welcome to our School."

Frau Eiermann turned to Sophie. "Under normal circumstances, I could not accept you—this is through no fault of yours. But Herr Dr. Bergen assures me that he, Ingrid, and Marie will do their utmost to catch you up." She quickly turned to me. "Is that right, Marie?"

"Yes," I shot back. "I will, I will," determined to do anything to keep my new friend by my side.

"In that case," now Frau Eierman was smiling, "you have been provisionally accepted, Sophie. Congratulations—but I need to see progress."

"I look forward to having you in my German class." Frau Sonntag turned back to me. "You wrote a *very* fine essay."

"Well done, girls," Vati said in the car. "You are off to a good start, and I know that Sophie can catch up." He stepped on the gas with enthusiasm and intoned, "*Ich hab mein Herz in Heidelberg verloren,*" steering the old Opel back through the wide-open gate.

22

MAMA'S DEPARTURE
AND THE KISS, 1954

"I am still waiting for my emigration papers. When I poured my heart out to Colonel Brown, he wrote a beautiful character reference for me and forwarded it to the Canadian officials. I hope that it'll do some good," Mama wrote from Garmisch. "*Dieses Warten ist zum Verzweifeln!*" All this waiting drives one to despair.

I felt for Mama. It didn't seem right that Ingrid and I were content living in our snug world with Vati and Tante B. while Mama was all alone. In my frustration, I half-prayed, half-sighed, "Lord, please allow Mama to emigrate. And please let her life in Canada be good." Thinking about Mama's life so far away, an unexpected sense of peace enveloped me—until I realized that the peace I felt was not for Mama but for myself. Shocked at my callousness, I fell on my knees to atone.

"Are you praying for our family?" Vati walked in unexpectedly. I flinched and quickly got off the floor, surprised at my own spontaneous foot fall. Old habits. Vati tossed a pack of cigarettes on the coffee table and fished one out without lighting it, all the while keeping his eyes focused on me.

Finally, he said, "Prayer is a good thing. It concentrates the mind; you might also say, it concentrates *the heart*." Vati lit his cigarette. "As a boy I prayed that God would allow me to become a priest. I wanted to be a priest because I wanted to be good. But you don't have to be a priest or minister to be good. We merely have to be conscious in all we do so that our actions don't hurt others."

Vati a priest? That sounded crazy, although I sensed that our father never attended to his patients' physical ailments alone. He touched their hearts and uplifted their spirits.

"What do I mean by being good?" Vati continued. "I don't mean polite behavior or obeying rules. I have known many so-called upright citizens who beat their wives or profited from the misery of others."

I sat up sharply, knowing instantly what he was talking about: The Sisters and the minister at St. John's! The teachers who let others torment us.

"Do you still pray and are you still a Catholic?" I asked.

"No, Marie. You might say I pray inwardly by concentrating on being helpful to others. And I am no longer a Catholic. God can't be divided into Catholic and Protestant. God is greater than all our segmented imagination. God is everywhere and everything. Look around you!" Vati sucked on his cigarette. His eyes and face were shining as if lit from within. "Look at the beautiful markings on the wing of a butterfly, the low swoop of a swallow to catch a fly, the dance of the bee to share the source of honey—listen to the beat of your own heart. That's God. God is in all of us and in all things. There is no heaven or hell. There is nature, the universe, our own earth. There are rocks, flowers, oceans, and you. Look for the blueprint, the idea. Jesus was a great man. So were Buddha and Socrates. Greater than you and I. But God is not just one man and cannot be defined. God pervades all."

Slowly, my father's teachings began changing my view of the world. Was it possible, I wondered, that the angry, vengeful God of the Old Testament might also be one of kindness and ingenious creation—a God who teaches bees to dance rather than demanding a human sacrifice?

"If we human beings have one calling," Vati continued, "it is to love. Love is giving. Never taking advantage. Love lets us understand why others act and feel as they do. Love is the answer."

Finally, Mama received her visa. Vati picked her up in Garmisch and brought her to Merkdorf. Though Vati wasn't earning as much as a representative for the pharmaceutical industry as he used to as a doctor, he treated Mama to a farewell dinner at the *Hotel Ritter*, one of Heidelberg's finest restaurants.

We girls and Tante B. stayed behind. I woke in the middle of the night, hearing muffled sounds as if someone was crying. I listened intently. There, a sniffle! Where was it coming from? I strained my ears. Ingrid, Sophie, and Tante B. seemed to be breathing regularly. I must have been dreaming.

The next day, Vati, Ingrid, and I saw Mama off at the train in Manheim that would take her to the boat in Bremerhaven. She kept rummaging through her handbag, making sure she had her tickets and passport. One moment she smiled, the next tears filled her eyes. She clutched the small Steiff teddy bear that Ingrid and I had given her as a good luck charm to her chest.

We hovered between relief and sorrow. We felt sad that our mother was about to leave family, friends, and Germany behind, and we mourned the fragility of our relationship that was full of tension and unfulfilled hopes.

"Don't forget me, Marie!" Mama clung to me. Tears rolled down her cheek—tears *without* anger, as if Mama were turning into a new mother, someone I'd never get to know because she was leaving.

"Never forget me. Don't ever!" Mama beseeched Ingrid.

Vati pulled out a handkerchief while Mama leaned out of the compartment window. Vati and Mama's eyes locked when the train began to move forward. Both must have been reliving what had brought them together so many years ago. Mama made the most of looking heart-wrenchingly beautiful, her face flushed, her large gray eyes glistening with tears.

For a split second I thought I saw the little match girl ghost across Mama's eyes. When I looked again the shivering waif was gone. The conductor sounded the whistle and the train moved forward; I could no longer see Mama's eyes, just her hand dabbing tears from her cheek. Ingrid and I sprinted along the platform until the train outran us. Our father had already fallen back. Later in the car, we were silent, wondering what the future would hold for Mama and for us.

Though Vati had looked deeply into Mama's eyes, he, too, seemed relieved. Holding on to the steering wheel, he must have known, I believe, that from now on no one would try to wrestle the wheel away from him again.

Mama's letters from the New World made waves in our family, especially when she included photographs.

My dearest Ingrid, dearest Marie,   Banff, 1953

I am sending you pictures of our flat in Banff. As you can see, it is quite cozy, but I need to make new curtains and pillow covers. Our refrigerator is as big as a wardrobe and almost as long as Bastian's car. Bastian loves his new Pontiac.

I miss you very much, and I miss Germany a little, but our town is beautiful, and I go for walks a lot. I'm helping out in a restaurant until my English is fluent. Then I will look for a better job and maybe get my Canadian driver's license. Your brother wants to go bear hunting this fall. I don't know if I like the idea. Bears are so cuddly. I miss you very much.

Your loving mother
P.S. Tell me about your fancy school.

Bastian had added a note for Ingrid: *Mom tells me you're studying English. That's great. You can put it to good use when you visit us. We'd love to see you. I really like it here. People aren't as arrogant as in Germany, and you don't have to go to university to succeed.*

I wondered why Bastian hadn't addressed me. Perhaps I should have started prep school with English like Ingrid, instead of Latin, but I really didn't want to go to Canada. After my baccalaureate, I planned to return to Falkenburg Castle to translate the illuminated manuscripts and unlock the mysteries that had captivated me throughout my childhood like the script on the gravestones of the Jewish cemetery.

Ingrid could not understand my interest in a *dead* language. At least English was spoken by American soldiers right here on Heidelberg's streets, and, of course, in Hollywood movies. Ingrid adored American movie stars, especially Rita Hayworth, Kim Novak, and Lana Turner, and swooned over Chuck Berry and Pat Boone. She and her gang of friends tuned in to AFN, the American Forces Network, to improve their English and be up on the latest pop charts.

Sophie turned the letter on its side where there was yet another P.S. This one said, *Be sure to pick English as your next language, Marie, so that you'll be able to get around when you visit us. Love, your brother dear.*

When he wasn't quizzing us on Latin declensions or holding forth on God and Nature, Vati was loading the old green Opel with boxes of medical supplies for his visits to other doctors' surgeries. Vati was so good to us, and life had become so much sweeter since his return that Ingrid and I liked to believe he had given up his medical practice for us and our new life in Heidelberg. Yet, every now and then, Vati seemed to be lost to the world.

"A peddler of wares. That's what they have reduced me to," I overheard him say to Tante B. in a bitter tone. It was the bitterness that made me pay attention. Only then did I realize that Vati was troubled. But I didn't know who "they" were and what he was referring to. And since I was so needy for peace and attention myself, I didn't dwell on it.

Typically, Vati took off from our suburban village amidst hugs and kisses while he reminded us to do our homework first thing after coming home from school. The moment he returned, and even before he had stowed away his large case of wares, he usually called out, "Tante B., please put the kettle on." After serving coffee, Tante B. sat at a safe distance from us while Vati launched into one of his sermons. While knitting or reading the daily tabloid *Bildzeitung*, Tante B. might look up now and then and even roll her eyes at Vati, when she felt he was too outspoken, but she never interrupted or criticized him.

Vati took a sip of coffee, struck a match for his first cigarette, and focused his blue eyes on us.

"Why does a baby smile?" he might ask.

"Because it's happy?" Ingrid ventured a guess.

"No, a baby smiles so that the male won't smash it against the wall!" Seeing our shocked faces, Vati flashed a smile of satisfaction.

"You don't believe me, do you? But it's true. Look at Nature. A mother bear hides her cubs from the male, so does a lioness and tiger because the male may kill the young." The flame of the match had flickered out, but Vati was on fire. He drew in a deep breath and rushed on, "The male has to be coaxed into accepting his offspring, while the female can't help but care for her child. She has been programmed to nurture it. Nature wants its young to survive. A father who holds a baby that smiles is less likely to harm it." Vati fixed his gaze on us to see if his message had sunk in.

"The mistake we humans make," he continued, "is that we think we are above Nature, but we are not." His voice was full of passion. "We are part and parcel of Nature. Our mating, breeding, and child-rearing practices are not so different from those of a wolf or a baboon.

"Take courting practices. Sand crabs build nests, then stand outside and wave to passing female crabs to attract their attention. Peacocks spread their feathers." Vati stopped, his eyes widened. "And what does the human male do? He drives a motorcycle or sports car and revs up the engine to impress the girls." We giggled. "It's the same mechanism, isn't it?"

"Oh, Onkel Karl, that's so funny!" said Sophie.

"Wait a second, Vati," I pleaded. "Can we go back? Did *you* ever feel like smashing us against the wall?"

"What a question." Vati took another drag from his cigarette. "No, I would never harm a child or any other defenseless being."

Following the dim, inner rhythm established at Falkenburg Castle, I took off every so often to be by myself, going for walks along the meandering Neckar River that formed the southeastern border of Merkdorf and flowed into the Rhine some fifteen miles from our village.

During the river's lively history, it had been navigated by the Celts and the Romans, by the Alemanni, and all the tribes and power players of the Rhineland up to Napoleon. Its military value couldn't have been outstanding—it wasn't deep, wide, or wild enough to serve as an imposing barrier, but it was and remained a busy water road. While ducks raised their young in the reeds, ships from Holland, Belgium, and France sputtered by, loaded with coal, oil, cement, and feed stock. Sometimes, the skipper's wife hung out laundry or a child played on deck. I often wished I could hop on board to see firsthand what it meant to be part of such a miniature, moving world.

On my return and still in a dreamy mood, I spotted Vati's car parked at the curb, climbed inside on a whim, and settled myself in the small luggage compartment behind the back seat.

Now I had gained a world of my own. Lying on my back, I watched the clouds move in the sky, letting my thoughts drift along with them. Were we really not different from peacocks or baboons, I wondered?

And what about courting practices?

Suddenly I heard the gate click and ducked down deeper. Vati and Tante B. got in. Vati slid the key into the ignition but didn't start the motor. I was about to pop up, when he said, "How many bills are outstanding?"

"Four," answered Tante B.

"And how many can we pay?"

"Two," she said, "at best."

"Can you talk to Herr Albert," asked Vati, "and see if he'll let us charge the groceries until the end of the month?"

"Of course. Herr Albert is a reasonable man. He'll give us an extension." Tante B. sounded confident. My heart went out to her.

"If only I could have my own surgery in two or three years," Vati sighed. "But eight years! An eternity."

"We'll be so busy, it'll pass quickly," said Tante B.

They fell silent. Then I heard Vati say in a near whisper, "Why don't you come along, dear? For just half an hour, then I'll drive you back to the girls."

"Come along." Vati's voice was soft and enticing. That sounded treacherous to my ears, disloyal to Mama and to us, too.

"All right. For just a bit," said Tante B. I heard some rustling, some moving about and then a kiss. Vati started the motor right after that smacking sound and took off for his place. As soon as he and Tante B. had disappeared inside the house where he lived, I climbed over the seat, opened the door, and ran. My heart beat so hard that it hurt.

By the time I reached Schulstrasse, I was out of breath and stopped to calm down, aware that I was too upset to go in, but where else could I go? It was already evening. I steeled myself and marched in briskly, not looking at Sophie who was scribbling away at the coffee table. I threw myself on the bed couch with my face to the wall and my back to the room and stayed there—oblivious to my friend and the falling light of the day.

My heart felt raw: I was losing faith in my father without whom I could not survive. Vati *had* to be steadfast and good. If he and Tante B. were more than friends, what did that mean for Ingrid and me? And, despite everything, I did not want Mama replaced by another woman.

"Are you feeling all right?" Suddenly Sophie sat by my side. I mumbled something.

"What's the matter?"

I wanted to tell her, but I could not begin to describe my feelings of loss, sadness, and anger. Sophie looked at me for a long time.

"They kissed!" I blurted out.

"What?"

"Your Mutti and my Vati—they kissed."

"Really?"

I nodded.

Sophie didn't seem shocked.

"Did they kiss *leidenschaftlich*?" Passionately?

"No."

"Well, then." Sophie sounded relieved.

"Your father is sometimes so sad," Sophie said, as if Vati's sadness had something to do with the kiss in the car. "Especially when he's packing his case to leave town."

"So, you noticed too?"

"Yes. He was our doctor in Falkenburg and always cheered everyone up; he still does, but not with the same exuberance." We both fell silent. Sophie took my hand. "Don't worry. Your Vati is a good man."

I snuggled against Sophie who seemed to block the swarm of winged creatures pursuing me. *Your Vati is a good man.*

When we were all already in bed, I heard Tante B.'s key in the door and saw her tiptoe across the room. I synchronized my own breathing with Ingrid's, pretending to be asleep, but watched Tante B. from beneath my half-closed lids. She looked calm while bending over Sophie and tugging the blanket more firmly around her. Then she settled me the same tender way. Her face and her hands were as reassuring as always. Part of me responded to her caring presence, but not all. When Sophie turned in her sleep, I rolled over, snuggled up against her, and finally allowed myself to let the world be.

23

Our Founder's Fate

Frau Sonntag taught history and German. In her German class, she emphasized essay writing, grammar, and style. If that were all, I might not have remembered her so fondly. But she did so much more: she awakened our love of literature by devoting the last fifteen minutes of each class to reading a poem, a fairy tale, or short story to us—transforming our drab post-war classroom into a magical place and transporting me back to the Treasure Hall of the Castle. Frau Sonntag's voice was like a musical instrument, expressing the full range of human emotions from the wrath of the gods to the lure of sirens, and the shy purity of a young girl like Gretchen in Faust.

Sophie, our classmates, and I were all ears when she announced she would read the signature poem of the *Romantic* poet Eichendorf to us during our third year at the school. Frau Sonntag waited until every girl sat at attention, then read the poem slowly, drawing us into the rhythm until we were breathing in time with her voice:

> *Schläft ein Lied in allen Dingen*
> *Die da traeumen fort und fort.*
> *Und die Welt hebt an zu singen*
> *Triffst du nur das Zauberwort!*
> *In all things a song lies buried*
> *As they dream away the time*
> *And the world breaks into singing*
> *If you find the magic rhyme!*

An image of Falkenburg's sweet-smelling manuscripts rose in my mind. I was sure that the rhyme was hidden among the thousands and thousands of words so carefully scripted by monks centuries ago. *Some day, I'll return,* I told myself. *And who knows? I may find the magic rhyme.*

Sometimes Frau Sonntag asked one of us to read out a text. When she called on me to recite a poem, I froze at first, but the words cast such a spell over me I forgot my shyness and read with a passion and enthusiasm that seemed to flow through me rather than from me. Sometimes, Frau Sonntag read one of my essays out loud. The first time, I stared at the floorboards and shifted in my seat, but finally I lifted my head and *listened*, surprised how confident the writer sounded. Deep down, I saw myself as merely besotted with language—be it Latin or German—giddy as a pollen-gathering bee.

For the first three years of *Gymnasium*—from 1953 to 1956, when I was between 10 and 13—we girls of the Elisabeth-von-Thadden-Schule dove deeply into Greek and Roman myths. From there, we moved on to Charlemagne, and the medieval Holy Roman Empire, led by German Kaisers and Kings, including the father of Falkenburg's Prince Henry. We learned about the culture of courtly love as well as knightly jousting, and the tensions between Pope and Kaiser. I was struck by the image of Henry III's knee fall before the Pope at Canossa. I wished he hadn't done that, but overall, I was once again being held captive by the long-gone past, especially the Middle Ages, which had witnessed the building of Falkenburg Castle.

My medieval dreams were interrupted when Frau Sonntag started her German class in early September with a solemn expression. "We are approaching the anniversary of Elisabeth von Thadden's death, the founder of our school, and a resistance fighter against the Nazis. I'd like to tell you more about her. She has been called a *reluctant* resistance fighter because she was against *any kind of violence*—above all, Nazi violence. That's why she did not join Count Stauffenberg's group that tried to assassinate Hitler on July 20, 1944. You all know about him and his tragic failure because our Federal Republic of Germany has designated July 20 as a national holiday." Frau Sonntag smoothed the skin of her forehead with two fingers and sighed.

"So what was Elisabeth von Thadden's crime? In the eyes of the Nazis, her first crime was upholding Christian values and continuing with prayers and Bible studies at her school here in Heidelberg." Frau

Sonntag straightened her shoulders and smiled at us. "I mean this very school, *your* school." Her smile dissolved, her eyes darkened. "The Nazis demanded that schools across Germany teach their racist ideology. This, Elisabeth von Thadden wouldn't do."

Again, Frau Sonntag massaged her forehead with two fingers. "Elisabeth had lost two brothers in the war," she told our attentive class. "She'd been close to them and became passionate about stopping the senseless slaughter of young men. And she was appalled by Nazi brutalities and how Nazi opponents and others were carted off."

Like our classmates, Sophie and I had no idea what "carting off" meant. Frau Sonntag did not elaborate.

"We don't know exactly how Miss von Thadden thought she could help stop the war, but she was in regular contact with British friends, letting them know what was happening in Germany, and she helped people escape to England. That was her second crime. Sadly, her circle of friends who met regularly had been infiltrated."

Seeing the puzzled expressions on our faces, Frau Sonntag added, "A Nazi spy had joined her group. He turned her in. She was arrested by the secret police, interrogated, imprisoned, and tried for high treason. Once in the hands of the Gestapo, she never had a chance. On September 9, 1944, Elisabeth von Thadden, along with some of her friends, was executed for allegedly having committed *high treason and undermining the fighting forces*." For a brief second, Frau Sonntag shielded her eyes with one hand, then said quietly, "She was beheaded."

We girls gasped. I dug my fingers into Sophie's arm. Sophie stared back at me, bewildered. Some girls moaned. *Beheaded?* For remaining true to her faith and *talking* to the British?

"We know from her last letters to her family," Frau Sonntag resumed, "that she accepted her fate calmly and gained much strength from her faith. She trusted in God, even in that terrible hour when she was led to the execution hall. Her last words were, 'Put an end, Lord, to all our suffering.'

"This coming Monday, we'll hold a commemorative service in the chapel. All students must attend. It would be nice if you'd wear your Sunday clothes, but not to worry if your mother objects. The most important thing is that you'll be there to honor Elisabeth von Thadden's courage and martyrdom. You probably know that she is buried next to the chapel and have read her name on the large grave marker."

We were shaken. The image of Elisabeth von Thadden under a guillotine was unbearable, even more so because she used to pray in the chapel where we were now praying, walked the halls we were walking, and broke bread in our refectory. I could no longer look at the grave marker, which we had first noticed during our entrance exam, without thinking of her gruesome death.

The next day, Sophie and I, still roiled by Elisabeth von Thadden's fate, asked Vati about the Nazis. "A bunch of hoodlums, that's what they were," he said with contempt, "but they made inroads into society, and once there, they took off."

Vati clapped his hands. "Where is Ingrid? It's time for a talk. Tante B., please put the kettle on," he called over his shoulder. Sophie reminded Vati that Ingrid had play rehearsal at school, prompting him to light a cigarette and ask, "And what was the basis for their power?" Vati looked to Sophie and me for an answer, but unlike Frau Sonntag, he didn't allow much time for us to respond. He took a deep breath and sailed right on. "There were two compelling reasons. One was Germany's defeat in World War I, the other was the most appalling poverty. Your grandfather on your mother's side, hothead that he was, never got over having lost that war. One reason he let out his anger on your mother, Marie."

I felt a pull whenever Mama's name came up, a mixture of sadness, guilt, and pain. Mama had always been an explosive force. And yet, from the first, I had also sensed a sadness in her that pulled me in—like the time she'd read the tale of *The Little Match Girl* to me. But then she did outrageous things like attacking Anna so that I wanted to run away and never see her again. I tried to imagine my angry grandfather, the Baron, whom I had never met, and conjured up a faceless, mustached man, wielding a riding crop.

"He was a cavalry officer," Vati went on. "Thought himself a hell of a fellow. And couldn't have been prouder of Germany. That's a dangerous pride." Vati leaned toward us. I felt his passion and his concern through the familiar screen of smoke.

"Never forget, girls"—Vati stabbed a finger at us—"that patriotism is the last refuge of a scoundrel, as the Englishman Samuel Johnson put it. All sorts of atrocities can be justified in the name of the fatherland, and they were under the Nazis." Vati blew smoke at the ceiling with a far-away expression.

"Yes, be weary when leaders keep invoking 'love of country' or 'making our nation great again.' Whipping up such emotions is used to get people marching. And who gains from wars? The existing power structure—be it a king, a bunch of nobles, or merchants—while the common folk die. It's the people who die."

Vati cleared his throat. "Well, Germany lost in 1918. The victors took everything and imposed heavy reparations. Many people were left without their livelihood. No work, nothing to eat. You can't imagine the times. The old and the young were especially vulnerable."

He took another drag from his cigarette and stared at the ceiling. We understood that he was back in those terrible times. He didn't even notice when Tante B. poured steaming black coffee into his cup.

"Children threw stones at me on my way to school in the 1920s because I was lucky enough to wear shoes. Our place was just outside town, and my way to school led through workers' quarters. They pelted me hard, those poor devils." Vati laughed. "That's how it was."

His laughter was short and without malice. I knew he wasn't trying to pass judgment, merely stating a fact, though to us he was conjuring up a foreign country. Sophie and I had never been hungry or had to walk barefoot. *Our* Germany, the Federal Republic of Germany, was a quiet and peaceful land where everyone had food on the table, a roof over their head, and clothes to wear.

"In any case," Vati resumed, "that's how they got in. The Nazis promised bread and pride in country. Hitler vowed that the humiliated Germany would rise again. He would make Germany great again, and every man, woman, and child would be fed."

Vati poured milk into his coffee and took a sip. "They were clever, focusing on the things everyone identified with: jobs, food—and the honor of the nation. And from there they rose, taking over every sector of the government and society, controlling everything until we woke up in a police state."

It didn't occur to me to ask Vati if the Nazis had ever appealed to him. His words showed too much contempt. I understood that he hated what they had done.

———

Ingrid met us at the door, her cheeks flushed, when Sophie and I came home from after-school choir practice.

"Mama called from Banff! She's coming for a *Blitzbesuch*—her words, not mine." I couldn't help giving Ingrid an "Oh, God-no" look. Without losing a beat, Ingrid understood. "I really think it will be all right this time," she said. "Not more than eight days, a lightning visit as she called it. Her friend Irma from Garmisch is getting married and wants Mama to be her matron of honor. Do you remember Irma?"

"Of course." How could I have forgotten Irma? She had helped Mama get her job at the PX, but she had also pressured Mama in the hotel lobby about something 'criminal' and disturbed me with her hideous grin.

"Irma even sent Mama some dollars to help with the trip. Mama was all gushy about that. Anyway, she asked if we could pick her up from Frankfurt airport; she'll stay in Merkdorf for one night. She'll go on to Garmisch the next day and spend no more than a couple of days with us *after* the wedding because she can't get more time off from work."

"Wow," Sophie said. "Mutti won't be thrilled." Ingrid and I didn't feel pure joy either, glad as we were for Mama.

24

MAMA'S FLYING VISIT

I stuck my head into the kitchen where Tante B. was grating raw potatoes for a scrumptious meal of goulash and potato dumplings. "Where's Sophie? She'd been doing homework before I went to the store and now I can't find her anywhere."

"She mumbled something about taking a break down by the river and for you to join her," said Tante B.

"Thanks. I'll look for her." I broke into a smile. "Can't wait for dinner. You make the best dumplings."

After running down the steep steps to the Neckar, I stopped at the edge of the river and took a deep breath, uplifted as always, when the land opened before me. Today, the river looked almost blue; the next day, it might assume a greenish color, and after a rain, a solid brown. Beyond the band of water, miles of flat land made up the Rhine Valley, orchards primarily whose frenzied spring bloom created a layer of white foam so delicate that the first burst of wind would blow it away.

Sleek, black fishing boats bobbed up and down in the reeds. I scanned the path. No Sophie. Which direction should I take? Perhaps toward Heidelberg. When I rounded the first bend, I spotted a slumped figure on the nearest bench and slowed down. Sophie looked up at me with teary eyes.

Impulsively, I threw my arms around her. "What is it, Sophie? What's wrong?" With her shoulders trembling, Sophie waved me off.

"Oh, come on. You can tell me. I tell you *my* troubles. In fact, what would I do without you?" Sophie produced a meek smile.

"Ellen's father came home from Russia."

"Oh, my God. What a miracle!"

"Yes," Sophie sniffled but was no longer crying. "Of course, I'm happy for her. At the same time, I feel crushed. Why couldn't my father have come home, too?"

Germany's chancellor, Konrad Adenauer, had negotiated the release of 15,000 German prisoners of war with the Soviet Union—ten years after WWII ended. We had heard that of the 2.8 million soldiers captured by the Soviets, more than half had died of hunger, cold, and exposure during the first year of captivity.

"I wish I could bring him back for you."

Sophie let out a sigh. "Mutti wasn't happy with my father."

"Did she tell you that?"

"Yes, she talks to me about everything in her life." I was surprised, considering how little I knew about Mama's life before she married our father, except that her parents hadn't given her any love. She *never* talked about her youth and certainly never about her first marriage.

"Still. Whether they were happy or not, I want to know more about him."

"Where's his family?"

"In Cologne."

"Right here in the West? I always thought they were in East Germany because your mother constantly talks about Silesia."

"That's where Mutti grew up and where she returned after my father went missing in action. She was very close to her family."

"We'll work on her and find a way for you to visit his family in Cologne."

"Last time I asked Mutti about my father," Sophie said, "she told me he had many talents. But his mother had spoiled him. She adored him and waited on him hand and foot." Sophie's face was beginning to smooth out, her shoulders straightening. "Later Mutti said that his mother set him up in business. It went well for a while, but then he started drinking." Sophie paused. "Though my father wasn't a saint, I wished I could have known him. Maybe he had a reason for drinking."

I put my hands on Sophie's shoulder and turned her toward me. "Tante B. is a kind person. Much kinder than Mama. Maybe she was scared your grandma might set you against her when you were little."

"Maybe."

"But now you're older and can make up your own mind."

"You bet!"

I couldn't imagine life without Vati; had he died in the sanatorium, all I would have remembered would be his smile and his sparkling blue eyes. That gave me the shivers. And here was Sophie who'd never even *seen* her father. I was convinced Vati would want Sophie to meet her grandmother, uncles, and aunts who could bring her father alive for her through their photos and family stories.

"Give me some time. We'll figure it out."

Sophie's eyes were regaining their spark while I was planning on enlisting Vati's help. I knew Tante B. would listen to him.

Sophie was scrubbing the kitchen sink while I piled food from our fridge onto the kitchen table. "I wonder if we've ever cleaned this darn thing since we moved in?"

"Mutti probably did some time ago," said Sophie, "but fridges are like little kids—always in need of scrubbing."

Ingrid appeared, her face red and sweaty. "I've washed the hallway, the steps, and mopped our living room, *as well as* Vati's and Tante B.'s bedroom. I need a coke." Ingrid drank greedily from the bottle I handed her.

"I sure hope Mama will be impressed with our spic-and-span place."

"I feel we should grow wings so that we don't have to touch our sparkling floors," said Sophie.

"Me, too. Can't wait to hop into our shiny Opel. Vati had it washed and waxed."

"All for Mama. I hope she will be pleased."

Our mother emerged from customs at Frankfurt airport in a deep blue, well-tailored suit with a fancy belt, held together by a sparkling brooch, and a fur cape around her shoulders. She stood still the moment she spotted our family, thrust one hip forward, and stretched out her arms to let us approach.

Vati presented her with a bouquet of flowers, and we girls lined up for a kiss. Mama beamed. She looked around to check if our tribute had been registered by others, and smacked her lips, satisfied. At home, where Tante B. had set an abundant table, the family toasted her health with champagne and offered her all the delicacies she couldn't find in Canadian stores: Westphalian and Black Forest ham, finely-ground calf's liverwurst, Harzer Roller cheese, and Black Forest chocolate cake.

"Everything is so much more modern in Canada," Mama told us while inspecting our kitchen. "I haven't seen such a tiny fridge and outmoded stove in a long, long time. This kitchen? Off to the dump, I say." I was glad that Tante B. was still in the living room and didn't have to hear Mama's put-downs.

"You look like a stork in this dress with your skinny legs, Marie. We'll have to let the hem down," Mama told me on the way back to the coffee table. I took note of Mama's smiling face and sweet tone. The Mama I remembered from Garmisch wouldn't have bothered with smiles.

"Let me tell you about that outstanding gel that could do wonders for your hair, Tante B. I am sure it would help you get rid of that dry frizz," Mama said in the same tone to Tante B., who blushed instantly.

"You'd better not wear such tight pants," she later advised Sophie, "because of your...well, your...derriere." Sophie winced; I felt angry, but managed to wink at Sophie.

By silent agreement, Ingrid and I wanted Mama to have a perfect visit, especially since it was so short, but Mama wasn't making it easy for us. We breathed a collective sigh of relief when she boarded the train for Garmisch.

Some three days later, Sophie and I were doing homework when the doorbell rang. We heard Ingrid call out, "Mama! We didn't expect you so soon! Vati said you'd phone from the station sometime this eve and he'd pick you up."

Sophie and I quickly grabbed our books, stowed them away, and threw an embroidered tablecloth on the table.

"I caught an earlier train," Mama said. "Aren't you pleased?"

"Yes, yes, we are pleased, but need a moment to get ready. Would you like some *frischen Kaffee and Kuchen*? Fresh coffee and cake?"

"I could do with a good cup of freshly brewed coffee," said Mama before she hugged me. "The stuff on the train was so awful I couldn't drink it."

We girls jumped into action. Sophie and I ran to the baker to pick up the plum cake and Streussel we had ordered while Mama headed for the bath to freshen up. While we were setting the table, we saw her disappear first into Tante B.'s and then into Vati's room. We didn't give her tour of our flat a second thought since Mama had always had free rein wherever she was. We were surveying our beautifully set table with a sense of satisfaction when we heard Vati and Tante B. return.

They called out their usual "Hello, children. We're home" in the hallway. Ingrid rushed out of the kitchen, saying, "We're just setting the table for Mama, who returned early," when Mama charged out of Vati's room like an avenging angel, her eyes on fire, her body rigid.

"Welcome back, Lilybeth," said Vati and stopped dead in his tracks. Mama was waving a flannel nightgown at him. He knew instantly that Mama was on a roll and told Tante B., "Please check the shirts on the laundry line." He turned to us. "Girls, off into the living room with you." We saw him take Mama's arm before the door closed.

"You double-crossing, dirty pig!" we heard Mama scream at the top of her lungs. "You bastard! Bringing your mistress into my children's home, neglecting them while you pump that Silesian slut. I found her nightgown at the foot of your bed!"

"You're out of your mind," we heard Vati say. "I wasn't even home last night. Sometimes Tante B. sleeps in my room since the window opens into the yard; her room is so small and stuffy. I was attending a conference in Karlsruhe. You can ask the girls."

Mama's screams stopped. Ingrid, quick as lightning, opened the door to Vati's room after a tentative knock. Mama's fists were still clenched, her body shaking. The nightgown lay crumpled at Vati's feet.

Ingrid mustered her courage. "Mama, we've set such a pretty table for you and poured fresh coffee. Please come along."

Mama froze and seemed confused. She scrutinized Vati's face. It had relaxed when Ingrid came into the room. In fact, Vati looked downright relieved. That drove her anger right up again.

She pushed Ingrid aside, picked up the plum cake, raced back, and threw it into Vati's face. My stomach turned and Ingrid doubled over.

"Here! Take this! There's the mess you deserve!"

Sophie and I couldn't help moaning, and Ingrid cried out, "Mama don't, please don't. We tried to make everything perfect for you."

Mama stared at Ingrid. Then she covered her face with her hands, the first signal that she was winding down. We hardly dared look at Vati's smeared face. And though I felt as sick to my stomach as I had when Mama had poured ashes over Vati's head in the car so many years ago, I managed to say, "Please, come to the table."

Ingrid took Mama's arm and guided her to the living room; Vati headed for the loo. Sophie offered Mama cream and sugar while Ingrid passed the plate with the Streussel. We three sat without saying a word, exhausted, yet alert, determined to avoid saying or doing anything that could set Mama off again. Vati and Tante B. stayed out of sight.

When would it ever end?

Ingrid walked Mama back to the Gasthaus where they sat down in the dining room, she filled us in later. "Mama ordered a glass of wine, and I devoured a bratwurst with potato salad. I don't know why, but I was ravenous," Ingrid said.

I knew why. We'd been thrust back to the days when the world was drowned out by Mama's screams, and there was nothing, nothing to hold on to. That's when you do anything—polish your shoes, water the flowers, or eat until you bust.

Mama insisted on walking Ingrid, Sophie, and me to the train station on the day of her departure. "You better go to school instead of riding along to the airport. I don't like dramatic airport farewells," she told us. Vati would drive her to Frankfurt midmorning. When the school train approached, Mama hugged Ingrid.

"Bastian and I can't wait for you two to visit," she said.

"I will," promised Ingrid. Vati had been called to a teacher's conference before Mama arrived and had not returned with a happy face when he learned that Ingrid's grades had been slipping in German, Latin, Math, and the sciences. Ever since, Ingrid had been grumbling about how the schools in Canada might be more inspiring.

"You must forgive me," Mama sobbed suddenly, looking directly at me, "if I lose my temper. I've had such a hard life. I never had love. But I love you. I love and miss you both so much. You must come and visit." Tears were running down her cheek.

"Promise?"

We promised. We were already on our train, the door hadn't closed yet, when Mama clutched my hand, pulling me toward her. "Be careful, Marie. Tante B. may try to poison you so she can have Vati for herself."

I looked into Mama's tear-stained face, into eyes that appealed to me as if I, Marie, had the power to set her free. The doors slammed shut. Mama's shoulders slumped. I couldn't believe what Mama had said—and yet her words touched a nerve. There *was* something between Vati and Tante B. I'd felt it ever since the kiss in the car. Ingrid shook her head as if to say *Good God!* I wanted to shake off Mama's words, too, but they kept haunting me. What if Tante B. *did* want Vati for herself? Where would Ingrid and I be then? I tried to push Mama's words away, but they wouldn't leave me alone, along with her wide-open eyes that kept pleading with me.

When Sophie and I came home from school, Tante B. let us in.

"Come and have some hot chocolate, you two. I've got fresh buns from the baker."

Sophie's face brightened, but I turned away. "I don't have time," I said, avoiding Tante B.'s eyes. "I've got to write an essay."

Then came the nightmares where a cloaked figure handed me a chalice that I knew contained poison. The figure loomed over me. I tried to push the chalice away, but my hand wouldn't move.

My screams were so loud that Sophie woke me, and Tante B. came running into our room. But how could I tell them about my fear of losing Vati's love, attention, and care? That I even feared losing Tante B.'s love? I craved and needed both. Vati and Tante B. were my anchors. And why did Vati kiss Tante B. in secret? Our Vati, my Vati could not, should never be dishonest. I felt hurt, lost, desperate, and confused.

Since Mama had left, I felt I was doing Tante B. wrong, and yet I couldn't help but be mistrustful. Everything I'd ever loved and trusted—Vati (while he was in the sanatorium), Anna, the Castle, our freedom—had been taken from me without warning.

To make up for Mama's plum cake explosion, Vati and Tante B. invited Sophie and me along to Vati's upcoming pharma visit to Munich.

We explored the famous English Garden, tackled Bavaria's famous *Schweinshaxe*—roasted pork knuckle—for lunch at the Hofbraeuhaus, and walked along the river Isar to return thoroughly exhausted to our meeting place in late afternoon. As evening fell, we curled up on opposite ends of the back seat of the car, each with a pillow under our head and warmed by a blanket.

I heard Vati's familiar voice. "Why are you so quiet, Tante B.?"

"Tired."

"Guess our travelers have fallen asleep." I let Vati's voice lull me toward sleep.

"Hm."

"What's bothering you?"

"I can't believe you allowed Lilybeth to upset our lives again."

"We've been through this already. I didn't invite her, but she is the mother of my children. I cannot shut her out."

"Even when she's creating havoc?"

"Look, she was all alone while I was...well, you know. She lost everything because of me. The least I can do is treat her decently while she is here."

"Do you still...care for her?"

I tensed like a bow and felt my blood rush to my head.

"I thank my lucky stars that she's content in Canada."

"Well, you sure don't show it when she is here."

"What do you expect me to do? Say right to her, 'I'm so glad you're living three thousand miles away?' You know what that would accomplish. She'd be back in Germany in a flash!"

I did not want Mama back in Germany. But the child in me wanted Vati to miss her. The old loyalty battle made me queasy. But more than anything, I wanted Vati's undiluted love.

Tante B. was sniffling. The part of me that did not believe Mama felt for her.

"Come now, Lena." Vati kissed her cheek. "Put your head against my shoulder," he said softly. "Try to sleep."

Maybe I could now go to sleep, too. It was all so...messy. I envied my classmates who had a father and mother living together. For a moment, I even envied those whose father had never come back from the war. They never had to take sides. Sophie was turning in her sleep. Her left arm landed on my hip. I felt soothed, closed my eyes, and was about to drift off.

"Lately, I feel like packing it in." I heard Tante B.'s voice. "Maybe I should pick up Sophie and make a new life for ourselves. At least it'd be real and not an illusion."

Oh, no. Won't they ever stop?

"Don't go there, Tante B. I couldn't bear it. The girls...the girls and I need you. You are our anchor, our lodestar..."

"I don't know, Vati...I really don't know."

Who wanted to pick up Sophie and make a new life? I was stirring but couldn't shake myself awake. Tomorrow...I would find out tomorrow.

The next day, when I caught Tante B. staring out the window, I touched her shoulder and asked what was wrong. Her big blue eyes ballooned out toward me, only now registering my presence. "Oh, Mariechen," oh Marie dear, she whispered, "if only you were older."

Vati must have noticed her absentmindedness, too, because he took her to the movies at least twice a week from then on. In fact, running away to the movies would become a family obsession, as if we'd discovered the existence of movie theaters only after Mama's *Blitzkrieg*.

The moment Vati gave us the green light on weekends, we three girls took off like a streak. Once we arrived at Heidelberg's *Bismarckplatz*, Ingrid broke away from Sophie and me to meet up with her best friend Eleanor and some other girls while Sophie and I happily moved on by ourselves.

Charlie Chaplin and the Three Stooges had thrilled us no end when we first arrived in Heidelberg, but could no longer hold our attention. We needed something stronger. Our hunger for heroics had grown in proportion to the helplessness we felt during Mama's visit. Hollywood lifted us above our own pressures and pain, at least for a while. *El Cid*, *Joan of Arc*, and *The Ten Commandments* empowered us. We sucked in their grandeur with the same abandon with which we sucked on our lollipops in the dark theater. We saw *The Ten Commandments* at least twice, mesmerized by Pharaoh's pursuit of Moses and the parting of the Red Sea.

Sometimes, Sophie and I ran into Ingrid and her friends at the ticket window. We smiled and waved hello, but we never sat with them, because we felt superior to Ingrid's swooning crowd. Though supposedly more mature than Sophie and me, they nursed childish crushes on Kim Novak, Grace Kelly, Cary Grant, Rock Hudson, and James Dean. They collected their heartthrobs' pictures and pasted them into photo albums, spending hours adoring the glossy portraits. And they devoured magazine articles that revealed details of their idols' private lives, especially love affairs, weddings, and divorces.

Sophie and I also had our favorite actors: Charlton Heston, Kirk Douglas, Ingrid Bergman, Jennifer Jones, and Katherine Hepburn, but we weren't interested in their private lives. We loved the *characters* they played. Like our celluloid heroes and heroines, we wanted to raise the oppressed, climb the highest mountain, and lead a people to the Promised Land. In the half-light of the movie house, we felt alive, strong, and capable of conquering the world.

At night, long after Ingrid had gone to sleep, we acted out our favorite scenes. Sophie reigned as El Cid, Spartacus, Prince Ironheart, and King Arthur, I as Joan of Arc and Mary Stuart. The basic plot of all our fantasies was simple: one of us was the hero, usually male, the other a more tender counterpart.

"Do you want to play Joan of Arc?" Sophie might ask.

"No, I don't want to face the fire tonight."

"Moses?" Charlton Heston had left an indelible impression on us.

"Not really." Sophie stroked my cheek.

"Let's make up a story then."

"Okay, I'm Prince Tamar." I came alive with every word. "On the eve of a decisive battle defending my kingdom. I'm really a princess, but my father passed me off as a prince since he already had seven daughters when I was born. He taught me fencing, jousting, and the art of politics, and I have become an accomplished sovereign. I'm in my tent on the battlefield. You are my opponent, Prince Harold. We've never met, but tonight we both decide to go swimming in the river."

"Right," Sophie carried on, "I'm already in the water." She made some swimming motions.

"A horse and rider approach!"

"Whoa! Whoa!" I called out and pretended to jump off a horse.

"I'm flexing my muscles," Sophie whispered, "then steady my feet. This could be an enemy soldier. Now the moon emerges from a cloud and I see the figure of a beautiful young girl. I stand transfixed—"

"While I slowly walk into the water. When I'm almost submerged..." I slide down the mattress, "I put my arms around you and kiss you." Sophie pulled me close and kissed me. It felt good to be held. I squeezed her back and we kissed tenderly. Then I gently pushed Sophie away.

"But the muffled call of a bird drives us apart," I said. "I jump on my horse and am off before you can follow me. Little do we know that we will face each other in battle tomorrow."

From then on, there was barely a night we didn't play movies. Ingrid got wise to us after a while, but Vati and Tante B. never did. We intuited that they might not approve of our pastime, so we waited until everyone was asleep, but deep inside we felt we had nothing to hide. Ingrid dismissed our games as child's play, but we knew better. As Moses or Saint Joan, we aspired to the highest callings of mankind, escaping the cold war threat of our time, and the tensions at home. We soared above reality to land safely, upon our descent, in each other's arms.

25

BASTIAN'S LETTER

Dear Ingrid,

Thank you for your letter. I'm glad and honored that you wrote to me in confidence because I think I can put your mind at ease. And I can't wait to welcome you to Canada. I KNOW you will like it.

Here up North, no one is judged by their education and class as people are in Germany. Our Vati is an exception, but I know darn well that Aunt Amalia and her brood, your classmates, and most of the Bergen family would see me as a failure because I don't have the Abitur and never went to university. But I'm making a living for myself and can see that my life is getting better all the time. People are much more open and friendly here than in Germany, and nature is breathtaking: clean lakes, rivers, waterfalls, and endless woods.

And, of course, schools are much more fun. They offer "drama" as a regular subject and more sports than you can name: gymnastics, swimming, basketball, tennis, hockey, and more. You love drama and sports and would have a ball. As regards French, one of your favorite subjects, you could travel to Montreal and Quebec and be in a "French-speaking world."

But I better get to your sore point: Mama. I was sorry to hear that she had another of her outbursts in Germany and know how devastated you and Marie must feel. Sometimes I get so angry I could whack her. I mean hard. But, compared to Falkenburg and Garmisch, she is a bit better.

School ends at three or four PM, depending on your schedule and play rehearsals or athletic training. Your guidance counselor helps build free times for you. You can use that free period to rest, buy yourself a Coke, or get your homework done. Oh, I almost forgot. Schools have cafeterias where you get a good hot lunch every day. Doesn't it almost sound like a hotel? German schools are much more rigid and don't care where you get your food, don't care about rest, and even less about having fun.

All this means that you would be away from Mama for the better part of the day. Mama found a well-paying job as a cook for the owner of a huge lumber business and doesn't come home until the evening. While we'd all be together on weekends, I'd make sure to do fun things with you like going to hockey games, which Mama can't stand, taking you to a drive-in, and spending time with friends—yours and mine. And I'll teach you to drive as soon as you've caught up on your sleep after your long flight. Ehrenwort! Cross my heart and hope to die.

Sure, we'd attend the occasional movie with Mama and we'll have some meals together, but if we are smart, we can arrange much of our schedule so that she gets to do what she likes to do (going to the hairdresser, shopping for clothes...) while we take off on our own and have some fun. And Mama really is better than she used to be.

So, what do you think?

The new world is beckoning you. Your brother loves you and can't wait to see you! And even though you write that Marie and Sophie are real close, she'll probably come and visit us in a year or two. Then the three of us would be together just like the "good, old days."

Please write soon when we can expect you. And give my best to Vati. I miss him. I do remember what a good Assistant Mrs. Borodny was at Vati's surgery. She has a photographic memory and never lost her temper. You guys are lucky. It must be so much more peaceful at home than it used to be.

Loads of love,
Your brother Bastian.
P.S. For heaven's sake, burn this letter!

26

INGRID DEPARTS AND SEX EDUCATION

Basti's letter hit the mark. Ingrid was sweet sixteen, but sixteen did not feel sweet to her. She felt restless and dissatisfied with school. She was not particularly interested in science or philosophy, not even in existentialism that was being debated all around us. Nor did she give much thought to God and the world. She did concentrate feverishly on her dashing young French professor, Monsieur de Remarque, a real Frenchman, adored by all the girls in her class and the entire school. That man could have started a harem had he not been inclined toward attractive young men, a revelation that would shake up the entire Elisabeth-von-Thadden community before too long.

Ingrid did like to read novels and she loved Hollywood movies. In sum, she eagerly swallowed Basti's lure that schools in Canada are fun and embarked on a campaign that slowly but surely wore our father down.

"If you want to take the plunge, so be it," Vati said finally. "But if you don't like it in Canada for any reason whatsoever, you always have a home here with Marie, Tante B., Sophie, and me!"

Ingrid pranced about, celebrating her victory. I was puzzled. Had she forgotten that leaving for Canada meant living with Mama?

"Don't you worry about Mama?" I asked her.

"Sometimes," Ingrid said, studying her face in the mirror, "but I don't take Mama as seriously as you do. And she can't shove me around anymore—I'm taller and stronger than she is. Bastian will stand up for me, too!"

Remembering the time Mama chased Bastian with an iron skillet, I was not so sure, but I believed in my sister's innate strength. "Mama likes you so much better than me," I said. "She loves your thick blond hair and your peachy complexion; your health, strength, and proud carriage. I'm a scrawny, clumsy failure in her eyes."

"Oh, come on now, sis. For a thirteen-year-old, you've developed quite a bosom. You aren't scrawny anymore, and you have beautiful eyes and shapely legs."

I blushed. We eyed each other. I felt certain that Ingrid must have been thinking what I did. *Wouldn't it have been great to compliment each other more often in the past?* I threw my arms around my big sister and squeezed her tight.

The next day, Tante B. and Ingrid carried a big trunk down from the attic and filled it with Ingrid's clothes, shoes, and jewelry, her white skates, her photo collection of movie stars, and her favorite novel, *Gone with the Wind*. Finally, Ingrid climbed on top of the heavy chest, pressing down with her full weight, while Tante B. turned the key in the lock that made a grinding sound. Ingrid and Tante B. shook hands; suddenly their smiles froze, they threw their arms around each other, and bawled.

That's when I finally accepted that I was losing my intrepid sister who had taught me how to read when I was just a squirt, who walked me down the Castle's hill to school, and who had tried to look out for me—at least when I was small and before Sophie joined our family. I also knew that we'd be fused forever because of Mama.

When the time came to take Ingrid to the airport, there was no room in the car for Sophie and me because of the mountain of luggage. The younger sisters had to stay behind and hugged Ingrid in the street. I pressed my favorite book, *The Cornet* by Rilke, into Ingrid's hand and Sophie slipped a small bracelet into Ingrid's jacket pocket.

"Back into the house with you two," Vati bellowed, "or you'll be run over by a car." Sophie and I ran inside and opened the windows wide. From there we waved until Vati's car had turned the corner, and we were left staring at the gray, empty street. Finally, we pulled in our heads. The house was empty—Ingrid's absence looming like a presence.

"Let's write her a letter," Sophie suggested. We rummaged for the thin airmail paper, reserved for Mama, smoothed it out, and uncapped our pens. Since Ingrid had only just left, we couldn't really tell her any news, so we wrote that we missed her. Writing that we missed her made us cry. Big drops fell onto the paper; it buckled, and the letters smeared.

Suddenly, by some unspoken consent, we headed for the kitchen to fix ourselves a potato salad, a thick mass of potatoes, chopped pickles, tomatoes, boiled eggs, onions, and fried bacon. We carried the heavy bowl back to the coffee table and filled the void in our heart with heaps and heaps of potato goo.

Ingrid wrote enthusiastic letters home, how she *loved* her new school, and was *auditioning for a big role* in a play. *I went to a drive-in theater last night,* she wrote, *and saw The Invasion of the Body Snatchers, which is fabulous!!!*

I couldn't have watched the film without Basti by my side—it's terrifying, absolutely nerve-wracking! You must see it when it gets to Heidelberg, which may take months. Germany's just too far off the beaten path when it comes to Hollywood movies. A boy in my school thinks I look like Kim Novak and it's not the first time I've heard that.

Sophie and I looked at each other and giggled. Of course, Ingrid was attractive, but Kim Novak? *I do miss Vati, Tante B. and you guys and my beloved French teacher, Monsieur de Remarque. I hope that he'll soon be your French teacher, too. I know you'll love him. Bastian let me steer his Pontiac on the way home and I will definitely get my permit this week! You can get a driver's permit here at age 16 instead of 18 like in Germany.*

In her next letter, Ingrid wrote, *Mama bought a new TV that's so amazing. I can get myself a Coke from the fridge or do some ironing while watching "Gunsmoke."* Sophie and I eagerly showed the letter to Vati upon his return from a Boehringer trip.

"You know how I feel, you two. Why would I need a TV? I can hear the news on the radio; and when I feel like seeing a film, I go to a movie house. Even if I were more interested in buying a TV, I wouldn't even consider getting one until you have finished prep school and successfully passed your Abitur."

We knew Vati wouldn't budge because school and learning were everything to him. So, radio remained king in our house as it did for most of our classmates. Vati and Tante B. regularly listened to the news and relaxing music and all of us gathered around the radio on New Year's for the countdown to midnight, champagne glasses in hand.

Sophie and I turned on the radio for news, political debates, and the occasional soccer game. And somehow, without ever making an explicit decision, we had begun to listen to the American Forces Network, ostensibly to improve our comprehension of English, but also to listen to the latest music, especially Swing and Rock.

We'd become enchanted with Johnny Cash and his ballads of Big Bad John, or How High's the Water, Papa? His songs told a good story, and his seductive voice, suffused with existential sadness, touched us to the core. All of it—the melody, the words, and the color of Cash's sound—seemed pure and straightforward to us, not artificial or contrived like so many German pop songs after the war. It was a new tone, and when we heard it, we couldn't help being flooded with melancholy and longing.

And we got most of our world news from the radio. Morocco's independence struggles, Khrushchev's unheard-of criticism of Lenin, the Suez Crisis, and the exciting events in Hungary where Prime Minister Nagy was trying to establish a more independent state within the constraints of the Soviet Union. Everyone in Germany saw the developments in Hungary as a risky undertaking, to be sure, but we all hoped that Nagy would succeed.

One afternoon, when spinning the radio dial toward AFN, young, excited voices caught my ear: "We beg you, brothers and sisters in the West, help us! Soviet tanks are rolling in our streets."

Sophie and I were alone at home. Tante B. was traveling with Vati much more often now that we were older and could take care of ourselves.

The voices sounded young, just like those of our classmates. There was an urgency to them but no outright fear. They said they were students who had taken over the radio station to call for help.

I listened as if my life were at stake. The transmission broke off for a moment, forcing me to kneel on the floor with my ear pressed to the speaker before the sound came back on.

"Nagy has fled. We're the only ones left. Shots and heavy artillery are coming our way. We can hear tanks approaching. Brothers and sisters in the West, please come quickly."

Sophie and I heard shots and explosions. We tried to imagine what it must feel like to know that tanks are rolling toward you. I buried my head in my hands. "Oh, please, God, let the Americans hurry. They, and only they can rescue these brave souls." Sophie was biting her fingernails. The sound of shots was growing louder.

"Surely, they will help. I mean the Americans will help, right?" My eyes begged Sophie for reassurance. "They will, they will," Sophie said.

"That's what America is about, democracy and freedom—they will, they must step in."

Sophie steadied my shoulder. "I bet we'll hear planes overhead any time now."

The explosions grew louder. Still, the voices broke through the clutter and noise. "Please come soon! Do not desert us."

Then no more voices, only crackling and breakage, followed by a terrible silence.

What was happening? Had the students been captured? Were they wounded? Or dead? And where were the Americans, where were we Germans, the British, the French?

Finally, an announcer came on, "This was the last transmission from Budapest. We have been unable to reach any of our contacts. It is feared that the Soviets have put down the uprising. It is feared that many have been killed, among them Prime Minister Nagy."

My heart was racing. Kneeling on the floor, with my face in my hands, the first bits of reality sank in. The Americans and we Germans didn't care enough. We didn't want to provoke the Russians. We preached democracy, but when confronted with such brutal force, we did *nothing*.

I needed to talk to Vati.

Sophie wrung her hands, then raised me up and hugged me. "I'll make us some hot chocolate."

"I don't want chocolate. I want people to live up to their own convictions!"

"What were you thinking, Marie?" Vati asked when we had finally settled around the coffee table after his return. "A war that might well have been fought on our own soil since we are wedged right between East and West. Nowhere is there greater danger."

"Of course, I don't want war. But, Vati, the Americans could have used air power. Their decisive response could have inspired the Poles, the Czechs, and the Yugoslavs to come to Hungary's aid. A chain reaction could have produced a massive uprising against the Soviet Union!"

"That's wishful thinking, Marie. The Russians have substantial forces on the Hungarian border. No one else is ready to fight. And apart from America, no one is as powerful as the Russians."

"What about the British and the French?"

"Up to their necks in the Suez Crisis. And Eisenhower is focused on getting re-elected. The Russians know what they are doing."

I heard my father but was not appeased. "We just let them be slaughtered."

"Yes," said Vati, stirring his coffee, "it's horrific. I admire—and pity—the brave fighters. Like you, I hate oppression, but had the West interfered, thousands, tens of thousands, and more would have died. War is a killing machine. I hope you'll never see it in action."

Meanwhile, our village of Merkdorf had a new scandal that seemed to overshadow the European tragedy, at least locally. Heidi, the fifteen-year-old niece of our landlady, had become pregnant. Everyone was talking about it.

"You'd think skinny Heidi had committed murder the way people are condemning her." I shook my head at Sophie.

"And to have to leave school," said Sophie.

"Even her friends are shunning her, but I bet their parents are pressuring them."

"Thank God, your Vati would never do that," said Sophie.

"What wouldn't I do?" asked Vati as he walked into the living room, having freshened up from his trip. I jumped up and gave him a resounding kiss and opened the door just wide enough to call out in a mock deep voice, "Tante B., please put the kettle on and call us when it's ready. We'll come and help."

Vati laughed.

"You wouldn't condemn Heidi, Onkel Karl, right?"

"Poor Heidi," Vati said, fumbling in his pocket for his cigarettes. "Her life in this village is over, at least her chance for a good life. No young man from around here will ever marry her. It's not fair, but that's how it is. Young boys will pursue a girl relentlessly, tell her she's beautiful, that they can't live without her to get what they want."

He tapped the end of a cigarette on the table, fished out a match, and lit it. I studied him. He was rigidly strict when it came to boys; he did not trust them. Sophie and I knew we wouldn't be allowed to date until we had passed the *Abitur*. I couldn't help but ask, "Why does everybody get so agitated over sex?"

Tante B. entered with a tray. Sophie and I set out the cups. "Will you join us?" asked Vati. "We are going to talk about sex." Tante B. stopped pouring, her eyes popping out. "In a little while," she said briskly and headed straight for the door.

Vati took a sip from his cup and fixed his eyes on us. "There is a force in men and women that is ruthless and self-serving and you must look out for it or you will be hurt. For the anatomical details, you can browse through my medical atlas, but there is so much more to this than anatomy." Vati, deep in thought, shoved the packet of cigarettes back and forth on the table.

"When I was your age, I had no one who talked to me about women and sex. I adored my mother and thought all women were like her. Hah!" He chuckled, shaking his head as if he still could not believe his stupidity.

"One of the strongest, perhaps *the* strongest drive in all of us is the drive to procreate. Consider the many seeds of an apple or a dandelion. Nature produces excess seed, with the goal that at least one will take. We human beings are part of nature; we are not different. All the flirting and dancing and courting between men and women has only one underlying cause: to reproduce.

"Most people aren't even aware of the incontrovertible drive to reproduce. Your mother wasn't. And I wasn't, at first. The individual usually looks for love. By that most people mean sympathy, excitement, and physical attraction. People fall in love, get married and have children, almost without exception wherever you look in the world, be it in bitter cold Alaska or the relentless heat of the desert, be it among Amazon tribes or urban centers. The drive to reproduce is so strong it is indestructible, in both women and men. Men are obsessed with it, in the form of sex. Much of women's energy goes into nurturing, in taking care of children. That offsets the harshness of the drive." Vati took another drag and held the smoke back for such a long time that I worried he might choke. Finally, he breathed out.

"Just think of Heidi. The boy probably told her he loved her. Often boys do, in fact, believe they love the girl they are after, but once the first excitement wears off, they're ready for another girl. Men are like the apple and the dandelion; they scatter their seed. The more they scatter, the higher the chance of producing offspring. Women have to be more selective because they carry the child for nine months in their body, give birth to it, then take care of it."

We were all eyes and ears, Sophie as wide-eyed as I, but less agitated. The more I listened to Vati, the more frustrated I felt. As always, Vati spoke with passion and sincerity, but I didn't want to see men as sex-driven monsters. The men I knew best, Bastian and Vati, were sensitive and kind. I felt all men should be that way. Vati made it sound as if there was no love in the world, only instinct.

"So men and women are really on two different tracks? Men want sex and women want men who can take care of a family?"

"Exactly!" Vati looked pleased that I had caught on. But I didn't want men and women to be on different tracks. I wanted them to be people! Before I knew what I was saying, I asked, "So what made you fall for Mama?"

Vati coughed and looked up. "That's an *ad hominem* question, but fair enough." He took another drag and looked out the window, turning abruptly back to me. "Where to start? I have to go back many years. Berchtesgaden, 1939. I'm returning from a house call to a hard-scrabble mountain farm, when a swoosh of color suddenly shimmered before me as I came out of a steep curve. A young woman in pink, clutching a curly-haired boy close to her body. I brought the car to a stop, vaguely aware that the young woman had jumped out of the way, which hadn't really been necessary. The moment I laid eyes on her, in her pink dirndl and a white, lace-trimmed blouse that cradled her breasts, I felt a jolt. And after she trained her beautiful gray eyes on me—they were childlike and searching—I was swept up by a force I could not name.

"I asked her with feigned nonchalance, 'May I offer you a lift home?'

"Your mother smiled. Oh, such a smile. 'Yes, thank you. Not home but into town.'

"I didn't know then that your mother had been married off to a much older man, a Lieutenant Colonel, who'd served with your grandfather, Baron von Baginski, in the cavalry during WWI. She lived with the Colonel in an imposing villa, at the foot of Obersalzberg.

"'Dr. Bergen,' I introduced myself. 'And who is this young, curly-haired man?'

"'This is my son, Bastian. Come on, Bastian, shake the doctor's hand.'"

It was sweet to imagine my big brother as a little boy, but strange to see Mama through Vati's eyes. Suddenly, and for the first time, I felt wiser than my father.

"Every time I saw her walk along the road in her pretty dirndl," Vati continued, "her head held high like a queen, holding on to your brother's hand, while stepping out in quick, springy steps, I could not help myself. I pulled the car over and offered her a ride to wherever she was going." He took a deep breath. "Well, that's how it started, anyhow."

I shivered and Vati fell silent, as if conjuring up the past had exhausted him. I also felt exhausted. Sophie broke the silence. "Goodness, I better study for our history test tomorrow."

"Do you ever want to get married?" I asked Sophie later that night. "Never."

"Me neither. I don't want to be a reproduction machine, popping out child after child because men want to satisfy their unstoppable lust. I refuse. I swear to you, I refuse."

27

SOPHIE'S GRANDMOTHER

Our last year of Home Ec. I could not wait to be rid of this tiresome subject, my worst. Our final project required knitting a pair of mittens. Sophie and I had bought the same wool in the identical color.

"How come yours look so neat and mine loose and lumpy?" I asked. "I *hate* knitting."

"That's it, that's why." Sophie smiled at me impishly. "I *love* to knit. Mutti taught me when I was little. First, Mutti would brew tea. Then she'd sit me down and we'd knit or crochet for hours. That's how she made most of our money before your father hired her. Mutti knit sweaters, socks, and caps; and embroidered tablecloths, then sold them. Between that and the jewelry from my grandfather's store in Silesia, we scraped by."

The doorbell rang. We looked at each other. "Vati and Tante B. already?"

Sophie got up and peered through the fine curtain. "Some woman in a suit and a fur around her shoulders."

I could feel myself blanch. "Mama?"

"No, no, older and no makeup." Sophie opened the window a bit. "Yes?" she said. "May I help you?"

The woman looked up, searched Sophie's face, and broke into a smile.

"You wouldn't by chance be Sophie, would you?" Sophie wrinkled her forehead. Out loud, she said, "I am. But I don't know who you are."

"Sadly, you don't. I'm Hildie Aldinger, your father's mother. May I come in?"

Sophie kept staring at her until I cuffed her. "We'll be right there to let you in," I called out over Sophie's shoulder.

"Sorry to arrive unexpectedly," the woman said after I led her into the living room. "A distant cousin of mine died in Mannheim, so I took the train down to attend the funeral. Then I thought, I'm only a few kilometers from my dear boy's only child. I haven't seen her since she was a baby. I must say hello."

Sophie was still staring at the woman, unsure what to think. The older lady was neatly dressed and looked us straight in the eye; her smile seemed genuine. Sophie stood upright and stiff like a soldier. I cleared my throat.

"We expect Sophie's mother and my father soon. When is your return train?"

"Eight PM." Mrs. Aldinger smiled at both of us. "I took a chance." She looked from me to Sophie. "May I sit down?"

"Please," said Sophie, and after the woman was seated, she finally added, "It's...good to meet you."

"And a great joy for me."

"Do you have other family in the area, Mrs. Aldinger?" I asked when Sophie remained silent.

"Sadly, no—and I have only a small nuclear family. My husband—your grandfather, Sophie—passed away shortly after the war. May he rest in peace. He was a good man. We had two children." Now she was smiling at Sophie. "Bernhard, your father, and a daughter, Karoline. Karoline never married. The man she loved fell in the Ardennes." Mrs. Aldinger walked over to Sophie and put her hands on Sophie's shoulders. "You, Sophie, are my only grandchild."

I saw Sophie's cheek muscles work. She nearly jumped up and embraced her out-of-nowhere grandmother just as I heard a car door slam and knew it must be Vati and Tante B. "Excuse me for a moment," I said, rushing out to warn them.

"She seems decent and was not pushy. So, we invited her in. Hope you aren't upset," I told Vati and Tante B.

Tante B. froze. Vati didn't exactly look kindly at me, so I added, "She immediately asked for you, Tante B. I'm sure she thought you were home." Vati put his arm around Tante B.'s shoulder. "This was bound to happen sooner or later. Let's look her over. Don't worry, dear. No one can take Sophie away from you."

"Sophie wouldn't let anyone take her away," I huffed. Tante

B.'s eyes dug into mine with a mixture of hope and concern. Vati led her inside.

After the introductions, we all sat down again, Tante B. right next to Sophie.

"Did your house survive the war?" asked Tante B.

"Yes, Lena. We were so lucky, one of only two houses standing on our street after a British bombing raid."

"I'm very glad to hear it. How is Karoline doing? And her young man?"

"Karoline is doing well, thank you, teaching fourth grade," Mrs. Aldinger lowered her eyes, "but her young man never came back from the war."

A shock ran through Tante B. "I am so sorry." She rose slowly, heading toward her mother-in-law.

"And I'm so terribly sorry, so terribly sorry," she started to shake, "about Bernhard." The two women were clutching each other before we knew it, both sobbing. We couldn't help but stare, aware that the two disparate souls were united by their loss and the unbearable sorrow of war.

"Let's make some coffee," said Sophie. Vati gave us an approving nod, and we fled to the kitchen. While I was pouring hot water into the filter, Sophie tiptoed back, listened at the door, and reported back, "They're like a bunch of school children, talking, shooting off questions, even laughing. All about surviving the war. 'Did Miller's house get bombed? And what about their sons? Did they come back from the Front?'"

Sophie hugged me. "Thank God!"

Inwardly, I blessed Vati, Tante B., and Mrs. Aldinger for being so civil. If Mama had been part of the scene, accusations would be flying, and someone would have already broken into tears.

"Do you like her?" I asked Sophie.

"I think so. Do you?"

"I do."

Sophie cheered up. She offered coffee to everyone before sitting down next to Tante B. and taking her mother's hand. From her chair she was watching Mrs. Aldinger's face, perhaps searching for a likeness to the face of the father she knew only from a few photographs.

I passed around a plate of cookies.

Finally Sophie spoke up. "Mrs. Aldinger," she stopped herself, took in a deep breath, and started again, "*grandmother*, please tell me about our relatives." Sophie's grandmother leaned back, eyed Sophie with satisfaction, and embarked on an exposition of their family tree.

Thank god, Vati kept track of the time. At seven, he offered to drive Mrs. Aldinger to the train station.

"Sophie, it was a great pleasure to meet you," Mrs. Aldinger told Sophie before getting into the car. "Your eyes are just like Bernhard's. I almost feel that he's with us when I look at you." She dabbed her eyes. Sophie was smiling dreamily and allowed Mrs. Aldinger to hug her. "I very much hope that you'll all visit us in Cologne soon," her grandmother said, turning to Tante B.

"We'll see when we can get away," Tante B. said quickly, not promising anything, but in a tone that was so much warmer than when she had first said hello.

"Will you see her again?" I asked Sophie as soon as the adults had left.

"I have to. She's my father's mother."

"Of course, you will, now that the ice has been broken."

Sophie threw her arms around me. I rubbed my forehead against my friend's and felt her tremble. "Yes," she said, "yes, I want to see her again."

I entered Frau Sonntag's private apartment in the *Herrenhaus*, her *inner sanctum*, as we students called it, distinguished by a fireplace, green velvet curtains, a comfortable velvet couch with matching, overstuffed chairs, and books wherever you looked. I had been in the inner sanctum several times before, practicing for a poetry evening or rehearsing small sketches to be performed on Parents' Day. Frau Sonntag's most recent invitation had come as a surprise.

"Have a seat, Marie. I have poured us some tea." She handed me a delicate porcelain cup and saucer.

"Thank you, Frau Sonntag."

Frau Sonntag looked at me with her warm chestnut-brown eyes.

"You're probably curious why you are here. It is a *personal* matter. I beg your forgiveness for that. Now don't you worry, you have nothing to fear. Knowing that your own mother is so far away, I felt I should take the liberty of playing mother just this once."

"Marie," she asked. "Are you happy at our school?"

"Yes," I shot back, my face assuming a puzzled look.

"I am certainly happy to have you in my German class," Frau Sonntag said quickly. "You are a fine student and write beautiful essays." I took a sip from my cup. "Next question. Is Sophie happy here?"

I looked at her in surprise.

"I know I should ask her directly," Frau Sonntag said, "but right now I'd like to hear what *you* think."

"I think Sophie's happy here," I answered, wrinkling my forehead.

"Did I hear a slight hesitation?"

"No, no," I said quickly—too quickly. I was alarmed.

Frau Sonntag offered me a plate filled with cookies, which I waved off. "Well, let me tell you how it looks from my perspective," continued Frau Sonntag. "You two are very close—you sit next to each other, walk in the park together, don't mingle much with your classmates, though you're not antisocial. In the afternoon, you get on the same train to the same home." Frau Sonntag cleared her throat.

"You've been here four years. It would be nice if you got to know a few girls more closely and enlarged your circle of friends." Frau Sonntag's face lit up with a smile. "There is nothing wrong with anything I've brought up so far, but there are consequences to such a close, I'd almost say *intimate* relationship." I bit my lips and felt myself blush. Frau Sonntag placed her hand on mine.

"Sometimes, when I put a question to the class and before I've called on any particular girl, I have observed, along with other teachers, that you might discuss the question with Sophie. Sometimes though not always, Sophie will then raise her hand and enthusiastically give that answer out loud." I had to smile against my will. Frau Sonntag did, too. "Sophie is an endearingly enthusiastic soul," she said.

"My fellow teachers and I also noticed that Sophie's strongest subjects are art—her watercolors and drawings are exquisite, and so is her knitting and crocheting. She has gifted hands, which raises the question if Sophie might not benefit from a school like the *Hans Holbein Gymnasium* in Manheim that furthers artistic students. While we cherish the arts at our school, our focus is really on *academic* subjects."

Frau Sonntag picked up the teapot and refreshed my cup.

I didn't know where to look. My heart was pounding. *Which raises the question if Sophie might not benefit from the Herbert Holbein Gymnasium in Manheim that furthers artistic students.* "They want to separate me from Sophie," I thought, my stomach rising against my chest. "I can't let that happen."

"Now, please give our conversation some thought," continued Frau Sonntag. "I felt it would be good to share some of my colleagues' and my own thinking with you before I speak with your father. You may discuss our conversation with Sophie if you like. You probably will in any case since you two are so close."

"Could you speak with Sophie *before* speaking with Vati?"

"Would you like me to?"

"Yes."

"I will then. In that case, I have a very big request. If you can, please don't discuss our meeting with her."

I stared at the fireplace, the delicate teapot, and finally at Frau Sonntag. "I'll try."

A good thing that Sophie was captain of the softball team that week, I thought on my way back to the classroom. She'll be too excited and exhausted to worry about my meeting with Frau Sonntag. I picked up my books and watched the end of the game in the yard.

A few days later, when we were finally alone at night, Sophie slipped under the covers next to me. "Boy, am I beat, but I have to tell you something extraordinary. Brace yourself," Sophie announced.

"*Raus damit!* Out with it!"

"While you were translating *De Bello Gallico* for Vati, Mutti took me aside in the kitchen. She hemmed and hawed a lot but finally fessed up that we're having money troubles, *bad* money troubles."

"Ever since we've left Falkenburg Castle, we've had money troubles," I said. "It's so distressing."

"Mutti says if Vati's mother, your grandma up north, won't help us out, they'll take our furniture, the car, anything that can be moved."

"Who's *they*?"

"The Internal Revenue Office." Mutti hemmed and hawed some

more. Finally, she said, "This private school of yours costs a lot of money. An awful lot. Marie seems to flourish there while Ingrid and you have had a harder time." Then she wiped a tear from her eye. "If you attended a public school like the *Hans Holbein Gymnasium* in Mannheim, which has a good reputation, but doesn't cost a penny, I think we could get out of debt."

I couldn't believe my ears. Was the whole world in on the plot to pry us apart? I pinched Sophie's arm so hard that she shoved my hand away. "You crazy?"

"No, it's just that when I was talking to Frau Sonntag last week..."

Sophie brushed me off. "Let me finish. I felt like I'd been hit over the head at first, but you know, since the first shock I've actually felt better. I'd hate for us to be in different schools, but if we could get out of debt that would be such a relief. And it's true what Mutti said about Ingrid and me. I like our school, but it doesn't fire me up like it does you. Each year is tougher than the last. I *have* heard they have great art teachers at that school in Mannheim."

"No," I interrupted. "We just need to set aside more time for revisions. We can do it. You and I can do it!"

Sophie shook her head. "I know what I know. Besides, we'd still have the afternoons, evenings, and weekends together. I'd like to give it a shot."

I said nothing. Finally, I pulled Sophie against my chest, "Oh, my valiant Prince Ironheart!" I kissed Sophie with playful passion as if I could bring back the times when we had "played Hollywood movies."

A month later, Sophie and I walked to the same station in the morning, but each boarded a different train. Sophie's was heading north to Manheim and mine south to Heidelberg. If we both managed to get the right window seat, we each followed the train departing in the opposite direction with our eyes for as long as we could.

On weekends, as we hunkered down in the plush seats of a darkened Heidelberg movie theatre—watching Sir Lancelot rescuing Queen Guinevere and Robin Hood fighting for the rights of the downtrodden while wooing Maid Marian—we picked out the scenes we wanted to enact later that night and squeezed each other's hand in anticipation.

In the meantime, Vati and Tante B. did indeed visit Sophie's grand-mother during a professional trip north and a few weeks later an invitation arrived for Sophie to spend the summer in Cologne with her grand-mother and aunt, and, if she liked it, perhaps even stay until Christmas.

Ingrid, Bastian, and Mama, in the meantime, had been bombard-ing me with invitations to visit. I was flattered, but not fired up. Ingrid persisted, "Why don't you come here while Sophie is in Cologne?" she wrote. "I'll take you for rides in Bastian's car and we'll see movies in the drive-in. I miss you!"

Tante B. encouraged Sophie, "The time for amends has come. It'll do you good to spend the summer with your father's people, Sophie."

"What shall I do?" Sophie asked me.

"Go, kiddo, go."

"And you?" I couldn't see myself hanging about all alone.

"I'll go to Canada," I said spontaneously. I wanted to empower Sophie, not realizing that I'd be split into two disparate souls from that moment on. One part of me was glad to see Sophie connect with her family, though that implied a long separation. The other feared that new reality. I felt like the sorcerer's apprentice who had invoked demonic forces he could no longer control.

Now Sophie became excited about Canada, too. Vati was already fired up. As usual, Tante B. joined the chorus. That short phrase *I'll go to Canada* had caught me in a sling.

"What a great opportunity to perfect your English," Vati rhapso-dized, "and get to see your mother, sister, and brother in the bargain. There is no better time to see the world than when you are young. We'll talk to Frau Sonntag to see if we can get a leave of absence for you."

Frau Sonntag, who believed in her heart of hearts that children should be close to their mothers, granted the leave and before I knew it, we were caught up in paperwork for my entry to Canada and were checking out transatlantic flights. My exodus had begun.

Sophie, on the other hand, didn't even need a reservation for her rail trip to Cologne. We would begin our life-changing journeys in early summer and return six months later, after the turn of the year. *Six months!*

Eager to hand over a well-groomed *young lady* to Mama, Vati and Tante B. bought me new sweaters and skirts, and had my hair styled in a hair salon and its color brightened. Tante B. was going so far as to pluck my eyebrows, penciling them darker, and persuading me to wear a lace garter and nylons with my new high heels. I felt like I did as a child when Mama forced those over-the-top hair ribbons on me.

"Could you quickly come to the post office with me?" Vati asked newly-refurbished me. "I haven't been able to find a parking spot lately with all this construction. I'll hover nearby while you run inside."

"*Ja, natuerlich.*" Yes, of course.

When Vati found a holding spot, I took the letter and hopped out of the car while Vati rolled down the window for a cigarette.

I'd barely taken a few steps when a shower of whistles rained down from the nearest scaffolding.

"*Huebsche Beine hat die Kleine!*" Nice pair of legs on that cutie.

"*Und 'n Busen zum Schmusen,*" and a bosom for schmoozing, shouted another.

More whistles.

I looked around to see who had attracted the construction workers' attention; the only people on the street were a man with a cane and a hefty middle-aged matron.

"*Aaaaw,*" boomed a voice, *Sie sucht was.* She's looking for something.

I stopped dead. They are whistling at *me.* Why? What's there to whistle at? I dashed forward and nearly collided with a young man leaving the post office. He took his hat off and bowed to me. "Allow me, my dear Fraeulein. It's an awfully heavy door." He held the door for me while I rushed past him in full flight.

Vati was standing next to the car when I returned. The moment he spotted me, he threw his cigarette on the ground and rubbed it out with his heel. Again, the men whistled, but no one called out little ditties. Vati was scowling. "Hop in and let's get out of here. Disgusting bunch, these men!"

"Were they whistling at *me*?" I asked.

"Yes, Marie. Be prepared to expect more of this. You are turning into a young lady."

"If this is part of being a young lady, I'd rather not be one!"

Vati laughed, "That's my girl. But we cannot change the nature of primitive men. They love attractive young girls."

I stared at Vati in disbelief. Did he really think I was attractive? Mama was attractive. Ingrid was attractive. Bastian, too. I'd merely been the family runt all my life. True, I'd filled out some since Falken-burg and Garmisch, but basically, I was me—Marie.

"Just remember what I've been preaching all those years. Most men are after one thing only. Be wary of compliments and praise. Remember the ulterior motive."

"Yes," I said, for the first time not smiling at Vati's "hang-up," but inwardly siding with him.

At home I caught Tante B. staring out of the window again for what seemed like an eternity. I touched her back lightly. "Are you missing Sophie, Tante B.?" She turned and looked at me with her large, protruding eyes. "Yes, I do, but I'm glad to have you around for now. It'll be so lonely after you leave."

"I'll write as often as I can. And remember, *you* can visit Sophie in Cologne now and then, which is something I won't be able to do." At that, my heart contracted. *Maybe I'll miss Sophie so much that I'll rush back to Germany before my six months are up,* I wondered. We'd never been separated for more than a couple of days.

Tante B. was stroking my cheek. "You have to give Ingrid the longest hug from me. Promise?"

"Promise."

"You two will have a great time."

I heaved a sigh. "I hope so."

"'Course you will."

BOOK V

Alaska Highway

28

ALASKA HIGHWAY

Standing in the departure hall of Frankfurt airport, both Vati and Tante B. looked anxious and pale. "I'm not emigrating like Mama and Ingrid. I'll be back in the new year," I told them, even though they knew that. They were so quiet. If they had said "stay," I would have thrown my arms around them and made a run for the car, but neither of them did.

The moment I set foot on the plane, I was greeted with unaccustomed deference, "*Good afternoon, Mademoiselle. Welcome aboard,*" and ushered to my seat with gracious smiles, making me feel quite grown-up. "*Drinks will be served right after take-off, Madame.*" I registered the promotion from *Mademoiselle* to *Madame* with smug satisfaction.

The plane rolled onto the runway and raced forward at top speed, the deep drone of the engines ratcheting to a howl. They'll burst! I grabbed my armrests and held on. When I felt the lift, saw the busy autobahn below floating away from me, clouds turning into mere shreds of mist, the foothills of the *Taunus* flattening, I felt at one with the plane. We were up, diving into space, flying away from everything petty and small. I felt released from the heaviness of everyday life.

Though I could not spread my arms as I used to on the ramparts of Falkenburg Castle—my seat neighbor was only inches away—I soared and kept soaring in my mind. After a few hours, the captain announced the scheduled landing in Greenland where we had to refuel.

We went through the same stages as during takeoff, only in reverse. Again, the engines howled as if they wanted to burst, and I clung to the armrests while eye to eye with earth. A few more seconds and we'll bang foreheads. My muscles tensed.

Just then I felt the wheels touching and grabbing ground, marveling at the skill of the pilot who had avoided a crash. The passengers clapped. The doors opened, and ice cold air rushed in. My fellow passengers and I were shooed to a snack bar hut, a dark island in a sea of white.

Though I was bundled up in my coat, my eyes and senses were fresh and open, drinking in the glittering snow, white arctic foxes flitting along the runway, and dark blobs of ice that looked like pools. The brisk air starched my lungs and seared my skin.

After the respite, I rushed up the steps to the plane, quickly fastened my seatbelt, and couldn't wait for liftoff—to be up in the air, once again soaring.

In Edmonton, where my eyes were able to feast on green again, I changed to a smaller aircraft for the flight to Fort St. John, my destination. The plane flew above Banff, Bastian's and Mama's original home in Canada. And, to my chagrin, that's where Bastian was working as a builder right now. It was a big promotion for him, one he couldn't refuse, but I wouldn't see my beloved brother until Christmas.

Slowly, the plane came to a stop in Fort St. John. I spotted Mama as soon as I stepped onto the tarmac. Her bright clothes, sparkling eyes, and jewelry outshone everyone, her bosom heaving, her face triumphant.

I rushed toward her, but when I saw the fiery eyes that had so often cut into me, the rouged mouth that disappeared into a thin line before she let loose the terrors of her heart, I froze. Undeterred, Mama pressed me against her chest. "At last," she breathed, "finally, you've left that manure pile of a village, your father, and all."

Of course, I hadn't left Vati, I was *visiting*, as she knew full well.

"Where's Ingrid?"

"At home." Mama's expression turned rigid. "She forgot to clean the refrigerator yesterday. So I told her to get it done right after school today."

My heart sank—was it too late to run back to the plane? "Mama, I've come to visit you, Bastian, and Ingrid, not things like a *refrigerator*. And wait 'til you see your presents." My flight bag was bulging with bottles of Tosca, Mama's signature perfume, and pounds of Belgian chocolate. Mama's face seemed to soften as I helped her heave my luggage into the trunk of the car. We were off.

I was on the lookout for Indians and Eskimos in my new town, but so far saw only pale faces. Still, the flat-roofed wooden boxes looked exactly like the houses in the Hollywood Westerns Sophie and I used to binge on. Mama turned off the paved road. Now the car was bumping along potholes and dirt, stirring up dust. I saw no trees, no town squares or stone houses—only more, ever smaller wooden ones.

"Where is the town?"

"That *was* the town," said Mama, "the stretch along the paved road. All the other streets are unpaved. God, how I hate this eternal dust!"

Mama worked as a cook. She would have never accepted a job like that in Germany, but here, where there were few class differences, and very few people with Mama's culinary talent, she was being well paid preparing meals for the richest business owner in town.

"Can you believe that I earn twice as much as I did at the PX? I've saved enough to buy a small house. Not outright, but I made a hefty down payment and got a good mortgage. It's such a different life here. If I hear of a better job in a different town, I'll put the house on the market, sell it in a snap, and go where the money is."

"And Ingrid?"

"She'll come along." Mama took a deep breath. "Our house is nothing fancy, mind you, but it is *mine*." Her lips receded into that thin line, her neck stiffened. "No one can take it from me." Mama pounded her chest. "But then your apartment in Merkdorf isn't anything to crow about, at least not when compared to Falkenburg Castle or the house we had built in Garmisch. But what can you expect with your father..." Mama stopped herself.

"What about Vati?"

"Well, with him having to go to a sanatorium and everything crashing down."

Mama was pulling into the driveway toward what looked like a miniature wooden house or fancy shed to me. Ingrid darted out of the house. I pushed the car door open and flew into my sister's arms. Ingrid's blond hair was tied into a swinging ponytail revealing an open, pretty face. She was quite a bit taller than I and striking in her bright red dress with its flowing skirt.

Ingrid carried my suitcase while Mama nudged me through the front door into the living room. There was no hallway. The table in the center of the room was so beautifully set with bright flowers, candles, and our grandmother's linen and silver that it sparkled like a jewelry box—odd being greeted in this dusty frontier town by the remnants of a more elegant past.

"You'll love it here, kid," Ingrid told me. "School is fun! Grades don't matter. There are so many cute boys!" After a pause she added, "Mind you, I'm a *good* student here."

The next morning, I dressed in my new dark gray skirt, a dark blue blouse, and my high heels.

"We have quite a walk," Ingrid told me. "Better wear your loafers."

"What loafers?" I asked while fishing for sturdier shoes.

"Never mind," said Ingrid, pointing to the shoes in my hand. "'Course you wouldn't have them in Germany. Yes, those will do."

We marched past dozens and dozens of small wooden houses, crossed a small park, and ended up in the *paved* part of town. Ingrid pointed out the town hall, a post office, a police station, a drugstore, and two churches.

"That's pretty much the town," she said. "Except for the big grocery store, the drive-in, football stadium, and hockey arena. They're spread out along the periphery, surrounded by huge parking lots. Everything around here happens in *those* places. And our school is just five minutes down the road, also surrounded by parking lots."

Ingrid introduced me to Mr. House, my homeroom teacher. I liked his square, handsome face, solid build, and friendly eyes. "Welcome, Marie," said Mr. House while Ingrid moved on, "our school and our country must still feel strange to you. But after a little while, you'll get used to us, I assure you. We welcome immigrants from all over the world, and I'm always amazed how quickly they settle in. Don't worry about a thing and please come to me if you have questions or concerns."

Off to a good start, I thought before I heard some girl behind me whisper, "Did you see her clunky shoes? Like a Russian babushka." Was the girl referring to me? I looked around. All the girls were wearing loafers or saddle shoes.

During break, someone nearby said, "And those dreary colors!

Haven't they heard of pastel in Europe?"

I blushed. Yes, I clearly stood out among the local girls who wore nothing but pastel sweater sets, saddle shoes, and skirts puffed by petticoats. Older girls wore makeup. Vati would have been called in for a teacher-parent conference if I had shown up with red lips and rouged cheeks at my venerable school in Heidelberg.

The height of frivolity, in my eyes, was the fact that girls clutched handbags all day long, but kept their books in a locker. What an up-side-down world! Wasn't school about books and learning, and not about lipstick and powdered noses?

"So, you ever meet Hitler?" a gum-chewing girl asked me on my third day in school. I cringed at the cursed name.

"I'm the same age as you are," I said coolly, hoping my answer would put an end to this exchange.

"Well, did ya or didn't ya?" the girl insisted.

"He died in 1945."

"Oh." The girl popped her gum, swung around in her petticoat, and pranced off. I had not made a friend.

"People here aren't big on European history," Ingrid explained. "They're not big on dates. If anything, they are totally focused on Britain and British history—they know *nothing* about the rest of Europe."

My next shock was the curriculum. German and Latin weren't offered; chemistry and physics only for three years, so much time wasted on homeroom, home economics, and typing.

"The place feels like a mixture between a fashion institute and a secretarial school," I harrumphed.

Ingrid looked at me with cool eyes. Her brow shot up. "That's just because you're such a...such a *blue stocking!*"

I heard Ingrid's mocking tone but accepted the term like a badge of honor. If nothing else, the Canada adventure taught me once and for all that learning was key to my sense of self. Vati's encouragement, the rigor of the Elisabeth-von-Thadden-School, and Falkenburg Castle's sculptures, tapestries, and manuscripts had shaped me for good.

Mama appeared to be in better control of herself than in Germany. After all, she was a success in the eyes of the new world and her own.

Bastian had helped her adjust and prosper as well, but she made the most of her changed circumstances.

She had bought a house, a car, a television, and was supporting Ingrid. She no longer had to wait for Vati or anyone else to come home for dinner, and she didn't have to share her bed with a cranky older man as she had been forced to do in her first marriage.

Meanwhile, Ingrid and I spent quite a few Saturday afternoons in the bleachers of the football stadium. My sister and her best friends waved pompons every time someone from "our" team scored and jumped up and down, cheering and screaming.

I had never seen an American football game nor attended a hockey game in my life and felt like a total idiot jumping up and down and screaming my heart out. When I told my sister during an intermission that I was leaving and got up from my seat, she yanked me down with such force I knew I'd have black and blue marks.

"You can't," she hissed. "Sit and cheer!"

Though a couple of boys asked me for a date, I couldn't make myself accept because of Vati's sermons and the necking I'd observed in the cars around us when Ingrid had taken me to the drive-in. Instead, I wanted to learn as much about the world and myself as possible. This turned me into a lonely trooper. I missed Sophie with every fiber of my being and turned her into my pen pal confidante.

Dearest Sophie,

Fort St. John feels like the Wild West except that it's northern oil country. The main road turns into a dirt road after a few blocks. On hot days, they pour oil on the surface to keep the dust down. People live in small wooden houses or these metal boxes they call 'trailers.' Each house, every metal box has prongs sticking out of the roof, antennas for their televisions. Life centers around their TV, Sophie. People are either at work, in their cars, or in front of their screens. They don't even turn the darned boxes off when they have visitors.

You sit on plastic chairs in restaurants. The flowers on the tables are made of plastic, so too the tabletops. I miss our plush Café furniture and the newspapers from Vienna, Paris, and Hamburg. And get this, the moment you take a seat in a restaurant, you are served a glass of water filled with ice cubes. Even when it's cold outside!

The countryside is endless, a thrilling experience. Once you hit the open road, you'll find no secondary ones, no fences, no church spires, no signs of human habitation. If I had a car, I'd just keep driving, hypnotized by the ocean of trees, the lines of the far horizons which rise, dissolve, and rise again, drawing you in as if you could drive to infinity!

Forests here are scruffy, full of underbrush, no paths for walking, and no benches. The Peace River is wild but shallow. It doesn't look navigable. I always thought our Neckar was rather puny compared to the Danube or the Rhine, but it is deep and dark compared to the Peace River.

The stars are incredibly bright at night. After the hot, dusty days, I like the nights best. Bastian wants me to go hunting with him when he comes for a visit later this year. I'm glad he's coming, because I would not dare to explore the forest on my own, I'd get lost, which is—believe me—no laughing matter, because there are wolves and bears here.

Ingrid has grown even taller and is one of the most popular girls in school. Her main interest is boys, which makes talking to her quite predictable. "What do think of Val, Marie? Doesn't he look like Montgomery Clift? And he's allowed to drive his father's Bel Air!"

The boys in school are very friendly; they talk about girls, cars, and sports, anything but politics, philosophy, books, and art.

I miss you, Tante B., and Vati terribly and would give anything if you could be with me. Please tell me everything, I mean everything, about life in Cologne. I'm sure it's smashing. Here, it's primitive.

Much love, Marie

Sophie's first letter from Cologne took weeks to arrive because her grandmother sent it by boat, creating a painful gap in our communication, but Sophie made sure to buy aerograms after that. I so missed her spontaneity and warmth. Canadian life felt strange, superficial, and uncivilized to me. I couldn't share my feelings with Mama and Ingrid because they seemed to be thriving in what felt like *wilderness* to me.

My life is weird, Marie, she wrote back, *everyone is taking delight in how I look. I almost feel like a display model. 'Look at the golden flecks in her eyes,' Aunt Karoline shouted right after she gave me a welcome hug. 'Just like Bernhard's!'*

My grandmother thinks I have the same eyebrows and high cheek bones as my father, and her sister, my great aunt, insists that she could have sworn it was Bernhard sitting across from her as we gathered around the coffee table. I no longer know if I'm Sophie or Bernhard, but it doesn't matter cause they're spoiling me rotten. I know I have the best mother and I adore your Vati, but it feels incredibly flattering to be so totally accepted for simply being who I am.

I put the letter down. Had I ever been accepted that way? Definitely not by Mama—and not by Ingrid, I felt. But, thank God, by Vati, by Anna, and by Frau Sonntag—and by Sophie, always, always by Sophie. If only Sophie could have come with me to Canada!

I think I could poop on the carpet and still be adored! Sophie wrote. I burst into laughter. *Anyhow,* she continued, *grandmother has already embarked on a campaign to have me stay throughout the school year, but I want to be back in Heidelberg as soon as you have returned.*

Dear Sophie! Though she was in a strange city among new people, at least she remained inside the home of our language. Meanwhile I had to cut a path through the jungle of English. Four years of formal British school English hadn't fully prepared me for the Canadian vernacular. I yearned for the sounds of my native tongue almost as much as I did for Vati and Sophie. Right after my arrival, English sentences kept speeding by me like clouds in a storm. But soon I spoke as fast as my classmates and everyone around me. Over time, I learned to love the wonderfully vibrant, malleable, and rich English language—rich in vocabulary, metaphors, and onomatopoeia—although surprisingly *simple* in its *grammar.*

During the second month of school, I woke up in terrible pain. The small bedroom swayed. My body contracted with such violence that I curled in upon myself—without finding relief. Since age eleven, I had to go through this menstrual torture every four weeks that reduced me to nothing but a throbbing clump of flesh. No thought, effort, or willpower could stop the ordeal.

I hated my helpless misery and couldn't understand why I had to suffer a pain that felt as strong as I imagined labor pain to be, whereas most girls, including Ingrid and Sophie, felt only minor discomfort.

Ingrid caught on immediately. "I'll go and tell Mom to call school, so that you can stay home. I'll make you tea."

"No tea yet." After hours and hours of contractions, a feeling of nausea finally signaled the end of my ordeal. After getting sick to my stomach, I could finally fall into an exhausted sleep.

"I'm so sorry." Ingrid patted my shoulder. "I hope it'll be over soon."

Wave after wave of contractions rolled over me, squeezing and wrecking my disowned body. Finally, I staggered to the bathroom, holding on to the wall.

When I returned, Mama stood next to my bed with a hot cup of tea.

"Why don't you stay here in Canada, Marie?" Mama's voice was soft, her eyes full of pity.

"I'd like to, Mama, but I'm homesick for Germany. I miss Vati and Sophie"—I almost said "and Tante B.," but stopped myself in time— "And I want to live in my own language!"

"I know, dear. I miss Germany, too, but less so now. It'll get better with time. I promise."

"I can't find like-minded friends. Nobody's interested in books, politics, even classical music."

Mama frowned. "Oh, come on, it's not that bad." She was annoyed but was trying not to show it, most unusual for her. She smoothed out her frown and was smiling again.

"Ingrid and I want you to stay here, and your brother can't wait to see you on Christmas," Mama continued. Now she had hit a soft spot. I also couldn't wait to see my goodhearted brother.

"And some of the boys have asked you out on a date, which is a compliment to you." Mama had never sweet-talked me before. What was up? I needed to shake her up.

"Only a desperate girl would want to date such boring boys," I countered and hoped she'd now abandon her "keep Marie in Canada" campaign. Mama's cheek muscles quivered, her eyes hardened.

"Well," she said, "well, let me ask you this then: why would you want to return to a father like yours?"

I couldn't believe my ears. The old warfare.

"What do you mean?" I asked coolly. "Vati's a good father, the best."

"He's rash and selfish."

"He's not." I sat up, clutching my stomach.

"And worse."

"How so?"

"He's a criminal."

"That's ridiculous."

Mama's eyes bored into me. "He's done things. Terrible things." Her bosom was heaving. "I've been trying to protect you and your sister for so long, but you are pushing me!"

"What terrible things? Tell me."

"All right." Mama straightened her back. "You asked for it." Her eyes filled with glee. "He committed murder!"

"He did not!"

"He did, too! Assisted suicide. And had to stand trial and serve a two-year prison term. That's why he is no longer a doctor." Mama smacked her lips. "We told you he was in a sanatorium. You were so young."

I froze. My stomach cramped again. Vati in prison? That would explain our abrupt move to Garmisch, our stay at the St. John's Children's Home, the taunting teachers and classmates, the loss of our house! She must be right. But she also loved to badmouth Vati.

I pulled the bedcover over my face because I could not bear to be seen by Mama nor look into her cruel, self-righteous eyes. In the stifled darkness, I sobbed and sobbed, trying to push reality away.

"We'll talk tomorrow when you feel better," Mama said and left the room. In the silence, her revelation crashed over me again. Vati imprisoned. The loss of our house in Garmisch. Bastian's forced return to his ancient father. And we—Ingrid and I—thrown into the "prison" of the Children's Home. Despised, beaten, and tormented, because the sisters, our teachers, and everyone in the town of Kempten, every single person who saw us being shepherded to school, knew that we had criminal parents—or at least one parent who had broken the law.

It must be true. Infuriatingly true. Mama *was* telling the truth. I had lived it without knowing why. But that did not mean she was right in a moral sense. Whatever had happened when Vati helped someone to die, I wanted to hear it from him. I knew both viscerally and intellectually that my father would never kill. All his energy had been dedicated to alleviating his patients' pain and healing them, whenever possible.

A furious anger flared up inside me. Anger at my mother's glee, her total disregard for my feelings or Vati's miserable fate. Though I understood that she wanted her disclosure to alienate me from Vati, she was achieving the opposite. Now, more than ever, I had to get away from her, my petticoat school, and this crummy place of shacks, dust, and oil that called itself a town.

When Ingrid finally tiptoed in at night, I sat up in my bed, my back straight, my jaw set.

"Why didn't you tell me, Ingrid? Why? Why would you let me hear it from Mama?"

Ingrid looked into my eyes. "You mean about Vati?"

"What else?"

"May I sit down?"

"Suit yourself."

"I didn't learn about it until Mama told me after my arrival."

"It was not murder, right?"

"'Course not. He helped a very ill man die who suffered excruciating pain. In the eyes of the law that is murder."

"So why didn't you tell me when I arrived?"

"Mama asked me not to. She said Vati wanted to tell you himself."

"And you trusted her?" Ingrid hung her head. "What else is there? What else are you and Mama hiding?"

"Nothing, Marie. I swear."

"You sure?"

"I'm sure."

I grumbled something about "having to get out of here."

Ingrid took my hand. "You will." She sniffled. "Please forgive me. I should have told you sooner." Ingrid heaved a sigh. "I've been so overwhelmed lately." My big sister sounded helpless. Not like her. I felt her distress. "What's the matter?"

"I'm falling in love with Val, and I don't know what to do."

"Does he care for you?"

"He says he loves me."

"Well? Then everything's all right."

Ingrid let out a moan. "Oh, you don't understand. He's pressuring me to go beyond kissing."

"You mean he wants to have sex with you?"

"Do you have to be so crude?"

"Oh, Ingrid! Vati talked our ears off that we cannot and should not trust young men. All they want is..."

Ingrid laughed, and I burst into laughter, too, despite it all, and took Ingrid's hand. "It's up to you, Ingrid. If he really cares for you, he'll listen. Tell him not until after graduation. That buys you time and you can see if he respects what you say."

Ingrid moved a strand of hair from her forehead. "Sometimes you're a real human being."

And sometimes you are my "kid" sister, I thought but didn't say so out loud.

The world had not changed the next morning no matter how much I wanted it to be a different world. Now I knew, but what did I really know? Vati had been convicted of a compassionate deed which the law considered a crime and had been imprisoned. But Vati wasn't a criminal. He was always soothing his anxious patients and doing everything in his power to cure them. He fought against death. I was sure he helped the man because he was in extremis and there was no hope.

I closed my eyes. Squeezed them shut. I had to find a way to get away from Mama and this cruel, cold, God-forsaken place.

The next morning, I made it a point to join Mama for breakfast and told her calmly and firmly, "I need to go home."

"I know how you feel, dear, but I have no money for your return ticket." By mutual consent, Vati had only bought a one-way ticket. Mama was to provide the return ticket, as she told me with a triumphant grin.

My heart convulsed. What next? Was there no end to it? Won't someone, anyone show some pity? How could Vati have agreed to this? I felt as low as I had when I played Russian Roulette by running into onrushing cars in Garmisch as a child. Except I was older now. And angrier. Angrier at the world, at Mama, even at Vati, at everything. I mustn't let Mama overpower me. I must, I would find a way back home.

Out loud, I said, "I'll quit school, find a job, and *earn* the money for my return."

"You do that."

Vati would have never let me drop out of school, I was sure of it, but Mama didn't see education as the foundation for a well-lived life. I could read her mind from the way she looked at me and knew that she believed I would fail. I was the dreamer in the family who loved books, movies, and fantasy games. I was not practical. She was sure I'd break down and give up.

But what Mama didn't understand was that I now had a mission: whatever it took, I was determined to return to my loved ones, my language, *and the civilized world.*

There was something else. In her latest letter Sophie wrote that not all was well between Vati and Tante B. Her mother had poured her heart out to Sophie during a visit to Cologne. Tante B. didn't feel as appreciated by Vati as she'd like to feel. She worried that he still carried a torch for Mama.

I think her anxiety also comes from the empty nest. Both she and your dad have always been focused on us, Vati preaching to us and provoking us to think for ourselves and Mutti cooking, baking, and homemaking, and now there is a void.

Wise Sophie.

During Mutti's litany of woes she also mentioned that she'd been hurt by your sometimes-distanced manner since your mother's "Blitzbesuch." Blood rushed to my cheeks. I felt terribly ashamed. It was true that there were times when I had been worried that Tante B.

might harm me, especially after Mama's warning that she may want to poison me. But now, shaken by Mama's accusations and glee, I couldn't believe that I had fallen for Mama's machinations.

When I got home from school, I sat down at the kitchen table and wrote Tante B. a letter.

Dearest Tante B.,

If only you knew how much I miss you, Vati, and Sophie! I can't wait to come back to Heidelberg and resume our family discussions around the coffee table—you knitting with an amused smile on your face, Vati and I sparring, supported or challenged by Sophie, but all of us glad to be with each other.

They say absence makes the heart grow fonder, and that is true, though I have always known that you are the kindest woman I have ever met. You have made such a difference in my life. Ingrid and I were pretty weary girls, constantly dreading outbreaks and beatings when you and Vati took us under your wings. You gave us peace.

I know there was a time after Mama's Blitzvisit when I turned away from you. Mama planted an evil seed in my mind, suggesting that you might want to poison me because you wanted Vati for yourself. She made this horrible accusation with the most pleading eyes, with assurances of her love, and a heartbreaking appeal to my pity. I didn't really believe her yet I was caught. It was a bad time and I have no good excuse except that I was young and vulnerable. But deep down, I did not believe her, deep down I was ashamed of myself. As I am to this day. Please forgive me.

I love you, Tante B., and thank you for the love, care, and patience you have shown us. You are a Godsend. I can't wait to come back to you, Vati, and Sophie in the new year!

With much love,
Marie

I sealed the letter and prayed that it would pour balm on Tante B.'s wounds. "I *do* love her," I whispered to myself. Not as unconditionally as Vati, nor as tenderly as Sophie, but with a grateful love.

Though I knew I was doing the right thing and felt calmer than before writing the letter, I hurried to the post office before Mama or anyone else could stop me from sending my letter on its way.

I also knew that no ten horses could prevent me from finding my way back to Germany.

When Mama told us "Basti will join us for Christmas," Ingrid and I jumped for joy like the time he miraculously appeared at our new house in Garmisch after his ancient father in Berchtesgaden finally let him join us so many years ago. Basti's presence made us stronger since he was so much older, wiser, and robust.

Ingrid and I knew we'd be laughing more when Basti was around. We would conspire. Not in anything mean, but in activities that excluded Mama. That alone made us feel lighthearted.

The moment tall, lanky Basti, half-hidden under a wide-brimmed cowboy hat, bounced down the steps from the prop jet and threw his strong arms around me, I melted. My brother, my friend. Though Basti—like Ingrid—did not like to ponder the mysteries of the universe or explore the texts of ancient manuscripts, in fact would rather attend a hockey game than lose himself in a poem, he did not grate on me. I responded to his congenial nature, and we were too far apart in age to annoy each other. Ingrid who was much closer to me in age, could irk me, and I knew that I irked her, too.

Basti pulled Mama's car into a small dirt parking lot off the Alaska Highway, set up for local hunters, and I braced myself. I had heard Mama confer with Basti in whispered tones when I came into the kitchen for breakfast, only to fall silent the moment I showed up. Later, she kept nudging him toward the door.

Basti turned off the ignition and offered me a chewing gum.

"Come on, bro, I don't chew." I quickly smiled because I didn't want to offend my brother who always had a packet of gums in his pocket. "Get on with it, brother dear. I saw Mama working on you this morning and know you're 'under orders.'"

Basti grinned. "Okay, okay. You're right. I always knew you were perceptive."

"Thanks to Mama."

"What?"

"Well, you had to read her constantly to know when to run. Over time, reading people's faces became second nature. And listening to the tone of their voice."

Basti burst out laughing. "Well, that's a novel way of looking at our fucked-up childhood. But you are right. I am supposed to help persuade you to stay in Canada, but don't worry. I'm more interested in learning how *you* feel."

"I want to go home. I hate this decrepit town, its worthless school, the silly girls, and the endless football and hockey games." Basti moved closer and offered me a hanky while stroking my hair. Only now did I feel tears running down my cheek.

"And most of all I hate what happened to Vati and the glee—the glee, Basti—in Mama's eyes when she told me about his downfall. She reveled in his misery. I don't want to be anywhere near her. Why does she even want me to stay?"

Basti put his arm around my shoulders. "That is a very good question and I'm not sure I understand it either." He shook his head. "It's in part about winning, I think. Winning against Vati. But there's more. She sees herself as a 'real woman.' And motherhood is part of womanhood." Bastian pulled a pack of cigarettes from his shirt pocket and lit one. Then he stared out into the dense woods around us. "In her own warped way, she does have maternal instincts...like a wolf." Bastian's face lit up as if he had just stumbled on a new insight.

"I'm convinced she would have defended us to the death when we were small...like a wolf mother." I nodded excitedly because I felt that strong instinct in our mother, too.

"What I can't understand," I said, "is why someone with any kind of maternal instinct is then beating the shit out of her children and making their life miserable."

Basti kept shaking his head in bewilderment. "I don't know. Maybe it has to do with hormones malfunctioning or something like that. I really don't know, Marie." His large gray eyes looked at me like Mama's when she was sad and yet our gentle brother was nothing like her. Strange how our family traits played out in us.

Basti lit another cigarette. He sat up straight. "I won't persuade you to stay and have known almost from the first that you are much more like Vati than Ingrid and I. Not in every way, but in your need for learning, your enjoyment in learning, your constant searching."

I must have looked at him with surprise. Basti smiled. "I'm gonna tell you about an incident that made a deep impression on me when I was about 13 and you four years old."

Now I am curious. "Four?" I asked.

"Yup. That's why I've never forgotten. Vati was quizzing me in the library in preparation for a Latin vocabulary test at school. We were seated at the round table in the corner covered with a long tablecloth."

I well remembered that table and could see it in my mind.

"Farmer," Vati asked.

"Agricola," I shot back. Vati was pleased.

"Soldier," he asked.

"Miles." Vati nodded with satisfaction and moved on.

"The farmer plows," he asked.

"Agricola," I began and could not come up with the Latin verb for 'to plow.'

"Well?" asked Vati and grabbed the pack of cigarettes on the table. While he fished out a fag, a hushed voice from under the table whispered 'arat.'

"Vati's face remained clueless and I quickly answered in a firm voice 'Agricola arat.' Vati's face lit up. He picked up the textbook again and asked a few more questions. I answered every single one. Whenever I hesitated, the small voice from under the table helped me out. Vati was clearly impressed, and I grew taller in my chair. Finally, Vati put the book aside and mumbled something like 'the end.' I didn't translate because I saw we were done, but the voice under the table didn't and whispered 'finis' into our silence.

"Vati's face lost its smile. His intense blue eyes searched my face. He lifted the tablecloth, bent down toward the floor, and said, 'You better come out, Marie.' Your scrunched-up figure crawled toward us. Finally, you were standing before us in your short, pleated skirt, which didn't cover your bony knees—with an expression of wonder on your face. And in those few seconds, Vati's face lit up with pure joy. His tender awe and pride blew me away. He lifted you up, pressed you against his chest, and slowly put you down again.

"'I see you have been practicing Latin with Basti,' Vati said. 'Well done, Marie. But you cannot prompt him when I'm quizzing him. Understood?'

"And you dutifully said, 'Understood,'" Bastian told me.

I was touched though I had no recollection of that scene.

"It's a sweet story, Basti, but all young children love to learn. It's not a big deal."

Basti shook his head. "Not that early and not that easily." He folded his hands. "That's why I understand that you want to return to your prep school, to Vati, and to our own language. I'll do what I can to help."

Basti had barely left for Banff again, when Fate stepped up and met me halfway. Mama was offered a job in an oil camp in the bush near a town called Fort Nelson, hundreds of miles north of Fort St. John—about 1,300 miles north of Vancouver. There she would cook for twenty men, earning even more money than in her current position.

This was my chance. Mama was so fired up, I knew she'd give in if I wanted to go there, too. I talked to Mr. House, the teacher who'd made me feel so welcome after I arrived, and together we researched the small town of Fort Nelson. With his help, I wrote to the manager of the Fort Nelson Hotel about a waitressing job; I finished the letter at home because I didn't want Mr. House to see that I had listed my age as 18 instead of 15. I wasn't too worried about my fib because I had always looked older than my age, and I felt my deception was justified in light of my desperate plight. The manager hired me sight unseen. Mama was impressed with my initiative, applauded me for making myself older—having been forced to work hard during her own life, she believed in the value of bone-breaking work and gave me the green light.

Since Mama would have to buy food for her oil camp in Fort Nelson, she told me, she'd be able to look in on me. That was fine by me. We found a room for Ingrid in a boarding house for students who lived too far away from Fort St. John to be served by a school bus. Ingrid knew she was being shoved aside to suit Mama's own purpose, but she was not upset because she would stay in the same town as Val.

In fact, she was downright cheerful.

I felt a little hurt by her happy mood, but not terribly so because I was now on my way. A few months of work and I should be able to buy myself a ticket home. Home! I felt like singing. And I'd come to realize that Ingrid and I were on different paths. They seemed to be more or less parallel in Germany but were now moving apart.

If Fort St. John was a dust town, Fort Nelson was the mere shadow of one. It consisted of a thin line of houses and wooden shacks, one filling station, and one store frequented by native people and a handful of white farmers who were trying to make a living in this harsh place. During the fur trading days of the 1800s, Fort Nelson had been a trading post, with the local rivers serving as trading routes.

In the 20th century, Fort Nelson withered away except for a glorious moment during World War II, when it prospered while the US Army built the Alaska Highway from south of Fort St. John all the way to Alaska in mere eight months, in the process creating the town's hotel with fancy columns out front and long barrack-like wings running toward the bush in back. Who would have thought that the same army that rained down bombs on Ansbach when I was born was also busy building a road in this God-forsaken wilderness that would become my home fifteen years later?

The fur trade had come and gone, and WWII had long since ended, but the vast, wild forests, rivers, and lakes around Fort Nelson endured, as had its moose, elk, wolves, and bears. Most people living so far up north, even its native people, didn't survive unscathed. Most of the women lost their teeth in their thirties and looked as if they were fifty. The few Anglo women had harsh expressions, as if they'd never been girls. All cheered the arrival of oil and gas explorers in the 1950s that promised a new life for the dying town.

My realm was an L-shaped dining room with plastic chairs and tables. I served my guests glasses of water with ice cubes and almost always cups of coffee while they studied the menu offering *hamburger, steaks, fries, meatloaf, fish*, and *pies*. Alcohol was served only in the bar across the hall.

Bobby, a skinny waitress in her thirties, showed me how to do my chores. I was terrified since I'd never held a job before, nor had any of my classmates in Germany. No one who attended a college prep school in Germany would ever dream of *working* while they were *students*.

My first customer gave me a big grin when I asked, "May I bring you a cup of coffee, sir, or would you rather have tea?" He looked around.

"Where's she from, Bobby?"

"Never mind where she's from, Jim. It's her first day on the job, so be nice to her."

"Scuse me for asking." He winked at me and ordered steak, mashed potatoes, and vegetables, blueberry pie to follow.

"Thank you, sir, I'll get your order right in." I turned, heading for the kitchen. He let me walk away for a few steps, then called me back.

"Little Miss Hoity-Toity? Aren't you going to ask me how I like my steak?"

"Oh, I'm sorry. How do you like your steak?"

"Raw and juicy, like my women!" he roared and slapped his thigh while I marked the order and took it back to the kitchen, wondering what weird and crazy place I had fallen into. Jim was the open, harmless sort. Other men leered at me, stared with a strange hostility, or even trembled when I spoke to them.

I asked Bobby if they had a fever.

"Fever? A fever? You're priceless, kid. It's you. You're the one giving them the fever," she chuckled. "They've been in the bush for months without women and now they see this fresh young thing. So what do you think happens? They get all worked up."

"But I'm just a girl!"

"You got it! If you were fifty, they wouldn't look at you."

I was offered half of a wooden house on the eastern side of the hotel, reserved for hotel staff. My first home! I was excited about my apartment with its kitchenette and its own TV. At night, when I thought back to Mama's revelation and imagined Vati locked up in prison, I was filled with such sadness that I couldn't sleep.

Finally, I turned on the TV and watched movies from my vast double bed until two in the morning, surprised how quickly I had taken to the medium I had pooh-poohed in my letters to Sophie only a little while ago. One night, when I got home after the evening shift, the television didn't work. Someone will get it straightened out tomorrow, I thought, and headed for bed.

Hearing a noise, I sat up in that murky state between waking and sleep. Footsteps breaking through the frozen snow were headed straight for my house. The manager had told me no one was living in the other half of the place, which he was reserving for his new bookkeeper.

Now I heard whispers. There must be at least two people. My heart started racing. How could I stand up against two men? I looked around for a heavy object, any heavy object, but could see none. Perhaps I should pretend to be asleep? Maybe they were only thieves who would take what they wanted and leave me alone. Then Bobby's words came back to me. "They've been in the bush for weeks and months without women..."

I froze, keeping my eyes glued to the doorknob. I had locked the door, hadn't I? While watching the knob, I glided ever so softly out of bed.

There was a shuffle by the door, then the knob turned. Oh, God. Please let it hold. What should I do? What in God's name can I do? How could Mama leave me all alone in this icy hellhole?

Tears welled up. I saw myself bleeding in the snow, crawling toward the hotel. My heart, that treacherous heart, beat so loud that it would give me away. There was no hiding place.

All the time, while feeling doomed, my mind kept working as if a separate part of me and suddenly I heard myself saying, "Who's out there? Are you the ones I served the T-bone steaks to?"

There was a terrible silence, then renewed shuffling. "We sure are. And how do you get into this place?"

The speed of my reply surprised me. "Easy. My mother locked me in for safety, but she keeps an extra key under the doormat of the door in back. Why don't you get the key from there while I get some beers from the fridge?"

The guys were giggling. Their steps stumbled forward, slowly at first, then they sped up as if in a race. One hollered, "Hey, Hal. Hold your horses. I'll blow your brains out if you shaft me."

Wearing my deerskin slippers, I unlocked the door as gently as I could, terrified I might look into the crazed eyes of one of the men but was met with only darkness and snow. I dove into the night at lightning speed, racing for the back door of the hotel. Just as I reached the door, I heard howls behind me, pushed the door open, and flew up the corridor to the front desk, gasping, "Help me please."

The night clerk and the manager dropped their jaws at the sight of me, but quickly settled me in a chair. I spit, blubbered, and sobbed out my story. The clerk made me a hot chocolate and the manager said firmly, "You'll stay here in the hotel tonight. And it may be a good idea to stay here from now on."

Though the men who tried to get into my place never came back to the hotel, I was relieved to be offered a narrow, drab room in one of the hotel's wings within shouting distance from the front desk. The room had a single, sagging bed, a dresser, and one chair that looked out into the fenced compound of the manager's prize-winning husky, Pasha, a white, blue-eyed male who paced his prison with powerful energy. My shabby room was smaller than Tante B.'s closet in Merkdorf, and the pacing dog squashed any peace and quiet with his restlessness.

By the end of my first week, I hiked up the window frame and stretched out my hand, barely touching the wire mesh of Pasha's compound. He charged at me with a fury like Mama's. "Don't you see that we're two of a kind, Pasha? We're both locked in." I pulled back.

Before leaving my shift the next day, I collected steak gristle and small bones that could be pushed through the wire mesh. I opened the window and rubbed the food against the screen. Pasha charged, then stopped dead, scenting the meat.

"There you go, Pasha," I said in a deep, reassuring voice and squeezed some morsels through the wire. He accepted the first one cautiously, all others with greed. My heart warmed as his bushy tail whipped up a frenzy. When the food was gone, he stood still, looking at me as if seeing me for the first time. I stuck my fingers through the mesh. He came close, opening his awesome jaw and licking, no, massaging my bony fingers with his rough tongue. I leaned back and closed my eyes. The cold air bit into my flesh so fiercely I had to pull back my hand.

At night in my sagging bed, I thought of Vati's sermons about sex. "There is a force in men and women that is ruthless and self-serving and you must look out or you will be hurt. All the flirting and danc-ing and courting between men and women have only one underlying goal: to reproduce." I remembered how I had fought Vati's message, but now saw it played out around me. All men wanted was sex, and local women produced child after child until they were formless and old, as if each child stretched them outwardly but left them hollow within. Or was it the endless white months of icy cold that compelled men and women to become bloated and succumb to drink?

One day, after my shift, I slipped out the back door to catch a breath of fresh air. The back belonged to the wild: stray dogs, wolves, and the odd bear fed off the hotel's garbage. The wolves appeared only at night and remained as shadows. I almost called out in surprise when I spotted a group of thick-furred horses rummaging through spilled garbage. They raised their graceful heads at the sight of me and whinnied, more like a warning, it seemed to me. I slowly walked back inside and asked Bobby about the unusual visitors.

"Yup, we attract horses. The farmers release them at the start of winter to fend for themselves. Beats feeding them. But they return to the farm in spring." I winced when I heard that and wished I could offer them shelter, just as I dreamed of releasing Pasha some fine spring day.

The next day I ventured out to the back again. The horses' warm breath hung like sheets in the arctic air. They shook their thick fur and flexed their powerful muscles when I came closer. They were so beau-tiful, I longed to touch them; gently, I moved forward step by step. Just when I thought I'd been accepted, the horses looked up, shook their manes, and cantered away. The backyard looked deserted and shallow without their dark, massive bodies.

Early in the new year, a tall young man—long legs, taut body, and narrow hips—sat down at one of my tables. He was polite and didn't tremble or wink. His black hair was curly, his dark eyes filled with a vague sadness that made me picture him playing mournful songs on a guitar. His gentle manner was such a relief.

"Bill's a real sweetheart," said Bobby. "Comes 'round every two months or so, leaves good tips, and never gives us trouble."

I must have smiled at him. When he came back for dinner, he asked me to go to the dance that was held once a month fifteen miles down the road. I didn't know what to say. I felt closer to the half-wild horses and Pasha than to Fort Nelson's women and men. After serving Bill coffee, I hurried across the restaurant to Bobby.

"Of course, you'll go! Bill is a love."

I almost said, *I'm only fifteen!* Luckily, I looked much older with my serious face and fully developed bosom.

"Will you be there, Bobby?"

"If someone asks me, hell yes," she answered. Then her face brightened. "You just gave me an idea, kiddo. I guess I can maneuver it, especially to keep an eye on you. Just you wait and see."

By the end of her shift, Bobby came running. "Cook will take me to the dance, old codger *loves* dancing."

I accepted Bill's invitation.

My date wore a neatly pressed shirt and jeans, cowboy boots, and a dash of cologne when he arrived to fetch me with his truck, his eyes shadowed by a cowboy hat. I had slipped into a party dress that Mama had bought during a sale at the Hudson Bay Company; it was made of green crepe, fit tightly over my bosom and developing hips, then flared out at the knees. Bill did a double take when I appeared, took off his hat, kneaded his hands, and let out a muted whistle. I flashed him a quick smile and turned my head away when I felt a blush coming on.

Bill opened the door to his truck, and I, amazed at the height of the cabin, had to climb up and into it, while trying hard to keep my dress from sliding up. Once seated, I felt like I was in a lookout tower—or back on the ramparts of Falkenburg Castle, except that there was no wide open view, but a thick rope of woods closing in on both sides of the road.

Open space—breathing room—was above us, a star-filled sky that cupped the truck, the highway, and woods, and showed up in slivers and patches—kaleidoscopic pieces—between and above the layers of hills as Bill drove north. I felt his chiseled face turn toward me every so often.

"When did you arrive here in Fort Nelson?" he asked, keeping his eyes on the road.

"Four months ago." He nodded. I watched the play of muscles under the cloth of his jeans. We remained silent for a mile or two.

"You mind if I smoke?" Bill asked.

Thinking of Vati, I quickly said, "Oh no, not at all." Keeping his left hand on the steering wheel and his eyes on the road, he fumbled for a pack of Marlboros somewhere between us and held it up.

"Would you like one?" This time he was looking at me. I shook my head. "No, thanks." I got the feeling my answer pleased him because a shadow of a smile flickered across his face. He lit the cigarette, drew in the smoke, and blew it out by turning his head away from me.

I appreciated his thoughtfulness and leaned back, hypnotized by the road peeled from darkness by the truck's headlights and abandoned to darkness again. I watched layer after layer of horizons form and recede as we rolled on, and could have gone on forever, riding high into the starlit night. I began to wish we would never arrive, when Bill steered the truck into the dance hall's parking lot.

Bill and I shuffled across the small square of the dance floor a few times. He barely led me, so our feet kept bumping into each other. During the band's break, when Louis Armstrong's thrilling *Blueberry Hill* made the jukebox and my lonesome self quiver, I forgot about my feet, closed my eyes, and sank into Bill's chest. In response, he moved gently toward me. Our melding felt so sweet and luring that I pulled back in surprise.

After we danced a little, Bill left our table to get a couple of beers. In a flash, half a dozen men sprinted over and asked me to dance. I didn't know where to turn, when Bobby appeared. "This young lady is with me and Bill. How about asking some of the gals lined up against the wall for a dance?" The men trudged off.

Bill had observed the rush on me, and we left shortly after we finished our beers. I took a big step up into the truck. Bill steadied me when I teetered backwards because of my tight dress, making my back tingle under the touch of his hand. I heard him breathe a sigh as he walked around the truck to the driver's side. Once off, we didn't speak. I thought I felt Bill's hand touch mine now and again, a touch so gentle I was not sure if I was merely imagining it.

At the hotel door, Bill bent down, ran his finger along my cheeks, and planted a chaste kiss on my lips. Teetering on my toes, I kissed him back.

"Let's go to the dance again next month," he said.

"I'd like that very much, Bill."

"And maybe have a bite to eat beforehand."

"Yes, that would be nice."

He climbed into his truck, and I waved as he turned onto the winding highway. So much had happened and nothing had happened, but I sensed that anything could happen, as early as tomorrow. If I wanted to, or worked at it, or just let it happen, I could end up here forever with someone like Bill. In a few years, I would look sad, fat, and empty like most of the women of Fort Nelson. I'd live in a shack or in a trailer, and at first my husband would take me to the dance every month, but later, as we spoke less and less to each other, and I'd have the kids to take care of, he'd take off on his own.

I was so wide awake I knew I wouldn't be able to sleep, so I ran to my room, slipped into my warmest boots, buttoned my coat, and was off into the night. Walking the icy highway through town, I looked up into the sky and back to the road, where starlight spilled onto the ground like frozen milk. I felt embedded in the crystal light and wanted to keep walking, but when I came to the last house, I stopped and turned back. I was not as brave as the wolves and thick-furred horses that made their home in that night. And I'd been branded by knowing that I was vulnerable.

I never saw Bill again, because Mama surprised me at the hotel three weeks later just after I finished my morning shift. I spread the money saved from my salary and all my tips out before me.

"You did extremely well," Mama said, her voice slightly shaken. "Much better than I expected."

"I am going home, Mama," I said.

"I suppose. But I wished you'd reconsider." Mama's gray eyes widened. She turned away from me, staring at the bills and coins on the table, gathering them in and creating a pile as if in a trance. Then she raised her hands and stared at her painted fingernails, stretching them out before her and pulling them back in. Like a cat.

Finally, Mama looked me in the eye. "You're rejecting me, aren't you? Choosing Vati over me."

"It's the dust, Mama, the oil, the crude men..." I was looking to my mother for help, but Mama's eyes stared straight ahead. I didn't even know if she had heard me.

"It's the endless winter, the unforgiving cold. And I need to get back to school."

"Why not go to school with your sister?"

"I don't fit in."

Mama's eyes said, *"You ruthless girl."* Her small cough set in.

"But I do fit in at my school in Germany," I said in a quiet but firm voice. I *had to* appease Mama—without giving in. If I gave in now, I'd be clawed by her forever.

I conjured up a smile. "Just think how much money you're making, Mama. You can now visit Germany much longer than the last time! And you can show me Berchtesgaden like you've always wanted to do."

Mama sighed. "What can I say? You're bullheaded, just like your father."

Her words were steeling my determination rather than undermining it, but my own feelings didn't matter right now.

"I'm sorry it didn't work out, Mama. I'll do my best to make you proud of me. And when you come over, you can show me Hamburg and Berchtesgaden."

Mama sighed. "Well," she muttered, almost in a whisper. Her small cough had stopped, her shoulders drooping. "I guess I'll call the travel agency tomorrow."

"Thank you, Mama." She took my hand in hers and I felt like I had so many years ago in Falkenburg when Mama suddenly looked so sad while reading *The Little Match Girl* to me. It was as if she had turned into the shivering girl before my eyes.

Mama straightened her back and pushed her chin up. "But you have to take a boat instead of a plane. It's cheaper."

The match girl was gone, leaving me the Mama I knew. "Fine," I said quickly. "A boat is fine."

I would have rowed back to Germany if that were the only way to get home.

It turned out that Mama's travel agent found a stupendously cheap flight to Amsterdam—cheaper than the boat. From there I could take the train to Heidelberg.

The hotel manager told me, "You've been a good little worker, Marie—and brought in business. You can have your job back any time." Mama beamed, but I knew I would never come back. I'd miss Pasha, the star-filled nights—and perhaps even Bill. But not this outback hotel and its crazy, starved men.

At Fort St. John's airport, Mama looked pale. She kept clearing her throat and clutching a hanky in her right hand. Ingrid was away, visiting Basti in Banff, courtesy of Val who was driving her there. We siblings had said a tearful telephone goodbye to each other. Ingrid's voice sounded sad but not too sad, but hearing my brother's voice breaking into a sob almost did me in. "You've got to come and visit us in Germany, Basti. Please promise."

"I promise," he said. "See you in Germany." Maybe I could have made a go of Canada if Basti had been with us in Fort St. John, I wondered, but quickly dismissed the thought. When the airport official opened the door to the tarmac, Mama charged forward and asked, "Can I walk my youngest child to the plane?"

"I'm sorry, Ma'am," the official said, looking *the youngest child* up and down, "it's against regulations, but do take your time in saying goodbye to the young lady."

Mama clutched me to her bosom, then looked at me the way she had when we had said good-bye at Mannheim's train station so many years ago. Her eyes filled with tears, tears *without anger*, and my heart surged with a pity-filled love that lit up like a flare only when we were about to part.

BOOK VI

Back in Heidelberg

29

BACK HOME

Sheets of rain were hitting my plane window so hard during the landing at Amsterdam's Shiphol Airport, they washed out the skyline, the terminals, and the hangars. I couldn't make out a single building until the plane had come to a full stop in front of my gate. New rivers of rain rushed down the windows of my taxi to Amsterdam's train station. I felt submerged in water. What did you expect, I told myself, this is *Holland* and, of course, Germany isn't really so different!

When the taxi approached *Centraal Station* in the heart of Amsterdam, the rains eased for a moment, allowing me to hustle into the arrival hall without being drenched. I set down my heavy suitcase, loosened my shoulders, and closed my eyes for a moment. Only eight hours away from Heidelberg—an overnight ride and I would be back home.

Instantly, the cavernous station became a welcome hall. Dutch sounds, so close to German, caressed my ears. *"Varweel!"* a woman called out, producing a crisp, guttural "r," the kind English speakers rarely manage, and a clear "l." *"Varweel,"* a man's voice answered. What a beautiful duet! When I put down my case on Platform 8 for the overnight train to Munich, a sweet voice said in German, *"Engelein, heb Deine Puppe auf!"* Pick up your doll, my angel.

I turned to the young woman who had just spoken. "Please say that again," I begged her and quickly covered my mouth from embarrassment. "I've been living on the Alaska Highway for months on end," I explained, "and haven't heard German for *so long*."

The woman's raised eyebrows relaxed. *"Ja, so was!"* Well, what do you know, she said, and repeated *"Engelein, heb Deine Puppe auf."*

"Hab ich doch schon," But I already did, a tiny voice piped up. The

girl's mother and I broke into laughter.

After finding my compartment and reserved window seat, I sat at attention, eager for the train to depart and carry me home. And for as long as daylight lasted, I looked through the train's window—first into Dutch and within the hour into German lands. My eyes clung to spires, bridges, and hilltop castles as if they had never seen spires, bridges, and castles before. The wheels moved too fast for my feasting eyes. Soon, the light-filled woods would shine with *Maigloeckchen*, lilies of the valley, and *Anemonen*, anemones. There were no pipelines, no underbrush, no wolves, and no bears in these woods.

Finally, I fell into unsettled sleep. But at a quarter to six I stood next to my luggage in the corridor, exhausted yet burningly awake, as the train approached Heidelberg Station. In just a few minutes I'll see Vati! Would Tante B. be by his side or was she still at Sophie's grandmother's house in Cologne "pondering her future" as Sophie had written? Sophie herself would not come back until the end of the school year because a school exhibit in May would feature several of her paintings.

When the train came to a stop with a screech, I stepped onto the platform, ready to behold what I most wanted to see, but there wasn't a soul in sight—just gray asphalt stretching into fog.

For an instance I felt bereft, then straightened my shoulders, lifted my luggage, and headed for the staircase to the great hall. Clattering steps came rushing down just as the conductor blew his whistle and the train began moving out. The steps stopped dead. Vati was standing before me, breathing hard from running, sweat on his forehead, his blue eyes lighting up at the sight of me.

"Marie, *mein Kind*! So sorry, I'm late."

"Vati!"

We threw our arms around each other and stood still in our embrace. Vati loosened his hold for a moment to take a look at me. "*Mein liebes, liebes Kind.*" My dear, dear child. "Du bist wieder da." You're back.

"Did you ever doubt that?"

"Deep down, no. But you are a young woman. Who knows, you might have fallen in love."

"Come on, Vati! With all your diatribes against young men...how could I?"

"There's a rebellious streak in you, my dear. Mind you, that's not a bad thing, but..." He smiled without finishing his sentence.

When Vati picked up my suitcase, I looked around for Tante B. No sign of her. *I'll ask Vati later*, I decided. After stowing the suitcase in the trunk of his car, Vati said, "I took the day off so you can tell me all about your Canadian life over breakfast at the *Strahlenburg*, a much less glorious, yet still worthy cousin of our own Falkenburg Castle. I quickly hugged him and climbed into the car, my mind already picturing the medieval hilltop castle with its fine restaurant that offered sweeping views of the Rhine Valley.

When we entered the restaurant and the maître d' asked for Vati's name, he broke into a smile. "Oh, Dr. Bergen, your party is expecting you." *Which party?* I wondered. The moment Vati stepped aside I looked into Tante B.'s round face, all smiles and red from excitement. Tante B. in a new, swanky suit jumped up, opened her arms wide, and I walked in. When we released each other, and I looked out into the land, my shoulders spreading and my chest expanding, I told her, "I'll never ever leave again."

The waiter filled my cup from a silver coffee urn, Vati offered me a basket with Broetchen and pastries, and Tante B. picked out the biggest boiled egg from the egg basket. "*Nu iss mal schoen, Mariechen, das ist das schoenste Ei!*" Now, eat, my sweet Marie. This is the best egg!

After I sipped strong, aromatic coffee—so superior to the brew on the Alaska Highway that always tasted chemical to me—I answered a never-ending stream of questions: "Yes, Tante B., Ingrid is blooming. She's even taller now than when she left Germany." "Yes, Vati, she is a *good* student and so good-looking and statuesque she gets to play the female lead in almost all plays."

"Have some *Schwarzwald Honig*, my dear. It's good for you!" Vati tempted me with a jar of deep green Black Forest honey. I took a spoon and dripped honey onto my crisp *Broetchen*. "And is your mother doing well?" he asked casually.

"Very well," I said. "Canada has been good for her. She's earning good money." I waved my egg spoon in the air. "I think Canada has been good for all of them—Mama, Ingrid, and Bastian. Of course, I didn't really get to spend much time with Bastian because he'd been offered a well-paying job in Banff by his old boss just before I arrived. That made me sad, but I was so busy, especially on the Alaska Highway, that I wouldn't have been able to see much of him."

"It was brave of you to work as a waitress," Tante B. said, patting me on the back. "Very admirable! Thank God your mother was by your side."

"By my side? She was some thirty-five miles away in an oil camp deep in the bush! I lived in a stinky little hotel room, hardly larger than a WC—"

Vati grabbed my arm. "What? What did you just say? Your mother wasn't in the same town?"

I flinched. Mama had asked me not to let on when writing to Vati that I'd be by myself in Fort Nelson to earn money for my return ticket. I blushed.

"Vati," I said, starting to stutter. "I wasn't supposed to...Mama had asked me not to..."

"*Raus mit der Warheit!*" Out with the truth. Vati bellowed in such a commanding tone that the waiter sprinted to our table.

"Everything in order, Herr Doktor? What may I get you?"

"More coffee," Vati said in a calmer voice, after exchanging long glances with Tante B. He put his hand on mine. "Tell us, *mein Kind*. I want to know everything."

I saw no anger in his eyes, only concern, so I told them about my little house where the men had tried to break in, my meager hotel room, my work, Pasha, the wild horses, and Bobby. I didn't utter a word about going to the dance with Bill. Vati was simply too paranoid about young men.

Tante B.'s eyes popped out and Vati's face blanched, reddened, and blanched again. I could almost feel his anger. *How could Mama expose his youngest to so much danger?* I read the concern in Vati and Tante B.'s eyes and felt uplifted and reassured.

30

Unbearable Truth

When I rejoined my classmates, I didn't let on about beery hockey games, sex-starved men on the Alaska Highway, or my job as a waitress. My classmates would have been utterly shocked.

No girl at the Elisabeth-von-Thadden-Schule ever held down a job—least of all in a dangerous environment. Their—and my—main task was to concentrate on our studies so that we would pass the *Abitur,* our ticket to university. That's what Vati and my classmates' parents expected. With only 5% of young people attending university nationwide, we were prepped to join our country's elite.

I did rhapsodize about Canada's rushing rivers, northern lights, vast woods, and many-layered horizons. And I dove with gusto back into Latin, German literature, and, of course, English. My prep school English class had progressed beyond basic grammar and was now tackling short stories, beginning with Steinbeck's *Red Pony.* I became a star in English, especially after I slid back into my formerly practiced British pronunciation.

How wonderful to be back home, in a real school, luxuriating in my native language. I had rejoined civilization. Riding high on my infatuation with everything German, the ancient castles, stone churches, light-filled woods, alluring poems, and soothing lullabies, I did not sense the past creeping up on me. Once again, I was blind—this time blinded by the joy of reunion.

My tall, congenial classmate, Gerda, who sat next to me, gave me the first warning.

"Remember, we have a retreat next month in the Odenwald," Gerda reminded me. The Odenwald was a hilly, forested region distinguished by mighty beech and oak trees, forest meadows, and clear brooks. The Roman Limes ran through these ancient woods, and you could still stumble across the remains of the wall.

"Great," I said, "I love the Odenwald. We'll go for long hikes and tell ghost stories at night."

"I wish," Gerda said. "But this retreat has no hikes. Our teachers want to finally reveal 'the whole truth,' all the gory stuff about the Nazis and the persecution of Jews, Gypsies, and other so-called *inferior* people."

We knew terrible things had happened under the Nazis, but we knew nothing about their scope or the depth of viciousness.

"Oh, dear. Sounds ominous."

"You bet. I've talked to some of the older girls who've been through it. They say it is horrible."

My classmates and I were born during the last year of Hitler's Third Reich. None of us had memories of the Nazis or the War, yet our teachers had not yet discussed WWI, the Weimar Republic, the Nazis, or WWII with us. Following the school's long established history curriculum, we were currently dwelling in the 1800s, learning about the peace treaty between Prussia and Austria; the power shifts in Europe; and the British colonies, including the rise of America. Still, we were being sent off to the retreat since the stalwart Elisabeth-von-Thadden-Schule had made it a tradition to offer this seminar to students in the 10th grade.

We had periodically been reminded of Hitler and the Nazis, usually on July 20, Count Stauffenberg's failed attempt on Hitler's life, and on September 9, the anniversary of the execution of Elisabeth von Thadden, the founder of our school. We had seen a couple of newsreels of Hitler's speeches. The Fuehrer's pathos, his screaming voice, and jerky motions, exaggerated by the jittery reels, made him look and sound like a caricature, more like Charlie Chaplin's Great Dictator than an idolized *Fuehrer*. Hitler's references to *Blut*, blood, and *Vaterland* that had stirred the hearts of men and women of his time sounded antediluvian to us. We could not relate to the pumped-up patriotism, originally fueled by humiliation and outrage at the Versailles Peace Treaty of 1918.

On the contrary, we had been brought up to *despise* war and be mistrustful of flaming patriotism, precisely *because* it can be whipped into aggression. We were baffled by the wildly gesticulating, grotesque man in the new reels. *This man* had terrorized Germany and Europe? It was *this man* who'd glorified war and death? We simply could not feel his demonic power. To us, he was a spectacle, not a specter. Had he given a speech in Heidelberg's market square, we would have turned our backs and left him to address the air.

The seminar began with long lectures on the Great Depression, hunger, and unemployment, followed by more lectures about the aims of the Weimar Republic, its constituencies, and the many political parties. The lecturer's voice was so monotonous, and he showered us with so many statistics that we began to lose interest and only revived when lunch was announced.

During the first hour after lunch, we were drowsy, but suddenly sat up straight and paid attention when the lecturer mentioned *plans for the eradication of Jews*. What? *Plans* for the *eradication* of *Jews*? Men and women who were German citizens? How could that be? To fight another nation is one thing, but to *eradicate* one's fellow citizens seemed absolutely crazy.

The lecturer stopped himself, searching our faces. He said again that there were plans, orders, and instructions in minute detail for the *eradication* of Jews, communists, Gypsies, homosexuals, the handicapped, anyone whom the Nazis considered to be *misfits*. I squirmed in my seat.

The speaker's face was pale. Beads of sweat were appearing on his forehead just below the hairline. He shoved away his notes and set up a movie screen.

"You will now see a film, a witness to the truth. Not your typical Hollywood movie, but a documentary, consisting of actual photographs, spliced together. A narrator will guide you and provide further details." The eyes that scanned us looked sad and resigned. "Brace yourselves," he said, "this is very difficult material."

He pulled the shades, and the film began to roll, showing a harmless, ordinary gate. A voice told us that this gate led into a concentration camp built to hold political prisoners and Jews—Jews who had *never broken the law* but had been *rounded up* and brought there *simply because they were Jews*. Why? Because the Nazis believed Jews were an *inferior race* and held them *responsible for Germany's defeat* in World War I and other national hardships.

I sat up as tall as I could and strained my ears because I had to be sure what I heard was actually being said. I could not make sense of the message.

The voice spoke of a *program of extermination*. I didn't know how to reconcile the clearly constructed sentences of the speaker with their destructive message. Words like *inferior race* and *vermin* cut through me like daggers, but my mind could not process them.

The next image showed the camp from the inside with barracks and guardhouses. I saw fences, barbed wire, and soldiers with guard dogs. The images, severe and static at first, suddenly surged with energy when I realized that everything had been designed to cut off movement, freedom—and life. *No one who entered left alive,* said the voice, with very few exceptions. Those who tried to flee were shot. Or torn to pieces by dogs. Or burnt to death by the electricity of the barbed wires. Or died of exposure during an icy winter night.

Torn to pieces? Burnt to death? Could something like this have really happened in our time? My stomach pulled against my breast-bone. I felt nauseous. I didn't want to imagine what I heard...but I did. Against my will, I did.

Already the screen showed bunker-like structures with arched ceilings, reminiscent of coal cellars of St. John's. I remembered how oppressive and scary it felt to be locked away in such vaulted enclosures.

In the next slide, the bunkers were no longer empty but crammed full with men, their heads shaven. They wore identical, prison-style outfits. They looked exhausted, dull, absent, as if they didn't care anymore. I felt sorry for them and slid into pity until I was drawn toward one with piercing eyes, looking right at me. *I dare you to see me for what I am.* I felt his despair, his insistence that I see him as more than a shaved head, more than a worn-out body in prison clothing, more than an animal herded into a corral to work and die.

"I do see you," I wanted to shout. "I see *You!*"

Each new image was more terrifying than the last one. Still by still, I was descending into hell, into the misery of women and men trying to hold on to their humanity. The voice insisted on leading me on.

It spoke of medical experiments, operations carried out on living people without anesthesia, of women pulled under icy water to see how long they could survive. I learned that every tenth inmate was shot, because one prisoner had tried to "escape" by throwing himself against the electrical fence to die.

As the camera zoomed in on the eyes of the prisoners, they grew larger, moving closer, becoming *my* eyes looking in on crammed quarters where people were packed together like livestock about to be led to slaughter, people so emaciated that they no longer looked like human beings. Hair gone, flesh fallen away, skeletons wrapped in skin.

I wanted to push the images away but could not. I did not want to believe what I saw though it was right before my eyes. This could not be real. This must be some horrible joke, a stage set for an infernal play.

The narrator's voice insisted that the photos were real and that they recorded the systematic, cynical rubbing out of the soul. Once that was gone, life became a living death.

Physical death followed closely behind. Up rose still photographs of a gas chamber, a shower room, where the Nazis herded the weak and dying, as the voice told me, but also the newly arrived, the still hopeful right next to those who had lost faith in any kind of a future, together with children who clung to their mothers.

I trembled from imagining what would happen after the doors closed on the still-breathing, still-feeling women, children, and men. Each image cut into me and drew me in, as if *I* was the one walking into the chamber with them, as if I was breathing the gas.

But I *was not*. I was pulled back to the present by the click of the lecturer's machine, uploading another reel. The gas chamber disappeared. The next frame showed piles of corpses. I was familiar with piles of coal, wood, and sand, but piles of dead bodies? Yes, there were piles and piles of bodies with jutting bones and eyes looking at me from cave-like sockets. Starved, broken bodies with wide, open eyes. They clung to me.

I felt I was no longer a person, only a filter, a receptacle for pain. I could not breathe, but when my breath returned after all, I wanted to disown it, because I no longer felt entitled to breathe.

Another shock ripped through me when I finally understood that it had been *my people, my own people* who had murdered women, children, and men as if humans were not fellow beings but *things*. The very *civilized* people I had run back to from the uncivilized Alaska Highway. But those could not be my people! *No one I know* would *ever* do anything like this. *No one.* Those who did were more vicious than wild beasts.

When the images on the screen showed more piles of bodies, I fled from the room. I couldn't take in anymore, felt wrung-out and cold. The eyes of the dead were all over me.

The void was back. The dreaded void that had no mouth devoured me; the dread that was ice cold, burnt like fire. It was there whenever Mama's fists became drums; it sprang from the switch of Sister Hedwig, the cold eyes of the minister; it broke down doors to rape and kill. The void was alive and breathing, not only back then, in the camps, but even now it hovered about us.

I ran. Outside, the embankment rushed at me and fell away. I no longer saw trees or their branches; I no longer smelled the scent of their pitch. There was no sky between leaves—just eyes, deep sunken eyes. The Nazis...*we...Germans*—had done this.

I knelt on the ground, desperate to feel dirt, stones, and earth— solid, *innocent* matter. I cried from horror, from not comprehending, but knowing and understanding, that even if I cried forever, it would change nothing. This had happened, could never be undone.

After a while, more girls came out, many crying, some smoking nervously—I had never seen them smoke before—some with their arms around each other. Suddenly Gerda hugged me. "It's over," she said and led me back inside.

A minister offered to pray. Where had he come from? Had he been there from the beginning? I couldn't remember, but even praying felt wrong. It was far too *passive*. What could prayer do *after the fact*? We needed firestorms, roiling seas, hurricanes to *destroy so much evil*.

When my classmates and I looked at each other, we saw our own horror and disbelief in the eyes of the other. We were united by what we had seen but alone in grappling with its impact. We now spoke in whispers as if to eradicate ourselves.

Somehow, we survived supper; the teacher said something about giving us time to recover and picking up again tomorrow after we'd had some sleep. But what good would that do? We'd never be the same. Life was not the same. God was not the same. God had not interfered. What had happened to God's power, compassion, and pity?

We put on our nightgowns and slid under the covers, but we could not sleep. Slowly, in twos and threes, as if by silent consent, we drifted to Monika's room. We didn't know what to say to each other. There was no one and nothing to help us understand.

Finally, Monika picked up her guitar and played a soothing evening song, *Der Mond ist aufgegangen*, The Moon Has Risen and Golden Stars are Shining. Gerda hummed along. Next Monika strummed *Am Brunnen vor dem Tore*, At the Well by the Town's Gate, and we all joined in, singing quietly at first, then more fervently. After we had sung every folk tune we knew and still could not part, someone blurted out a sailor song. Monika, startled at first, accompanied the crude song with her guitar. And all of us sang the absurdity, the gruesomeness of life out of the window into the night.

The retreat continued for another day, but the projector and film cans had been put away and were not brought out again. The lecturer discussed the course of the war and Germany's surrender. Then it was over.

Still, we could not believe that anyone we knew and loved could have had anything to do with such abominations. Our parents protected us, fed us, and tucked us in at night. They had taught us to care for each other, for neighbors, for friends. They worked hard for us. Right after the war, when there wasn't enough food, our parents had put more food on our plates than they took for themselves.

Only later, after the terrible knowledge began to work on us did we ask more questions. What did my parents know about this outrage? And if they did know, what did they do about it? Why did they not speak up when the discrimination against Jews and other "enemies of the state" began?

The retreat took place while Sophie was still in Cologne and Vati on the road. When I got home, I asked Tante B., "Did you know all *that* was going on?"

"We didn't." Tante B.'s large blue eyes filled with tears. "When people were taken away, we believed they were going to work camps. And Germany had become so unfriendly to Jews that many—" Tante B. sobbed so hard, she could not go on. She wiped her eyes with her bare hand. "We thought many were emigrating. Even today, I cannot make myself believe what happened. If someone had told me *then* what was really going on, I wouldn't have believed it, but no one did tell us, Marie. Most people were kept in the dark." Her words left me exasperated—and angry. The anger had little to do with Tante B. I believed her. But something in me refused to accept a reality where atrocities happened that no one thought possible and that remained unimaginable even after they had happened. What kind of world was this?

I could not reconcile this horrible truth with my love of learning, with the idea of progress, with the energy that made life worthwhile. I felt drugged with despair not unlike the time in Garmisch when I had given up all hope of Vati's return and had run into onrushing cars.

"I'm off to Heidelberg," I told Tante B. out of the blue. "I'll be back before dark."

"Wait," Tante B. called after me. "Just hold a second. There is a letter from Bastian for you. Take it along." I stuffed it into my coat pocket. In town, I walked about aimlessly, but I could not run from the void. Next thing I knew, I was on the Ernst Walz Bruecke, a bleak, modern bridge spanning the Neckar River.

The river below reflected a gray sky above, colored it even dirtier with its rain-silted waters. A cold wind whipped up small waves and blew under my coat. I shivered, but kept staring into the waves and back into the dirty sky. I felt enveloped by the cold, drenched by dread silting my soul.

"I should jump. Get out of this world without compassion." The thought floated itself from the waters, the sky, and from within.

I grabbed the banister, leaned forward, and stared into the river. Waves of gray. Dirty gray...everywhere.

Stepping back, I placed my hands on top of the banister, pushed, and heaved myself up.

The river below me was swirling, making me sway.

They gassed children, made victims dig their own graves before they gunned them down...

I took a breath and bent my knees for the jump.

"Halt!" Two strong arms locked around me.

"Let me be!" I struggled against the embracing vise. "For God's sake, let me be."

The arms lifted me and set me down on the ground.

I looked into the shocked eyes of Monsieur de Remarque, Ingrid's disgraced French teacher, who had been dismissed from his post not long after she had left for Canada. Paragraph 79 of the legal code: Homosexuality.

"Monsieur de..." I mumbled. "Oh, Monsieur de...I want...I can't stand," I sighed, cursing my failed escape and somewhere, below the layers of anger, frustration, and pain, even this man's ruined life.

"Shush. Shush. Take a deep breath. Lean against me."

I could feel his heart beat. He unbuttoned his coat and wrapped it around me. I was still shivering, but the warmth of his coat began to revive me.

Somehow, he managed to flag a taxi. He walked me firmly to the car door, released me from his coat shelter, and maneuvered me inside.

"To Café Schafheutle," he directed the driver. "Let's have a hot chocolate," he said to me. "And you tell me what's on your mind." I was crumbling inside, couldn't say a word, but leaned into his arm around my shoulder.

At the Café, he located a table in a back corner. No one was near-by. "Tell me what troubles you," he asked after putting his coat over my knees.

I spewed out my despair as if a vomit of words could wipe out the sickening swirl of knowledge though I already knew that I'd never be able to free myself from what I had come to know.

I could neither rub nor burn it out of me.

He listened with eyes that seemed to say *keep talking,* and some-where behind the pigment of their soft brown, they also said, *I know. Yes, I know.*

When I was spent, he started to talk. "My family and I lived in Par-is during the war. I was only a teenager, so I escaped the draft. It was an anxious time; we witnessed German brutalities and experienced some chicaneries ourselves but nothing life-threatening.

"One day, my mother slipped in the middle of the avenue and was sideswiped by a passing car. The driver, a German in uniform, stopped and attended to my mother. He happened to be a doctor and did all the right things until an ambulance arrived. The doctor followed the ambulance to the hospital and stayed with Maman until she received her diagnosis of a dislocated shoulder and Papa had arrived.

"After she was released, he appeared at our door with a bouquet of flowers, some wine, and more importantly, a picnic basket filled with butter, eggs, honey, ham, cheeses, and even a plucked chicken, the kind of food we rarely found on our grocery shelves in those days. Of course, my parents invited him in. They, that is we—I was called in and duly introduced—chatted with civility. He politely declined our dinner invitation as he wanted us to be the sole beneficiaries of the basket, he said in perfect French.

"Over time, a tentative friendship grew between my parents and him, both parties acutely aware of the delicacy of the situation. The doctor always appeared at dusk, and we never saw his car parked close to our front door. We, in turn, never discussed his visit with our French friends.

"When his wife and son arrived in Paris, shortly before he was transferred to Belgium, the doctor brought them along on his farewell visit. That's when I met Wolfgang, a stunning young man who towered above his father. Despite his perfect athletic build, he moved like a panther. It was the panther who captured me, though Wolf's large violet eyes seemed to look into my soul. I felt known, more known than I had ever been, and was gripped by such a sense of loss when they bid us farewell that tears rose in my eyes. 'We've all grown fond of Monsieur, le docteur,' my mother tried to console me with watery eyes, tousling my hair and rushing off to the kitchen to compose herself."

Monsieur de Remarque raised his hand to attract a waiter and ordered another hot chocolate for me and a cognac for himself. His face was flushed.

"We learned, after the war, that the doctor had been killed in the Battle of the Bulge. His wife and son survived the war. Wolf and I visited our respective homes during school holidays over the years, and I later decided to study at Heidelberg University where Wolf was a medical student.

"Now you know more about myself than you bargained for. Please tell me about *your* family."

"I will in a moment," I said and felt a blush coming on while I mustered the courage to ask, "Are you trying to console me for what my people did by telling me about some *nice* Germans?"

"Not at all," said Monsieur de Remarque calmly. "I only wanted to say that 'the German people' or 'the French' are made up of individuals. It matters how individual people behaved."

He took my hand. "But I understand your uproar. I, too, was horrified when I learned about the concentration camps and mass murder of so many innocent people. And yet I chose to live here in this country because of my ties to *some* German people and..." Monsieur de Remarque blushed. "And because I fell in love, as you probably know."

I nodded.

"Now it's time to turn the tables. Please tell me about you and your family."

I sighed. "That's a complicated story because my family is all broken up. But I'll try."

We talked for another hour or so, then Monsieur hailed a taxi for me. "You will go home directly, won't you?"

"Yes, please don't worry," I told him. "I'm all right now." I took a deep breath. "Thank you, Monsieur."

When I got home, Tante B. met me in the hallway. "Thank God you are back. I was getting worried. Are you all right?"

"Yes, Tante B., I'm better." She scrutinized my face.

"Come into the kitchen where it's warm and cozy. I'll make us a cup of tea." After she poured us our tea, she asked, "What did Bastian have to say?"

Bastian's letter! How could I have forgotten about his letter? He hardly ever wrote. What could this be about?

"Would you believe I forgot about the letter?" I fished it out of my pocket, ripped open the blue airmail envelope, smoothed it against the kitchen table, and read out loud,

My dear Marie,

I bet you were surprised when you saw my handwriting. Well, this is a special letter, not exactly a happy one but not

that bad either, or we would have phoned you. Ingrid and I are fine, but Mama has been "under the weather" for a while. First, she caught pneumonia at her oil camp way up north.

Tante B. grabbed my arm, her bulging eyes full of concern.

They flew her to a hospital in Fort St. John. That helped with the pneumonia. But somehow, she fell into a deep depression and can't seem to shake it. They had to put her on intravenous feeding, are trying out some medications, and have her under constant observation.

Tante B. called out. "Stop for a moment. Can you believe it? Pneumonia? Depression? Intravenous feeding?"

I patted her hand while eager to read on. "Let's find out more, Tante B."

At first, the doctors thought that something must have happened at the camp. Maybe some men hurt her or somehow terrorized her, but she spoke well of them. They kept sending cards and the big boss even phoned a florist in town and sent her a big bunch of flowers. So, that didn't seem likely.

Now the doctors think she is just terribly exhausted, and the exhaustion together with her menopause, which had caused some problems before the pneumonia, derailed her body and mind. They feel that she will come out of it and are doing all they can. In the meantime, she is finally getting the rest she needs.

I'm telling you so that you know what's happening. It's so unlike Mama that Ingrid and I are dumbfounded, but we trust the doctors. We also thought it would be great if you would write to her soon and perhaps send a book, some romantic novel by Courths-Mahler or such. She loved that syrupy writer. I hope to send you the hospital phone number in my next letter. Maybe a phone call from you would help snap her out of it. We're just trying to think of anything that could help.

If the situation gets worse, we will phone you, but I don't think that will happen. Ingrid sends her best.

> *Be hugged, little sister, and be kissed by your*
> *loving brother Bastian*

> *P. S. In her rambling, she keeps asking for "Herr Jensen."*
> *Ingrid thinks he was her favorite teacher. Do you know any-*
> *thing about him?*

While Tante B. poured us more tea, shaking her head and clicking her tongue, I took a deep breath and, for the first time that day, almost forgot what had led me to the Ernst Walz Bridge. I didn't truly forget, I would never forget, but I pushed my own turmoil into the furthest corners of my mind. What Bastian described did not sound like Mama. Mama hated being idle, rarely ever sat still, and she didn't take to bed except for a few hours after her outbursts. But never day after day. And she loved food. Even during our darkest times, she had never lost her appetite. A gnawing feeling of guilt crept up from nowhere. Could my leaving have contributed to her anguish?

Then the extraordinary rescue by Monsieur de Remarque pushed thoughts about Mama away. It *was* extraordinary. To think that he was crossing the bridge the moment I... And now Mama in the hospital with pneumonia and depression. How can life be so crazy?

When I felt Tante B.'s concerned look on my face, I picked up the letter again. Perhaps I could do *something* for Mama. It would not change the past, could not change the past, never outweigh the past, but perhaps it could make a dent in the present.

I visited Heidelberg's largest bookstore the next day to find some romance novels for Mama. And I would talk to Vati about menopause and depression. Something deep inside me locked on to this mission of mercy. Not as a conscious distraction, though it was that, too, but as something concrete, something small I could do.

Yet all the time, while sipping my tea with Tante B. and trying to think of ways to help Mama, some part of me kept standing on the Ernst Walz Bridge, staring into the cold gray of the river.

31

My Classmates
and Heinrich Speer

After our return from the seminar our teachers continued with the regular curriculum. Frau Sonntag and our homeroom teacher, Dr. Schmidt, offered to meet with any girl who wanted to talk about the retreat. No one I knew took up their offer because they hadn't been with us in the Odenwald, and we were too shattered, too roiled.

We *did* probe and wonder within our own families and among close friends, but *only* close friends, as if these unimaginable, outrageous crimes had been committed by someone *within*. And they must have. Some second or third cousins, or perhaps even a father or uncle of one of our classmates must have known something, must have acted as some cog or even principal within this massive murder machine. But certainly *no one in our own family*. No one we knew. That was impossible.

Something else kept gnawing at me. I didn't know who was guilty and who was not. There was no mark on the forehead of those who had participated.

I scrutinized the faces of middle-aged and older men rushing past me as I made my way to the Café *Neckar* to meet up with Gerda and Monika, our first get-together after the retreat. Who were these people? Most looked preoccupied and dull, their faces closed off. Were these same dull people capable of torture and murder? What would they answer if I asked, "Did you ever work in a concentration camp? Did you supervise slave laborers? What do you know about the Warsaw Ghetto?" Had people's faces been more open and friendly before the Nazis came to power? At what point did they become what they became?

Checking face after face, I almost bumped into a man in a Bavarian Loden coat who returned my searching glance with such indignation that I stopped and stood still, only to find myself looking into the display window of Café *Neckar*. Already, an attentive waiter opened the door for me. "We'll be three," I told him and followed him to an alcove table. I sank into the warmth of the Café and picked up the *Rhein-Neckar Zeitung*, Heidelberg's daily, grateful for the chance to catch up on the news before my pals showed up.

How stupid of me to think I could recognize Nazi criminals, I scolded myself, and did a double take as I was faced with a large photograph of a young Albert Speer, Hitler's architect and Minister of Armaments and War Production. The newspaper article said that Speer had now served thirteen of his twenty years in prison. Influential people, among them General de Gaulle, were working for his early release. If they succeed, he planned to return to Heidelberg.

I felt the hair on the back of my neck stand up. I didn't know much about Speer, but he had been Hitler's Minister of Armaments and War Production. How could he even conceive of living here among us as if nothing had happened? As if one shocking piece of news wasn't enough, the article right below the one on Speer claimed that 92% of Bavaria's judiciary were former Nazis. That was almost everyone, I thought, and could very well mean that Vati's prosecutor and judge had been gung-ho Nazis.

When shadows fell on my paper, I looked up into the faces of my two friends, all pink-cheeked from their walk from the train. "This whole retreat was too devastating," said Monika, a tall, long-limbed girl with an impressive forehead, right after kissing me on both cheeks and before collapsing into her chair. My cherished seatmate Gerda, with her brown bangs and large brown eyes, buzzed my cheek, too, and plopped into the Café's plush chair.

Monika's family belonged to the landed gentry in East Prussia and some of her relatives had been part of the von Moltke group plotting the June 17 attack on Hitler, which so tragically failed. She dabbed her forehead and sighed. "I wished I'd never heard about the camps and never ever seen that documentary. My mother feels our teachers should have prepared us better before showing us such horrendous material."

"I know. I'd give anything not to know," I said, becoming aware that Monika's eyes were filling with tears, which shook me up because Monika was one of the most composed girls I knew. "But we have to know," I stuttered. "Because..." I looked to my friends to help fill in the right word, but they—and I— could not come up with any.

"What did *your* father do in the war?" Monica asked me and I answered quickly to give her a chance to recoup.

"He served on the Western Front—as a doctor. 'Nothing prepares you for war,' he always told me. 'It's brutal, inhuman, a horrible waste of human life and yet,' he also said, 'it creates bonds between men that are unbreakable. Often, a buddy will sacrifice himself for another without the slightest hesitation.'"

Now I could feel myself getting worked up and turned back to her. "And your father?"

"Fought in Africa. He was a friend of Rommel's. My mother takes it as a blessing he was killed before the Nazis forced Rommel to commit suicide. They might have come after my father, too." Monika was silent for a moment. "Of course, he'd be gone either way, but my mother is grateful that it was *fate* and not a Nazi-thug taking his life." Monika swept crumbs from the coffee table and kept sweeping even after there were no crumbs left.

"I cannot remember my father," she finally said softly, "but I love the face that is looking at me from the pictures all over the house."

Warm-hearted Gerda put her hand on Monika's shoulder, and I placed mine on top of hers, feeling utterly helpless. "I'm sorry you never knew your Vati. And I feel for your Mutti."

Monika shrugged. "It can't be helped," she sighed. "I don't think my mother will ever marry again. She loves him still."

"And your father? What did he do?" Monika turned to Gerda.

"He fought in Russia at Leningrad," said Gerda.

"Boy, was he lucky to get out alive!"

"I know," Gerda said. "Sometimes I wonder if it was Leningrad that made him so bitter and taciturn."

I had been a guest at Gerda's house and had been troubled by her father's closed, rigid face. Now, after having seen the emaciated victims of the concentration camps, I wondered if Gerda's father could have witnessed...or worse, unthinkably worse, even have actively participated in...

"Has he ever told you any details?" Monika's mind was clearly on the same track. "About freezing to death, eating dead horses and...?"

"He *never* talks about it." For a second, Gerda's face looked as closed as her father's. "When someone mentions Leningrad on the radio, he turns it off. And then he leaves the room. Sometimes even the house."

I shuddered. Vati had told me that between 1941 and 1944, the duration of the siege of Leningrad, 800,000 people had died and there had been 2,000 civilian arrests for cannibalism in the city.

"My mother," said Gerda, shifting the focus, "grew up in the East in one of those ancient German settlements in Romania. She learned German before Romanian and attended a German school. She said she was proud of Goethe and Schiller, proud of Bach, Schubert, and Beethoven and always felt that Germans had contributed so much more to civilization than Romanians."

Blood rushed to my face. Once again, I felt ashamed of my snobbish disdain for the Canadian North. How I had longed for my cultured Germany where even people with little education scraped their last pennies together to attend concerts and operas. How I had longed to return to my poetry and music-loving nation, not that barbaric Nazi beast that devoured its own humanity in order to maim and kill.

"Mama was jubilant at first when the Germans took over," Gerda continued, unaware of my inner struggle, "but when they rounded up people like cattle and mistreated them, she was aghast. Her family became divided. Her older brother joined the underground. Mama loved him for that, but her younger one fought for Nazi Germany. The younger survived and has never shaken his guilt."

We three remained silent. What could we say when we could not bear much less understand our country's outrage? We couldn't begin to fathom Hitler's appeal nor his ritual drumbeat "of making Germany great again." No one we knew, no one of our generation had ever sung the "German National Anthem" or saluted the German flag. And now we had even more reason not to do so.

I was sure if my friends and I had lived in the Germany of the thirties and forties, there would have been no Hitler, no death camps, and no war. I was certain of that.

"I don't understand the Nazis." Monika interrupted my mulling. "Do you?" Gerda and I shook our heads.

"I heard from my parents that political leaders are discussing an early release for Albert Speer. If he gets out, they'll allow him to live right here in Heidelberg," Gerda said. "Why should we be forced to share our town with a man from Hitler's inner circle?"

"I gotta run," I said abruptly, not knowing how to deal with distressing news from all sides. I was shaking inside, checked my watch as if I had another commitment, and jumped up. "I'm late. Sorry to run." I grabbed my satchel and stumbled out of the Café. Thank God, it was raining outside. That would help cool me down.

Ninety percent of all prosecutors, judges, and court lawyers in Bavaria, the largest state of this new Republic of West Germany, were former Nazis! Today. In our *democratic* Germany.

I resolved, on my way to the train station, that I would never join any political, religious, or "social" organization that discriminated against anyone. If I hadn't known I'd make a spectacle of myself, I would have knelt down right on *Hauptstrasse*, Main Street, raised my hand to the heavens, and sworn a holy oath.

Finally, Vati came home from his latest Boehringer trip. I couldn't wait to ask him about the Nazi atrocities. And about our own childhood and how Ingrid and I had ended up at St. John's Children's Home because Vati had been convicted of manslaughter. I was anxious, impatient, felt almost incorporeal, yet couldn't have been more present. While Tante B. put the kettle on, I asked him about the concentration camps.

"Sit down, Marie, that's an infamous story. Tante B. told me about your retreat when I phoned home. That must have been very difficult."

I nodded while tears rose against my will.

"An abomination," Vati continued while fishing for his pack of cigarettes. "*Homo homini lupus est.*" Like a wolf, man preys on his fellow men. His blue eyes seemed to darken—I remembered the hurt in them when Mama had thrown the ashtray in his face so many years ago. "And yet there are good, decent people everywhere, a few good people—even in war."

I waited until he had lit his cigarette and inhaled before asking, "How could you *not* have known about the concentration camps?"

"We knew there were camps, but we believed that they were forced labor camps and that some of them were for real criminals. We had no idea about the systematic slaughter of people." Vati blew out smoke. "In retrospect, we should have been much more alert and suspicious. Many of the leading Nazis of Ansbach, for example, were callous and made noises about destroying all 'enemies of the Reich,' inside Germany and beyond. I considered them braggards. Now I know some, maybe more than 'some,' must have also been insiders.

"I did what I could to counteract their actions, which amounted to precious little. I didn't attend rallies. I treated Jewish patients at night. Your mother was furious with me. She was terrified of what the Nazis would do to us if someone turned me in."

He paused, staring into the distance, inhaling again, then looked me directly in the eye. "When I was young and naïve and away from home for the first time at the University of Munich, I took a wrong turn. I couldn't wait to go to the famous Ratskeller and other Munich pubs. I enjoyed my visits to a certain smoke-filled Café where a svelte brunette belted out French chansons."

Vati stopped himself—whether from the pull of the past or a sense of embarrassment, I couldn't tell.

"I was a cocky young man and on my own for the first time in my life," he continued. "That was intoxicating. At home I was Bergen's 'Charlie,' but here I could be whoever or whatever I wanted to be. During my first semester I fell in with a group of young Nazis. They drank and sang rousing songs, primarily *Wanderlieder*, songs for hikes in nature. They believed in their own strength and in a strong Germany. And they admired Hitler because he promised to make Germany great again." Vati lit another cigarette.

"They invited me to join the SA and I did. Because they were friendly, because they drank and sang, and because I wanted to be part of a group. Remember, I was brought up in an austere household. My people were sober and didn't sit around the fire at night, singing or telling stories. My parents rarely gave parties. The few I remember were rather formal."

"But when my new Munich friends started provoking people they didn't like and bashed in the heads of some communists one night, I dropped out and never returned. I did my best from then on to avoid their ilk. It wasn't so easy when I was a student, but later, as a doctor,

I had plenty of good excuses to stay away from meetings and rallies, because I had to deliver a baby or attend to a dying patient."

Vati sucked on his cigarette as if he wanted to draw its smoke out all at once. His eyes were searching a past that both pulled and repelled him, I felt. He wasn't hiding his emotions, nor was he sharing them beyond what he had already told me; he simply kept pressing down on the cigarette between his lips.

"*Der Mensch*," Mankind, he said slowly and thoughtfully. "*Der Mensch*," and fell silent.

32

ALL SECRETS REVEALED

"What time is it?" Tante B. asked for the second time within the hour.

"Only ten 'till one," I said. "Still two hours before Sophie's train arrives in Heidelberg."

"How about a good cup of coffee?" suggested Vati. "That'll keep us fresh and will help pass the time."

When Tante B. didn't perk up, I took her arm and walked with her to the kitchen where a beautiful *Schwarzwaelder Kirschtorte,* Black Forest cake, graced the table.

"But we won't touch the cake."

"Of course not! We'll save that for Sophie."

"What was prison like, Vati?" I asked after setting down my cup, aware that I was putting Vati on the spot. I wanted to clear the air before Sophie returned and had planned to ask Vati the night before. But when I had seen his distress over the Nazi past I no longer could.

Vati looked up sharply, scanning my face. "Who told you, Marie?" He fumbled for his cigarettes.

"Mama did in Canada."

"That's another difficult topic," he said with the same sad expression that filled his eyes when he spoke of the war. He inhaled deeply. "I have often wondered if I had to do it over again, knowing that it would destroy my professional life as well as my marriage—though the marriage was pretty much over before that—I fear I'd still help that dying young man."

"Tell me about him."

"His sister Barbara came to me after surgery hours one night. She couldn't stand his agony. He was dying from sepsis, a horribly painful death. He walked the floor at night with his cane, letting out terrible moans and muffled screams. Refused to have his leg amputated after the war."

Barbara? Barbara...and terrible moans? Suddenly, I saw the low-lying farmhouse with its dark corridor and milk-can-filled kitchen before me. And remembered those gut-wrenching groans coming through the wall—and the raised fist of farmer Fritz as Vati and I drove away from the farm.

"Vati, I know who Barbara is. And farmer Schmidt. I was with you when you made a house call not long after their little girl was born."

Vati studied me. A quick smile lit up his face. "You're right! I had forgotten about that. You couldn't have been more than five." He cleared his throat. "In any case, I agreed to help. He passed away peacefully. Barbara's husband Fritz ran to the priest and the priest turned me in." Vati fell silent for a moment. "Fritz himself was ruthless—he'd forced himself on Barbara far too soon after childbirth. As for the priest and the judge, they should have remembered the role of their own institutions under Hitler!"

I felt my anger rise thinking of Speer and Bavaria's judiciary. If 90% of all the bakers in our state had been former Nazis, they would, nevertheless, be baking their cakes and breads with fresh flour and fresh eggs. Bavaria's lawyers and prosecutors, on the other hand, had not been issued new minds and hearts after the war.

My fists were clenched. I wanted to get hold of Fritz and bang his head against the barn, I wanted to confront Vati's prosecutor and judge, and at the same time I wanted to comfort Vati and be comforted by him.

I didn't know where to turn. I needed fresh air.

No, I needed a new mind, a mind that didn't know so much.

"Come and sit by me," Vati said.

I merely stared at him.

Vati picked up a cup, filled it with hot coffee, and held it out to me. "Come, dear. This will do you good. And perhaps a slice of bread." He settled me on the couch, steadied my chin, and put the cup to my lips.

When Tante B. appeared with more coffee, Vati asked her, "Could you bring us a slice of bread and honey? I think Marie could do with some food. We've been talking about my trial and the people who put me in prison." Tante B.'s hand stopped pouring.

"Marie brought it up. Her mother told her in Canada. It's only fair that she knows." Vati stirred his coffee, while Tante B. headed back to the kitchen. He put his hand on mine.

"Oh, I hated them. Hated the judge and the priest, believe me, Marie. There were nights when I swore revenge." He coughed. "But I overcame that. Thank God I did! Revenge and hate only hurt the one who feels those emotions." I didn't need to look at his face to know that he was speaking the truth. I had never seen hate in my father's eyes.

"What was it actually like in prison?" I asked, recalling the nights on the Alaska Highway when I had tried to picture my father's life behind bars.

Vati bit his lip and lit another cigarette though his last one was still smoldering in the ashtray. "Prison is hell. You need to be ruthless or very shrewd to survive." He sipped more coffee and laughed, but not the bitter laugh from before.

"I survived by paying attention to the prison staff's aches and pains, helping wherever I could, and by dealing in cigarettes smuggled in by my loyal patients. That provided enough protection."

My thoughts returned to the camps. Vati's compatriots had killed millions of innocent people and only a few years later they had thrown my father into prison because he had helped a dying man. Who gave the guilty the right to judge? Shouldn't *they* have been locked away? What kind of world was this?

I didn't want to accept what had been thrust on me. I wanted to shout at God and even at Vati, "Keep your horrid world. I want no part of it."

Though I knew that Vati had suffered from this world just as I had, even more so, I still felt he was tied to it by the mere fact that he, his generation, and his elders had bequeathed this nightmare to us. Many by helping create it, others by not speaking up or working against it.

"It was heartbreaking to see our Vati behind bars." Tante B.'s warm voice broke into my turmoil. "He looked so pale and thin. When word got out what had happened, several of Vati's patients—us women mostly—got together to brainstorm how we could cheer him up. We decided to visit as often as prison regulations allowed, and that we would always bring cigarettes, cakes, and fruit."

Vati put Tante B.'s hand on top of mine and enclosed both with his. "I'll always be grateful to you for that, Tante B., and to you, Marie, for your questioning mind and for your empathy. That's all we can do in the end—try to understand one another."

I heard Vati and was touched by his words. I let my hand sink into his and Tante B.'s, and felt some solace, but I could not find peace. While we'd been talking, a cloudburst washed our windows with a furious onslaught. I wished for more onslaughts just as I had as a child when Mama had thrown a fit in the car that almost ran us off the road—torrents and torrents of water that would wash all the blood and ashes away.

Vati, Tante B., and I huddled together on platform 6, looking for the 5:17 PM train from Cologne that would bring Sophie home. We shifted our weight from foot to foot and craned our necks in the direction of the train. After a while, I started pacing. Would Sophie and I slip back into our own world and resume our movie games? A new wave of French, Italian, and Swedish films with their stark realism was taking Western Europe by storm, making our former Hollywood spectaculars look like child's play. Perhaps Francois Truffaut and Ingmar Bergman would change our view of the world. I was dying to learn what Sophie thought of Kafka and Albert Camus, and I couldn't wait to introduce her to the Café Schafheutle.

Finally, the train from Cologne was announced. Vati hung back while Tante B. and I moved closer to the tracks. The wheels screeched, doors flew open, and the platform turned into a mass of moving bodies. A young woman in jeans, an expensive leather jacket, and a beret caught my eye. She was dressed much more flashily than the Sophie I remembered and was nearly pulled to the ground by her heavy case. Already I was flying to her side. Sophie and I were holding on to each other with a joyful tenderness that fused us into one.

Bursting with motherly love, Tante B. pressed her way into our embrace, but we gave way quickly and let our arms hug whomever they found. That night, Sophie and I stayed up until early morning. We were catching up on the days, the weeks, and the months we'd been apart.

"I'm sorry you had such a hard time in Canada, Marie. Makes me feel guilty about my coddled time."

"No guilt trip, please. I'm glad for you. And it wasn't all terrible for me either. I liked my fellow waitress Bobby, and tall, gentle Bill, and Pasha, the powerful husky...I liked the night sky, the woods and animals—just not the *culture* of the place. I'll show you some photos of Pasha tomorrow. And I want to see your paintings. And the photos of them in the newspaper."

"Every member of the Aldinger family saved their paper as a memento. And Grandmother is shipping the originals to us. I couldn't carry them all. It was so fabulous to win first prize."

"I always knew you were a genius!"

"Good," Sophie said with a wide grin. "About time. But seriously, I understand you so much better now. I used to be a perplexed when you suddenly disappeared into your dad's car or retreated to a bench by the Neckar River and returned with pages full of scribbles. Sometimes you'd read them to me, your poems and stories. But just as often when I asked to hear what you'd created, you'd wave me off. 'It's not good enough yet. Needs more work.'" Sophie smiled at me. "Now that I feel the urge to paint and become ever more accomplished, I can see where you were coming from."

I felt a special glow and was filled with gratitude to have my best friend Sophie in my life again, along with the new 'artistic' Sophie.

Sometime between midnight and morning, I told Sophie about the Odenwald retreat. The more I revealed the more I came undone. When I couldn't continue, but kept stammering, "Their eyes, their wide open, dead eyes..." Sophie shushed me. "Not tonight, Marie. It's too painful. For you and for me, too. We did learn some about the camps in my Political Action Group, but not in such graphic detail." *Lucky you,* I thought. Sophie kept stroking my hair. "Let's hold on to the glow of our reunion and face everything difficult tomorrow."

Her strong arms held me, making me feel loved. Through her

presence alone, Sophie calmed my inner storms, at least for a while. Though Sophie and I were as close to each other as we'd always been the night of her return, our old romantic games stayed where they belonged—in our *childish past*. Reality had put too heavy a hand on us; we were no longer mere girls.

BOOK VII

Present, Past, Present, Final Revelation

33

A Formidable
Young Man

Just months after our retreat, everyone in my class enrolled in dance class organized for young women and men in prep school by a local dance studio. Concerned that young men would distract me from my studies, Vati offered me 200 Deutsch Mark if I did *not* enroll.

"Go out and get yourself anything you want," he said sweetly. I did.

I bought a volume of Rilke poems, Camus' *La Peste*, and, together with Sophie, a beautiful reproduction of one of Emil Nolde's watercolors, entitled *Red and White Amaryllis*, a vision of exuberance. To Sophie and me, Nolde was as fresh, vibrant, and mysterious as Johnny Cash. He had recently been rediscovered, and we viewed his first post-war Heidelberg exhibition together. Sophie was so inspired she pulled out her watercolors the moment we got home from the museum.

I felt virtuous about turning Vati's bribe into art and books until my school friends began to invite me to their parties. Of course, they also invited the boys from dance class. Since I did not know how to dance and didn't know any of the boys, I always declined.

Vati's impassioned sermons on the irrepressible sex drive and my own mistrust of marriage had made me immune, I believed, to being trapped by 'the same old game'—that's why I could not understand Vati's fears.

And yet, at times I was gripped by strange longings. When the first tender green broke through the dark brown earth and the willows lit up with an orange hue, I had to run outdoors, stretch my arms toward heaven, and recite poetry to the wind. I'd walk the fields, even in fierce weather, captivated by the glistening earth of freshly plowed fields and feeling a kinship with the crows that danced rough with the wind.

At night, especially when Sophie was at one of her political meetings and Vati and Tante B. were on the road, I'd put Liszt's *Hungarian Rhapsody* on the record player, play it over and over again until I couldn't stand it anymore, light a candle, throw off all clothes except my petticoat, and dance to its rising beat, swirling, twirling, moving wildly and softly, letting the music take over every part of me.

To calm down, I threw on a blouse and jeans and ran out into the night, filling my lungs with the scent of wet leaves and grass, gazing up to the stars, not sure what it was that drove me there. Sometimes, when the yearning was almost unbearable, I'd hug a tree, any gnarly, old fruit tree. Vati might have diagnosed my yearnings as sexual, and they were, but they also sprang from a desire to lose my burdened self and be swept up by a force that could set me free.

Finally, Gerda shook me out of my self-imposed exile. She invited me to her next dance party and was clever enough to appeal to my chivalry by asking me to help keep her precocious brother—who could be a real stinker—in check.

But Vati wouldn't let me go. "Dance class and parties often spell the end of an academic career for a girl," Vati pontificated. "Suddenly a girl's focus shifts. She wants to be popular. Her mind wanders away from books to looks—with the eventual goal of marriage."

"Don't be absurd, Vati. No one in my class is thinking of marriage."

"Not consciously, my dear. Not consciously. But the hand holding, flirting, and maybe a little kissing is winding her clock. The young woman may not know it, but from now on she is primed to find herself a mate."

"Vati, I'm not going to hold hands, kiss, or have my clock wound. I just want to be with Gerda and my friends."

I took a deep breath and looked Vati straight into the eye. "And with all due respect to your objections, Vati, I *am* going to the party."

My eyes must have shot fire and my voice reverberated with determination, because Vati's expression suddenly changed.

"All right," he said in a low voice. "Go! And if you are foolish enough to latch on to one of those pimply young men, you may, if you must, go out on a date once every couple of weeks or so."

"I'm not interested in any pimply young men," I grumbled, pleased with my victory though not yet fully appreciative of the enormity of my father's about-turn.

Gerda greeted me enthusiastically. I talked with her mother for a while, a warm-hearted, unpretentious woman who exuded a calm inner strength. I was bound to adore her. Why couldn't Ingrid, Bastian, and I have had a mother like this? Instantly, I felt guilty and silently asked the fates that Mama's interest in the novels I had sent meant that she was getting better. Gerda's mother soon declared, "I'll now leave you young people to yourselves" and withdrew to her own quarters. I dutifully took my seat next to Horst, who was surveying his sister's guests from a barstool in the party room. Not ten minutes into my conversation with Horst, one of his buddies stopped by and abducted him to work on a school project, leaving me bereft. *Serves you right*, whispered something inside of me while I kept a discreet eye on my partnered classmates, *you shouldn't have come.*

My classmates seemed to be all giggles and coyness, preoccupied with their dresses and hair, flipping their curls this way or that, sometimes flirtatiously, sometimes nervously as if the lock on their forehead or the crease in their skirt spoke more eloquently than their words. They struck me as wound-up dolls, programmed to carry out a few ritual motions over and over again. They never behaved like this when we were by ourselves! My next thought bothered me even more: on that particular occasion, there was no difference between my cherished classmates and those superficial girls from Fort St. John!

After one of the 'pimply young men' put on a Chubby Checker record and turned up the volume, I fled to the library where a young man with reddish-brown hair was stretched out in an armchair, leafing through Konrad Lorenz's *On Aggression*. It was the book, rather than the young man, that caught my attention. Vati and I had discussed Lorenz animatedly since my return.

"Doesn't Lorenz shake you to the core?" I asked the young man. His eyelids fluttered for a moment while he assessed me with a cool and steady gaze. "For example," I went on, "that geese, and even we, will attach to anything as newborns, be it a mechanical doll or an alien from outer space, as long as the object of our fixation makes the ritual 'mother' noises and gestures. We can't break that bond even if it harms us." A shudder went through me as I thought of Mama. I cleared my throat and went on. "Right after birth, we are stuck for life."

The young man laughed. "You mean if our mother turns out to be a mechanical doll? You are right. If we are programmed to attach to whoever 'mothers' us first, then some of us may be in for a rough ride. But I'm more inclined to think," said Herbert, "that most of us are lucky." He pointed to a chair next to him. "I'm Herbert. Will you sit down or have you promised a dance to someone?"

"Goodness, no!"

When he got up to pull out a chair for me, I saw that Herbert was quite a bit taller than I with broad shoulders and well-defined cheek-bones; his hands looked strong; they were well manicured and struck me as appealing. I felt surprised how quickly the word *appealing* had popped into my mind.

I sat down, arranged my skirt daintily around me, and said, "My name is Marie."

"Pleased to meet you, Marie!" We shook hands. "But whether Lorenz is right or not, and I suspect he is, we have to free ourselves from our parents. That's always been true, but it's even more necessary for our generation."

"Why?"

"Because of the Nazis." He nailed my attention with those four words.

"What if our parents weren't Nazis?"

"Doesn't matter," he said curtly, then, looked up, flashing a brief smile. I leaned closer.

"Why not?"

"Firstly, hardly anyone admits to ever having been a Nazi. But even if our parents weren't, they acquiesced. They didn't stop brutality. On one level or another they are all guilty." A sharp crease had appeared on his impressive forehead, and for a moment, he scrutinized me as if to make sure that I was not one of "them."

"But the worst is that the Christian Democrats have embraced some of the old Nazis," he went on. "Not the most notorious ones, of course. Still, it's a national disgrace that today, in the 1960s, we still have former Nazi judges, lawyers, and politicians playing an active role in our society."

My feelings, exactly. Herbert's term "disgrace" nailed down Ingrid's and my experience in the children's home and Vati's trial and imprisonment. I felt contempt for my country's politicians and for the many voters who tolerated and thereby protected former Nazis. More often than not, they were affiliated with the Christian Democrats. That's why Sophie had joined the political youth group, aligned with the Social Democrats. It turned out that Herbert had been one of its leaders in Heidelberg while in prep school.

While Herbert was talking about the need to reject the lies and shameful behavior of the older generation that had failed to take responsibility for its actions, the music upstairs had stopped, and the house began to empty.

"Can I walk you home?" asked Herbert. I checked my watch. Good God! I had promised to call Vati when I was ready to leave and knew that he would have conniptions if I let a young man walk me through town at night.

"No, thank you. I'll help Gerda clean up. And I promised to call my father. He has only just given me permission to go out every two weeks, a huge concession from his point of view." A shadow of a smile flickered across Herbert's face.

"Will you give me your telephone number, then? I would like to see you again."

"Oh? All right." We parted, shaking hands with a warm smile.

I was smitten with Herbert—not in love but smitten, because he saw through the old power structure, because he knew what it meant to be part of our generation, and because he believed in himself.

It seemed to me that everyone was ambiguous, except perhaps Sophie. Life was ambiguous, truth was elusive, yet here was a young man who knew his own mind, knew German society, and wanted to do something about it. Though taken with Herbert, I also observed the censor in him, which reflected a cool, judging mind.

Herbert studied engineering and business at university. He had carefully plotted out his professional path, which seemed appropriate for a twenty-one-year-old young man. I, on the other hand, did not yet know exactly what I wanted to be. In essence, and not unlike Goethe's Faust, I wanted to know what "holds the world together." I wanted to put my finger on the truth beyond appearance. I would never have invoked *Faust* publicly for fear of ridicule, yet I fully identified with his relentless quest. And I wanted to return to Falkenburg Castle after university to decipher its manuscripts and search for the "hidden rhyme." There must be a connection, I felt, between the *ultimate truth* and the rhyme that makes the world break into song.

Herbert called exactly a week after the party. Would I like to go for a hike? I told Vati about my conversation with Herbert and proudly referred to his involvement with the SPD. After a pointed silence, Vati gave his blessing.

"Do you mind if I go hiking with Herbert this weekend?" I asked Sophie.

Sophie locked eyes with me. "Why do you ask?"

"What will *you* do?"

"Go down to the Neckar and paint."

I heaved a sigh of relief. Sophie had started to take drawing lessons from her art teacher after school. "Herr Muller wants me to focus on water; how it reflects the light and mirrors the world, especially clouds and the sky."

"Sounds like a challenge."

"I like to be challenged."

"Where was God in the death camps? Why didn't God interfere?" I pressed Herbert on a mild spring day as we climbed up *Heiligenberg*, Holy Mountain, that faced Heidelberg's castle on the opposite side of the Neckar River.

"I can't accept the existence of God," he said, "at least not the existence of a benevolent God. Not after all that happened. On the other hand, it doesn't make sense to believe in an evil God. Good and evil are within us, I suspect."

"If there is no God, then what is there? Just us and an uncaring universe?"

"Why not?" Herbert sounded impatient.

"Because of the *need* to believe. And our desire for something greater than ourselves." We were walking along *Muehlbach*, a swirling brook on its way to the Neckar River, but paid no attention to its rushing flow.

"That can be explained, too. After all, we are herd animals. Herd animals need a leader. And we have all been children. Children need a protector, a guiding, powerful force. All that translates into a desire for something 'greater than ourselves.'"

"That may be true," I answered, "but I don't feel that's all there is. There is a spiritual force, something deeper than the need to be guided." Herbert said nothing but took my hand and pressed it against his cheek.

I felt both stimulated and protected in Herbert's presence.

We were now walking under chestnut trees, holding hands on the way up to Heiligenberg. At times, Herbert's shoulder brushed against me accidentally, whereupon he stopped, touched my cheek, or brushed some hair out of my face. When he spoke, his pronounced cheek muscles worked energetically as if they were pushing his thoughts from his mind to his lips. I liked his full lips and breathed in his scent, a bitterish concoction with an edge of chamomile sweetness to it.

While his character and his mind appealed to me, I was not so sure of his passionate self. The part of me that danced to Liszt's *Hungarian Rhapsody* and the part that ran out into the night sought ecstasy and abandon. Somehow, I worried that Herbert might be so solidly constructed that he was incapable of losing himself.

"Even if we assume there is a God," said Herbert, "we have no influence over what God does, since he is, by definition, all-powerful. But we can influence society. The most important task for our generation is to break up the entrenched order. It is time to rid ourselves of the old guard and empower the Social Democrats who are concerned with the common good and not just the elite. I don't mean the communists—they only represent another form of totalitarianism—but the social democrats."

"True," I said. "Communism has been discredited since Hungary at the very least." I still couldn't forget those last calls for help from radio Budapest in 1956, when I was kneeling in front of our radio, while Russian tanks rolled through the streets. "How we betrayed people's hopes. We just sat there and did nothing!" I said with contempt.

"I agree with you," Herbert said quickly. "It was terrible. No one wanted to risk another world war."

He looked tenderly into my eyes, like a priest about to bless a child, took my hand in his, closed his eyes, and kissed my fingertips as if my fingers were something otherworldly. I almost smiled, and watched his devotion with curious fascination, surprised at the effect of my presence on him. Vati had so ridiculed the courting game that I could not enjoy it freely, but it moved me nevertheless, especially Herbert's sudden shifts from strength to tenderness.

I loved it when his green eyes grew soft, when he seemed to see something so rapturous in me that he had to yield. Although I believed that there was nothing intriguing about me, I was moved and flattered, and afraid of the moment, which was sure to come, when he'd find out that I was just an ordinary girl. We walked through woods where Roman soldiers had piled stone upon stone to erect the *limes*, their barrier against rebellious Germanic tribes. I wondered if the soldiers had dreamt of sun-drenched Rome while upending rocks from the soil of our cold and wet German earth. Did they march on to Britain where they built another *limes*, the barrier against the Scots and the Celts? Our path moved along their crumbling wall. If I stooped down and lifted a stone, would I touch palms with a soldier now buried along the Thames or in the Teutoburg Forest where Roman troops had met their doom?

On the other side of the hill was a Nazi reconstruction of a Germanic meeting ground, now overgrown. We left it by the wayside. After we reached the top of our steep climb, we gazed silently at the ruins of a Benedictine monastery and rested on an overturned pillar, breathing the rich air of decaying trees. A sheet of beech seedlings covered the floor of the former apse, glistening in the sun.

"Come," said Herbert, taking my hand and pulling me deeper into the woods through underbrush. He headed for a small clearing, covered with fern.

"Let's rest."

He took off his jacket, spread it out as a blanket while he sat down on a pillow of moss. I put my head in his lap. Letting my eyes run up the shafts of swaying trees, I caught a piece of blue sky that opened to an even deeper blue, a sky beyond the sky, a receding spiral of space. Suddenly the world spun away from me, rising above my body like smoke over a field while the weight of my body seemed to sink deeper into Herbert's lap.

When Herbert gently outlined my eyebrow with his fingertip, my body surged toward him, stirred by his touch. We kissed tenderly at first, then urgently, with Herbert pushing his tongue into me as if he wanted to reach the sky through the roof of my mouth. Embracing earth, sky, and a wildly beating pulse, I soared into a space of longing and letting go.

For a blissful moment, I was at one with the world. Then a branch crushed by the foot of a passerby broke with a loud crack, and I slipped back into fragmented me.

34

THE PHONE CALL

I woke in the middle of the night, hot and disoriented. The phone in the kitchen was ringing. The alarm clock showed 2:00 in the morning. Vati and Tante B. were on the road. What if a sleepy driver had plowed into their car? Or their brakes had failed? I sat up, stumbled past Sophie's rhythmic breathing into the kitchen, and lifted up the receiver.

"Hallo?"

"Is that you, Marie?" I was surprised to hear English. "Did I wake you?"

The voice was higher than my sister's. Must be...Mama! "Yes, you did, but that's fine. How are you, Mama?"

"Not yet well. The doctors don't know how to help me. Nobody knows how to help me...."

"Oh, dear. Are you still in the hospital?"

"Yes. My neighbor has a phone and was kind enough to let me call you."

"That's good."

"No, it's not good at all. Nobody loves me. You don't love me. My parents didn't love me, they hated me and beat me. And YOU rejected me."

"No, Mama, I rejected Canada."

"What?"

"I rejected the icy North. I wasn't made for a life in Fort Nelson. I'm sorry."

"You're sorry?"

"Yes. But please tell me are Ingrid and Bastian visiting you every day?"

"I think they do."

"Because they care for you."

"They care for me?

"Very much so."

"Do you care for me?"

"Yes."

"Then come back and get me out of this place."

I woke, lying on the cold kitchen floor covered in sweat with Sophie bent over me.

"What's the matter, Marie? Did you have a nightmare?" Sophie looked at me with Tante B.'s motherly eyes while I sat up. "The phone. Did you hear the phone ring?"

"No."

"Was I on the phone when you came in?"

"No. You were just like this, stretched out on the floor."

"Mama called. From Canada."

"I don't think so."

"No, no. I spoke with her."

"I think you had a dream. Let me help you up and let's slowly walk back to bed."

"Mama sounded so distressed." Sophie put her arm around my waist. "The phone is still in its cradle. You must have fallen before you reached it."

I shook myself. "Maybe...I did dream it all."

Sophie walked me back to bed. I couldn't wait to be under the covers and pulled the feather down all the way up to my ears.

"There. Stay put. I'll go and get you a glass of orange juice. And tomorrow we'll try to call Bastian or Ingrid to get an update on your mother."

When no one in Fort St. John answered the phone next morning, I decided to stay home from school and try a few hours later. I knew Vati would write an excuse for me once I explained the situation.

Could I really have had such a realistic dream? And what was it trying to tell me that I didn't already know? Mama—our life with

Mama—remained a festering wound in my life. I hated her fury, and I bled for her helplessness.

Finally, I reached Bastian in the early afternoon.

"Basti? Is Mama all right?"

"Not quite yet, but there is hope. Your parcel arrived and Mama actually started reading one of the Courths-Mahler romances. The doctors take it as an encouraging sign."

"Good. Will the doctors let her take some of the elixir for post-meno-pausal women Vati sent along?"

"They're checking it out. Thank you for everything. Maybe we're over the worst."

"Basti, does Mama have a phone in her room?

"Yes, but it's for in-house calls only. If you call the hospital the switchboard will connect you to her room."

"What about her roommate?"

"Same thing. Why do you ask?"

I told my brother about the nightmare. He was silent for a long time.

"Basti, you there?"

"Don't let her destroy you."

"Mama?"

"Who else? She wreaks havoc wherever she goes. It took me a quarter century to say this out loud, but deep inside we three know, don't we?"

"Yes."

"Why do you think I hated studying? Before your Vati came into our life, Mama beat the shit out of me whenever I made a spelling mistake or couldn't decipher a word."

"Oh, Basti. How awful!"

"We've all been through it."

"Yes—and yet..."

"What?

"I've always felt that she cannot help herself. That she is possessed. Once a certain trigger is activated, she's like a wound-up toy that has to go through programmed motions, come hell or high water."

"Sounds like her."

"She has no control. But deep inside her, there's this sadness..."

"I don't know."

"I don't *know* either, but I *feel* it."

"Maybe." My brother fell silent for a moment.

"Basti, it's like a chain. Mama got beaten up by a mother who was mistreated by her parents. And God knows what violence Grandma's parents endured. Thanks to you, the doctors, and Vati, we're not coming after her; we're breaking that chain." I heard him take a deep breath.

"Maybe." He stayed silent for a moment, then said firmly, "Right now, she needs positive reinforcement, the doctors keep impressing on Ingrid and me. And, in her restless sleep, she still keeps mumbling 'You must tell them, Herr Jensen. Tell them, please.' Mr. Jensen could make a real difference here. See if you can find him."

"I'll start sleuthing. Do you or Ingrid have any idea where he might live?"

"Try Hamburg-Altona where she grew up. He may not even be alive anymore what with the war and the firebombs. Start with the Hamburg phone book and call us as soon as you learn something."

"*Ich werde mein Bestes tun.*" I'll try my best.

Already during the call, and even more so now, I felt as if I were entering new territory, something not yet known but beginning to show its contour.

We *had to* help Mama. She had always worked hard for us. I could have never survived in her jobs. She fed us when we had little money in Garmisch, and she provided a home for as long as she could. She never considered giving us up.

I knew I would never live with Mama again because of her outbursts but also because we had so little in common. My mind and soul were starving in Garmisch when she was our only parent. She was not interested in discussing God and the world. And she didn't want to hear the questions that wouldn't let go of me—*Why are we here? What is the meaning of our existence?* She didn't love Rilke's sonnets, Schiller's plays, or Goethe's *Faust* that set my soul on fire.

But I also believed if the three of us didn't try to help her, then we couldn't move forward ourselves. It wasn't about Bastian, Ingrid and me, but it was *also* about us.

35

RETURN TO FALKENBURG CASTLE, 1961

"I've been waiting for you," Sophie said when I came home from school. "Mutti and I have been invited to our former landlady's golden wedding anniversary in Falkenburg. She got Vati to agree that I can take next Friday off from school and come along." Sophie stopped herself and looked coyly at me. "And..."

"And what?"

"And *you*"—Sophie paused, watching me like a hawk—"*you* have received your father's blessing to come along as well."

I sank down on the couch. *Back to Falkenburg.* My first—my one and only home. *"Echt?"* Honestly?

"Echt. And Mutti wants to ask our former landlady if you can attend their party."

"Thank you, that's sweet of her, but please ask her not to. I need some alone time with my Castle. Oh, Sophie, I can't wait."

When Tante B. finally turned off the Autobahn, a freeway without speed limits, she breathed a long sigh of relief and celebrated her escape from big trucks and crazy drivers by pulling into a rest area and lighting a cigarette.

"Hast Du fein gemacht, Mutti," applauded Sophie. "You did a fine job." Squashing my impatience, I chimed in, *"Ja, Tante B. Sehr fein."*

Some twenty minutes later, Tante B. turned onto the two-lane road from Noerdlingen to Falkenburg, and my excitement soared. It had been far too long, years, since I had set eyes on Falkenburg Castle—my stone mother, my teacher, my friend.

"I can't believe they've turned Round Tower and those two dilapidated buildings into Falkenburg Castle Inn." Tante B. smiled at Sophie and me in the rearview mirror. "But how nice that we can stay there."

I didn't warm to the idea of a Castle Inn where any stranger, anybody at all, could make himself at home in what had once been part of my realm, but at least the Inn allowed us to stay within the Castle's walls.

I scanned the horizon. My Castle, my home, was bound to appear any moment, yet curve after curve held back its presence, until the car emerged from a sharp turn. Then, without warning, it rose before me—magnificent, massive, and timeless, lifting its six towers deep into the sky.

My whole being expanded from knowing I was this Castle's child. Tante B. shifted into a lower gear for the steep hill that I had raced up and down with Vati so many times.

"Please drop us off at the outer gate, so we can walk in," I begged her.

Once outside, I stood still, taking in the moat, the East Wall, and several towers. Motioning Sophie to follow, I walked slowly into the fortified gate, took a deep breath, and ran my hands across the stones of its walls, savoring their rough surface, reading them like a blind man reads words, and stretching upward to let my fingers slide along the arch until it stretched beyond me.

"*Ihr seid's noch.*" It's still you, I whispered.

In the inner yard the Castle's towers, halls, and balustrades enclosed me just as they always had. They had remained steadfast, untouched by time and circumstances, while I'd been buffeted about. Not a line on the horizon, not a single shingle had changed. I thrust my arms up into the sky in an ecstatic, open embrace.

Together, Sophie and I walked toward the Castellan's house, our former home. The gate to the garden path was locked, and a strange woman looked out the upstairs window.

"Do you want to see if she'll let us in?" Sophie asked.

I shook my head. "No need. I used to spend every free moment in the Treasure Hall, on the ramparts, and in the chapel—not at home." I was going to say "because of Mama," but felt reluctant somehow because of Mama's health struggles in the Canadian North. And suddenly I wondered if Mr. Jensen might mean to her what my Castle meant to me. I knew so little about Mama's childhood.

Sophie and I climbed the incline to Wolf Gate where the skull had been baring its fangs at me ever since I became aware of the world. On this gray day, its bleached bones looked brittle and weatherworn to me.

Fuerstenbau, housing the great hall and ducal apartments, rose before us. "Come to me," it seemed to say. "I know you." Sophie and I climbed its outer staircase to the entrance door, but when we turned down the massive handle, it wouldn't open.

Even the chapel door was locked. Here we were, so close to all I had known and loved, and yet we were shut out. The arms of the willow by the chapel door moved in the breeze. I brushed away their leafy branches, stepped inside its tent, and leaned against the trunk while Sophie walked on. "Come here," she called out to me. "Look at that sign!"

I saw her pointing to a massive sign in front of the granary. *SCHLOSSFUEHRUNG*, guided Castle tour. "We've missed today's tours. But guess who'll be there for the first *Schlossfuehrung* tomorrow morning?" Sophie jiggled my nose with her index finger just as Bastian used to do. And suddenly I missed my brother with such vehemence that a shiver ran through me. It was Bastian who had enlightened me about the history of Falkenburg Castle before my Castle began speaking to me on its own. And now he was prompting us to look into Mama's history.

We walked across a stone terrace toward Falkenburg Castle Inn. The Inn had been a service building for most of its 800-year-old life with much lower ceilings and smaller windows than the princely apartments or Treasure Hall. And while we lived at Falkenburg, it had been in such dilapidated condition that its front gate had been nailed shut, and a big DANGER sign put up.

But here it was, all whitewashed, the windows enhanced by freshly painted shutters, and young linden trees rising from its open veranda. I rejoiced in its thick stone walls and solid, stone stairs—true hallmarks of my Castle. The Inn's crowning glory was Round Tower, rising above the main structure and forming part of the Castle's defensive wall.

Tante B. awaited us in the lobby. Her cheeks rosy, her eyes bulging, she was bursting with good tidings. "We got the tower room." The moment I was enclosed by the tower's round walls, I knew I had come home. If Prince Henry had turned me into stone that instant, to meld into the tower forever, I would have been perfectly content.

The next morning, Sophie and I returned to the granary and rang the bell for the *Schlossfuehrung*. The guide, a middle-aged gentleman, searched my face. "Wait, don't I know you?" He broke into a smile. "You're one of Dr. Bergen's daughters! The little one?"

"I am."

"You have Herr Doktor's eyes! How you've grown. You were an itty-bitty thing." He bowed. "My name is Weber. I'll be your guide." He leaned toward me and said in a soft voice, "We sure miss Herr Dr. Bergen. Best Doktor we ever had. You can ask anyone!"

"I believe you."

Following Herr Weber through the yard into *Fuerstenbau*, I recognized the grooved banister, the polished floorboards, and every crack in the wall. In the past, there had been no locked doors. Now strangers had to let me in, and I had to pay for the privilege of visiting my favorite places.

"The main building, *Fuerstenbau*, was renovated under Count Gottfried, who lived here from 1534 to 1622—except for the top floor with its elegant stucco ballroom and reception hall. That was erected by Duke Ernst II in the eighteenth century"—Herr Gruber stopped himself and smiled apologetically—"but you know all that, Fraulein Bergen."

"No, not the dates. I remember the shape, the feel, and the scent of each hall, but I wouldn't have known about its history or architectural style as a child."

"*Count* Gottfried?" asked Sophie. "I recall a courteous old gentleman, the *Duke*, from my Falkenburg days, not a Count."

"Your memory is correct," said the guide. "But the counts of Oettingen-Oettingen weren't elevated to the status of dukes until 1674."

"Oh, only as recently as *that?*" Sophie chuckled.

Herr Weber smiled while I thought back to the past with its endless battles. Competing dynasties. Ferocious wars between Protestants and Catholics, culminating but not ending with the Thirty Years' War.

When we finally entered my Treasure Hall, I was stunned by its transformation. The heaps of strewn-about treasures had been cleared away, placed on shelves, locked behind glass doors, or hung, neatly framed, from the walls. No open boxes of manuscripts, stacks of paintings, or rolled-up canvases were waiting for my touch. Life that feeds on disorder and dust had been sanitized.

My childhood hall had been rich, fertile, and chaotic—just like Falkenburg's crazy history with soldiers from all over Europe storming its walls, tumbling off, and storming them again—and like the crooked path of my family.

"A whole army of archivists and historians achieved a great victory here. Everything is now in order," Herr Weber proclaimed with pride and for a split second I imagined his arm flying up in a Nazi salute.

I shook myself. "Maybe that's our problem," I whispered to Sophie. "God damn order."

When Sophie took off with Tante B. for the golden wedding reception, I was free to wander about the Castle—at least to the parts that had not been closed off. Thank God, no one could lock me out of the heath. I headed out through Hubertus Gate, across the moat, and left the road for the shepherd's trail as soon as it came into sight.

The heath cushioned my feet as it had always done. I inhaled its dry, sweet scent with languor. Then I ran, ran as fast as I could, jumping over scrawny bushes, hairy thistles, and pointed rocks like I had done as a child.

I ran and ran—until it faced me: the tall cross with the suffering Christ. And I remembered how Anna and I had stopped there to pray on that special berry-picking day. It had pained me to look at the crucified Christ, so I had focused on the inscription above his head: INRI. I already knew that words had power and wondered—feverishly hoped—that if we could call out the word that INRI spelled, maybe we could release Christ from his pain.

But Anna didn't know what INRI meant. And no one else did.

Now I knew. **I**esus of **N**azareth, **R**ex **I**udaeorum. Jesus of Nazareth, King of the Jews.

How could it be that so many women and men had forgotten that

God's son was a Jew?

Christians fell on their knees before Jesus and prayed to him. They prayed to a Jew and glorified a Jew, but no one seemed to remember that under Hitler. Perhaps that wasn't really surprising, since their priests and their church had also forgotten that fact and had sanctioned the persecution of Jews for centuries. Not only in Germany, but all over Europe.

Where was our "Christian" compassion when contemplating the crucified Christ? Where was our empathy? Had we become so inured to blood and thorns that we registered his suffering as a mere given, an artifact—hardening our hearts to the point where the killing of thousands and thousands of his brethren and sisters, God's children, could become norm because we saw people as things rather than living flesh and blood?

Back at the Castle, I headed for the well at the center of the inner yard that reached all the way to the river Woernitz below, supplying the Castle with water, even during a siege. I used to throw pebbles into its depth and listen to the long silence after the stone had disappeared into the darkness that shrouded its plunge toward the river. It had seemed endless to me, that silent falling, until finally I heard the echo of a sound. Too faint to be called a *splash*, more like a *whoosh*. I picked up a pebble, but when I reached the edge of the well, I saw that it had been sealed off with a metal lid.

If only I were Hercules! I'd lift off the lid and roll it around the courtyard like a wheel. I shook off my frustration. Weren't all these changes merely superficial? Did they really matter?

Hadn't the Castle inspired me to learn and keep learning? Hadn't it taught me that history was in flux? That progress was slow? That Christians were not Christians when they lacked love and compassion? That we killed God whenever we killed a man, any man, woman, or child, no matter their color, their creed, or origin?

Yes, the Castle had taught me all that by making me hear, feel, and see, by luring me into words that floated from the chapel's pulpit and by seeding awe and curiosity through the vellum manuscripts in the library, the swirls on the gravestones of the Jewish cemetery, and the spirit of Prince Henry.

I no longer felt closed off but embraced, even strangely uplifted. Ah. How long had the organ been playing? I walked toward the green veil of the willow by the chapel's door, pressed down the handle, and felt it open.

Count Gottfried and his two wives were still standing under the choir balcony, the fading eye of Jehovah still looking down from high above the altar, and St. Michael and Mary with the baby Jesus still facing each other in the chancel. I slowed my step and approached the altar just as the organist intoned *"Ave Maria,"* rarely played in my Protestant childhood days. All the better! The song's dulcet tones drew me in. Might they also lure Prince Henry, or were they too sweet for him?

"Not too sweet…" whispered the Prince while the organ came to a crescendo.

Where was he? The light had not changed around the altar, and yet I felt his presence.

"Good." The candles on the altar flickered as if a door had been opened.

"Life is not sweet," said the Prince. "Too often, it's bitter."

"Yes, it's often bitter."

I strained my ears, listening for the Prince's footsteps. Would they head for the crypt as they had so many years ago?

"So what to do?" I whispered, as much to myself as to the Prince.

His voice came closer.

I heard him whisper *"help"* but could not understand the words that followed. A few more steps and the Prince had come so close that his breath brushed the shell of my ear, creating a current that rushed from the crown of my head through my spine directly into what I had always known deep inside.

A hush, then a whisper. "Help, then make your way."

Make my way?

I reached for the Prince. While I was lifting my arm, I felt him moving away. Not away—*upward.* Something was stirring the air above me. I turned my head as high as I could, looking directly into Jehovah's eye as a shadow clouded its contour.

"Come back!" I implored him, falling to my knees. When only silence answered, I muttered, "Too late!"

And then I heard him again. Not from the altar, not next to me, and not from above, but from inside myself.

"Not too late to move forward!"

During the long drive back, the Castle's pull wouldn't leave me. Everything in me reverberated. Images and feelings rose and dissolved as if in a dream. I remained in a trance, interrupted now and then by Sophie squeezing my hand.

In the evening, while Sophie and Tante B. picked up their knitting and settled around the living room table, I left for the kitchen. Something inside me kept churning. I turned on the radio and sat down in Vati's chair. My fingers were drumming on the kitchen table when something made me sit up and pay attention...something dulcet. Gounod's *Ave Maria*, the song the organ had played in my Castle's chapel. Instead of losing myself in its sweet melancholy, I became filled with purpose and inner clarity: I must find Mr. Jensen to help Mama recover, that much I already knew, *and* I must turn to Herbert to connect me with young social Democrats. That was my new insight. I picked up the phone and called Herbert.

"I can't wait to show you my Castle," I gushed, "but that's not what I'm calling about tonight. I need to ask you for a favor."

"Ask away."

"You know many of the young Social Democrats at Heidelberg University. Will you please introduce me to some? I need to become more active politically."

"Absolutely, Marie." Herbert's voice was filled with enthusiasm.

"And learn more about the machinery of our democracy, which is about time. I'm four years older than our *Grundgesetz*, our post-war constitution."

I thought I heard Herbert chuckle. "I promise that you will learn about that machinery and make great friends in the bargain."

"As long as I have you," I said quickly, sending kisses down the line, and hanging up. I stood up and stretched. Good intentions and mere enthusiasm would not be enough. I knew that now. And sadness and despair, however justified, would change nothing. Sophie, Herbert, my schoolfriends, and I had to organize and work together to make sure that our country would stay on a firm course of "never again."

Before falling asleep that night I asked Sophie. "Tomorrow we must try to find Herr Jensen. You game?"

"Absolutely. As soon as our parents have left for the road."

36

MR. JENSEN

Our household's phone book covered Heidelberg and Manheim only, so I dialed Information for the telephone number of a Mr. Jensen in Hamburg-Altona.

"First name?"

"We don't know."

"Street address?"

"Unknown."

"Is this a hoax?"

"No. Please don't hang up!" I spilled out Mama's story, hoping to move the heart of the operator who could make all the difference. No luck. After that, Sophie and I took turns calling Information in ten-minute intervals, hoping for a different, more kind-hearted operator. Eventually, Sophie succeeded. The woman told her, "I've copied the phone numbers of all the Jensens who live in Hamburg-Altona; there are nine. Write quickly or I'll get into trouble."

Sophie thanked her warmly, wrote down every single name and number, and handed the list to me. I dialed the first number with Sophie giving me thumbs-up.

"I am the daughter of Lilybeth von Baginski, whose teacher in Hamburg-Altona in the 1920s was a Mr. Jensen. My mother adored him and still speaks of him," began my well-rehearsed spiel that ended with, "Do you remember a Lilybeth von Baginski?" One voice after another answered in the negative, some with indifference, others with regret. On the seventh a man's voice said,

"Yes, I remember Lilybeth von Baginski, such a beautiful...*tortured* girl."

Oh, my God, he knows Mama.

"Please give me your name again and that of your father," the deep, pleasant voice requested. "It would be easier to talk in person. Can you come and see me?"

I spelled my name three times before Mr. Jensen repeated it correctly. There was no way we could have a real conversation with him except face to face. *"Ja, ich komme gerne vorbei,"* Yes, I'd be glad to come by, I said quickly. "Our mother, I mean Lilybeth, is suffering from a serious depression. My siblings and her Canadian doctors—she's been living in Canada since the fifties—hope that you would be willing to talk to her by phone. She keeps uttering your name."

"Suffering from depression?" His voice filled with concern. "Of course, I'll talk to her. I've always been fond of her. She used to visit me for years after she graduated, together with her baby son, who turned into a charming little boy, but we lost touch not long after she married the Doktor."

"That would be my father."

"I see."

"When would you like me to stop by?"

"How about the day after tomorrow for afternoon tea?" Mr. Jensen suggested.

"Day after tomorrow for tea is wonderful. *Und darf ich meine beste Freundin Sophie mitbringen?"* He answered in the affirmative.

Sophie and I danced around the room. We had found Mr. Jensen. Perhaps now we could truly help Mama overcome her depression.

Sophie robbed her secret stash, funded by her doting grandmother, so that we could buy train tickets to Hamburg, and we arranged lodging through a cousin of her father's who lived in Hamburg.

The next day I phoned Vati's hotel and left a message with the name and address of Sophie's cousin, along with a few words about our mission. Vati would understand. He had always tried to help Mama, supported her Canada plans, ferried her about whenever she visited, and, unlike Mama who never missed an opportunity to put Vati down, he didn't speak ill of her in front of us.

I stared at No. 69 Hartmann Street in Hamburg-Altona, a drab apartment building, a cement block really, one of thousands erected in bombed-out cities all over Germany after WWII when speed was the driving force, not pleasing architecture. They served their purpose, these dull buildings, providing a sense of security and long-lost privacy to hundreds of thousands of citizens and refugees from the East who were emerging from rubble basements, displaced persons' camps, and cramped quarters.

I rang the bell to No. 32, *Jensen*. Sophie and I were buzzed in almost instantly. Our steps echoed in the stairway as if we were being followed. How many ghosts were still haunting Hamburg, I wondered? So many bombings, including the infamous firestorm of July 1943, *Operation Gomorrah*, when 35,000 civilians died and 125,000 were injured, leaving Hamburg in almost total ruin.

On the third floor, a tall, older gentleman with thinning white hair, beautiful violet eyes, and long, curved eyelashes came forward. *Valentino eyes*, I couldn't help thinking, remembering how Mama had swooned over that Hollywood star at Falkenburg Castle. Herr Jensen was wearing a gray cardigan over a neatly ironed white shirt and sharply creased gray slacks; the only off-note in his dapper presentation were his felt slippers; he must be suffering from swollen feet, I guessed.

"You must be Marie, Lilybeth's daughter. Your eyes." I was amused by how quickly people assigned me to Vati or Mama, in each case based on my eyes.

"Please come in. I've made some tea, and my daughter has baked an apple pie." Herr Jensen led us through a spotless sitting room full of books and modern Danish furniture into a dining room. The table had been set like Mama used to do at Falkenburg—white linen tablecloth, matching napkins, and a sprig of orchid blossoms in a delicate vase. After serving tea, Mr. Jensen asked about our school and our interests. We, in turn, learned that his wife had died a few years ago, and that he had one daughter who lived nearby. I tried to be patient during these pleasantries, but prayed he'd soon come to the point.

"Yes, Lilybeth von Baginski," Herr Jensen finally said, addressing me. "I was a young teacher then, still figuring out how to best deal with teenage girls. Your mother was my student from age ten until she graduated at sixteen. She was a beauty who turned heads. Lilybeth was not unaware of this effect. Still, I must say, she was closed off." Herr Jensen smoothed out his hair with his right hand in a slow, deliberate motion, as if massaging his memory. He looked me over, from top to toe, then continued. "Because there was so much pain."

I leaned forward, eager to learn more.

"But first...you said your mother and father are divorced?"

"Yes."

"And you live in Germany with your father?"

"Yes, together with Sophie and her mother."

"Unusual."

Herr Jensen's eyes filled with a curiosity that was gentle and far from off-putting.

"Can you tell me why?" he asked. "But you don't need to."

"My father has always been the more nurturing parent. Our mother, we call her Mama, wasn't." I couldn't go on. This man was a stranger to me. Yes, he appeared to be a dear gentleman, but...

I had never talked about Mama to anyone outside the family, not in school, not at St. John's, and not in Canada. It felt like treachery. Herr Jensen rose, then sat down again.

"You've come a long way," he said softly. "All the way from Heidelberg."

I nodded and started over. "Mama has always seemed possessed by some furious anger, a rage that often consumes her. When her anger explodes, she lashes out at everybody, but especially at those close to her. She becomes physically violent."

I swallowed. Already, my voice was unsteady. I didn't want to break down in front of Herr Jensen, and I didn't want to overwhelm him. I lowered my eyes. Sophie touched my ankle with her foot. I noticed Herr Jensen running his fingers ever more firmly over the hot teapot. He looked directly into my eyes.

"So she hurt you?"

I nodded.

He stared at the tablecloth and said nothing. For a very long time.

"Even when you were small and helpless?"

262

"Yes."

"I see."

Now he knew. I felt for him. Maybe I shouldn't have told him. He nodded a slow, deliberate nod and got up. "I'll just make us a fresh pot of tea."

When he returned, Herr Jensen said, "I have a feeling she didn't tell you much about her childhood."

"No, not much except for one phrase, *'Ich habe keine Liebe bekommen,'* I didn't receive any love."

"Yes," he said and sighed. "I'm afraid it's true. She didn't." He let out another sigh. "It's all so long ago. At first, I only saw her as a beautiful young girl, but soon I knew she had problems. Every so often she came to class with a black eye or welts across her arms or calves."

Herr Jensen looked distressed, as if seeing Mama right before his eyes. "I had a brutal father," he said, "and knew right away that she was being beaten. I asked her to stay after class one day and tried to get her to talk. Of course, she wouldn't. She was terrified."

I couldn't imagine Mama being terrified. The mother I knew was fearless, always on the attack and asserting her right.

Watching me closely, Herr Jensen touched my hand for just a second. "Let me tell you about her childhood, stories she told me when she visited me from Berchtesgaden with her young son Bastian. I hope my account won't upset you too much. It is not pretty."

"No," I assured him, seeking Sophie's eyes, "please go ahead."

"From what I can tell, your grandmother gave birth to your mother at age 16 after having been seduced by an orchestra conductor in a small town in Saxony."

What? Mama, the haughty baroness, illegitimate? Mama who commanded, or rather demanded instant attention because she was "higher born," i.e. "better" than anyone else? The bosom buddy of Countess Amalia? The noble lady who so moved the Duke's heart that he offered us housing at Falkenburg Castle? I couldn't believe it.

"Illegitimate children were seen as *bastards* in those days, not considered full human beings. And a girl who gave birth out of wedlock was treated like a whore and became a social outcast. So your great-grandparents hid your grandmother away in their own home so that no one would ever know she was pregnant."

I tried to picture my sixteen-year-old grandmother shut in for days, weeks, and months—facing her parents' anger, disappointment, and contempt. Every day anew.

"They made her work hard, doing laundry, ironing, and cleaning, but kept her inside. Food was her only consolation. She gained so much weight that baby Lilybeth weighed eleven pounds at birth. Your grandmother cursed your mother and never forgave her for her suffering. Little Lilybeth was put up with an aunt who lived in another town. The aunt had no children and was happy to take her in. Lilybeth stayed there for some four years.

"Meantime, your grandmother made her way to Hamburg where she met and married Baron von Baginski, a shady character, who'd been a cavalry officer in WWI. Long after the war, the Baron still flaunted his status by wearing riding britches and boots and carrying a riding crop. He adopted your mama. Yes, the Baron gave her his name, but he didn't give her any love. Neither did your grandmother, who blamed Lilybeth for every hurt and humiliation in her life."

"Didn't her aunt love her? What happened to the aunt?"

"I believe she did. But when your mother was five, the aunt became pregnant and her husband pressured her to return Lilybeth to her real mother. From then on, your mother's life became a nightmare." Herr Jensen poured more tea. "If you were older, I'd offer you a shot of cognac to fortify you. As it is, tea will have to do."

I was already horrified by what I had learned but sat up straight like a good soldier. Herr Jensen resumed, "The Baron was an alcoholic and a gambler. He worked at a casino and your grandmother may or may not have been..." Herr Jensen coughed, looked away, then cleared his throat. "It's possible that your grandmother was forced...into some terrible situation when the Baron couldn't pay his gambling debt."

I stiffened. Sophie took my hand. My grandmother bartered to strangers by her own husband?

"Though arrogant and cruel, the Baron was a good-looking fellow who could charm people when sober, but he wasn't often sober and died of alcoholism before your mother was married."

I breathed a sigh of relief. I had never liked the man Mama or Vati described as my grandfather. Now I was grateful his blood wasn't flowing through my veins. But I still couldn't believe that Mama was a commoner.

Herr Jensen moistened his lips with a bit of tea and continued, "While her parents spent nights at the casino and days asleep, Lilybeth had to fend for herself. Often, there was no food in the house. Her parents found fault with everything she did, and the Baron took his riding crop or the dog leash to her at the slightest provocation.

"During the Depression, the casino closed down. The family was forced to move into very modest quarters, and your grandmother had to take in laundry. She did the laundry in the kitchen where your Mama had a cot for the night."

My eyes were glued to Herr Jensen, Mama's teacher from grade 5 until her graduation. Mama had never breathed a word about those times.

"That winter was one of the coldest in living memory," Herr Jensen resumed. "The kitchen walls glistened with ice, the windows froze and didn't melt for the long weeks the cold spell lasted. Your mother didn't have enough blankets and no winter coat for her long walk to school."

I jumped up. Herr Jensen's eyes filled with concern. Sophie was already by my side. "Are you all right?"

"Yes, yes," I whispered. Suddenly something in me clicked... a childhood scene flashed through my mind of Mama reading the story of *The Little Match Girl* to me about a girl who had to sell matches out in the bitter cold. I shared this memory, adding, "Mama had looked so inconsolably sad and distressed that I've never forgotten."

"Yes, I can see Lilybeth identifying with the poor match girl." Mr. Jensen was rubbing his chin. "I'll add just two more stories and then we'll talk about that phone call to Canada, right?"

"Right."

"Your mother was briefly lifted out of her miserable existence when she was about 12 after she came down with diphtheria and was isolated in a children's hospital. She didn't even remember how she got there. The nurses feared she'd lost her will to live and was hovering at death's door. But Lilybeth pulled through. The nurses cheered her and took pleasure in spoiling her. She was allowed to eat anything she liked and was offered second helpings. She was given nice warm baths and gently toweled dry. Both the doctors and the nurses were touched by the lovely, emaciated girl whose body and spirit began to revive before their eyes. 'I wish I could stay here forever, Herr Jensen,' she told me when I visited her in the hospital." Herr Jensen wiped tears from his cheek. "Please excuse me," he said. "One does get a bit more emotional as one grows older."

I couldn't stop my own eyes from watering up while picturing Mama's life that had been so cruel that a hospital felt more like a home than her real home.

"That's when I sought out the principal of our school to see what we could do to get her away from her parents," Herr Jensen continued. "I'm ashamed to admit I didn't get very far—children had no rights whatsoever in those days. Lilybeth's father was a Baron and cavalry officer. The principal was terrified we might have the army and the aristocracy on our doorstep if we interfered and forbade me to take any further steps. I felt helpless, furious.

"But I did speak to the doctors and nurses who arranged for Lilybeth to spend a couple of summer months at a Prussian estate to recuperate. Lilybeth thrived there and would return for several more summers. She formed a close bond with one of the daughters of the estate...I think her name was...Anna, no, not Anna. Annagret? No, no."

"Amalia?" I suggested.

"That's it." Herr Jensen patted my hand, while the news sank in that Mama and Aunt Amalia had known each other since they were teenagers. Only now could I appreciate how devastating it must have been for Mama when Amalia left Garmisch right after we had moved there. I could almost taste Mama's despair.

Everything inside me ached. Hitting Mama with a dog leash? Making her sleep in an ice-cold room during one of the coldest winters of the century? Hitting and humiliating her when she needed comfort? If I could have rolled back time, I would have rescued Mama.

Then, a new, violent shudder ran through me when I thought back to Mama's explosions. I winced, no longer for myself, Ingrid, and Bastian, but for Mama: every time the demons finally let go of her, she must have been devastated to know that she was doing to her own children what had been done to her.

Or wasn't she?

In Basti's, Ingrid's, and my own life, it was Mama who wielded the riding crop. My head dropped to the table. Herr Jensen patted my back and whispered, "Shsh, shsh."

A grandfather clock chimed six times. "My goodness, that late?" Herr Jensen broke the silence and stood up. "Let's make our phone call tomorrow. You have so much to digest and I'm a bit shaken, too. We'll call your mother when we are fresh, if that's all right with you." Then, with a smile, he added quickly, "But I'm not too tired to fix us a sandwich supper. How about that?"

"You're very gracious, Herr Jensen," Sophie answered, "but we must get back to my father's cousin. We're expected for supper."

We insisted on clearing the table, fixed a time to meet in the morning, and bid Herr Jensen goodbye.

In the echo-filled staircase and on the way to Sophie's cousin's house, I kept shaking my head. So much violence. So much pain. No wonder our mother became what she became... Still! How could she do to us what had been done to her? I felt as if in the grip of a fever. Then, out of nowhere, Vati's words rose up in my mind, "That's all we can do in the end—try to understand one another."

Perhaps that is all. And yet, the nervous anticipation that life can explode at any moment and that there was nothing, absolutely nothing I could do to change that, no matter how well I behaved or how fervently I prayed; that fearful anticipation of disaster thrashed into the child Marie by Mama had never left me. It had seeped into my veins and scarred them for good.

To weep for Mama and at the same time wish that I'd been born to any other woman on earth was the deepest sadness of all.

Sophie's cousin opened the door and beamed at us. "My wife is ready to serve the soup. Let's move to the dining room." He bowed toward Vati, winked at Sophie and me, and offered his arm to Tante B., leading our procession to our first hot meal of the day.

The next morning, back at Herr Jensen's, we wasted no time in calling Mama.

"Lilybeth? *Spreche ich mit Lilybeth von Baginski?*" asked Herr Jensen. Hearing her maiden name briskly pronounced by a German speaker must have gotten Mama's instant attention. If only I could have been in the hospital room to watch her face.

"This is Karl Jensen, your middle-school teacher." Herr Jensen's face lit up. "You recognized my voice after all these years? How wonderful!"

There was a pause. Herr Jensen looked up at me and motioned me to move closer. "Did I recognize yours? Of course, my dear." I understood that he was repeating some phrases so I could follow the conversation. Herr Jensen cocked his head. "When did we last see each other? Not since the war, my dear Lily. You used to visit about once a year with your little boy when you lived in Berchtesgaden. Then, after you married the doctor, you moved, and we lost track of each other."

"How is your son?" Herr Jensen was smiling at me. "Right in the room with you and doing well. Please give him my best. He must be in his twenties, right? Twenty-five! My goodness!"

I felt like snatching the phone from Herr Jensen and whispering to my brother, *We did it, Basti, I can't believe we got them together. And once Mama is out of the hospital and reconnected with her beloved protector, we can get on with our own lives.*

"Do you remember when I brought you fresh cherries to the hospital?" Herr Jensen's cheeks were aflame.

He was talking to the tortured girl he had tried to protect. He was talking to her in the same compassionate tone and with the same good will she must have felt so many years ago.

"I have never forgotten you, Lilybeth," he said softly. "I hear you're in the hospital but getting better because you've decided to eat again." What? Is this ingenious teacher using a ruse? I told him that Mama did not want to eat. That's what worried the doctors and us.

"Keep it up, my dear girl, because I want to see you when you next come to Germany. Is there a chance you'll visit this year or next? You could stay at my place, Lilybeth, saving on hotel costs. I have a spacious guest room. You'd be most welcome." He listened again. "You promise, Lilybeth? Please don't tease an old man. Old people need hope just like you young people—in fact, we need hope even more than you."

Mama, a young person? I chuckled inwardly but was full of admiration for Herr Jensen. What an incredible teacher he must have been.

"In spring? I'm so thrilled. I bet each of us has a sack full of stories to tell." He cleared his throat. "You know how I got your phone number? No? Well, I'll tell you. From your valiant son Bastian, whom I met as a baby, your daughter Ingrid, and your daughter Marie. They were deeply worried about you. In your feverish state, you kept mentioning my name, and they picked up on that. In fact, your daughter Marie is sitting right across from me. We're having tea together talking about those dark times of the depression and the days of your youth."

Suddenly blood drained from Herr Jensen's cheeks, his eyes widened. "What? What are you saying? Oh, no. You misunderstand." He stiffened, shook his head, moved the receiver away from his ear, only to yank it back and listen again. Still shaking his head, he hung up. His shoulders slunk, his cheeks hollow.

I walked to his chair and put my hand on his shoulder.

He whispered, "Give me a moment."

What could have happened? All went so beautifully—better than I ever imagined. And now? I heard Herr Jensen clear his throat. He looked at me with sorrowful eyes. "I don't understand. She was so happy, talked like a young girl, and promised to visit no later than next spring, but when I told her you were here in the room with me, talking about her childhood, she stopped in the middle of her sentence. I could hear her breath quicken, and then..." Herr Jensen was massaging the teapot as he had done when I had told him about Mama's violent outbreaks, "and then she shouted. 'Oh, no! *The shame...* you traitor!' and hung up."

I felt hot and frustrated. Herr Jensen's phrase "and when I told her that you were *in the room with me,* she said, *'The shame' and 'you traitor'*" wouldn't let go of me. What smacked of betrayal in what Herr Jensen had said to her? Of course! I hit my forehead; I was so mad at my stupidity. To all the world, Mama was highborn. A Baroness. That's what she'd told us and every single person throughout her life—and what she liked to believe herself. She'd swallowed her own lie to claim an elevated status. And now she feared or even believed that Herr Jensen had revealed her illegitimate birth to us, leaving her naked and exposed as nothing but an ordinary girl. Worse, a girl born out of wedlock—to be despised by society and her own family.

"Oh, God!" I heard myself sigh out loud. Then I grabbed hold of myself. "Dear Herr Jensen, I think I know what's happened. Mama feels unmasked. She's afraid you told us about her illegitimate birth.

She doesn't want anyone, especially her children, to know the circumstances of her birth. That's why she spoke of betrayal."

Herr Jensen picked up on my energy and sat up straight. I rushed on. "We have to assure her that you did *not* tell all. And how could you have? As it is, you were *selective* in what you told Sophie and me. So, now you need to tell her that you spoke about the beatings she received and the hard times during the depression but NOT A WORD about her birth. Then we'll be back on track. Can you do that?"

Herr Jensen looked from me to Sophie and back to me again. Then he nodded calmly. "I fear you are right. It never mattered to me if she was of noble birth or not when she was a girl, so why should it matter now? But I see your point. Your mother's self-worth needs that noble status. And who can blame her under the circumstances? She had nothing else. And technically, she is right. The Baron did adopt her." He let out a deep sigh. "Yes, the poor dear had nothing else, no love, no care, no real nourishment." A tear was running down his cheek; he took my hand. "Now *you* have taught me a lesson. I'll call your mother back tomorrow before you come and let her know her secret remains a secret. Later in the day, we'll call her together."

We were connected quickly when we called Mama back the next day—after Herr Jensen had called her by himself to reassure her that we remained in the dark about her illegitimate birth. He dove right in as if there had been no interruption before. "I forgot to tell you, Lilybeth, that the tower of the Nikolaikirche, Church of St. Nicholas, where you were confirmed, is still standing. Oh, we'll explore Hamburg together and walk along the Elbe River." The to and fro went on for a while before he turned to me. "Of course, you can talk to her. Just know that I can't wait to see you. I'll write to you; Marie has already given me your address. Take good care of yourself."

Touched by the tender, intelligent love of this extraordinary man, I managed to sound upbeat. "Hello, Mama. How are you?" I heard Mama sniffle, but her voice was neither dull nor apathetic when she replied, "I'm so much better now that you found Herr Jensen. I can't wait to see him."

"I'm so glad, Mama. It was Basti who called our attention to him.

We'd been worried about you and wanted you to gain back your strength. I know you'll love Herr Jensen's apartment, Mama—to say nothing about his wonderful pastries and cakes." I heard her turn away and relay the message to Bastian.

Then she returned to the phone. I could hear her breathe. In, out. In, out. Finally, "I hope you know, Marie, that I couldn't...couldn't help myself all these years back." Her voice was small, almost inaudible. "My entire life, nothing but hardship. I couldn't...couldn't deal with it all. I never wanted to hurt you. I'm sorry." Mama sniffled, then added, "I love you all."

I swallowed. Mama had often told us she loved us, though she might bang our head against the wall an hour later. I understood that she believed what she said, but what kind of love was this? I took a deep breath and said as softly as I could, "You've had a terrible childhood, Mama. Such brutal parents. I wished I could undo it." Mama was sniveling.

"But that's long ago. We want to stay in the present. Please try to get well now, so you can visit this coming spring."

"I will."

I handed the phone to Herr Jensen. The moment he had placed it into its cradle, I made my way to him. He opened his arms, and I squeezed his still-formidable ribcage with every bit of my strength.

"You're a miracle maker," I muttered into his gray sweater. I was certain that Mr. Jensen's kindness had filled Mama with joy—and was brightening his own life. Now he could look forward to that special "girl's" visit. That's what Mama would be in his eyes forever—the beautiful girl whose bruises spoke to him of her pain.

I wondered if knowing her pain would make a difference to us, too. It must, I wanted it to. We finally knew the underlying cause, that terrible impetus for her violence. But I also felt that this deeper understanding could not erase the past or heal our gashes and scars. They would remain.

But something had changed. Bastian, Ingrid, and I were no longer mere victims of the past, but were taking charge of our lives. And we were leading our mother to a source for good. Violence and Herr

Jensen were mutually exclusive. I was sure that in his presence at least her demons would have no sway over her.

Herr Jensen's heart was beating against my chest, drumming up another memory—Vati's return to Garmisch after the absence of two long years when he held on to Ingrid and me. Vati and Herr Jensen. The priest doctor and the teacher-healer. We must get them together. And Monsieur de Remarque.

During the turmoil of helping Mama, I hadn't stopped to consider how blessed I was, how I'd been strengthened by my three guardian angels. And always by incomparable Sophie and kindhearted Tante B. And last, but not least, by Herbert, my newest, most muscular angel. While I had been taught as a child in Falkenburg that every person has one guardian angel, I now realized that I'd been granted far more than my share.

The world I never wanted to inherit had stopped for a moment to let me exhale. The world I'd never wanted to inherit was still orbiting its ancient sun in its prescribed ellipse—with its course changing ever so slowly, infinitesimally slowly over millennia because of the impact of one object on another.

ACKNOWLEDGEMENTS

Writing *Stone Mother* felt at times like squeezing blood from a stone for all the known existential and mundane distractions: the challenges of a professional life, the end of a marriage, and the death of one's parents.

Once I began enrolling in writing classes, workshops, and conferences in mid-life, my efforts began to take a fuller shape. Jane Vandenburgh and Arnost Lustig, my first teachers, were both passionate and brilliant mentors, inspiring through their own work and their creative energy. Arnost, a holocaust survivor, provided encouragement in his heavy Czech accent and Jane, a survivor of family catastrophes wrote in one of her first comments, "This is...a beautiful piece of writing...." Far too soon, both moved away from Washington, D.C. where I live. I was able to reconnect with Jane over a decade later and am immensely indebted to her in-depth mentoring.

The writer Hildie Block had the same galvanizing and nurturing effect on my writing career as my first mentors through her own work, the many inspiring discussions on *Stone Mother* as it went through several incarnations, and through her teaching skills. Hildie's intelligence, passion, creative talent, friendship, and wit remain a guiding light until today.

Ramona Ausubel, Richard Peabody, and Pam Houston formed another trinity of enlightenment. I am grateful for their energizing and intelligent support as I am to Stuart Dybek, Sally Rider Brady, Liz van Hoose, Fred Leebron, Jim Mathews, Paula Munier, and Mark Sarvas. The writer-teacher Barbara Beste Esstman completed the cycle of reviews with a calm, critical eye distilled from a successful writing and teaching career.

My warmest thanks go to my friends and fellow writers—Maureen, Karen, Rosmary, Jill, Adele, Rose and Pam— and to former assistant Kimberly, artistic neighbor Judy Leyshon, and tech genius Janey

Junker without whom *Stone Mother* would have crumbled. I thank each and every one of you with all my heart.

Finally, I benefitted from the wonderfully talented professionals at Atmosphere Press, beginning with acquisition editor Kyle McCord and editor Tammy Letherer and moving on to managing editor Alex Kale, production manager Erin Larson-Burnett, cover designer Ronaldo Alves, and interior designer Cassandra Felten to digital director Evan Courtright and book publicity director Cameron Finch.

....You are the best!

ABOUT ATMOSPHERE PRESS

Atmosphere Press is an independent, full-service publisher for excellent books in all genres and for all audiences. Learn more about what we do at atmospherepress.com.

We encourage you to check out some of Atmosphere's latest releases, which are available at Amazon.com and via order from your local bookstore:

Icarus Never Flew 'Round Here, by Matt Edwards

COMFREY, WYOMING: Maiden Voyage, by Daphne Birkmeyer

The Chimera Wolf, by P.A. Power

Umbilical, by Jane Kay

The Two-Blood Lion, by Nick Westfield

Shogun of the Heavens: The Fall of Immortals, by I.D.G. Curry

Hot Air Rising, by Matthew Taylor

30 Summers, by A.S. Randall

Delilah Recovered, by Amelia Estelle Dellos

A Prophecy in Ash, by Julie Zantopoulos

The Killer Half, by JB Blake

Ocean Lessons, by Karen Lethlean

Unrealized Fantasies, by Marilyn Whitehorse

The Mayari Chronicles: Initium, by Karen McClain

Squeeze Plays, by Jeffrey Marshall

JADA: Just Another Dead Animal, by James Morris

Hart Street and Main: Metamorphosis, by Tabitha Sprunger

Karma One, by Colleen Hollis

Ndalla's World, by Beth Franz

Adonai, by Arman Isayan

ABOUT THE AUTHOR

Malve Burns' earliest memories are of living in a thousand-year-old castle in Germany. Before moving to the United States for graduate studies, she grew up in a silent country that did not acknowledge its horrific past. Malve has led the life of an academic, teaching and managing study abroad programs as well as working in think tanks and in development at Cornell, USC, Ithaca College, Johns Hopkins, and GWU. Her short story, "A Hot Munich Afternoon," appeared in the collection *Defying Gravity*. Czech *Playboy* published some of her short stories in translation. Malve lives in Washington, D.C., in a hundred-year-old condo castle.

Printed in the USA
CPSIA information can be obtained
at www.ICGtesting.com
LVHW041603030923
757103LV00038B/560